THE LAWMAN

LAWLESSNESS & THE LAW BOOK 2

AMI HICKEN KING

Illustrated by
ROLAND DALQUIST
Edited by
TERRY CUMMINGS

To those who represent home
And
To those loved and lost during this novel's gestation:

Dolly Tokunaga, my cutest and most enthusiastic super fan
My mom—her house drama inspired, well, house drama
Flanders, a good boy and writing buddy

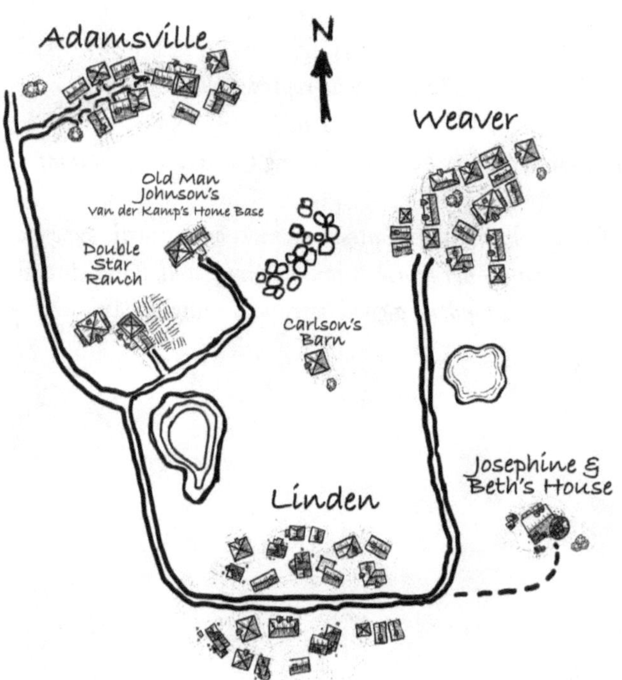

Adamsville
N
Weaver
Old Man
Johnson's
Van der Kamp's Home Base
Double
Star
Ranch
Carlson's
Barn
Linden
Josephine &
Beth's House

CHAPTER 1

1879, ARIZONA TERRITORY

The door slammed behind Josephine with a sickening finality, making her jump as she stumbled down the front porch, desperate to escape conflict and further humiliation. Flustered by anxiety and blinded by scalding shame, she scurried across the street as quickly as possible. It was bad enough she had to take in extra sewing, ever dependent on the whims and goodwill of the town's matrons. Her situation was made worse by Mrs. Cooper slipping in extra work after payment had been negotiated then threatening to complain to Mrs. Patterson if Josephine didn't comply. That was lower than Josephine could imagine, her throat tightening at the deceit. Foreboding flooded her while the growing wind discombobulated her. Her feet automatically took the shortcut to Main Street while the quiet afternoon streets helped mitigate the echo of Mrs. Cooper's shrill voice in her head. Josephine kept her head low, snugging her packages closer to her breast as if they would somehow protect her.

Fighting back tears and wanting to rush home before anyone saw her, she was unaware of company until she ran into it. The packages popped out of her arms and landed on the ground, creating puffs of dust that the increasing wind blew away. Immediately, a stocky, unkempt man grabbed her upper arms and gave her a once-over. The close-set eyes assessing her had a deadened look to them. Josephine shivered and leaned away from him, realizing too late she should've been more aware. An icy chill ran through her, cutting through the heat of the day.

Leering, the stocky man called over his shoulder to two men leaning against a building. A taller and tidier third man was propped against a wooden pillar smoking.

"Look what I found, boys! Ain't this sweet? A little afternoon treat." The first man's eyes locked with hers. "Now tell me, darlin', what do they call you?"

Josephine swallowed hard. Fear bubbled up, but she could neither scream nor move. She helplessly watched over her captor's shoulder as his three companions sauntered closer. Her heart beat so hard she thought it would move up through her throat to escape. The stocky captor became irritated with her distraction and gave her a good shake.

"I asked you a question, kitten. What's your name?"

"Jo-Josephine." Her head swiveled around, and her eyes grew larger as she took in the men now surrounding her. Rooted to the ground with fear, she was too afraid to pull away. Tremors came as she watched them communicate silently with one another. The stocky, unkept man pulled her close despite her arms reflexively pushing back at him. The men laughed at her feeble attempt.

"She's real pretty. Do you think Van Der Kamp will let us keep her?" The tidy blond with a neatly trimmed mustache reached out to brush away a lock of hair the wind had blown into her face. She tensed, and his eyes darkened, taking her in. His voice dropped lower, "Very pretty."

"I think we should leave her be. Van Der Kamp don't like no funny business. You know what happened to Wrighty when he crossed the line." The scrawny man-child croaked his protest, then looked around as if he half expected this Van Der Kamp to come around the corner and yell at them.

"Shut up, Harry." A scar-faced man reminded the gangly, awkward teen, "You're the one still in trouble with Van Der Kamp for the outhouse incident. Quit worrying." He looked back at Josephine. "I think we should take her out behind the saloon and see what she's made of."

Josephine flinched, her throat threatening to cut off her air supply, making her feel lightheaded. The tidy mustached man guffawed as if he had told some hilarious joke, but his tinny laughter stoked Josephine's hysteria as she tried to squirm free from the stocky man's grip and the men's intrusive gawking.

A gust of wind kicked up more dust, and everyone closed their eyes and ducked their heads. Josephine's skirts tangled around her legs and her captor's, intimately connecting them and teasing him. He was much too close—she could feel his legs—escalating her worry that someone would walk down the residential street, or that Mrs. Cooper would look out her window. Not wanting to be seen or become town gossip, never mind the harm to her person, Josephine was pushing even harder at her captor when the darker man with a scar grabbed one of her arms.

The two were pulling at Josephine in a tug-of-war when a lone rider interrupted their tussle.

The rider's deep voice carried over the wind. "What are you doing there?"

Startled out of their struggle, but still holding Josephine, they watched the large man trot over on a huge, glistening, coal-black horse. It kicked up even more dust as the man pulled up his reins a few yards in front of them. The pair created a wall blocking the west wind. Josephine's heart pounded harder as she saw the rider's partially shadowed face. But despite his hat pulled low and the fading sun at his back, his strong jaw and firm lips jutted out, refusing to hide. The man struck an imposing and intriguing figure, magnified by his snorting beast. Josephine's heart raced even faster.

"Ah, Jimmy—why don't you just head on back to your horses? We're doing just fine. Your help isn't needed here."

The men chortled and guffawed.

Undeterred, Jimmy leaned over the saddle horn. For as high up as he was, he managed to move into Gus's space without dismounting. Even the horse somehow crowded Gus without shifting.

"Who've you got there, Gus?"

Gus stood taller, preening. "Why, this here is my new girl, Josephine." He pulled her closer and away from the tidy mustached blond, who was still holding her arm and shooting Gus a dirty look.

"Don't look like she agrees with you, Gus, and neither does Cy."

The rider nodded at Josephine, who had stopped struggling but had become as stiff as a corset with one more man to contend with. One lesson she had learned very early was if she made herself real small or didn't move, she could pass unnoticed. She was praying for some invisibility right now.

Ned stepped forward. "Now, look here, Jimmy. Just because Charlie and Wrighty are gone doesn't mean you have to go provin' yourself or anything. Just go on and leave us be. We're loping along just fine." He nodded, although mostly to himself because everyone else was eyeing Jimmy.

"Can't do that, Cy. Miss Josephine here doesn't look too

comfortable, and it's starting to get late in the day. I'm sure her people are going to be wondering where she is if you keep holding her up like this."

When he knuckled his hat back and revealed his face more clearly, she was surprised to see he was younger than three of the men.

"Those your packages?"

She nodded feebly.

Facing the scrawny teen, Jimmy said, "Harry, pick those up for her, will you?" It wasn't a question.

Harry bent down and reached for the bundle closest to him, but Ned kicked it away and gave Harry a shove. He hollered at Jimmy, "Who died and left you boss? We don't have to do what you say.

Jaw clenched, Jimmy stared back at Ned. He gripped the reins tighter and paused before answering. "No one, but this is not how we treat ladies." He threw his leg over the saddle and landed softly. "Now, let's do the right thing. I'm asking politely." The last bit didn't sound as friendly or polite as he had been up to that point.

Harry's head swiveled between Jimmy and Ned before he bent down again to pick up the packages. Ned yanked Harry back, using the momentum to propel himself at Jimmy, but Jimmy was too quick for him. Raising his left arm, he blocked Ned's punch while swiveling from the right with an uppercut that landed under Ned's jaw. Ned stumbled backward, arms flailing, as Cy jumped Jimmy from behind and sucker punched him. Jimmy arched back, contorted in pain, before twisting to face Cy. Grabbing Cy's arm, Jimmy pulled it behind his back and yanked upward. Cy howled but couldn't retaliate.

Gus was pulling Josephine away when Jimmy barked, "Let. Her. Go!"

Gus sneered. "Says who? You?" He laughed hysterically. "That's a good one, son."

When Gus spat out the word *son*, Josephine noticed an almost imperceptible flinch from Jimmy. He straightened to his full height, eyes pinned on Gus. Heaving a heavy sigh, he said, "All right, then."

But as he tossed Cy in Harry's direction, Jimmy lunged at Gus, who threw a punch that missed. They circled each other without advancing. Cy righted himself and charged at Jimmy's middle while Gus went for his head. Jimmy had the advantage of height on both, by at least a half a foot on Cy and a little more on Gus. The pair soon found themselves toppled on each other. When they tried to get up, Jimmy knocked their heads together, dropping them in a heap at his feet.

Jimmy picked up the packages and shoved them into Harry's arms.

He threw his thumb over his shoulder. "Put those in my saddlebag, please." Addressing Josephine, he doffed his hat. "Jimmy Stapleton. I'm going to take you to your people. I promise that you're safe with me."

Jimmy inclined his head toward his horse, Coal. "May I?"

Josephine gnawed at the inside of her cheek, but she gave a partial nod and moved toward the horse. Jimmy's hands encircled her waist. With a gentle hold, he lifted her onto the saddle. She reached down to adjust her skirts, but Jimmy beat her to it with a gentle but improper tug.

"This'll be fast but not as comfortable for you, I'm afraid. Hitch your leg around the pommel and scoot as far forward as you can."

Josephine felt the heat rushing to her face but dutifully obeyed. Jimmy was behind her in a flash. Her body felt consumed by fire in a way she had never felt. This was the closest she'd been to a man—ever. Her father hadn't been very demonstrative; she hadn't grown up with boys; and she generally steered clear of others.

Ack. Uncomfortably close.

Attempting to move forward even a little was impossible, as she was wedged in between the pommel and Jimmy. Her default to stillness didn't work, either. Despite Coal's smooth gait, she still rocked against this stranger, heightening her discomfort and dismay. Trying to create more distance between them without being obvious was impossible, so she made only a half-hearted attempt. Admittedly, there was something nice about his protective nature as well as his muscular thighs pressed against her. She compressed her lips, wishing herself small for her wayward thoughts and in the steady fear that they'd be seen together like this.

Jimmy cleared his throat and waited. Josephine stiffened but didn't speak. They were in a sort of standoff of politeness and propriety until, finally, Jimmy took control.

"Which way should we head, Miss Josephine?"

"I live off the road into Linden. The one intersecting the mercantile end of town. But ..." Her voice dropped lower. "Could we please not ride through town?" Josephine dropped her head. "Maybe take the back way to that road?"

Jimmy kept Coal at a walk without responding. Curiosity and nerves were getting the better of Josephine, so she sneaked a peek at him. His face was impassive as he watched the road ahead, his dark eyes scanning their surroundings. Josephine took that moment to observe her savior. Or at least, she assumed he was saving her. She didn't bother to question him because she was happy to be away from the others and their disturbing behavior. At least he had manners.

With that said, this Mr. Stapleton was a beast of a man. She'd never seen someone as tall or broad as him— at well over six feet tall, unnaturally large compared to the men in town. While she didn't really fit in the saddle with him, initially she didn't think she'd fit at all, given how large he was. Even the man's presence took up a lot of space. All she noticed was his size and agility. She would've been hard-pressed to describe him if asked. Now, as she quickly looked closer, she realized how handsome he was, an odd contrast to the initially frightening figure who rode in and defended her.

His kindness was clearly evident. It wasn't just his words and polite attitude toward her, either. He didn't do anything rough or quick. Even when he lifted her so high onto his horse, his grip was gentle. Conversely, a lot of masculinity was mixed in with the gentle nature and boyish face. Without realizing she was doing so, out of the corner of her eye, she studied his dark hair and eyes and the bit of shadow growing on his square jaw and high cheekbones. No one would ever mistake him for a woman despite his thick, long lashes and his lush, wavy hair. Everything about him was solid and full or broad and expansive, whichever way she looked at it. He was like the great protector with his eyes always watching and aware. His horse mirrored this compelling mix of masculine and protector.

Jimmy startled her out of her gawking, but she watched his full lips move as he spoke instead of meeting his eyes. "I know a back way. Are you avoiding someone in particular, or are you afraid someone will see you with a stranger?"

Stunned by his astute observation, Josephine needed a minute to gather her senses. "We haven't been properly introduced. I don't want to borrow trouble." Thinking herself tart, she quickly added, "I also don't want to be the subject of gossip, especially since there's been a lot of strangers passing through town these days. Everyone is watching."

Nodding, Jimmy kept silent until they were on the road

out of town. He had cut behind the businesses before giving Coal his head. Josephine noticed the horse had released some pent-up energy after moving into a fast trot. His massive shoulders relaxed beneath them despite moving. After a few minutes at a good clip, Jimmy slowed the horse.

"How far out are you?"

"About two miles. You'll see a giant cottonwood. That's our property on the left."

Coal's rhythmic clomping eased the tension between the strangers. It helped that Josephine had finally relaxed after they were out of the populated part of town. She was relieved no one had seen them, at least that she was aware of. There wasn't anything between the town's shops and her family home, and Jimmy was a quiet man, so she was happy to be in the clear and looked out into the distance.

Jimmy shattered her illusions with his next question. "You walk all that way by yourself?"

Panic set in. She didn't want to explain her situation to a complete stranger. Honestly, she didn't want to explain her family situation to anyone. Her mother had maintained a tightly controlled version of who and what their family was, one she wasn't allowed to add to or elaborate on, ever.

Instead of betraying herself with her voice, she nodded her head. She frequently walked because Beth often took the only horse they still had. *No one's business that they had to sell their horses and livestock just recently.*

"That's a decent walk, especially carrying all those packages." Jimmy's head swiveled around as he took in the surroundings. "You have a gun, or at least a knife?"

Josephine recoiled at the thought. She'd travelled that road so many times and never thought twice about anything like that.

"No. It's perfectly safe."

However, doubt began to creep in because she was just

accosted one street over from Main Street. That doubt increased again when she thought of all the strangers who had been coming to town and lingering. They wouldn't do anything productive aside from going to the saloon, at least according to the town gossips. Then, after varying amounts of time, they'd disappear without word. None of them had Jimmy's pleasant or friendly look, either. Just passing those strangers on the street didn't feel safe like she was feeling with Jimmy. She shuddered.

"Well, you can never be too sure. You are a ways out."

When they reached the old-growth cottonwood, Jimmy turned Coal toward the property but eased him to a halt. Josephine turned as much as she could, wondering why he had stopped so far from the house. Then she noticed his narrowed eyes in the fading light.

"What's wrong? Do you want me to get off here?"

"No. I'm going to have a look around. It's too quiet. Where is everyone?" Jimmy had already dismounted before she could protest.

"But—"

He reached up for her and placed her gently on the ground. Too scared to reveal she was alone right now, but also scared about what Jimmy had seen, she didn't know what to say. She was relieved that he had already started to walk away.

Speaking over his shoulder, he said, "I'm going to have a look around. It's unnaturally quiet. I want to make sure everything's okay. Stay with Coal. He'll protect you if anything's around here."

Jimmy's long legs took him out of sight before she could figure out what to say in response. Josephine grabbed handfuls of her skirt, bunching them then smoothing them while darting looks around the property. She couldn't see what Jimmy saw, and that fear was eating at her. Taking a step back, she bumped into Coal, who turned his head to give her the side-eye. She realized, as they stood so close, that Coal was far larger than any horse she'd ever encountered, a complement to his overgrown master. She widened her eyes back at him. In response, he bobbed his head and snorted at her in what she deemed to be disgust.

Goodness. Judged by a horse. This has certainly been a day.

Jimmy had made good time and returned to find Coal and Josephine still eyeing each other suspiciously. He pushed Coal's head away. "Be nice." Looking at Josephine, he said, "It's all clear, but who lives on the property? It doesn't look like anyone's been here for a long while."

"That's really none of your concern, sir."

Jimmy looked taken aback at her crisp tone. Accustomed to men and horses, he was used to speaking plainly if not politely.

"I don't mean to pry. I suppose what I'm getting at is it's dangerous to be way out here all alone and walk those miles by yourself. I just saved you from some unsavory men. Who protects—" He broke off as her frown increased. "I mean—"

Josephine crossed her arms over her stomach, trying to stifle the queasy feeling. No one had ever cared for her safety before. Before her parents died, she hadn't gone to town as often and rarely gone unescorted. She certainly hadn't been allowed to walk or, worse, walk alone. She had usually stayed home and done chores because that's what her mother had wanted her to do.

Now, Jimmy's concerned look was doing her in, and she was struggling with what to share. Indecision and a tightly held mix of emotions—sadness, loneliness, fear, to mention a few—were choking her. It was safer not to feel, to tuck everything neatly away from sight. However, this was difficult with Jimmy poking at some tender spots with kindness and concern, both of which were foreign to her. She needed to say something to make him leave.

"My sister, Beth, will be home very soon. I appreciate your concern. I really do. But I should go in and start supper. I'm a little late getting home ... I ..."

Jimmy's lips pressed together as if he didn't like that answer. "Maybe you should've waited for your sister so you could return together. That'd be safer." Josephine's eyes went wide, and Jimmy backtracked. "Look, I'm-I'm making a mess of this. I know I don't know you, but you seem real nice, and I'm worried about your safety. You've met a couple of the men I travel with whose scruples I question. The rest of us aren't like that, but even that doesn't matter. Lone women aren't safe." He made firm eye contact. "Do you have someone here to keep you safe?"

Josephine's lip began to quiver, and she looked at the ground. Jimmy's kindness was undoing her. Kind people did that to her because that's not how her family had treated her. She crossed and uncrossed her arms because she didn't know what to do with herself. She wanted to run away. Not trusting her voice, she gripped her skirt to keep her hands busy, tilted her head to look Jimmy in the eye again, and spoke anyway. He needed to leave before she completely fell apart.

"You are very kind, and I appreciate your help and concern. There really isn't much you can do for me, and as I mentioned, my sister will be home soon. Thank you for all your help."

In a hasty escape, Josephine turned and made a beeline for the front porch. Jimmy took a few long strides and caught her shoulder before she could go far. Surprised, she whirled back around.

"Sorry." He released her. "You forgot your packages." He raised an eyebrow. "I'm still unconvinced that everything is all right here, but I have to take your word for it. I'll walk you to the door. Just make sure you get a lamp lit and lock the door before I leave."

He nodded at her before walking back to Coal's saddlebag and retrieving her packages. Holding his hand out to indicate she should proceed, they silently walked to the front of the house before Josephine tried to take the packages from Jimmy's hands.

"I'm walking you to the door and making sure the lamp is lit, remember? It'll make me feel better. Don't worry. I'm not staying."

Hesitating, she opened the door and continued into the house, then felt on the entryway's side table to find a lucifer. The house was so quiet that the striking sound felt like it echoed. She lifted the glass and lit the lamp. When she inclined her head toward the same table, Jimmy placed the packages next to the lamp and doffed his hat.

"Lock the door behind me, Miss Josephine. I won't leave until I hear it latch." He watched her for a moment before heading out the front door, quietly pulling it shut behind him.

Josephine stood staring at the door for a moment, knowing the gentle giant remained on the other side waiting for her to comply. Swallowing, she scurried to the door and twisted the lock before leaning her shoulder against the door and pressing the top of her head to it. Sighing, she stood there for a moment before saying aloud, "I was going to do that anyway, Jimmy Stapleton."

CHAPTER 2

Gus and Cy had been gone for hours, and Van Der Kamp was fed up with their nonsense. Damned Gus was getting to be about as bad as Wrighty with all the rebellion. The gang was supposed to be lying low in this town, but those two kept living large at the saloon. Who knew what other trouble they were causing? Van Der Kamp gave his word to Sheriff O'Donnell, from Weaver, that they would be out of his hair and out of sight, but it seemed this town brought something out in those two. Van Der Kamp was sure Ned and Harry were with them, followers that they were.

"Jaems," Van Der Kamp called down the hallway.

"Yeah, boss?"

"I need you to go look for Gus and Cy. I'm betting they're in town. Hope they're not causing trouble."

"On it, boss."

* * *

WHAT JAEMS FOUND when looking for Gus and Cy surprised the hell out of him.

"What in the Sam Hill happened to y'all?" Jaems jumped off his horse before it stopped completely.

Propped up against the boardwalk were Gus, Ned, and Cy while scrawny Harry crouched in front of them. He was handing Gus a handkerchief when Jaems rode up. They looked a little sheepish, except for Gus, who was full of fire. Jaems cocked his head at them.

Holding the cloth to his broken nose, Gus barked, "That damned Jimmy picked a fight with us."

Clearly, he spoke before thinking because Jaems quirked his eyebrow at them and rubbed his chin. Before he could say anything, Cy chimed in.

"Jimmy was putting his nose where it didn't belong. That's what happened."

Jaems looked around and then went pale. "What'd you do with the body?" He whispered so loudly it was comical.

"What? There is no body, you fool."

"Well, then—where's Jimmy?"

That's when they all looked like fools. They realized they were doomed no matter what they said. Harry finally decided it was better to confess.

"He's with the woman, Josephine. Took her home."

"What woman? What she got to do with anything?"

"Uhh—" Harry looked at the others as if they could help dig him out of this hole.

"Go on. You better tell me because Van Der Kamp has his nose bent out of shape about something. I'm thinking y'all have something ta do with it." When no one spoke, Jaems said, "Harry, you know you're already in a heap of trouble for the outhouse incident."

Harry turned red and cleared his throat. He had pulled a childish prank that had gotten out of hand. No one had let him forget about it because Van Der Kamp had caught wind of it. Gus shot him a dirty look out of the corner of his eye.

"Well, there was this pretty woman we was watching …" Cy shook his head at Harry, but Harry kept talking. "Gus thought we might want to get to know her a little better."

Jaems crossed his arms over his chest. This was exactly what Van Der Kamp was afraid of. Shaking his head, he said, "Go on."

"Well, Jimmy rode up and interrupted our getting to know her, you know?"

"No, I don't. Get on with it. Van Der Kamp is waiting, and you know he ain't patient."

"Jimmy asked if we knew her, and the next thing I know, he'd coldcocked Gus and was pummeling Ned. He said he was gonna take her home."

"Whaddya mean, 'take her home'?"

"Just what I said. He put her on his high horse and took her home. Left Cy and me to do cleanup and all."

"That's totally unlike Jimmy. What else did he say?"

"Well, we're's not to bother her no more."

Jaems looked around at the four of them as if to confirm what Harry had said, but they were either looking sullen or looking away. When he realized what had happened—that one man had taken on these four men and whooped them— well, that was too much for him. He threw his head back and guffawed, sounding like a braying burro, until tears rolled down his face.

Gus sneered at Jaems, which only caused Jaems to point his finger at him. "You think you're all high and mighty yerself. How many times didya taunt and beat poor Jimmy when he was growing up? Huh? Every time Charlie wasn't looking, for sure. Every time." He took off his hat and slapped it on his thigh. "'Bout time you got some of it back. Whooo-eee. Jimmy's outdone himself." Shaking his head with a mixture of mirth and disbelief, he shoved his hat on his head. "Well, you sorry souls better git on back to camp. Van Der Kamp's expecting y'all. You can tell him why yer all beat up."

Snorting to himself, he gathered the reins to his horse and climbed back on. He pointed at them and said, "I wouldn't dawdle none, neither. Van Der Kamp's in a snit."

His chuckling trailed after him as he rode off the way he came.

While riding back through town to Old Man Johnson's, or home base, as some of them called the ranch, Jimmy didn't see Gus and his cronies, nor did he encounter any trouble. He had started to relax on the homestretch when a wolfhound came barreling out of the tree line toward him.

Coal reared up, but Jimmy pulled on the reins and called out, "Whoa!"

Greeting them with a hearty bark, the dog danced around them until Jimmy dismounted. He recognized the dog. It was the same one that had run toward them when they first came to town. Gus and Cy had taunted him and chased the poor dog off by throwing rocks at him. Jimmy was surprised to see him again.

He held his hand out flat for the dog to sniff. "Hello there. I'm surprised you came back after the other day."

The dog snuffled and licked his hand, tail furiously wagging all the while. The dog leaned into Jimmy, looking up at him.

"I'm telling you, I think God has a funny sense of humor

sending you back this way. Those men you encountered the other day are real curs." He could've sworn the dog smiled back at him, jowls pulled upward in a kind of doggy grin. Shaking his head, Jimmy gave him some more pets and scratches. "I don't know where you've come from, but they need to feed you more."

Reaching into his saddlebag, Jimmy pulled out some jerky and fed it to the scrawny dog. The dog took it gently then devoured it as if he hadn't tasted food for weeks, slobber flying and mouth smacking.

"Easy there. I have another piece you can have, but then you need to get on back to where you're from."

He pulled out another jerky strip from his saddlebag and tossed it to the ravenous beast. Jimmy patted the dog's head one more time before mounting. The dog remained where he was, chewing away as Jimmy rode off at a slow canter. He hadn't gone far before the dog had caught up, running alongside him. Choosing to ignore the dog so as not to encourage him, Jimmy kept his pace until he reached the barn. He walked Coal to his stall and began removing his tack for his rubdown and some oats and water. The dog followed him all the way to the stall and lay down in front of it. The other horses watched the pair with curiosity.

Jimmy ignored the dog, hoping he'd get bored and leave on his own. The scruffy beast had already been subjected to Gus and Cy's brutality when they first rode to town, and he didn't want a repeat of that. Jimmy was brushing down Coal when an annoyed voice interrupted him.

"There you are. Where've you been?"

"Who's asking?"

"Van Der Kamp." Jaems hissed at him.

Van Der Kamp's name was one that made everyone look alert, Jimmy included. He finally turned around. He dropped his hands to his sides, looking down at the dog who was now next to him, then back at Jaems, whose brow was furrowed.

Jaems nodded toward the dog. "What's that?"

"A dog."

"I know that, you numbskull. What's it doing here?"

"Dunno. He caught up with us just outside the property and followed us. I told him to go back."

Jaems snorted. "You and the talking to animals." He was about to go on, but Jimmy's face darkened like a thundercloud. Jaems raised his hands defensively. "Didn't mean no harm, Jimmy. You're good with the animals, that's all. No one else can do what you do."

"So you all say, but you don't listen to me."

Jaems understood where Jimmy was coming from. The men bossed Jimmy even when Jimmy knew better. And when it came to horses, Jimmy always knew better. Jaems had heard what happened with Dobbin that morning because Dobbin had come back to the bunkhouse carrying on about being done wrong. He had claimed that Jimmy roughed him up and wouldn't listen to reason. When the gang found out Dobbin had taken Winnie, they knew why Jimmy was mad. At the same time, they were shocked that he had taken out his feelings on Dobbin, even though they knew Dobbin had deserved it.

Jimmy usually didn't react, and they had never known him to act in anger. He was generally very quiet. But this time, he did all the things that were out of character for him, including leaving without telling anyone. These events surprised everyone.

"There's the rub, ain't it? Expectin' you ta do all the heavy work and not paying you no never mind. It's 'bout time you gave them all what for. I juss can't believe you finally did it, Jimmy, that's all. And more than once." Jaems shook his head and smiled wistfully. "Ten or so years of quiet, then—boom—

you shake everything up like an earthquake." Jimmy's jaw ticked, but Jaems was quick to add, "I support ya, Jimmy. And that's not just because Gus has it coming to him, neither. I suppose it's just … it's so sudden and twice. In the same day." He nodded, punctuating his point.

Surprised by a rush of relief, Jimmy grunted at Jaems. Unused to validation and agreement, words failed him. Jaem's wasn't a gossip and generally kept to himself, so his unlikely support sparred with Jimmy's agitation. The empowered feeling he had developed by taking control worried him. His father had been a heavy-handed man who didn't consider those in need. This new turn of events troubled him.

Jaems intruded on Jimmy's thoughts. "You best git goin'. Van Der Kamp's in a snit. Don't want to keep him waiting."

"I have to check on the horses and brush Coal down."

"I already had Thom and Buford do the chores. You must've run Coal. He looks to be in a good mood. I can brush him."

Jimmy hesitated, hating to skip his chores, which Jaems had anticipated.

"Go on." Jaems waved him off and started to turn toward Coal.

Wavering, Jimmy looked down at the dog, back up at his horse, and glanced back at Jaems, who nodded his head. He walked off to the main house, glad the dog stayed behind, and the horse didn't pitch a fit, all the while questioning what was going on with Jaems. And with everyone for that matter.

CHAPTER 4

Feeling leaden, Jimmy trudged up to the house, his heart burdened with shame and regret. He'd broken his rule against violence today—not once, but twice —plus Van Der Kamp's order about lying low. Van Der Kamp's voice echoed in Jimmy's head, and Jimmy realized he was the one who had made a mockery of that rule this afternoon. His footsteps plodded as he chewed on what Van Der Kamp had in store for him.

The main house was dark and quiet. Convinced that Van Der Kamp was having one of his migraines, a "gift" from the war, Jimmy stood up straighter while blowing out a deep breath. He didn't know what sort of mood he'd find Van Der Kamp in, and he wanted to remain focused. That meant leaving his own troubles at the door—a door he stared at, undecided as to how hard to knock.

Jimmy paused long enough debating with himself about knocking, when Van Der Kamp barked out, "Come in!"

Unphased, he stepped into the room and waited.

"Sit down." Van Der Kamp was leaning back against his

chair, his elbow on the armrest, with his forefinger and thumb cradling his head.

The chair squawked, protesting Jimmy's tight fit and making him flinch at the sound. He watched Van Der Kamp watching him. Time felt momentarily stopped despite the loud ticking of the grandfather clock reminding him that time, in fact, was marching on. Van Der Kamp had the kind of eyes that saw everything with the added benefit of being so icy they created a pause in those watched. However, Jimmy was an excellent observer in his own right, and what he saw surprised him, mostly because Van Der Kamp didn't allow others to see him when he felt low. Van Der Kamp's skin was pale, lines creased his forehead, his eyes were sunken. His strength belied his naturally wiry frame. When standing, he was six foot two. Today, however, his shoulders curved inward as if he'd lost some of the army starch in his posture and were reflecting his forty-five years.

Blinking, Jimmy conceded the staring contest. Van Der Kamp pulled in a long breath that scrunched up the right side of his face. He paused a beat before speaking. "Heard you had a busy day."

Jimmy nodded. "That's about right."

"Care to elaborate?" Van Der Kamp's eyebrows raised with his question.

Huffing out a sigh, Jimmy dropped his head a moment before looking back at Van Der Kamp. "Where do you want me to start? With Dobbin taking Winnie when I told him not to, or Gus, Cy, Ned, and Harry harassing a young woman in town?"

"Start where you want. It's your story."

"I'm tired of the men treating the horses like tools." Jimmy sighed. "Been tired. When I say one needs rest, it needs rest. They have needs just like we do, but Dobbin's too dim to understand. He took Winnie, continued to ride her while she struggled. I don't even know what he needed her for, but he went behind my back and took her." Jimmy cleared his throat. "I may have expressed my displeasure with more than just words."

"Mmhm. Dobbin bears watching. I agree. Don't like that he's mistreating horses, either." Van Der Kamp widened his eyes with a look of "I'm waiting" when Jimmy remained silent.

"I took care of Winnie then decided it was best to leave to avoid doing something I'd regret because a burning rage washed over me. It was uncomfortable—all-consuming and out of control."

Van Der Kamp nodded while Jimmy bolstered himself for the remainder of the story.

"That's when I came up on Gus and his cronies, and I didn't like what I saw there, either. They were scaring some poor woman, and Gus was pawing at her like an animal."

"And?" The corners of Van Der Kamp's lips looked like they were tipping upward, but it was hard to tell in the low light.

"And ... I asked them to pick up her packages that were on the ground and let her get on her way." Jimmy stopped as if he were finished. Van Der Kamp, however, was not finished listening.

"Go on," he drawled.

"My asking didn't have much of an effect, so I decided they needed to understand that asking politely is a courtesy."

Van Der Kamp couldn't stop his smile this time, despite pulling his lips together. Jimmy raised his eyebrows in confusion, forcing a barking laugh out of Van Der Kamp, who leaned forward, putting his arms on his desk.

"Might as well tell it all, Jimmy. I heard what happened. I want to hear how you see it."

Jimmy sighed in exasperation. "Well, I took matters into

my own hands, so to speak. Made it clear that they weren't to be bothering poor Miss Josephine again and that I was taking her home safely. They chose not to listen, and I decided to show them I mean business." He shrugged. "Tired of being ignored, I suppose."

"'Bout time, Jimmy."

Jimmy's eyes widened, but he remained quiet.

"You've been taking a lot of heat from all of them, and it seemed to get worse after Charlie left." Jimmy opened his mouth to interrupt, but Van Der Kamp stayed him with his hand. "Go on and do what you have to do to get your work done. You do fine work around here, and the horses sure do appreciate it. They've never looked happier or healthier since you got a hold of 'em."

The right side of his face scrunched up as he inhaled deeply through his right nostril—a tick of Van Der Kamp's. He did it when he was thinking, but that habit wasn't limited to being thoughtful and sometimes veered toward danger-ous. Jimmy always considered it his thinking sniff. He was sniffing out the right thoughts to share, especially since he shared so little. "Need-to-know basis", as Van Der Kamp liked to tell everyone. He tapped his pointer finger on the table.

"I don't like what I've heard about the horses. They need to be treated well and kept healthy–can't be having anything different going on."

Jimmy's nostrils flared, thinking about the horses. Keeping his anger in check, he pressed his lips tightly and gave a curt nod.

"Like I said, do what you need to do. If anyone questions you, tell them I said so, or just give them a good setdown. They can't mind just me, and only when I'm looking. A couple of them are behaving like children, and we need to weed them out. I'm cleaning house, Jimmy, and you're going to be an integral part of that."

Van Der Kamp stretched his hand outward, palm up. "They think because Wrighty is gone they can screw around? Just because he was the first to throw fists doesn't mean it's okay for the rest of them to flaunt the rules and bully others. This isn't a hazing, and it's not their turn. Catch my meaning?" He raised an eyebrow at Jimmy.

Jimmy inhaled deeply, giving another curt nod.

"What, exactly, do you think I mean?" Van Der Kamp canted his head, his eyes shrewd.

"The men need to toe the line, or they're out. Where the horses are concerned, I get to dole out justice as I see fit."

"Not just with the horses. You get to dole out justice, period. Even at twenty, you're more even tempered and fair than the others. You do what's best for the group, not just yourself. Just be aware the others won't take this kindly and may come after you, especially after this morning."

Van Der Kamp rapped the desk twice with his knuckles then pointed his finger at Jimmy. "I have plans for you."

"I—"

Jimmy was cut off by a God-awful howling and commotion out front. His face fell, and both men ran out the front door to see what was going on.

Outside, Gus, Cy, and Ned were circling around the wiry wolfhound that had followed Jimmy home, while Harry stood nearby. They were taunting the poor creature, kicking him and poking him with sticks. One threw water at him. They were laughing and taking pleasure in their cruelty, showing themselves to be the bullies they were. The dog held his own, hackles raised, teeth bared, but refused to attack. Jimmy's fists went tight, and his face flushed scarlet.

"Stop!"

Everyone froze, shocked, looking toward Jimmy. Jimmy's

voice cut through the ruckus, but the biggest surprise was that he was front and center.

Jimmy marched toward them, shoving Gus away from the dog. "What in the hell do you think you're doing?" Caught off guard, no one spoke. "I asked you a question. Remember what happens when my questions don't get answered?"

"Step away, Jimmy. This mongrel needs to be put out of his misery." Cy flung his arm toward the growling dog. "Look at him. He won't even stand up to us."

He shifted to kick the dog, but Jimmy's arm shot out faster than Cy could move. Jimmy twisted Cy's arm behind his back, bringing him to his knees.

"I'm guessing you don't rightly understand how I feel about you bullying the innocent and the weak. Consider this your last warning. I don't cotton to that kind of behavior." He dropped his voice. "Understand?"

Cy didn't immediately respond, so Jimmy jerked his arm up harder, making him wince before nodding his head. Jimmy's outstretched arm, finger pointed, slowly moved across the group. They looked back at him with fresh, wide-open eyes.

"Are we in agreement?" They continued to stare until he torqued Cy's arm again. "I'll gladly repeat this afternoon's lesson if you like."

Gus glared but managed a curt nod. The others followed suit. Van Der Kamp remained at a distance, arms crossed, watching everything play out. Gus dared to shoot a look at him, but quickly turned away from Van Der Kamp's piercing eyes. Jimmy released Cy's arm and brushed his hand off on his leg as if to get rid of the filth. Then, although he didn't need to, as the dog was so tall, he put one hand on his knee and held out the other for the dog. He gratefully trotted toward Jimmy, who gave the dog a few pats and a scratch behind the ear before he straightened. By then, Van Der

Kamp had moved closer to the cluster of men. A scowl etched his face. He gave an angry nod before speaking.

"You yahoos interrupted our conversation." As if nature bent to Van Der Kamp's will, everything went silent—even the wind died down. "From here on out, you better start paying heed to Jimmy."

Van Der Kamp turned to walk away, paused, and tossed over his shoulder, "Stop harassing the weak and the less fortunate. That's not the purpose of this gang. Best not forget that, either." He continued to walk away but kept speaking. "If you can't bother to follow the rules, find your way out, or we'll find a way out for you." Taking a few more steps, he added, "I can promise you won't like what we'll do to you, either." He nodded to himself, mostly as a force of habit. Also force of habit was the men minding what he said. If Van Der Kamp said it, it was law.

Jimmy walked off without another glance at the men, the dog happily following him.

* * *

WHEN HE WAS out of earshot, they grumbled among themselves.

"What the hell just happened?" Cy hissed.

"Hell, if I know." Harry shrugged.

Gus kicked the ground while shooting Cy a dirty look. "What just happened is Van Der Kamp has raised Jimmy in the ranks. Didn't you hear him? We interrupted their meeting." He sneered, glaring at Jimmy's back.

The dog turned at that moment and looked back at them. He gave a protective growl, clearly aligning himself with Jimmy.

"We should've killed that stupid beast the first time around. Damn!"

"Yeah, he's like hell." Harry whispered, mostly to himself.

Cy looked confused. "Who's like hell?"

Harry had a bemused look as he watched the others walk off. "That dog is following Jimmy around, kind of like hell's been following Jimmy since Charlie left, that's all."

Gus shoved Harry's shoulder. "You're an idiot."

Cy said, "He's kind of right. Some kind of hellfire has been burning inside Jimmy since Charlie left. I don't think it's Charlie's leaving him that has him feeling that way, neither."

"Well, Jimmy packs a wallop, that's for sure. I'm not in the mood to eat his fist."

Harry nodded before walking away, leaving the men scratching their heads at his proclamations. Still growing into his manhood, Harry was a scrawny teen and a follower; however, his observations demonstrated stronger insight and wisdom than those he blindly followed.

CHAPTER 5

Josephine was at a loss. Her day had not gone as planned. Not even close. Opening one of the packages Jimmy had carried in, Josephine unfolded and spread out the fabric. She methodically gathered the thread, scissors, and pins to begin her commissioned work, but found she couldn't summon the focus to start Mrs. Patterson's dress. The banker's wife had chosen a beautiful fabric with silver threaded through it, which shimmered in the lamp light. Normally, that alone would be enough incentive, but everything about Jimmy had disarmed her.

When her heart finally settled to a normal pace, she still couldn't get him out of her mind. She rolled his image around, replaying the events of the afternoon. Awareness of Jimmy as a man, not just a savior, was at the forefront of her thoughts, pushing aside the frightening memory of being accosted and feeling helpless. Shaking her head, she began to refold the expensive fabric.

I'll get to this in the morning. I'll be fresher then.

Her usual mode of chastising herself was terminated

before it could begin by the sounds of horses and voices outside. She froze, straining to make out their words.

"Come on, honey—just one kiss good night. There's no harm in that." A slow-talking man spoke in slightly slurred words.

"You know there is. It's bad enough you followed me all the way out here. You shouldn't be here." Beth's tone belied her words.

Josephine fumed. *Of course Beth would giggle inappropriately. There's nothing appropriate about this, and she knows it. Beth was supposed to be home hours ago. She said she needed to go "help" her friend Clara, who had just had a baby. "Help" my foot. That girl wouldn't know what help meant if it slapped her in the face.*

Huffing, Josephine stomped to the door ready to fling it open. But just as she turned the lock, the door pushed into her, and Beth came stumbling in after it.

They stared at each other, Beth wondering why Josephine was at the door, judging by her look of surprise, and Josephine wondering who rode home with Beth, especially since Beth had the wagon and no packages. Their faces mirrored their surprise until it was broken when Beth turned up her nose at Josephine, and Josephine glared back. Beth skirted around Josephine as Josephine peered out into the darkness trying to catch a glimpse of the man who was riding away.

Josephine's attempt brought her nothing. The light was liminal, and the yard was empty. She slammed the door while pivoting toward Beth. Unsettled by earlier events and upset that Beth would risk her reputation by allowing a man to escort her home, her voice raised uncharacteristically. "For land's sake, who was with you, Beth?"

Beth casually turned around, tilting her head and clasping her hands. She affected the innocent look with ease, blinking her eyes. "That was Clara's brother, Ralph, making sure I made it home safe." The corners of her mouth tilted up, imitating a smile.

"That's nonsense, and you know it. That was a man, and he was asking for a kiss! How could you, Beth?" Josephine's voice came out strangled.

Men had been a huge issue for them since their parents had died. There were a few who circled like vultures, especially since the Snyders were well off, and all three sisters were pretty in their own way. But since Essie was already married, the attention was on Beth and Josephine. The attention, however, was more hurtful to Josephine. She'd always been treated like a social afterthought by her family as well as some of the men in town, especially a couple of them who hadn't been complimentary to her prior to her parents' deaths. One man made it a habit of calling her "Little Joseph" because she was more boyish than her sisters.

The male population and finances are where Josephine and Beth could have used some of Frank's help, but their new brother-in-law was nowhere to be found when it came to that. He showed himself only when it was to his advantage. In fact, Josephine was pretty sure she had heard Frank laugh when she was called Little Joseph because of her boyish figure and that he was spreading nasty rumors about Beth. Unfortunately, Beth's current behavior didn't help her cause.

Beth shrieked, "You were spying! How could you, Jo? You're such a busybody, never leaving me in peace. Why?" She stamped her foot in anger and frustration. "You ruin everything."

Josephine jerked back as if Beth had slapped her. Simultaneously, the flat of her hand went to her chest, accompanied by an audible intake of air. "You know that's not true. I—"

"It is true. You never let me have any fun." She narrowed

her eyes. "Always watching me like a hawk. You're as bad as Frank and Essie with your judgment. Worse, maybe, because you're the youngest. You're just jealous that you're not as pretty as me." Beth tossed her head and stormed off, leaving Josephine with teary eyes and a tightness in her chest.

Ever since Essie got married, it was the same argument, at least the no-fun portion of it. The *not as pretty as* her beautiful sisters had been going on for as long as she could remember. They had *figures of real women*, with *hair spun like gold*. Even the townspeople referred to Essie and Beth as the *Nordic beauties*, whereas Josephine was the *unfortunate one* with mud-brown eyes and hair a shade of floundering blonde that bordered dangerously on the brown and red sides. Not statuesque, but average. She couldn't possibly be one of the Snyder sisters. People joked that she was the "cousin."

Josephine's eyes spilled over with tears as she remembered the taunts and whispered comments behind her back —the sort of whispering that was not intended to be a secret. A pain she thought she had purged long ago returned with a vengeance, along with the sick churning in her stomach that threatened to rise. Rubbing small circles on her stomach, she sniffled, looking around before walking back to the master bedroom. Again, her work could wait until tomorrow. She was too weary to even walk up the stairs to her own room.

Josephine couldn't sleep or rest. Muffled thuds as Beth threw things around mixed with her angry stomping resounded through the ceiling. Why Beth was so angry, Josephine didn't know. After a restless couple of minutes, Josephine still didn't have an answer, but it dawned on her that Beth probably hadn't put the horse or the wagon away. She came inside too quickly after her arrival. Resigned, Josephine rolled herself off the bed and trudged outside.

Sure enough, Beth had abandoned Daisy and the wagon

between the corral and the barn. Josephine found a drowsy Daisy waiting patiently for someone to unhitch her and put her up for the night. Daisy glanced at Josephine, bobbed her head, and nickered a greeting. The horse's sweet face calmed Josephine, as it loosened the grip of her frustration.

Josephine reached up to scratch Daisy behind the ear. "Oh, dear. Why does Beth always do this to you? You poor baby," Jo cooed at Daisy, who ate it up. Grasping Daisy's harness, Josephine led her into the barn. "I hope she didn't drive you hard or mistreat you while you were out." Josephine scrutinized Daisy, while stroking her cheek. Reaching the barn, she unhitched Daisy, leading her into her stall. After filling Daisy's feed bag and hanging up the harness, she set to brushing Daisy down. "You know I love you, don't you, Daisy? You come tell me when Beth's being a bully, and I'll take care of it. I will." Kissing the horse and hugging her neck, she whispered, "I promise."

* * *

Jimmy walked back to the barn to check on Coal and make the rounds on the other horses. Even though Jaems said Thom and Buford checked on them, he didn't really trust anyone else to do the job. At least he didn't trust anyone to do the job correctly. He had watched the way some of the men treated their mounts when he and Charlie were first kidnapped. It wasn't right. These were beautiful, intelligent creatures that deserved respect. Everyone deserves respect, but a few of the men gave theirs only to Van Der Kamp, and only because he had rules, and he expected them to be obeyed. He ran his gang better than the army did their soldiers.

The dog continued to heel by Jimmy. He almost laughed when the hound had turned around and growled at that jackass, Gus. As if Jimmy couldn't hear what they were saying. They spoke loud enough to wake the dead. It's funny because the dog had more sense than they did and seemed to know they were talking a load, too.

Finished with his rounds, he looked down at the expectant dog sitting next to him wagging his tail. He was slobbery and wide-eyed, smiling at Jimmy with the kind of devotion that comes from being a good dog. Jimmy sighed.

"All right, big fella. I guess we're stuck with each other." Jimmy reached down and scratched the dog's head, roving to the sweet spot under his neck, much to the dog's delight. "You get to bunk with me, but you're gonna need a good brush-down before you can come inside. Bath tomorrow."

Jimmy leaned his head forward and furrowed his brows, aiming for his best fearsome look. Somehow, he had a feeling the water would be more of a battle than an actual cleansing. Regardless, he didn't have the energy for it right now. It had been a long day, and he needed time alone with his thoughts. His time was usually spent alone. Somehow, today he'd been exposed and pushed out into the open for all to see. He didn't like it. Not one bit. He was too busy with new tasks to be collecting evidence to use against the gang. Being so close to Van Der Kamp had its disadvantages as well. He may hear more, but he was also more vulnerable.

* * *

VAN DER KAMP watched Jimmy and the dog. He shook his head and suppressed the mirth bumping against the migraine's remnants. He always knew deep down Jimmy was still a softy but was endeavoring to hide it with impassive looks and detached behavior as he grew older. After years of trying to remain invisible, Jimmy's immediate defense of that poor girl and the giant mutt proved he was a fierce protector of those in need and whatever he deemed right. Jimmy was a study in contradictions, that one.

Van Der Kamp's shoulders relaxed. The job of destroying Mack Pennington's web became a mite easier with Jimmy at his side. Jimmy had a fire in his belly and a taste for revenge —he could feel it. But if Jimmy knew about Pennington and his hit on Jimmy's father, he'd go off half-cocked, and Van Der Kamp couldn't have that. But if he gave Jimmy all the opportunities to do the work he needed to do and slowly fed him information, he'd have a powerful tool at his disposal down the line. Yes, Jimmy would do just fine. He might even be a sight better than Charlie at this stage in the game. It'd be a slow game of chess, but Van Der Kamp played to win, no matter what the cost. Pennington was going down.

CHAPTER 6

The smell of coffee—not the fact that chores needed to be done or that Josephine might need help with breakfast—drew Beth downstairs. Exhausted, Beth plopped herself on the chair, slumping forward with her head in her hands.

"Jo, will you pour me some coffee, please?"

Josephine looked at her as if she'd grown a second head. Instead of answering, she turned back to the stove and continued cooking.

"Jo-oh, I asked you a question." Beth was pathetic. Not only was she whining, but she still wore her robe and slippers, looking as bedraggled as something the cat had drug in. "Jo." This time, Beth clipped out her name.

Jo slammed down the wooden spoon and turned to face a surprised Beth. She jammed her hands on her hips just like their mama used to do when she was getting ready to verbally tan their hides—of course, only when no one else was around. That wouldn't be ladylike. Josephine pointed a finger at her sister.

"You've done nothing but complain about me for months. Months." Jo's voice rose on the second *months*. "Now you expect me to wait on you hand and foot? You couldn't even bother to take care of poor Daisy last night. You left her outside, still hitched up!" Jo leaned forward, arms spread wide as her voice grew louder. "You have a lot of nerve, especially the way you treated me last night." She tossed a dismissive hand at Beth, while returning to her cooking.

Beth watched Jo banging around the stove, moving meat off the pan, flipping the eggs, and slicing the bread so hard it folded in on itself. Josephine roughly brushed it off the cutting board, slammed the knife down, and returned to the now smoking eggs. All the while, Beth looked on with her mouth agape. She was barely awake when she had come downstairs. Now, she was waking up to the horror that was her normally sweet and compliant sister. Incrementally Beth straightened in her chair, looking ready to run at a moment's notice.

"Jo," Beth asked softly, as if she were trying to gentle her, "is everything all right? Are you feeling well?" Beth leaned back, biting her bottom lip. Her hand went to her cheek.

Jo spun around and barked, "No," before whirling back to the pan and dumping burnt food on the plates next to the stove. Smoke was rising, and it was making Beth's eyes burn, but she was too afraid to say anything. She was pretty sure her sister lost her mind during the night. Treating Jo as if she were a wild animal, Beth made slow movements and quiet sounds. She was easing herself off the chair when Jo practically tossed the plate of burnt food at her, making it clank on the table. Some of the eggs rolled off the plate. Horrified, Beth looked between the plate and an enraged Jo before slowly lowering herself back into her seat.

"Eat!" Jo pointed at the plate of food as she shoved a fork in Beth's direction.

For once, Beth did what she was told, but chewed slowly, watching Jo the entire time. Finally, she couldn't take it anymore. "Jo, honestly, what's got into you?" Her throat worked hard to swallow the overcooked food before she could continue. "You're kind of scaring me." She leaned away from Jo, gripping the fork, just in case.

"You know, you think you can just do what you want all the time, and when you don't get your way, you holler and throw a fit. When I point that out to you, you tell me"—she jabbed her finger at her chest—"*me*, I'm the horrible one. I do more than my fair share of work around here. Why is it that I have to walk into town to pick up parcels of work? Why is it that I have to put the wagon up and take care of Daisy after you took them into town doing Lord knows what? Of course, that's after you come home late and accuse me of ruining your life."

Jo slammed her hand on the table in sheer frustration. The plate and cup jumped along with Beth. Jo had never vocalized her feelings this way before. In fact, until Jimmy the Stranger said something about her situation and showed more concern about her than her blood relatives ever did, she had never bothered looking at how things stood. She hadn't ever complained, had always done what she was told, but was forever reminded to be grateful for what she had. But when she thought about last night, she didn't like what she saw: an overworked and underappreciated sister trying to keep things together when everyone else seemed to be working against her. When Beth yelled at her and then said she was ugly, it was the last straw. Jo wasn't the only ugly one. Things were going to get really ugly before they got better.

Beth stared in shock. Jo had never raised her voice. She had always backed down at the first hint of confrontation.

Beth cleared her throat before quietly speaking. "Jo, I never knew you felt this way. I—"

"You don't trouble yourself wondering what I think or even care, Beth. It's always been about you and who's paying attention to you." Josephine spoke sharply, startling Beth, who jerked her head back.

"That's not true, Jo. You're not being fair!"

Jo raised her eyebrows at Beth. "Really? You're not being fair, throwing my looks into every argument you're losing. Honestly, Beth. I'm not that ugly."

"I never said—"

"You're always implying it, if not saying it outright, as is Essie. Come to think of it, so did Mother and Father. You all call me that behind my back." She threw her arm out toward town. "There are men out there who don't think I'm ugly, just so you know."

Beth's face clouded over. "What do you mean by that, missy?" She leaned forward with a furrowed brow, her words sharp.

"I had to hurry home before it got dark, and I wasn't paying attention to where I was going. Because of that, I ran into some men, and they seemed to think I was pretty."

"What do you mean 'ran into'?" The edge in Beth's voice reminded Josephine of their mother.

"I physically ran into them, knocking my packages everywhere." Josephine explained as if speaking to a child before her voice took a sterner edge. "The packages I shouldn't have had to carry all the way home, Beth. What did you bring home, except a man?"

Beth's fists balled up and her face went red. She was near shrieking again. "I told you—that was Clara's brother! He was seeing me home, safe. More than you did for me."

Finally, Jo shrieked. "I let you have the darn wagon!" She

threw out her arms in exasperation. "Someone is always 'seeing you home.' You're safe from everyone but yourself, Beth. Who looks after me? I'm here working all alone most days. I walk to town and back home alone. You'd never be the wiser if I disappeared, unless you were looking for clean clothes or a meal."

Jo stalked out of the kitchen, stomping up the stairs. She slammed her bedroom door before Beth realized she had been bested by the meek one. Practically growling, Beth clenched her fists, blowing out a hard breath before storming up the stairs after Jo. She pounded on the door with her fist, hollering, "What do you mean by men?! Open this door and tell me what men would cavort with you."

Josephine threw open the door, her beet-red face reflecting her fury. Beth wasn't ready for the door to be opened or with such force, and her foot caught on her skirt's hem, sending her to the floor. Josephine jabbed her finger at Beth.

"See? That's what I'm talking about. You can't possibly imagine that some man, let alone men, would have any interest in me. Ugly, plain, boyish old me."

"Don't start with that tired old nonsense. Poor you."

"Poor me, nothing. You always throw that in my face— 'You'll never get married, so you might as well be the one to do all the chores because you'll be doing them all alone for the rest of your life anyway.'"

Beth's words, when spoken by a screaming Jo using falsetto, sounded so horrible. It was like a slap in the face hearing them spoken back at her.

"You can't possibly know how, how ... *awful* ... it is to be told you're ugly your whole life." Jo's voice was strangled. Her breathing came in gasps—the precursor to her tears—as she crossed her arms protectively over her belly, hunching forward. She choked out, "Especially wh-when beauty is held higher than other, m-more important traits. By the p-people who should l-love you the most, no less." Jo turned away, sucking in a stuttered breath. "Just go," she whispered. When Beth didn't move, Jo spoke a little louder. "Go. Away. Do something useful for once, like clean up the kitchen."

Jo remained where she was until she heard Beth get up and leave. Only then did she turn around and gently close the door. Tears were streaming down her face as her body gave up trying to keep the sobs to itself.

* * *

BETH'S HANDS WERE UNSTEADY, reflecting the way she was feeling. She plunged them into the lukewarm water and tried to scrub the burnt egg off the cast iron skillet. Raising a soapy hand, she brushed an errant strand of hair from her face. Jo's behavior threw her off. She had plans to flirt with John in town to see where that would lead. That had blown away with the wind. She had to do these few chores so Jo would calm herself down. *I still don't understand why Jo was in such a lather this morning.* Beth shook her head as she scrubbed. Something else must've happened because Jo usually let words thrown at her slide off like water off a duck's back. Blowing another strand of hair from her face, Beth looked down at her hands, grimacing.

Ugh, my hands are going to look so pruney by the time this is done. Jo should've been watching what she was doing. Beth glared at the pan and the bits of burnt egg covering it. *I couldn't even eat it, and now I'm cleaning up after her. She's wasting time with whatever nonsense she's gotten into.*

Scrubbing harder because she really wanted to get out of the house and back into town, a strange thought came to her. *Jo must be making it up, or these men are new to town ...*

By the time Beth had finished the dishes and straightened up as little as possible, Jo had returned. She stood watching Beth with her arms folded across her chest, lips pursed. Her eyes were swollen and red from crying, but she stood erect.

"Jo … are these men new to town? Have you seen them before?"

Josephine made a guttural sound. "I've never seen them before." She suppressed the urge to roll her eyes. "Don't worry. I'm not trying to steal any man's attention from you."

"Jo." Beth huffed out her name in exasperation. "That's not what I was saying. I'm wondering if more trouble has come to town. Ever since Frederick Reinhardt's cowboys returned, things have become rough. That's all."

"Don't talk about the menfolk like you know their business, Beth. It's unbecoming." Jo frowned.

Beth rolled her eyes. "Quit being such a prude." Huffing again, she threw her rag into the sink. "I'm concerned, that's all."

"For whom?"

"For all of us." Exhaling, she whipped her head toward Jo. "They didn't try anything with you, did they?" Beth sounded concerned for all of a split second. Then she went on, washing away any sliver of concern she might have had. "Everyone says Frederick Reinhardt and Sheriff Colter are up to no good. We all know that Frederick is angry and frightening. What if Frederick has more men coming to town? I think something's off about the sheriff. He's ignoring the cowboys' goings on."

Jo's face softened, despite their bickering. "Beth, I know you miss Matthew. Maybe—"

"We're talking about the so-called sheriff, not Matthew." Beth was not opening up to anyone until she got some more answers. She also noticed Jo didn't directly respond to her first question. "What aren't you telling me about these strangers, JoJo?"

"Nothing. I've told you all there is to tell. Besides, you're speaking about things I don't know anything about."

Beth snorted. "Whatever you say. Now you're acting more like the sheriff with your avoidance." She wiped her hands on the apron she was wearing, removed it, then handed it to Jo.

"Why are you handing me this?"

"It's yours, isn't it?"

"Well, yes, but—"

"Well, nothing. You've got a lot of work to do today. You said that Mrs. Patterson was in a hurry for that nice dress you're making with all that fancy new material, and that Mrs. Cooper needed you to help with some mending. Right?"

Jo was stunned. After their tussle this morning, she would think Beth would have been more contrite, or at least have some more sense. Apparently, she had run out of that along with clean aprons. Jo shook the apron out in disgust and turned on the ball of her foot. She marched out of the kitchen and up the stairs to retrieve her sewing basket. It wasn't that Beth was correct that angered her so much, as it was her complete disrespect in the allocation of work. Beth thought she had done her day's work by cleaning up the kitchen, and Jo was as sure of Beth's thinking as the sun rising each day. Beth thought about only Beth.

Josephine's assumptions proved correct as she came down the stairs and watched Beth go out the front door, shutting it none too gently. After waiting for five or so minutes, curiosity got the better of Jo.

She peered out the window, waiting for Beth to emerge from the barn. *Wagon or saddle? Interesting, saddle. Beth must be in a hurry today. I wonder who she's meeting?*

Jo shrugged. Exhaustion washed over her, so she let it go.

She hadn't felt this worn out in a long time. At any rate, Beth was right—she had a lot of sewing to get to in addition to the regular chores. She'd wait to collect eggs until she was ready for a break from sewing. Bread could wait, too.

She was sure Beth wouldn't be home at a reasonable time tonight, either. Why would she? *And she had Daisy to keep her safe*, she thought bitterly to herself.

CHAPTER 7

$\mathcal{A}$ bead of sweat trickled between Beth's breasts, fueling her agitated state. Her skin felt like a frying pan rapidly heating up for cooking, and her patience had evaporated before she left the house. It was entirely too uncomfortable to be out, but Beth was determined to try and catch John at the livery. They had some unfinished business, and she was impatient.

Darn Jo and her inconvenient feelings, anyway. Why now?

A strand of hair kept tickling her nose. Frustrated, she alternated between using her hand and blowing harder and harder to keep it off her face. Daisy took advantage of Beth's distraction, slowing herself to a lazy pace. Beth's irritation had her pushing the mare faster than normal, all because Jo's behavior had surprised Beth and sucked up most of the morning. Well, that and getting up a little later than usual. But Jo was primarily at fault.

We count on her to be consistent.

Their mother's voice popped into her head, sternly admonishing her and Essie about JoJo's place as helper. Beth's lips pressed together tighter. Since Essie was always considered the prettiest, it made Beth feel a little lost between the two sisters. It seemed the family couldn't really count on much these past few years, but she was hoping to change that. If anything, she could count on herself to get to the bottom of what was going on with Sheriff Colter. Beth was going to keep talking to the men and find out what they knew, even if it looked like flirting. Let everyone think what they will. She couldn't stop them from thinking or doing what they did, nor could she stop the gossip if she tried.

Daisy brought them to the edge of the town's business area and took herself to the nearest trough. When Beth dismounted, the horse blew a sigh of relief as she lowered her head to drink her fill. She was so thirsty that the sigh ended as blowing bubbles in the water. Beth was too preoccupied to notice. She scanned the street and boardwalk, shielding her eyes from the sun as Daisy slurped away. Even when Daisy raised her head and blew, shaking water from her chin, Beth didn't pay attention.

"Well, good morning, Miss Beth."

Beth whirled around, the flat of her hand pressed against her chest. "Oh," she gasped on an intake of breath. "Mr. Draper! You startled me." She exhaled loudly while dropping her hand. "You should probably practice announcing yourself before approaching someone from behind." Realizing she was being tart, she softened her words with a smile.

The other men called Terrance Draper "soft hands," among other things, because he had the look of a dandy who didn't do real work. He dressed in fine suits and was better groomed than some of the women in town. The saloon owner and mining speculator openly appraised Beth. She had become accustomed to that of late despite how much she disliked it.

His eyes took in the length of her, lingering on her ample bosom in a way that felt much dirtier than when the other men watched her. Despite knowing someone had spread rumors about her loose nature, Beth felt Mr. Draper's behavior went beyond the rumors, and not just because Jo repeatedly expressed her dislike of him. He didn't gawk like the others did. His gaze was more of a sense of entitlement or even ownership. It sent a chill down her spine even as the sun slowly scorched her skin.

"Yoo-hoo!"

Mrs. Clarksen's greeting interrupted any excuse Beth scrambled to formulate to get away from Mr. Draper. While she appreciated Mrs. Clarksen's interruption, Mrs. Clarksen wasn't one of her favorite people at the moment. Beth seemed to have an ever-growing list of them right now. Her desperation to find John was hounding her more than the heat. Plastering a smile on her face, she turned to face the town gossip.

"Hello, Mrs. Clarksen. How are you?" Hands clasped in front of her, Beth's knuckles turned white. She concentrated on her hands to keep her mouth out of the equation.

"Beth, whatever are you doing standing out in the noonday sun? Your skin is going to burn to a crisp! Goodness." Mrs. Clarksen shook her head, her lips pressed downward.

"I was just watering Daisy before I started with my errands. Thank you for your concern. I suppose I really should find some shelter." Beth's eyes darted around, looking for some shady place to escape but not finding any.

Mrs. Clarksen continued to stare at Beth, which made her feel like squirming—and not from the rumors. They hadn't been on very good terms the past couple of years. In fact, Mrs. Clarksen wasn't just staring. Her eyes were boring into Beth. She suddenly felt guilty even though no one knew what she was up to. She shifted her feet, gesturing toward Mr. Draper.

"Mr. Draper was wondering what I was up to as well."

"Well, I wonder how you know that since I didn't get a chance to ask you."

He cast a side-eye at Mrs. Clarksen even though he was responding to Beth. They had a well-known dislike of each other. He didn't like her busybody nature, and she didn't like his saloon or airs. On top of that, he shunned church and all church-related activities.

"Mr. Draper should let the unmarried ladies be, Beth. What you're doing is none of his business." Her eyes didn't leave Beth's, but the words were really a warning for Mr. Draper. Her body and presence seemed larger with her bold statement, her neck stiffening with indignation.

"Mrs. Clarksen should know that gentlemen like to give ladies a hand when needed. You looked like you might need some assistance. It is very warm out, and you look flushed."

His voice dropped on *flushed*, causing both Mrs. Clarksen and Beth to do exactly that, flush. This was the kind of behavior Mrs. Clarksen objected to. He was continually testing the limits of propriety. In addition to being the minister's wife, she was still quite proper by her own admission. In fact, she was more proper than her husband, which made a lot of tongues in town wag.

Knowing this would turn into a battle of words and pride, Beth cleared her throat to stop its progression. She'd already had her fill of discord for the day. Straightening, she gestured toward the livery. "I hate to interrupt, but I need to be on my way. Hot sun and all. Have a good afternoon." Nodding, she turned on her heel but took only one step before Draper's hand was on her elbow. Looking down at it and back at his face, she yanked her arm back. "Wouldn't want to burn."

Mrs. Clarksen's smile at Beth's bold move fell when Beth added the bit about burning. Draper laughed at Mrs. Clarksen's expression, and she scowled in return. However, instead of sending him vitriol, she sent it Beth's way.

"Yes, you best be getting on your errands. Wouldn't want to keep JoJo waiting for you. She's always working so hard, and it would be nice for her to get some help." Beth's eyes hardened as Mrs. Clarksen added, "Do be a dear and tell JoJo hello for me. Tell her I'll be out sometime for a nice visit."

Beth didn't respond. According to Mrs. Clarksen, JoJo could do no wrong, whereas lately she had a lot of criticisms for Beth. Instead, she grabbed Daisy's reins and led her down the street. While her head was high and back straight, her retreat still held an air of defeat. Mrs. Clarksen's commentary generally had that effect on her.

* * *

Mr. Draper and Mrs. Clarksen watched Beth and Daisy for a moment before he broke the silence.

"Don't know what she ever did to you, but you didn't have to set her down like that." The pair looked back down the street before looking at each other again. "That was uncalled for."

"Kindly keep your peace on what you don't know."

Draper watched her for a moment before proclaiming, "Well, I better get a move on myself. I was thinking of riding over to Adamsville. I should get down to the livery, too, and check on my horse."

Draper made to follow Beth, but Mrs. Clarksen stopped him.

"If you have business in Adamsville, Mr. Clarksen could help you with it. No sense in you riding all the way over there when he's already going." A thoughtful smile crossed her face, changing her entire demeanor. "I'm sure he'll be going over there today or tomorrow to help save the souls of some of our poor brethren."

Visiting the soiled doves is more like it. Draper was disgusted with Mrs. Clarksen's praise of her husband and all his good Christian works. He couldn't figure out how she didn't know the "good reverend" was a cheat and a liar. As much as he didn't like Mrs. Clarksen, he did feel she was the good Christian of their family, for what it was worth.

"Mrs. Clarksen, you are too kind. I could not impose on your husband's time. He's tending his flock between two towns—two." He ruefully shook his head, placing his hand on his heart. "That's too much of an imposition. I could no more make that than I could ask him to give up his heavenly service to the almighty." His hand dropped. "Well, I must be on my way."

When Mrs. Clarksen looked as if she would pitch a fit about him following Beth, he added, "Perhaps I'll give my errand a day or two. No need to run around in this damnable heat."

The look of outrage on Mrs. Clarksen's face was worth the blasphemy, not that he was worried about that, either. Smiling, he tipped his hat at her, walking back to the saloon.

* * *

A SQUAT MAN leaned back against the building, his red, bulbous nose in the air as he exhaled from the cigarette he was holding between his fingers. Tucked away in the alley, George Watkins was watching the smoke billow as he waited for Ian to return. He didn't trust Draper as far as he could throw him, and not just because Mack Pennington had sent him. That man was up to something with the Snyder girl, and he wanted to know what. If he was sniffing around the skirts of that one, something had to be up. Rumor had it that she was free with her wares, but Draper was persnickety in his ways. He liked the challenge. Things weren't adding up. Watkins snapped out of his slouch when he heard footfall.

"Boss. Sheriff hasn't left his office all morning. Draper and Miss Beth were just ribbing Mrs. Clarksen. Get a load of this—"

Watkins held up his hand. "I don't pay you to bring me gossip. Are you sure they didn't say anything important? What's Draper doing with Beth Snyder?"

"He snuck up on her. Kept looking at her like she was dessert, but I'm also thinking he's suspicious of her."

"I kind of wondered what she was up to."

"Well, she wasn't saying, and that's when Mrs. Clarksen ran over and tried to get into their business. Them women had themselves a little cat fight." He chuckled before noticing Watkins's narrowed eyes. Clearing his throat, he shrugged.

"That's it?"

"I'm telling you—they didn't say much. They were having some sort of standoff on Main Street before Miss Beth left. He tried to follow Beth to the livery with his own excuse of going to Adamsville, and that's when Mrs. Clarksen offered up the reverend to do Draper's errand for him." Ian resisted the urge to laugh, clearing his throat instead. "Their bluffing is better than some of the poker players in this town."

Watkins took a long drag of his cigarette, watching the smoke unfurl from his mouth but careless of how low the end burned between his fingers. The pair remained silent as the smoke curled upward before dissipating. He took in a long breath before asking, "You sure there wasn't more to it? There wasn't any legitimate business he was trying to get done?"

"Sure of it, boss. In the end, he was trying to get away from Mrs. Clarksen to follow Beth, but Mrs. Clarksen wasn't havin' it." He shook his head slowly. "That woman can make the milk curdle in a cow. Draper don't want any part of that. He was just making an excuse to go to the livery because she interrupted his talk with Miss Beth." He snickered, his head bent, fist over his mouth. "She actually yoo-hoo'd them." Looking up, he guffawed.

Watkins's expression didn't change, but he watched Ian closely. He took another drag of the cigarette before flicking it to the ground and grinding it under his boot. He blew smoke out his nostrils like a dragon from some frightening fairy tale. Specifically, a demon dragon. He was dirty, dank, and dangerous. People, even those with a criminal nature, gave him a wide berth.

"I'll take your word for it this time." Watkins didn't bother keeping the sarcasm out of his tone. "Better keep your ear to the ground with Draper. He's up to something, and I want to know as soon as someone figures it out. I don't want him to know I'm coming for him. You hear?"

Watkins shoved past Ian and into the street, heading straight for the livery. He was going to find out for himself what Draper was up to right now. It'd probably take some piecing together what that crook was planning for the long game, but he had plenty of time to wait that bastard out. And wait him out was what he was going to do.

CHAPTER 8

Rays of light barely illuminated the yard as Goat banged around in the kitchen. Used to outdoor cooking, he didn't think twice about the noise level. His morning helper didn't seem to mind, either, and was content to lie on the floor nearby and watch Goat do his thing. Somehow, the dog got out of Jimmy's room and joined Goat in his morning ritual. They were an odd and wiry-haired duo, but aptly named: the dusty, scraggly dog that was much taller than an average-sized child waiting patiently next to a gray, overgrown, bearded old man named Goat.

He didn't have to wait too long before Goat, thrilled with his new companion, cackled and began throwing him bits of bread and bacon, and telling him stories as he worked. The dog would occasionally turn his head to the side or rotate an ear toward him, as if he were truly interested in the nitty gritty of the conversation. When Jimmy walked in, Goat and the dog simultaneously looked over their shoulders at him like a pair of conspirators.

"There you are, Dusty. I was wondering where you got off to. How'd you manage to get out of my room?"

Goat cackled, "Dusty." He pointed his spatula at the dog who had trotted over to Jimmy, bumping Jimmy's hand with his head for scratches. "That one there is wily. He can open doors hisself, don't you know?"

After a few good scratches and pats, he went back to his post with Goat because Goat had the food. And Goat spoke with his spatula, causing bits of food to drop to the floor that the dog happily lapped up.

Jimmy stifled the smile that wanted to break through. "No, I'm supposing that I didn't know. That's why I was asking."

Goat's face dropped, then he burst out laughing. "Oh, you had me there, sonny. You did. You must've gotten a good night's because you've got some extra sass in ya."

The smile won out, and Jimmy shook his head as he scratched the back of his neck. "I'm supposing I did. Don't know why, though. Yesterday was a long day."

"Ooh-wee. I heard about a little scuffle in town. Them men were a-talkin'. What happened?"

Goat leaned forward, eyes wide, like the old gossip he was, anticipating juicy tidbits from the brawl in town. He knew what he had heard. Now he wanted to hear what happened from not only a reliable source, but someone who was actually there. The others who were there weren't talking, ironically. And they always talked.

Jimmy paused, looking at Goat. Goat's eyes were shiny with interest, and he had a half smile on his face, which was saying, "Well, now. Go on. I'm a-listenin'." Jimmy couldn't resist Goat in anything because he had always stood up for him and Charlie. Besides, despite his eccentric nature, he really was a good man. He was kind of like the crazy uncle family members tended to ignore. That also made him an invaluable ally because he was able to hear things people didn't want others to know and to get things done that others couldn't.

Sighing, Jimmy shook his head. "There was a tussle in town. That's all."

Goat made an exaggerated sound of clearing his throat while throwing his hand at Jimmy. "You know that ain't what I want to hear. Spill the beans before I grow any grayer."

Jimmy narrowed his eyes because he wasn't much of a talker—and Goat knew it. He certainly wasn't a braggart like some of the other men.

Heaving a sigh as his shoulders slumped, he humored Goat. Dusty got up, and trotted over to Jimmy, nuzzling him. "Gus and his cronies were in the middle of the street harassing some young lady. Knocked her packages all around and wouldn't let her be."

Goat waited for the details he so desperately wanted, but Jimmy didn't give them up. He crossed his arms and asked, "And?"

Jimmy huffed. "And I asked them to let her be." He paused as Goat eagerly nodded at him, so Jimmy added, "They chose poorly."

"Ah-haa!" Goat slapped his thigh and pointed his spatula at Jimmy. "Then you showed them the error in their ways."

Jimmy blushed to the tips of his ears. He stared back at Goat and finally said, "I suppose I did. Who knows whether the lesson will stick or not." He shifted his feet. "Then, when I was talking to Van Der Kamp, they were harassing him." Jimmy pointed at the beast that was now leaning his entire body against Jimmy's leg. Dusty looked pretty content sitting there and began thumping his tail as if he knew he was being talked about.

"Oh, I was a-wonderin' 'bout that. That damn commotion could've woke the dead last night." He looked from the dog to Jimmy. "Woke me—that's close enough." He guffawed at that, shaking his head. Turning back to the stove, he said, "Coffee's 'bout ready. Help yourself."

"Don't mind if I do. I have quite a day ahead of me. Big boy here is getting a bath." The dog visibly shrank at that, looking up at him with half-moon eyes. Without looking at Dusty, Jimmy said, "Don't look at me like that. It won't work. Not from the horses and not from you."

"You're going to have your hands full with that one." Goat smiled at Jimmy. "Been a long time since we've had a dog 'round here. Gonna be nice." He nodded, turning back to his cooking. "Real nice."

Jimmy watched Goat work for a moment longer, wondering what he was thinking. Shrugging, he poured himself a big serving of coffee and dropped himself into a chair. Dusty laid his head on Jimmy's lap. He absentmindedly stroked the dog's head, eliciting a contented sigh from him.

The hot brew soothed Jimmy's throat, even though Goat made it strong and proclaimed it "put hairs on yer chest." He inhaled the pleasing aroma. It was a peaceful moment in the early morning until Dusty tensed. His hair was so wiry and matted it was impossible to see his hackles, but Jimmy felt the change and the rumbling low growl from Dusty's chest. Jimmy knew why before he heard the voice.

"Isn't this cozy? A boy and his mongrel."

Multiple sets of footsteps followed the voice. Jimmy figured it was Gus's entire crew. He didn't shift or acknowledge them in any way. Bringing the mug to his lips, he took another big mouthful of coffee and swallowed. He continued to pet the dog, so Dusty stopped growling. However, he didn't let down his guard and shot them a narrowed side-eye. While Dusty may have trusted Jimmy and Goat, he certainly didn't trust the others.

"You finally found a friend, Jimmy?"

Behind Gus, a smattering of chuckles broke out, and

boots clomped. When Jimmy didn't answer, Gus came around to taunt him face-to-face. "Nights aren't so lonely anymore now, are they? Must be nice being in the big house with your new friend."

The men roared with laughter. Jimmy didn't carouse like the others did. They sometimes called him "The Monk" behind his back because he mostly kept to himself, didn't drink, and didn't sleep around. They teased him about being untried. The thing was, Jimmy didn't trust others too terribly much. His meager experience had taught him that few people were trustworthy. People he should've been able to openly trust had let him down too many times. His own father had been the main culprit, and the last was the family preacher, before Jimmy was kidnapped.

He wasn't interested in any of the women the gang purposely sought out because they had to fight for their basic needs, too. Loyalty was slim. What exactly he was waiting for, he wasn't sure. All he knew was he wasn't in a hurry. Jimmy took a deep breath as he sat up straighter.

Saluting Dusty with his mug, he said, "I did find a good friend. More than I can say for you, Gus."

Gus's eyes narrowed. "What do you mean by that, Jimmy? I've got friends. You're the one who doesn't."

"I don't have to bully others into doing my business or following me around. Either they do or they don't."

Gus's face fell, but he quickly recovered. Laughing, he said, "Do you hear that, boys? Thinks he knows everything."

Harry looked decidedly uncomfortable, making himself even smaller than the young, underfed teen that he was, as he sidled over to the coffeepot to help himself. He looked sheepishly at Goat, who gave him an odd look. Shrugging, Harry turned around to look at Jimmy. Jimmy glanced at him then back at Gus. No one had responded to Gus.

"What I do know is right from wrong. You ought to learn that for yourself."

Jimmy got up and refilled his coffee. He nodded to Goat and walked toward the kitchen door. As the dog followed, Gus threw a kick at his hindquarters. He missed, but Dusty still turned around, growling, and lunged at him. Gus jumped back, arms flailing. He didn't expect such a bold reaction from the dog since the dog had endured their abuse earlier. Finding a protector in Jimmy seemed to have emboldened him. Jimmy turned around and snapped his fingers at the dog. "Here." He pointed to his side, and Dusty trotted over and sat next to Jimmy.

"That's what I'm talking about, Gus. Leave him be, or next time I'll let him loose on you."

Gus scoffed. "As if that old bag of bones could do any harm. He's all bark and no bite. He's just being brave because you're around."

"That's where you're wrong. Maybe he didn't feel like he had a reason before. He was starving. Some fool didn't take care of him, but now he has someone who will—and for him to care for in return."

"Pfft. You?"

"Yeah, me. Everyone needs someone to care about and something to fight for. He has me now. Got a problem with that?"

Jimmy crossed his arms, shifting his legs apart slightly. He'd had a taste of beating down Gus yesterday, and it sparked something in him. Jimmy's chest expanded, broadening his shoulders, as he straightened to his full height. Whenever Jimmy did that, everyone backed down. He was no small man. In fact, he was practically a giant, right down to his hands. They were like the smithy's—the size of a dinner plate.

"Settle down. I didn't mean any harm. Take that fool dog

with you and git." Gus made a shooing gesture, but his voice still had an edge of panic stemming from yesterday's beating.

"Sure thing, Gus." He raised an eyebrow. "And don't be kicking him anymore. He doesn't like it."

"Oh, for God's sake, Jimmy. Now you're talking for the damn thing? Take your hellhound and go on."

Jimmy walked off without another word. He looked down at Dusty as they headed toward the barn. "You did good for yourself back there. I think we're going to make a right proper team."

The dog barked at him, trotting along, happy as could be. It really did seem that he had found his person and was plenty pleased about it. Jimmy didn't feel too burdened about the situation, either.

CHAPTER 9

$\mathcal{J}$immy wasn't going to take his chances by bathing old dusty dog in the barn where he could potentially upset the horses. Recently stressed about their new location as well as with the general unrest of the gang, he felt they were finally settling down—except Winnie, thanks to Dobbin. Intuitively, Jimmy knew the dog's first bath was going to be more of a battle, so he needed to be strategic about it. One spooked horse was bad enough—but all it took was one horse who wouldn't settle to send unrest rippling through the herd.

Instead, Jimmy went farther out from the town proper to where the river ran wider. He didn't want to cause any unnecessary ruckus over water. Neither did he want any undue attention drawn to him. The longer ride was worth the hassle. Jimmy decided he might as well strip down and bathe himself since he was pretty sure Dusty was going to get him soaked anyway. He chuckled at that. Dusty.

Every time he touched that darned dog, clouds of dust came off him in little puffs. Jimmy had taken to calling him Dusty in the barn, and it seemed to fit. The dog must've agreed because he'd been answering to that name all morning. Unless he was just gleefully responding to the new hand that fed him.

They reached the river's edge, and Jimmy looked around, making sure no cattlemen were out and riding this way. So far, they hadn't seemed to at this time of day, which is why he waited, but why borrow trouble? Tossing the bar of soap on the ground, Jimmy shucked his boots, followed by his clothing. Dusty was already at the river's edge lapping up water. When Dusty looked fully absorbed, Jimmy gave the giant dog a shove into the water and followed him. Dusty howled as if he were being murdered, but Jimmy grabbed the dog under his belly, keeping his head above water. Dusty barked furiously and thrashed until he realized Jimmy was talking to him and had a good hold on him.

"Now Dusty, remember the deal we had? You were supposed to be having this here bath if you want to bunk with me. If you don't want to bunk with me, then I'm leaving you to fend for yourself with Gus and the other nitwits who follow him around."

His eyes narrowed at the dog, and that was about the time Dusty resigned himself to his fate. He certainly didn't look thrilled, but at least he was no longer thrashing, hollering, and carrying on as if he were dying. Jimmy walked around the river with him like that for a few more minutes, giving his fur a good soaking.

"All right then, we need to lather you up, or you're just going back to smelling the way you were, and that won't work for me. You hear?"

Dusty stilled, looking at him with his big old moon eyes, but Jimmy wasn't having it.

"Nope, big guy. Soap and cooperation. Then some grub."

Holding Dusty, Jimmy walked back to the river's edge and set him down. He grabbed the bar of soap, lathering it as

Dusty tried to skulk away. Jimmy snapped his fingers at the dog, pointing in front of him to stay. Sighing and hanging his head, Dusty stood in front of Jimmy, waiting for his fate.

"Come on. It's going to be fine. When have I done you wrong, Dusty?"

Dusty sighed once more as he hung his head lower. He stood rigidly while Jimmy lathered him with soap and gave him a vigorous scrubbing. As he realized this wasn't his mortal end, Dusty changed his tune and shifted to soft, happy moans and groans as Jimmy's hands worked their loving magic with the scrubbing and massaging. The corners of Dusty's mouth pulled back, and his teeth were showing, looking like he was grinning with joy as dirty water dripped off his coat.

"Good Lord, Dusty. You sure were a mess. Look at all that dirt. Now don't go telling me a bath doesn't feel good. A little more love, and you'll be back in shape in no time. I don't know what fool had you before, but it's his loss. Huh, good boy? Yes, you're a good boy—"

The sound of a horse coming down the trail interrupted them, and Dusty tensed, hackles raised. Quickly dipping his hands in the water to rinse them, Jimmy turned around and stepped out of the river, struggling to pull on his pants and shirt as quickly as his wet body would allow.

An older man sat atop a quarter horse and looked down at the pair. He bore an odd expression but didn't speak as he observed the two carefully. Dusty was attentive, but not defensive, which was noteworthy. Jimmy watched as the man slid off his horse and walked closer to them, hand extended.

"Douglas Elliot. I own the Double Star, the ranch just west of here."

"Jimmy Stapleton. Just arrived." He nodded in greeting.

Fortunately, Jimmy was a calm man who had a good poker face benefitting him in situations like this. Underneath, he was worried the rancher was going to start asking questions Jimmy didn't have the answers to. It'd be another strike against him with Van Der Kamp's edict about lying low. Jimmy also didn't want to be forced to leave before he rinsed Dusty. Odd thing to worry about, but he'd become attached to the expressive creature. Just not his current odor.

"I know. Been watching."

Surprise flickered in Jimmy's eyes, but quickly extinguished itself.

"We've had some water issues here in the past, men trying to divert it. Just making sure everything's doing fine. Also, had some rustling issues. Nothing new, but there's been a lot of newcomers lately." He continued to size up Jimmy as he spoke.

"Sorry to hear that. I'm unfamiliar with cattle. I work with horses." When Douglas didn't respond, Jimmy tilted his head, adding, "I don't care much for people because they lie. Animals are truth tellers."

Douglas's mouth opened wide, but instead of a retort, barking laughter deep from his belly rang out. "Now you sound just like my foreman, Lars."

Dusty joined in with some howling of his own. Jimmy gave Douglas a half smile because he felt a kindred spirit with the rancher despite feeling tested. Not many people understood animals the way he did. The gang was always giving him grief for all his fussing over the horses and their care.

When Douglas finally stopped laughing, he said, "Didn't have to tell me that. I could tell by the way you're fawning over that old cuss there." He pointed at Dusty, who cocked his head in response. "Never seen a man bathe a dog like that."

"Well, you didn't have to smell him, so there's that."

Douglas chuckled and knocked his hat back on his head.

"I suppose you have me there. You were taking some extra care with him that most people don't do. Looks like he could use some extra grub, though."

"Yeah, well, that's the way I found him. Actually, he found me. Followed me home. Whoever had him before didn't bother to care for him. Seems to be a real fine dog—someone's loss."

"He's yours now. I can tell already."

Jimmy looked down at Dusty, who stretched his neck out, tossing up his muzzle and giving a low woof in response. "Yup. We belong together."

Douglas nodded, tipping his hat before adjusting it squarely on his head. "I'm going to finish my rounds but thought I'd make my presence known, if you know what I mean." He locked eyes with Jimmy for a moment—doing double duty, assessing as well as issuing a warning.

"I do. You won't have any troubles with me. I keep to myself and the horses."

"Much obliged."

Douglas put his foot in the stirrup and easily sprang into the saddle with the grace of a man half his age. Jimmy and Dusty watched him ride off before looking at each other.

"I know. That was odd."

Dusty's ears pointed forward, focused on the rancher riding away before relaxing. He did a little hop into the water that made Jimmy laugh.

"Yup. Let's get that finished. I promised you some grub when we were finished. Let's get on with it."

CHAPTER 10

*V*an Der Kamp was sitting on the front porch with a cup of coffee, keeping an eye on the surroundings. He could hear the pair coming in but saw the dog first as it rounded the corner of the house. Dusty was still damp from his bath but happily trotted up the stairs and plopped himself down next to Van Der Kamp. His tongue was lolling from the morning exertions, but he was happy as could be. Van Der Kamp looked down at his feet with a rumbling chuckle.

"You've found a loyal pardner there, Jimmy." Van Der Kamp raised his mug toward Dusty when Jimmy joined them a short bit later.

"Yup. He's a good one. Finally gave in to his bath without too much trouble. Lot of carrying on at first, but he settled himself."

"He knows who's boss."

"At least the hand that feeds him." Jimmy smiled before turning serious. "Say, met a neighboring rancher today. Has his eyes on us—more of a warning than anything."

Van Der Kamp "hmm'd" in acknowledgement before

scrunching up the right side of his face for his thinking inhale. "Which direction he come from?"

Jimmy pointed southwest. "Double Star Ranch. Douglas Elliot."

Not that there was anything to see from where they were, but they both looked in that direction.

"I suspect another gang is in town. If Pennington's got good sources, that is. See what you can find without drawing attention to who we are. You may want to check on that girl of yours, too."

Jimmy jerked his head back. "Sir? I have no girl."

Van Der Kamp slowly nodded. "You do. The one you saved yesterday. She's yours."

"No, I protected her from Gus and his followers. I helped her."

"You sound like Charlie now. Go on, git. Find out how she's doing and what she's up to. Make sure she isn't being bothered by those half-wits. Speaking of which—heard about breakfast. Good job putting them in their place. Let's keep it that way."

Jimmy's lips went flat, but he nodded curtly. He went inside and up the stairs to change. His mouth open in a semi-smile, Dusty looked at Van Der Kamp before following Jimmy. Van Der Kamp chuckled to himself and took a sip of coffee.

"That damn dog." He shook his head with mirth. "He knows more than he's letting on."

* * *

JIMMY RODE into town with Dusty trailing behind him. The dog was so happy to be on an adventure that he was all over the place. Running ahead of Jimmy, stopping to sniff something important, then meandering behind him, yipping along the way. They were surprising sounds from such a large dog, but noises bursting with life. Jimmy, however, slouched and wasn't paying much attention to the dog's joy.

Normally, he'd be smiling along with Dusty, but being told Josie was his girl felt like a rock in his belly. Now he felt trapped in a role he didn't want, tense and out of sorts, like a day being stuck indoors did to him. Not only was he in charge of keeping the peace with Gus, but he had a woman to look after. He was saddled with tasks that were the opposite of what he wanted to do—get justice for all the victims of this gang. For his murdered parents and for the years he lost with his loved ones. For being forced to live with the gang after his kidnapping and for the years of harsh treatment he'd endured at the hands of Wrighty and his bootlickers. He wasn't even sure why Van Der Kamp had put him in charge of these things. There were plenty of others who could put Gus in his place. Plenty of people who'd be happy to lend a fist to that cause.

I'm sure Van Der Kamp is up to something. He always is. But why me?

As for Josie, he had planned on checking on her anyway, but just to make sure she was all right. He wouldn't put it past Gus or even Cy to find out where she lived and force himself on her. His face froze, although his eyes continued to narrow. For a moment, he held his breath. His mind went back to the night Wrighty had dragged Charlie and him back to camp after they had tried to escape. Wrighty had beat him so badly he couldn't walk for a week. Jimmy expelled a big puff of air. As quickly as the image came, it left.

It wasn't until he felt a familiar throbbing pain that he realized he was grinding his teeth. Years of holding his tongue and his breath created a painful habit of clenching and grinding his teeth. Both took a toll on his patience and his jaw. Moving his jaw around to loosen it up, he sat up straighter, resigned to do his duty. They had reached the edge of town, so he forced himself to pay better attention to his surroundings.

Since the gang was brand new to this area, he still got looks from the townspeople. His sheer size was most likely the primary reason, but he suspected the townspeople weren't too keen on newcomers in general. Douglas Elliot hinted at that. He couldn't blame anyone. Jimmy headed straight for the mercantile to get some supplies as well as a feel for the heart of the town. People talked, and he needed to hear some things.

CHAPTER 11

*L*inden's main street was filled with many storefronts and a flurry of people bustling by. But as they walked along, they avoided eye contact, and only a few were talking or otherwise engaging with each other. The situation struck Jimmy as odd as he rode by and took in the mix of cowboys, miners, and passers-by. The town sat in a rich mining and ranching valley nestled between two sister towns, Adamsville and Weaver. The river and stagecoach route kept these towns alive and brought in visitors.

Besides this lack of interaction, Jimmy noticed the seemingly casual postures of some of the men—pretending indifference while carefully observing. They behaved very much like the scouts in the Van Der Kamp gang when they went into a town. He watched a woman with a basket on her arm pop into the bakery just as a man emerged from the alley, hat pulled low. Farther down the street, a man leaning against a hitching post took a long drag of his cigarillo, pretending to ignore Jimmy while keeping his eye on a man coming out of a restaurant. This was exactly what the Van Der Kamp gang was doing by coming here—hiding in plain sight. Something that criminals or others on the run would do. And no one was paying attention, except those paying attention—those of more suspect nature.

Coal moved slowly by a man and woman walking with their arms linked who stopped to gawk at the incoming trio. Coal blew at them but didn't break his stride. Jimmy and Coal were used to the gawking. Dusty, however, took issue, giving the couple some side-eye, but had enough sense to keep with his pack. As usual, Jimmy's size made people notice him. Add to that his twenty-hand, jet-black horse and a wolfhound mix that stood as tall as a foal, they made for an impressive sight yet looked out of place on the dusty road. Jimmy was polite, nodding to those who made eye contact and ignoring those who didn't, before steering his group to the closest trough.

Jimmy slid off Coal and made a sweeping glance around at the storefronts. He was allowing Coal to drink his fill but finally put a stop to the watering when Coal nudged Dusty and Dusty returned with a nip and shove of his own. He wasn't in the mood for their shenanigans. Jimmy pushed Dusty away from Coal and turned the horse toward the mercantile. He looped the reins around the hitching post, when Dusty bumped his leg. He reached out, scratching the wiry dog behind his ear. Dusty's hind leg moved back and forth as he leaned into Jimmy even more. He grunted with pleasure, wagging his tail enthusiastically.

Pointing to the ground, Jimmy said, "You stay here. I'll be right back."

Dusty sighed but flopped himself dramatically on the ground. He looked up at Jimmy with sad, rounded eyes.

"Nope. Don't even try."

Jimmy walked away without looking back. Otherwise, Dusty might have gotten the wrong idea.

A chiming bell announced Jimmy's arrival at the door, followed by several sets of eyes turning his way. Filling the door frame, Jimmy doffed his hat as he entered and scanned the quiet surroundings. He nodded to a pair of ladies, walking directly toward the older man at the counter, who nodded and called out to Jimmy.

"Morning, sir. What can we do you for?" A tidy mustache above his smile enhanced the congenial face of Harold, the mercantile owner.

Once again, Jimmy nodded politely. "I'm needing a fresh shirt and some waist overalls, as well as some soap and several cans of beans."

"Well, you're no little un, are ya? I'll see what I have in the back. We may have to measure you and have something made. You in town for a while or just passin' through?"

"I'm here for a while."

As Harold collected the clothing items, Jimmy called out, "Might as well add some tobacco for my friend." His decision was a spur-of-the-moment one. He didn't have a list, but thought it was a good purchase for Goat. Goat had always been good to him, and he really enjoyed his tobacco.

"That's mighty kind of you."

"Well, he doesn't get around real well, and it might cheer him up in what idle time he has."

He heard a feminine chorus of "aw" nearby. Jimmy stifled a smile at that. It'd been so long since he'd been around flatterers or admirers—a lifetime. His childhood held the days from high society, and he didn't go to brothels. Jimmy was never one for flattery or false words, especially the kind those places conjured. Flatterers, false words, and the past could stay away. However, having his kindness acknowledged this time around was nice. It smoothed the edges of the more odious task of playing keeper of Gus and company. He grimaced thinking about them.

The pair of finely dressed women had been keenly observing him from the side of the store, and the older of the two stepped closer. Gasping, she asked, "Are you all right, sir? Is it your friend you're thinking about?"

"Excuse me?"

Jolted out of his reverie by this forward woman, Jimmy locked eyes with a curious set of blue ones. The sooty coloring rubbed onto her lashes made them stand out even more. She was watching him with a little too much heat, leaning toward him inappropriately close.

She must've read his mind because she leaned back. "I apologize for being forward. It's just that you suddenly looked a little ill or upset. I was just concerned. Please, forgive me." With a flick of her wrist, her fan snapped open. She fanned herself a beat or two, coyly waiting for his response.

"Thanks for your concern. It's nothing. I was just thinking is all." He turned to face the counter, hoping she'd get the not-so-subtle hint. He considered busying himself by calling out more items, but he was pretty sure these women were taking close note of his purchases.

Another voice chimed in behind him. "Please forgive my aunt. She speaks her mind, always has."

Jimmy stifled the sigh that was begging to break free. Instead, he inhaled deeply and silently released it before turning to face the younger woman who just spoke.

Flashing one of his rare and brilliant smiles, Jimmy said, "No need to apologize. I'm used to women speaking their minds."

The air went still as the women's eyes widened, not knowing how to take the remark. They looked at each other then back at Jimmy. Women in the West were more practical and heartier than the high-society women back East, at least what he remembered of them. But they still had polite manners and rules to follow. Jimmy felt they interpreted his words quite differently than he had intended. What Jimmy was really thinking about was his brother's love, Annabelle. She had no problems speaking her mind. Even more humorous than her outspoken ways was the thought of her being surrounded by a hardened gang and eventually running the camp in a way she saw fit. It made him chuckle.

The aunt's face slowly transformed into a mask of haughtiness, complete with turning up her nose. And it changed to one of fury and indignation as she responded with clipped speech. "We're not those kind of women, sir. I certainly hope you do not associate with them." She threw her shoulders back, eyes piercing him with challenge.

Jimmy made a choking sound but quickly recovered. "I do not" were his only words, but his voice was low, steady, and equally clipped, tinged with a deathly chill. He didn't appreciate having his morals questioned or being judged, especially by some forward women he didn't know.

The younger woman's brows knitted as she shot her aunt a fix-it look. The older woman huffed back but responded by using more formal etiquette. They were a confusing pair—the women looked closer to being sisters than aunt and niece.

"I'm sorry, sir. Please, let us begin again." The flat of her hand tapped her chest as she said, "I am Nora Reinhardt." That hand then introduced her companion. "And this is my niece, Lillian Reinhardt."

Jimmy stared, considering his options. He came here to get the lay of the land and to find out whatever he could but didn't relish the thought of revealing too much to these obnoxious women. They wanted something from him, and whatever it was, he wasn't planning on giving it to them. However, he needed to hear the town gossip, and who better to provide that than two young busybodies?

Clearing his throat, Jimmy responded, "Jimmy Stapleton." He gave a slightly angled nod. "How d'you do?"

The women bowed their heads slightly in response, then the three of them stood looking at each other in awkward silence. Everyone had gone about this backward. Jimmy was grateful when Harold came from the stockroom carrying an armful of garments and interrupted their standoff.

"Well, I have some of these that were for another fella who didn't come back for them. He's 'bout your size." He held up the shirt and Jimmy nodded. "You may want to go back there and try it on, just in case. If this doesn't work, I have some material that Frannie could whip up a shirt from."

That made Jimmy think of Josephine and her armful of parcels. Just as he was conjuring her up in his mind, Harold snapped his fingers in the air, interrupting Jimmy's thoughts.

"You know, JoJo's an excellent seamstress. Josephine—we've always called her JoJo—she's looking for some extra work. You may want to ask her. Mmmhmm."

Shaking out the shirt, Harold nodded to himself, handing it to Jimmy, who was pleased that something finally was going right today.

The whole situation felt much smoother until Nora burst out, "Oh, no! You don't want her to do his fine work. Frannie is a professional and a much better choice." Her face puckered into a frown, as if she had tasted something sour. She snapped her fan open again, this time furiously fanning herself.

Lillian nodded. "Yes, Frannie does most excellent work, and she probably would have no problem putting your clothing at the top of her list. It seems you have some need of these things."

Jimmy looked down at his dusty clothing stretched across his broad frame. His shirt and pants looked worn but serviceable. The vest was fairly new. Despite being twenty, he recently had a growth spurt, and looking down at his clothing right now, he noticed the fabric had become a little stretched. Not too appropriate for socializing, but that didn't matter. He never had a need to impress anyone, as he was always out working with the horses and didn't go into town when the others did. This wasn't a social call, either. This was his first real foray into town, and he could only imagine what these women saw.

When he looked back up, he saw Lillian smiling coquettishly and Nora watching knowingly. He turned to look at Harold, who shrugged his shoulders, frowning, looking somewhat at a loss. *No help there.*

"I appreciate you finding something. I know I'm a hard body to clothe." The women tittered, and Jimmy ignored them. "I'll try these things on, and we'll go from there. If I need something made, I'll be talking to Miss Josephine."

He shot a narrow-eyed look at the women when they looked to object. They were being catty and proprietary, and he didn't appreciate it. *A couple of spiteful gossips who probably don't have any valuable information for me, anyway.* Huffing, he stalked to the back area to change, his patience eroded by senseless people.

* * *

"Well, I never." Nora's fanning sped up. "Of all the nerve."

"I'm sure he meant nothing by it. Why, he can't even know JoJo. How could he? He must have barely come to town. I've never seen him. Right, Harold?" Lillian looked over at him, hope in her eyes.

"Leave me out of this, ladies. I don't know what it is about JoJo that has you in such fits. Just because you're mad that Essie married the most eligible bachelor in town, and Beth has all the men falling at her feet doesn't mean she's like them. She's not."

Harold turned around. These women tired and annoyed him. They did nothing productive in town aside from stirring up trouble. Bored and irresponsible, they left the Reinhardt spread to create problems for others. Frederick Reinhardt, Lillian's father and Nora's brother, was a heap of trouble himself. Harold wouldn't be surprised if Reinhardt was part of the horse thieving and cattle rustling that had broken out in the past few months. He'd always been devious and too big for his britches. Lazy as well. Harold stacked the beans and soap on top of wrapping paper, lost in his thoughts, while the women spoke in hushed tones.

"I think he's quite handsome, Aunt Nora."

"Don't call me 'aunt.' You know I don't like it. We're too close in age for you to be using it."

"Well, I mean to find out more about him, and you're going to help me. Should we wait for him to be finished and follow him out, or should we leave now with an air of mystery?" Lillian giggled, mostly to herself. She had read far too many romances and dime novels about bandits, which adversely affected the way she saw the world. If it weren't for her more worldly aunt and ruthless father, she probably would've been taken advantage of long ago.

Nora sighed while giving an exaggerated eye roll. "Don't go getting all starry-eyed over him. While he's a marvelous example of the male form"—she motioned her fan vertically, mimicking a head-to-toe perusal—"we know nothing about him. Besides, I'm thinking that your daddy has someone else in mind for you."

"Hmph. Daddy has no taste. I want a man of my own— one that I get to choose."

"Right." Nora rolled her eyes again. "Then you better be minding your P's and Q's, so to speak, if you want that to happen. You keep putting yourself in harm's way." She quirked a brow at Lillian, tapping her with the fan. "Remember? That's precisely why I'm back in this God-forsaken territory—to keep you from self-disaster. You can't seem to control yourself when it comes to male attention."

"Pshaw." Lillian flipped her hand dismissively. "Nothing doing. I'll be fine."

Jimmy's return interrupted their tête-á-tête.

"Shh, here he comes." She straightened up, looking anything but the casual affect that she was trying for. "How did the clothing fit, Mr. Stapleton? Do you need any alterations?"

"I didn't realize you worked here, Miss Reinhardt." Jimmy shifted the neatly folded stack of clothing from one hand to the other, away from Lillian, when he saw her eyeing it.

Lillian coyly covered her mouth as she giggled. "No, silly. I'm being neighborly. If something didn't fit, I'd be more than happy to walk you over to Frannie's shop." With an exaggerated motion, she leaned forward, pointing down the street. "I could put in a good word for you so she'll get working on your things straight away." Straightening, Lillian batted her eyelashes at him as she smiled.

Jimmy ran a hand down the front of his face as he looked at the floor. Taking in a deep breath and sighing, he remained calm as he said, "That's proper kind of you now. However, I think I will go with Miss Josephine, who seems to be needing some extra work. I'm always happy to help someone in need." When Lillian's eyes narrowed, he responded, "It's the Christian thing to do, ma'am." Nodding at the astonished pair, he walked around them and up to the counter where Harold was waiting.

"I'm sorry to say these don't fit. They're on the uncomfortable side of tight. I'd certainly bust a seam." Behind him, he heard gasps. Exasperated, his head fell back as he looked up at the ceiling. Harold barely contained a snort at it all. Jimmy met Harold's eyes and said, "I'd also like to take that material you were talking about, and if you could send me in the direction of Miss Josephine's, I'd be much obliged."

"Absolutely." Harold slid the tobacco across the counter. "Might want to keep that in your pocket for your friend. Don't think Miss JoJo will appreciate it being wrapped up with the material and thread." Jimmy looked confused before Harold responded, "I'm going to add some heavier thread for your work clothes. She's been doing a lot of mending for the ladies. Not sure if she'll have the correct thread on hand. If she does, you can always return it. No sense you making two trips out there."

"Out there?"

"Yes, out there. She lives about a mile or so outside of town. While it's not far, it's the opposite direction of every-thing around here."

Jimmy nodded. "Which direction do I go?" Naturally, Jimmy remembered but wanted to protect Josephine from gossip. He also didn't want to blow his potential cover.

"Head toward the saloon and keep riding down that road for about a mile or so. You'll see a giant cottonwood. Take the path that veers off behind it, and you'll find their spread."

"I appreciate it. What do I owe you?"

They completed the transaction, but the ladies hadn't moved. They were still gawking at Jimmy. He returned his hat to his head, tipping it as he walked past them out the door. Like ducklings, they followed him. When Dusty saw Jimmy coming out of the mercantile, he jumped up, wagging his tail until he noticed the women. Dusty took one look at them and emitted a low, rumbling sound.

Jimmy looked over his shoulder, confirming what he suspected. He was indeed being followed. *Unbelievable.*

"Dusty, no!"

The women gasped and sputtered at the giant dog blocking their path and growling at them.

"Get that thing away from us!" Nora commanded.

Lillian shrieked, "Oh, he's going to kill us!" She clung to Nora in terror.

"Leave him be. He's harmless." Jimmy looked over his shoulder at them. "Have a nice day, ladies."

After that, Jimmy ignored them. He was sure they were wearing matching pickled looks on their faces and were even more disgusted that he really was going to Josephine's and not their precious Frannie's. He wasn't sure what to make of that, but it gave him the perfect opportunity to check on Josephine without being improper or calling too much notice to his actions. He wondered why Harold would send a lone male stranger all the way out to Josephine's, but he would figure that out later. After loading the saddlebag, Jimmy easily pulled himself into his saddle. As Coal began a canter, Dusty happily followed, forgetting all about the nasty women in front of the mercantile.

CHAPTER 12

Josephine was in the side yard hanging unmentionables when Jimmy rode up on his jet-black devil horse. An unbelievably large dog trotted next to them. Jimmy raised his hand to wave, but instead of returning his greeting, Josephine made a choking sound from the back of her throat and scrambled to finish hanging the items she was clutching. Flustered and fumbling, she jabbed a clothespin at the apron on the outer line trying to create a shield for the undergarments. No matter how she tried, her efforts were unsuccessful. Panic set in as Jimmy's long legs brought him in direct line with the very items she sought to hide.

Unsure of what to do, Josephine froze. Politeness was in order, but she couldn't stand the thought of him catching sight of the items. So, there she remained, staring wide-eyed at Jimmy, waiting for shame's arrival. However, she was unprepared for what came next.

Jimmy wasn't focused on what Josephine was doing. Instead, his eyes roamed her face while a gust of wind blew wispy strands of hair across it, tickling her. Watching

Jimmy's eyes follow her dancing hair, Josephine hesitated before brushing the offending strands aside. His eyes followed the motion of her hand. Too enthralled by the way he watched her, she was unable to move. He bore an appreciative and wistful look, mingled with something else she couldn't readily identify.

Jimmy's scrutiny coupled with her desperate need for propriety scorched her skin, a nervousness calling out for her to do something. In response, she returned to wrangling the apron. Her agitated movement and increased flush snapped Jimmy out of his observation and longing, which were replaced by a look of sudden understanding. Instead of speaking, he let out a strangled grunt. Whipping off his hat, he nodded to her.

"Miss Josephine." Jimmy gripped his hat tighter. "I'm sorry to have interrupted …" The tips of his ears turning red, he continued. "Uh … morning chores …" Josephine put extra effort into her apron fight while trying to hide the remaining undergarment in her hand. Failing miserably, the bloomers dropped to the earth with a puff of dust. They both looked down at the pantalets before looking back at each other. Their motions were perfect mirrors, right down to their tandem embarrassment and mortification. Two incredibly shy and somewhat socially awkward people stood trapped in their private hell.

Jimmy had struck Josephine as a take-charge kind of man, but this time he looked awkward and unsure, like a hesitant child. He flushed a deeper shade of red as he cleared his throat. Lord only knew what he could be thinking. Josephine's stomach churned.

"I—"

Dropping his hat, Jimmy walked up to the line, gently took the apron and the clothespin from Josephine's hand, and with concentrated focus proceeded to hang it on the line. That gave Josephine her out. She swooped down, scooping up the offending garment and tossing it into the laundry basket. She slid the basket behind her with her foot as she folded her hands in front of her. Jimmy exaggerated the motion of pushing the clothespin down in a nearly comical way, which she took to mean he was really trying to avoid looking—at anything. When he finished, he backed away from the clothesline and picked up his hat. Mercifully, he kept his eyes averted.

Josephine looked down at the ground, swiping away some wispy strands from her face again before looking up at Jimmy. Her smile faltered because he was attractive and put her on edge. Not the dangerous edge that some of the other men in town did, specifically Terrance Draper, but on edge, nonetheless. Her hands trembled slightly, and her heart picked up speed. She didn't want to explore why that was. It just was. "Thank you." Clearing her throat, she asked, "You're a ways out from town. Is everything okay?"

Jimmy nodded. "Yes. I'm sorry to barge in on you like this." He shifted his feet. "I wanted to make sure you were doing okay. I'm sure you had quite a scare with Gus and his cronies."

Josephine didn't know how to respond. So much had happened since she had been accosted, including standing up for herself with Beth. Never questioning and always compliant, that wouldn't have happened before meeting Jimmy. He brought something out in her. Bravery? A sense of value? Something had changed. She shrugged her shoulders, more to herself, but Jimmy needed confirmation.

"You look a little unsure. Are you okay? Did you need me to do something for you?"

"What? No, no. I'm fine. Thank you very much, Mr. Stapleton. I appreciate you checking on me, but you really should go. It isn't proper for you to be out here."

Josephine was pleased that Jimmy left her an opening to send him on his way without being too terribly rude. Even way out here, she was afraid of being seen with a male stranger.

"Well, about that, Harold from the mercantile mentioned you might want to take on some more sewing. I need new waist overalls and a shirt, and he didn't have anything that fit." Jimmy's lips turned upward on one side as Josephine involuntarily eyed his clothing.

"Does he know—" Josephine's hand reached for her skirt, clenching it.

"No. As far as Harold knows, we've never met. I wanted to keep it that way because I didn't want you to be worried. But it was a convenient excuse to come out here. He gave me directions." Jimmy looked pleased at how things had worked out, but everything he was saying only fed the hysteria growing inside her.

"Does anyone else know you're out here? Was there anyone else at the mercantile when you were there?" Her tight voice betrayed her anxiousness.

"Actually, this aunt and her niece—"

"The Reinhardt women." Josephine's voice went flat, and her stomach felt like a sinking stone. Of course they had to be there. They're always around when trouble crops up.

"Yes." Jimmy's brow wrinkled. He had no idea how awful these women could make her life.

Josephine expelled a breath that was somewhere between a huff and a cry. "Now everyone is going to be talking about you being out here." Her head swiveled around as if she expected to see people lurking in the bushes. "You're very kind, Mr. Stapleton, and I appreciate all you've done. But really, you must go."

Jimmy looked at her dumbfounded. Josephine's throat

constricted, making her voice sound higher than normal, edged with panic, her body agitated.

"I don't understand."

"But I do. The Reinhardt women are the biggest gossips. They'll twist whatever they hear to suit their needs." Josephine covered her mouth with her hand. She didn't know if she wanted to shout or cry at her predicament. "They're one of the reasons I take in only women's clothing or mend the husband's clothing of the same women." She took a couple of steps backward. "And that's only if they insist—"

"Hey, now. Slow down, you're getting all worked up."

Jimmy reached out and took her hands in his, holding them gently. She resisted the urge to pull her hands away because there was something calming about his touch.

"Take a breath."

He modeled it for her, then took long breaths with her until she settled. His trick worked. The hysteria that was clawing at her settled itself. Jimmy's thumbs stroked the backs of her hands, soothing her while his calluses made her shiver.

Lowering his voice, he gently asked, "Why would they spread rumors?"

"Did you actually meet them?"

"Unfortunately, yes. They were horribly forward and unpleasant women. They were adamant that I go see Frannie. So much so that they offered to take me to her." He narrowed his eyes. "But what do they have against you?"

This time, Josephine did try to yank her hands away from him like an animal caught in a trap. The situation was even more insulting than she had first realized. She made little huffing and squeaking noises as she yanked. Jimmy loosened his grip without completely letting go, then spoke softly.

"Josie …" He stretched out the nickname. "I asked you a question. I can't help you if you don't answer."

Josephine stopped struggling and looked up with surprise. The center of her chest went warm, and her body relaxed just a little. "No one's ever called me that. They usually call me Jo or JoJo." She paused, and her voice became barely audible. "Or other horrible things." Her lips quivered as she recalled taunts and threats from days gone by, primarily from those who should have protected her from the abuse. Old heaviness pervaded her body. She sighed, shoulders slumping.

"What horrible things, and who? Those Reinhardt women?" Jimmy's face took on a fierce look.

"It doesn't matter. I'm sure you'll hear them talking soon enough." Josephine shook her head. "Let's just say I fall short of all the womanly expectations this town has. My sisters are the ones to look to, not me."

She tried to turn away, but Jimmy wouldn't let her. He put his finger under her chin, tilting her face back at him. He searched her eyes for what would've been an uncomfortable amount of time if she hadn't gotten lost in the speckled flecks of gold glimmering in his rich brown eyes. Yesterday evening, she assumed they were black. In the bright daylight, coupled with the kindness of his expression, they were a warm shade of brown, and the gold seemed to twinkle at her. She knew she should move away from him but couldn't make her feet move or words come out of her mouth.

Jimmy leaned close as if he was going to kiss her. Her lips parted, but she wasn't sure if she was going to speak or make contact with his full lips. She'd never, ever been this close to a man's face. Her mind and body were of two differing opinions as to the soundness of the moment. Her eyes unfocused. Some sort of pull was drawing her and Jimmy together, and they were uncomfortably close for a breath longer before he pulled away. He looked as surprised as she felt. Leaning back, she put a hand to her heart trying to settle its rapid beating. While stopping was for the best, she still felt the familiar sting of rejection.

"I'm sorry, I—" Jimmy stepped back. "Josie, I won't let anyone do you any harm. I protected you the other day, and I'll continue to do so—as long as I'm here. You need to tell me if someone treats you poorly." His lips flattened as he inhaled deeply and exhaled. "I'm not having it. No one should endure mistreatment." Jimmy's eyes went a shade darker as his voice took on an edge.

Unsure what hurt worse, that he was only being kind because he cared about everybody, and she misinterpreted his kindness, or the fact that he came close to kissing her and then changed his mind. Either way, she once again felt like the ugly little girl her mother told her she was. Her throat tightened and she was unable to respond.

"Josie, promise me you'll tell me if anyone comes out here and tries anything with you, or if they speak badly of you in town. I'll take care of it." He cupped her face with his hand, holding it there for a moment until she nodded in agreement. He tilted his head forward, pressing her with another look, searching her eyes until she nodded again. "That's my girl." He straightened up and stepped away while clearing his throat and visibly swallowing.

"Now, how about getting me on the road to something fresh to wear?" Raising his brow, he gave himself a once over. Looking down the length of himself and back up at her, his bright smile rooted her where she stood. With that, he walked back to Coal and pulled a parcel out of his saddlebag.

Coal tossed Josephine a look and snorted hard with a shake of his head, causing her to jump a little. She considered his reaction violent and took it to confirm her opinion of him. *Devil horse.* Nodding, the horse continued to eye her as if he read her mind.

Conversely, the giant dog jumped up and pranced excitedly around Jimmy, making him laugh. "All right, all right. You can come"—Jimmy held up his finger—"for a minute."

Turning to Josephine he said, "Watch out. Dusty's smitten with you and wants to say hi."

Jimmy barely got the words out before Dusty had descended on Josephine, wagging his entire backside, prancing with unbridled joy, and begging for affection. He was a welcome distraction for Josephine. Dusty's enthusiasm chased away her shame and disappointment, for the moment, as she gleefully returned his affection.

CHAPTER 13

$\mathcal{D}$usty trotted toward the barn to explore as Jimmy and Josephine entered the house. Being in Josie's home seemed too intimate, given the thoughts he was having about her. He couldn't help but stare as she moved through the room ahead of him. She was much prettier than he remembered. Then again, a couple of days ago, he was driven by a surprise attack of rage upon seeing the men harassing her. Something about her quiet and gentle nature brought out the protector in him.

She had looked like a forest fairy with her blonde hair shimmering gold and red in the sunlight, rogue strands of which danced around her delicate features and distracted him. Being somewhere more private didn't seem right, and having to be so close to Josephine as she measured him would be even more unnerving. He nearly kissed her outside while telling her he'd protect her. If he had kept staring at her, he just might have. *First the anger, now this, whatever this is.* Jimmy shook his head. I need to get it together.

Jimmy watched Josie scurry upstairs to get her sewing basket. He knew she was worried about propriety, but her worries rolled off her like a frightened mare during an impending storm. He didn't understand where all her fear was coming from and why. He had been careful about keeping their initial meeting a secret, and he felt he did right by her by having pretended he hadn't previously met her. What she was expressing was more than fear of breaking social rules. He couldn't just leave her like this.

I wish Travis were here. He'd know what to do about Josie. Then we could get on with the business of collecting evidence against the Van Der Kamp gang. Jimmy couldn't get too involved in anything because Van Der Kamp kept everyone in the dark about his overall strategy, and Jimmy didn't know how long he'd be with Van Der Kamp. There were too many variables and unknowns to make promises or get attached. Jimmy spent another moment thinking about how dealing with all these people was becoming complicated. In less than three days, he started with his anger and ended with strange and overly protective feelings for Josie. Hell, he'd even given her a nickname for crying out loud. He looked up the stairs, wondering what was taking her so long.

"You doin' all right up there?"

"Yes, I'm just looking for my measuring string. I'll be down in a minute."

He was growing impatient with waiting and the unknown. So just as Josie started down the stairs, Jimmy bounded up them to help her with the basket.

"Thank you for your help, but I'm doing just fine, Mr. Stapleton."

She tried to pull the basket back, but succeeded only in making his hand brush against the bottom of her breast. Both jerked back at the contact. Just as Josie let go, Jimmy yanked harder. She gasped when the contents popped up but returned safely to the basket. Alarmed, Jimmy didn't wait but pivoted to go back down the stairs. The tips of his ears burned red as he white-knuckled the basket. He was breaking out in a sweat.

Diverting from the situation, Jimmy said, "I sure wish you would just call me Jimmy. No one calls me Mr. Stapleton." His voice went lower. "No one." He continued to face forward because he feared he might burn up completely if he looked at her now. "Everyone calls me Jimmy."

"All right, then … Jimmy. I suppose you should call me Josephine or Jo."

It thrilled him that she allowed this familiarity, but he also knew what it cost her. He suspected that calling her by his nickname had caught her off guard, too.

"Sure thing. Although I'll probably end up calling you Josie. I can't seem to help myself."

"I noticed. Why's that?"

They stood at the bottom of the stairs. With an outstretched hand, Josephine indicated moving into the parlor. Jimmy followed her into the tidy room before answering.

"Josephine's so formal, and Jo doesn't quite suit you. Josie's nice and feminine—like you." He froze when he realized what he had said, and once again, the tips of his ears turned bright red. This seemed to be a pattern between the two of them. Josephine's eyebrows shot up, then she stilled, except for her face. It went pale before she blushed completely red, and she had to wait a moment before she could croak her words out.

"I don't believe you meant to use the word *feminine*. That's not how I'm usually described." She swallowed hard. "But thank you anyway." Her voice stayed tight, words strained.

Dumbfounded, Jimmy needed a moment to recover. "You mean to tell me that people don't think you're feminine … or that you don't think you are?"

"Well, I—"

Jimmy eyed her before shaking his head. "Doesn't matter. I think you're feminine. And I rarely care what others think." Josephine's eyebrows raised. "It's a learned habit. One that's served me well." He looked around the room, unwilling to follow that thread any longer. "Where do you want me?"

Josie watched him for a moment before pointing toward the window where the sunlight came pouring in, and there was room for them to spread out.

"Please stand still while I get you—" She looked up at him. While taller than some women, her five foot five inches wouldn't come close to his six foot four. "You're a mite tall for me."

He chuckled, a deep rumbling sound that warmed her from the inside out. "Spread your arms wide and hold on to the end of the tape, please." She slipped the end between his fingers. "Just stand still and keep your fingers tight so it doesn't fall."

Stretching the tape along the underside of his arm, she stopped where the cuff would end. She walked back to where he was holding the tape and pulled it taut. Then she measured each arm individually, followed by the chest, length, and neck, making notes as she worked. It was a pleasant silence until she had to measure his inseam. Flushing, she stood in front of him. Jimmy noticed Josie's habit of looking around to see if anyone was nearby even when they were alone. It reminded him of beaten-down animals. He wondered how long she'd had it.

"Um, I need to measure you for your trousers. I—"

"It's fine. Do what you need to do." He cleared his throat. "I'm cooperative, aren't I?"

A happy laugh snuck out of Josie. "Why yes. Yes, you are." She kneeled on the floor, tucking the end of the tape under his shoe. Her face flushed red, and her voice came out in a whisper. "I have to reach—"

"Oh." Jimmy snapped his head forward. "I won't move. Promise."

"I'll try to be quick."

True to her word, she measured as quickly as she could, but she sure came dangerously close to the family jewels. When her little hand brushed against the inside of his thighs, he flinched. Jimmy was gritting his teeth while breaking out into a sweat. And here he thought he'd done so well when she had him sit to measure his neck and was so close to his face that he could feel her breath and smell her hair. He could slap himself right now, but couldn't help himself, either.

At this point, he was rushing past embarrassed. He tried to concentrate on all the anger he was carrying or the chores he had to do—anything to distract himself from where her hands were. As soon as she stepped away, he blew out the breath he had been holding and took a step back. Shaking out his arms, he thought he'd turn blue in more ways than one. He urgently needed to change the path of his errant thoughts. Fortunately for him, Josie was returning the items to her basket and not looking at him. She appeared a little unsteady herself. At least he wasn't the only one.

"How long do you think—"

The front door crashed open, and a shrieking voice called, "Whose horse is that out there?" A moment later, a wild-eyed Beth stomped into the parlor, gaping at them. Staring in disbelief, she finally pointed a finger at Jimmy after what felt like an eternity. Her voice took on an even shriller tone, if that was possible. "Who are you?"

Jimmy shook his head. He felt like his ears were ringing.

"What are you doing here?" She shifted toward Jo, her

voice barely softening. "What's going on? Is this the man you bumped into yesterday?"

Jimmy watched her, shocked. *This is the pretty sister? She's a harridan.* When she started her attack on Josie, his senses caught up to him, and he intervened.

"No. I am not." He pierced Beth with a look that had her reconsidering her stance, but only for a moment. Before she could get her dander back up, he continued, "I'm the one who saved her from that man."

It would've been polite to introduce himself, but he didn't feel inclined to do so. This day had been something else with all these crazy and forward women he had to deal with. Aggravated, he reminded himself that's why he liked to stay at base and care for the horses. Horses and other animals, he understood. This nonsense? Not at all. What he did know, however, was fur was about to fly.

Straightening to his full height, his hands went to his hips, and his legs shifted into a wider stance. Beth's behavior triggered something in him. His jaw clenched as his cheek muscles began flexing. Glowering down at Beth, he said, "You need to treat your sister with a lot more respect."

Beth's mouth dropped open as she stared at him, looking as if she'd been slapped. No one had ever told her no or even corrected her. She almost always got her way. It took her a full minute before she regained her stride and fury. Her lips clamped shut, and her eyes seared Jimmy. Leaning forward with her fists clenched, she stamped her foot.

"No one tells me what to do. Do you hear?" Her voice wasn't as shrill this time, but it was certainly full of white-hot anger.

Jimmy raised one eyebrow before evenly responding, "I just did."

"Why I—" She raised her hand to slap him, but he stopped her with his words. "I wouldn't do that if I were you."

"Why not?" She sneered. "Not man enough?"

"Because you'll hurt your delicate hand. You don't seem like the type who does much work."

Beth gasped with outrage while Josephine stood immobile, watching with eyes as wide as saucers. Jo's gaze shifted to Jimmy, and he winked at her. Beth caught it and commenced shrieking.

"You set him up! You told him to tell me these awful things, Jo! You're so mean to me." Beth wailed as if she were the victim and not the instigator.

Jo moved to console her, but Beth pushed her away. "No! You always do this, Jo. You make my life miserable."

Jimmy had had it by this point. The ridiculousness of this day frayed his last nerve. The women in this town were incredibly irrational, aside from Josie, who seemed generally worried and fretful but calm in the face of her raging sister.

"Apologize now," Jimmy barked, making both Beth and Josephine jump. They snapped their heads toward him. "Apologize." His voice went lower, drawing out the word when he repeated it.

"I—"

"That's the problem. You don't see any need. You feel like the wronged one. You feel and you take, but you don't listen or contribute—you, you, you … Josie works hard. It doesn't take a genius to see that. I came here because I was told she was looking for extra work. When I got here, *she* was the one hanging laundry. When I intervened yesterday, *she* was the one bringing home an armful of work—a home she had to walk to as it was getting dark. Then she came home to a dark house. Where were you?" Ticking from the grandfather clock emphasized the fact that Jimmy had silenced the sisters. They had been running amok since their parents died and didn't know how to handle each other because no one had taught them. Jimmy had a sinking feeling that for whatever reasons, their parents had pitted them against each other. He was at least sure Josie hadn't been treated well, judging by Beth's actions. And that just didn't sit well with him. Not one bit.

"You have no right to talk to me like this. Tell him, JoJo." Beth looked at Josephine while gesturing at Jimmy.

Jimmy shook his head. He was inadvertently back to teaching lessons because he was fed up with all the selfish behavior. "Well? Are you going to do it, or do I have to make you do it?"

Josie reached out, placing a hand on Jimmy's forearm. "It's okay. She doesn't have to apologize." Josephine worried her bottom lip, looking up at him with a furrowed brow. She shook her head, distressed by the confrontation. It was clear to him she caved in the midst of conflict, avoiding it at all costs.

"I won't hurt her." He cradled Josephine's hand in his. "I don't hurt women, but she needs to treat you better and pull her own weight."

"I—" Josie began to defend her sister, then hedged.

"Don't, Josie. You can't deny it. It's plain she does nothing around here. Her attitude says it all. I said I'd protect you. I promised to as long as I was in town. That protection includes this." He cocked his head in Beth's direction without looking away from Josie. "You deserve to be treated fairly and much, much better than you are."

Beth glowered at the pair, her arms tightly crossing her chest, her toe tapping. "But, why?" Jo paused, squeezing his hand. "Why are you doing all of this … for me? You don't even know me. You have no obligation to help."

"I can't put words to that, Josie. All I know is you're a kind and generous woman. I don't like how people are treating you—or how you let them. I've lived a lifetime of being treated miserably, and I no longer stand for others to live the same way. Not when there's no need."

Jimmy turned his head toward Beth, speaking to her. "There's certainly no need to be treated like that from your own family, one that you seem to be so worried about." For once, Beth didn't have anything to say. She just stared at the pair, stunned. Josie hung her head for a moment, trying to hide her welling eyes. Her sniffing gave her away. Jimmy relaxed his posture, shifting toward her to lend comfort.

He placed a hand on her shoulder to get her attention and changed the subject. When Josie raised her head, he looked her in the eye, his voice soft.

"When do you think I could expect my new duds, Josie? I'm looking forward to seeing what magic you create with that old material Harold sold me."

Josie looked up with watery eyes and a grateful smile. "I suppose I need a few days, but I'll work real hard to get it to you soon." Pausing, she clarified, "May I have a week? I still have other chores to do, as well as Mrs. Patterson's new dress. Although she said I could have until Sunday prior to the dance to work on it. That's in a month. Would that work for you?"

"What chores need doing? I'm sure your sister could help you."

Simultaneously, their heads turned toward Beth, whose arms were stiff at her sides. Her eyes narrowed before she spat out, "Yeah, sure. I'll help, but don't go getting all bossy on me. I'm not your slave."

Rushing blood roared in Jimmy's ears, and his entire body tensed. If anyone should know what an indentured servant, a near slave, felt like, it was him. But he would never compare himself to a slave—never. He had been beaten and ill-used, but never beaten as badly as some slaves were. Even when Wrighty beat him so badly that he couldn't walk for days, he wouldn't possibly think to make such a comparison. For

Beth to be glib about both slavery and doing some chores stoked his anger.

"Watch your mouth," he said to Beth, his voice and jabbing finger decimating the room's quiet. Beth jumped back at his harsh tone. "You have no idea what you're talking about. Do some honest work, and don't speak of what you do not know."

Jimmy's jaw worked and his face hardened. His eyes had gone dark in anger, giving Beth pause. It was like the white-hot anger he had thrown at Gus yesterday. She took a step back, nodding her head. It was the most cooperative Beth had been. She looked as if she meant to keep her promise.

Blowing out a harsh breath, Jimmy turned to Josie. "You can take all the time you need. However, you need help around here, and she's going to give it to you." He threw his thumb in Beth's direction before saying over his shoulder to her, "You hear?"

Beth made a sound of disgust at the back of her throat but responded. "Yes. I hear."

The sarcasm wasn't lost on any of them. Jimmy pulled in another long breath while jabbing his hands on his hips. He pursed his lips and was just about to say more to Beth when she interrupted.

"You aren't the one who said Jo was attractive, are you?" Beth's face scrunched up as if she tasted something awful.

Jimmy's eyes narrowed at Beth's derisive tone. At the end of his rope with her, he said, "No, I'm not."

Beth's eyes flared in triumph. She stood taller while Jo simultaneously shrank. Seeing Josie shrink like that loosened Jimmy's normally tight lips.

"I don't know her well enough to do so. If I had the opportunity, I'd tell her she's beautiful—inside and out."

Beth frowned, her bravado deflating. Josie froze before

flushing to the roots of her hair. Jimmy looked at Josie, and Josie met his gaze, stunned.

"It was her inner beauty and strength that caught me. I didn't realize how physically beautiful she was until I saw her shining in the daylight today."

Beth's face burned with anger, an ugly flush consuming her exposed skin while her face contorted. She stamped her foot, pivoted, then stomped up the stairs. She hollered down at them, "I don't think what you two are doing down there is appropriate. You should leave, Mr. Whatever Your Name Is." She was hissing the words by the time she finished.

Jimmy chuckled. "Why would I use manners to introduce myself to a shrew like that?"

A giggle escaped Josie's mouth, despite her hand trying to muffle it. She was happy and joyful, the opposite of the scared and suspicious woman at the clothesline and the accommodating and shrunken sister in the parlor. Partly due to his own familial bias, he was convinced Josie was taking on more than her share of the family responsibilities, and that, somehow, the family was pressuring or bullying her just by her reactions. It seemed that no one supported her in ways that made her feel worthy. He tucked that thought away for later, instead enjoying how Josie had brightened with his teasing. Picking up his hat, he played with the brim. He wasn't sure what to do, so he impulsively bent down and gave Josie a lightning quick peck on the cheek before jamming his hat on his head.

"I better get a move on. Had enough of forward women for today—first the Reinhardt women and now Beth. I honestly don't know how you live with her. She's shrill." He poked his finger in his ear, wiggling it. He pulled a face, then smiled.

Josie laughed, looking lighter and freer, and followed

Jimmy to the porch. Her hand went to the porch pillar, and Jimmy kept walking toward Coal. He turned around, tipping his hat before sliding into the saddle. Jimmy whistled for Dusty. He came running enthusiastically from the back forty, tossing a bark Josie's way before running around Coal and taking off toward town as if they were racing.

* * *

JOSIE WATCHED Dusty lead the procession down the road, a jumble of emotions swirling around like a dust storm inside her. Sighing with a satisfied smile stretched across her face, she turned around, startled to find Beth watching her with crossed arms and a pinched look.

Beth scrutinized Jo's face before saying, "Do you think you're in love with him or something?" Huffing, she added, "It'll never work."

Jo's smile fell. Swallowing, she couldn't immediately respond. She crossed her arms and asked, "Why do you always poke at me? What're you saying that for anyway?"

"JoJo, why would a big hunk of a man like that take to you? He's more man than you could possibly handle. Besides, he's up to no good."

"What would make you say that, Beth?"

"Look at you, Jo. What do you have to offer him? Besides, he's probably just drifting through like all the other eligible men. They all have better places to be. If anyone's new in this town, they're hiding."

Beth walked off, leaving Josephine feeling more miserable than after their argument the day before. Why Beth constantly jabbed at her inadequacies, Josephine would never know. She was working hard for two of them to survive. All she did was work. If they didn't bring in more money or get Frank, their brother in-law, to change his mind about their living alone in the house, they were going to have to make some serious choices. None of which were appealing or good for them. Beth didn't seem to understand or care how dire things were. If she did, Josephine was sure she wouldn't be fighting her so hard.

CHAPTER 14

Dusty led the way for a good quarter of a mile before realizing Jimmy wasn't going to chase or play, so he circled back, making a couple of passes under and around Coal before falling in line. Even Coal wouldn't play because Jimmy was so deep in thought. They rode in silence, Jimmy a little too relaxed in the saddle and not paying attention to the route. He didn't even realize he was allowing Coal to find his own way.

His focus was inward, replaying his visit. Why was it so easy to be around Josie?

Images of her sweet face shining in the sun popped into his mind, pulling the corners of his mouth upward. Thinking about Josie's cute blush made him laugh out loud, snapping him out of his daydreaming. Lightning quick, his head darted around to make sure no one had heard, which was ridiculous. They were still over a mile outside town. Shaking his head, he sent his thoughts into facts, not this silly daydreaming.

First of all, he barely knew Josie, despite her feeling so familiar. These feelings confused and distracted him. Also, he was supposed to be watching out for her, not ogling something that wasn't for him. He had no home and no job. He rode with a gang he was planning to bring down, and until he brought that gang down, he was charged with keeping order within their ranks and bringing any helpful information back to Van Der Kamp. It was a lot of conflicting tasks and obligations, and there was no room for whatever this affliction that had come over him was. He nodded his head just because, and Coal followed with a snort.

That's when he felt something else entirely—a tingling at the back of his neck signaling danger. He widened his eyes to take in as much of the landscape as he could without being obvious. Glancing at Dusty confirmed he wasn't the only one who felt it. Dusty's ears were perked, as were Coal's. On high alert, Dusty swiveled his head back and forth. Jimmy shifted in the saddle to signal Coal to look alive, and they continued their march toward town.

He felt more watched than threatened but remained cautious as he retraced his ride from earlier that afternoon back to the mercantile. If someone was watching, he didn't want them following him to Old Man Johnson's. Taking his time looping the reins around the hitching post, Jimmy glanced backward but saw only late afternoon shadows growing behind him. A few pedestrians and workers moved on the street beyond the mercantile. Dusty remained on alert, standing next to Coal. With one last glance around, Jimmy spoke in a low tone to Dusty. "Watch." He entered the mercantile to see if the view from the large windows produced any answers.

"Mr. Stapleton! Did you find Josephine all right?"

"Yes, sir. I did."

"She doing all right out there? Been a while since her parents passed." Harold shook his head. "I worry 'bout her. She's a good girl. Beth, however—"

Jimmy made a noncommittal sound.

"I take it you've met Beth, too."

"I guess you could say that."

"She flirt with you?" Harold blurted out.

Jimmy looked aghast. "Lord, no."

"Not like those Reinhardt women this morning?" Harold chuckled. "They're something else, too."

"Yes, I've had more than my fill of women for the day. Especially shrieking women."

"Well, I heard them screaming about your beast, but—" Harold's eyes went large. "You didn't try anything with our JoJo, did you? Beth didn't walk in on anything inappropriate?" His face was turning a darker shade of red the more he spoke, the ends of his mustache twitching.

"What? No! I would never do that to a lady or any woman. I don't take what's not mine." He went stone-faced at the thought of a woman being forced. "I protect women, not abuse them."

"I'm sorry. It's just that Beth usually flirts—especially with brawny men like yourself. In fact, you're the type she seems to flirt with when they pass through town. Then you said she was shrieking … Sorry. I jumped to conclusions." He looked thoughtful for a moment. "Why was she shrieking?"

"I told her she needed to help Josie with the chores."

Harold's eyebrows shot up to meet his hairline. "No one tells Beth what to do. She doesn't do well with that. Always got her way, that one. Or forced it." He nodded.

"Not with me."

"Who put you in charge of that family?"

"Me. Josie needs help, and her sister is a coffee-boiler. She's tart and lazy."

Harold let out a deep breath. "Looks like you have your hands full. She's not one to cooperate, and, most likely, JoJo is going to bear the brunt of her displeasure."

"Not happening." Stiffening, he remembered the physical pain of Wrighty's displeasure, having been both the catalyst and innocent bystander. He wouldn't let that happen to someone else, not if he could help it.

"You're pretty sure of yourself, mister. What makes you think you can make her do what no one else has?" Harold rested his bent arm on the counter, leaning toward Jimmy. "You ain't going to beat her, are you?"

"Heck, no." Jimmy jerked back in repulsion. "What's with all the beating of women?" Harold looked surprised at that question. "You aren't the first to mention it. I'm sure you won't be the last."

"When women get out of line, some of the men around here feel it's within their husbandly rights to show 'em who has the upper hand. Why ya surprised by all this? Nothing new." Harold stood up, stretching slightly backward.

"I don't cotton to beatings." His lips compressed and his brow furrowed, squeezing intensity out of his eyes. "Of any kind."

"Well, don't go giving me the stink eye. I didn't say I agreed to it or anything. I just said that there's some here who do. Couldn't do much about it even if we wanted to."

Jimmy's eyes narrowed, and he leaned his head toward Harold. "What do you mean by that?"

"Just that the sheriff don't do nothin' about it. 'Specially when the men do it at home. Woman can bring a black eye to church, and the pastor just looks the other way. Sheriff's no better. That's all."

Jimmy shook his head. "The two men whose duty it is to protect the so-called weaker. How many women?"

"There's a couple. Remember the Reinhardt women from earlier?"

Jimmy rolled his eyes. "How could I forget them?"

Harold chuckled. "Yeah, they're a pair. Lillian's mother

died a few years ago. That's why Nora's back here—to keep her in line. She's real similar to Beth, if you know what I mean." Jimmy nodded. Not hard at all to imagine the ways in which they were alike, given their behavior this morning. "Rumor has it, Frederick Reinhardt killed her. Broke her neck while beating her."

The cords on Jimmy's neck strained, and his jaw clenched, but he didn't say anything. He didn't have to—the flint in his eyes did the talking.

Harold leaned forward across the counter. "Sheriff went out to investigate, had the coroner bring in the body for an autopsy like he's supposed to, but no charges were ever filed. They had a closed casket for her, and nothing else was ever said. As if she never existed. Even Lillian doesn't talk about her mother." Releasing a huff as he looked off in the distance, as if conjuring the woman in his mind, he repeated to himself, a little softer, "It's as if the woman never existed." He shook his head, voice firmer. "Damned shame. She was a real kind woman. Not sure how she ended up with the likes of Frederick. What little manners Miss Lillian shows come from her mama. Her brashness is all her father. He allows her to do whatever she wants—until the men come sniffing around." He frowned.

Jimmy didn't say anything, hoping Harold would continue.

"She flirts with them and leads them on, the wrong men, that. She's been known to get in a bind or two. Lucky for her, everyone's afraid of her daddy. Otherwise, they'd take what they thought they were promised, so to speak." Harold shrugged his shoulders. "She don't know any better, but neither does her aunt. She's only a handful of years older than Lillian anyway but has years more experience, if you know what I mean. At any rate, they're spoiled and sheltered—live in their own little world."

Before Harold could spill any more beans, the bell on the door chimed behind them, causing them to turn around.

* * *

Harold straightened up, pasting a smile on his face. Jimmy's head cocked in question. Harold gave him a side-eye glance, silently shushing him. Shrugging, Jimmy stepped away from the counter, allowing an imperious Mrs. Clarksen to hold court with the mercantile owner. The air around them shifted partly because of her haughty nature and partly due to the smell of her toilette water. The mercantile was hot, intensifying her strong floral scent. Jimmy nodded at her and stepped farther away, allowing her plenty of space to conduct business and to steer clear of her aroma.

He was pretty sure he'd hit the payload with this woman, as she carried herself with the kind of self-importance usually lending itself to gossip. Despite a day of annoyances and not much information about the other gang, he was willing to see where this went if he didn't start sneezing from her strong fragrance. He suspected she wouldn't be any less aggravating, but Van Der Kamp had expectations of him and didn't like to be disappointed. Especially since he hadn't heard tell of another gang yet.

Mrs. Clarksen gave Jimmy the once over, scrutinizing him from boot to head. Her face was stern and arrogant until she reached his face, then a smile brightened it, and her muscles relaxed. She was an attractive middle-aged woman, but it seemed that years of being judgmental had put a slight tarnish on her good looks. And judgmental she was. Jimmy was sure she smiled only because others considered him attractive and mannered. Ironically, what he noticed was how much prettier she was when she smiled.

"Harold, good afternoon. Who do we have here?" She bobbed her head at Jimmy.

"Mrs. Clarksen, this here is Jimmy Stapleton. Brand new to town. He was just in to purchase some new clothing, weren't you, son?"

Jimmy briefly tensed at the term *son*, but quickly recovered. That had been Wrighty's pet name for him. "Nice to meet you, ma'am."

"Well, aren't you a handsome young man. My husband is Reverend Clarksen. Are you married?" She pried with such undisguised curiosity that Jimmy was taken aback by the question.

Clearing his throat to hide his dismay, he shook his head. "No, ma'am. Can't say that I am."

"Well, you just haven't found the right young lady, yet. I can help with that. Why there is—"

Harold quickly interrupted. He didn't want a repeat of this morning. He knew how uncomfortable the Reinhardt women had made Jimmy feel. For whatever reason, he had taken a liking to this gentle giant. Truth be told, he was still reeling from this morning as well. The Reinhardts' machinations didn't sit well with him. It was like feeding time at the trough.

"Now, Lettie. Let the young man be. He just got into town —let him get settled before you go matchmaking. I'd tell you not to go matchmaking, but I know you'll do it anyway. Give him some space."

She tittered as if Harold had given her some sort of compliment. She had made some good matches, but for the rest of the townspeople, it didn't make up for her horrid behavior the other days of the year. Especially when she was talking about her "saint" of a husband, Reverend Clarksen. There were some who weren't convinced he was even an ordained minister.

"Oh, Harold." She batted her fan toward him. "You're such a charmer. When Francine passes, I'm going to find someone more—"

"Mrs. Clarksen, enough!" Harold's cheek's flushed; his lips pressed together, and his mustache turned downward. "Do not speak of my wife in that way."

She looked both surprised and hurt that he'd admonished her, especially in front of a stranger. Harold generally felt bad for Lettie, but she had sharply crossed the line with her dismay regarding his wife. Lettie was probably jealous that his wife had more freedom than she did. The intensity of Lettie's meddling had grown in proportion to her husband's increasing absences from town. It was as if she couldn't help herself. She needed to put her attention somewhere. Unfortunately for Harold, that landed on his unusual marriage, unusual only for Mrs. Clarksen.

"Harold, you know that I mean well—"

"Then please keep those thoughts and opinions to yourself. Especially in front of others." He tilted his head toward Jimmy.

Jimmy's face was neutral, but he was watching Mrs. Clarksen like a hawk would its prey. He was trying to get a good read on her. She was confusing and rude, but he reserved judgment as to where the conflicting source of her behavior lay. Since according to Harold her husband turned a blind eye to wife beating, he had no idea what she endured at home.

Clearly flustered by being called out, she fluttered about for a moment, like a fish out of water. A slight flush washed across her before she regained her composure and straightened.

"My apologies." Turning, she said to Jimmy, "And to you as well, Mr. Stapleton. I hope you find our growing town to your liking." Smoothing out her skirts, she spoke in a more subdued tone. "Harold, I've come to see if my order has arrived yet. I noticed the wagons arrived yesterday with some deliveries."

"I haven't had a chance to go through the boxes yet. Chester had to go visit his parents on their ranch. They've been having some problems with rustling, I think. He didn't quite say, but it seemed urgent, so I let him go. I'll try to get to them this afternoon. If it's in there, I'll drop it off to you. Will that be acceptable?"

"Of course, Harold. I'd send David, but he's been so busy of late with his parishioners over in Adamsville." Her hand went to her chest. "Poor souls. They have no one to lead their flock." As she shook her slightly tilted head, her eyes softened with compassion.

Jimmy looked past Mrs. Clarksen at Harold to get a read. Harold shot him a skeptical look, rolling his eyes. Jimmy almost snorted—it was such a comical gesture coming from the straitlaced man.

"He'll be back in a couple of days. A woman needs her baby christened, and there's a man who might need last rites. He's going to wait and make sure he's there for the poor soul in his hour of need."

"It's no problem, Mrs. Clarksen. If it's not in this shipment, you won't be seeing me today, so please don't worry. I'll drop it off when it does arrive."

"Bless you, Harold. You're ever so kind." She placed a delicate hand on Harold's arm before turning her head toward Jimmy. "It was nice to meet you, Mr. Stapleton. I hope to see you again soon."

With a graceful turn, she was off into the sunlight, the door chiming at her departure. For such a small woman, there was a flurry of energy following her out the door. The men stood there for a few moments before Harold started back up. He was in a chatty mood for some reason.

"That woman." He shook his head. "She's an ornery one and a busybody, but oddly enough, she means well."

Jimmy wasn't so sure about that, so he didn't respond.

Harold went on, "It's just too bad about her husband." The lines around his eyes tightened as he grimaced. "I hate to speak badly about a man of the cloth, but he sure doesn't behave like one."

Jimmy perked up at that. He wasn't a fan of the preaching variety, but there were times when they gave good advice. "What do you mean?"

"He's not serving the flock in Adamsville. It's more like he's servicing the flock, if you catch my meaning." He flushed at the impropriety of his own words but widened his eyes in a "if you know what I mean" manner.

Jimmy choked. He was pretty sure he knew what that meant. "Does Mrs. Clarksen have any idea?"

"That's a good question. I don't think so. She thinks that man walks on water—pardon the blaspheming."

"Or she's a good actress."

"Perhaps, but she tends to speak her mind about everything else. I'd find it hard for her to keep quiet about him even if it's humiliating to her. Everything tends to fall out of her mouth like water in a bucket with a giant hole in it."

"Mmm. Yes, she's pretty forward."

Laughing, Harold said, "You must think all women in Linden are forward. Aside from JoJo, that's all you've encountered."

"You have me there."

"Son, I like you. Hope things work out for you here. It's been a little rough around the edges of late, and the town's growing fast, but there's still some good left." He looked lost in his thoughts for a moment before he asked, "So did you come to return the thread, or does JoJo need something else? How'd you like her? She's a real nice gal, that one."

"I, uh—"

Harold's smile was mischievous, "Real pretty, too."

Jimmy just bobbed his head up and down slowly as he couldn't sort his thoughts enough to respond to him.

"Seems the cat's got your tongue—and it gave you her nickname. Josie?" Pausing, he made a swipe at his mustache to avoid laughing outright at the poor young man. "Couldn't let that one slide." Harold winked. "That's all right. She'll do a fine job for you, and you'd sure be helping her out. If some of your people needed extra help, keep her in mind. She's a hard worker—even more so since her folks died."

"How do you know—"

He waved his hand at Jimmy. "You look like the type of man who supports others. Don't rightly think you'd travel alone. Especially since you look like you're on some mission of sorts." Before Jimmy could interrupt, Harold held up his hand. "Not saying that you are. You just look like you have things in this life you need to do, that's all.

* * *

THIS TOWN WAS KEEPING SECRETS, that much Jimmy could gather. Harold gave him plenty with the Reinhardt and Clarksen gossip. He'd also have to alert Van Der Kamp about the sheriff. However, there was still the matter of the hidden eyes on him. They were still there when he left the mercantile, despite gabbing with Harold much longer than he had anticipated. In fact, he'd talked more today than he had the past two weeks. His jaw hurt, and it wasn't from all the tongue-biting these women forced him to do. His patience was running desert dry dealing with all these people.

Shaking his head, he continued riding out to base. He wasn't ready to call the place they were currently staying at home, nor this town, even if it was the closest thing to "home" he'd had in a long time. They had moved into the actual home of one of Van Der Kamp's old friends, the one they called Old Man Johnson. He was back East visiting his sister, so Van Der Kamp had the run of the place. It was an easy decision for him to move the gang from the abandoned mining camp in Weaver to Linden.

However, things weren't as they seemed in this town, and Jimmy felt like it was distracting him from the surveillance Travis had asked him to do. The plan was for Jimmy to continue observing the gang for Travis, an undercover marshal who was extraditing Wrighty. Jimmy was a natural observer, and searching for extra information was important to him. Not only had he promised to help Travis, but he also wanted to prove he could do this and help bring the gang down. That's one reason he wouldn't leave with Charlie and Annabelle—he had to do something. He didn't like the idea of anyone thinking he was incapable or adding to the litany of things allegedly wrong with him. Oddly enough, he liked Van Der Kamp as a person, but his gang was going down, if Jimmy had anything to do with it.

They had ambushed his family, killed his parents, and kidnapped him and his older brother, Charlie. It didn't surprise Jimmy that his father had been a dubious busi-nessman who tried to cheat the wrong man. Jimmy was oddly detached from losing his parents. His life with them felt like it belonged to someone else. They cared more about appearances than other people, including their own children. Jimmy was always deemed too sensitive, asking problematic questions about the welfare of others, and they duly punished him for it. He was angrier about the two of them having been held against their will and the abuse they had suffered, and others had suffered, at Wrighty's hands. *They never should've forced Charlie to rob the mercantile by threatening me. That's the worst of it. That, and holding Charlie back with my fear. I was too afraid of Wrighty to do anything, and Charlie suffered for it. Why didn't Van Der Kamp do something about Wrighty sooner?*

As for today's mission? He'd have to sift through the day's events to see if he could find any patterns. Certainly, the abuse of women was something Van Der Kamp needed to hear about. And he wouldn't like it, either. *I suppose that's the best place to start, and we'll see where that leads us. I'm not liking what I'm hearing, and neither will he.*

The fresh air, horses running, open space—Jimmy felt good. He woke up ready to get some honest work accomplished. It felt right to be back in the pen working with the horses. The area was peaceful even when some of the mares were bitey with each other. Daylight and no chatter. These two things made Jimmy' shoulders relax, and his soul feel good.

Hoping he brought sugar cubes with him, the horses trotted over to the railing of the corral where Jimmy stood. The day after vigorous training, he usually brought an expected "surprise." He figured they worked hard and deserved an extra treat. True to form, a couple of the mares were pushing each other to get to Jimmy first, making him laugh. As long as they didn't start kicking, he was fine with a little friendly competition.

The last horse to come up to him gently nuzzled his neck before putting her head on his shoulder for pets and scratches. Her lips pulled back into a semblance of a smile as they flopped around in delight. Her eyelids went heavy in a blissful state, nearly closed with pleasure. Jimmy was the only person she'd allow to get this close when unsaddled, especially after Dobbin had run her so hard. That still made him angry. Winnie felt him tense, nudging him as if to say everything was okay.

"You're a good girl, aren't you? You know I do everything in my power so you can stay safe."

Winnie bobbed her head and gave a little snort.

"I gave Dobbin what for for riding you so hard. He'll think twice before he tries a stunt like that again." He leaned his head onto hers, running his hands along the top of her head and behind her ears. "In fact, things are going to change around here, so don't you worry. I'm going to take care of it." He gave her a couple of good pats on her neck, sending her on her way. The moments he spent like this with the horses did him as much good as it did them. Stretching, he turned around to find Douglas Elliot watching him.

"You sure do love your horses, don't you?"

Jimmy nodded, thinking that was obvious. He was also wondering why Elliot was now on their property after issuing his earlier warning by the river.

"You in charge of them all, or was that your mare?"

"I'm in charge of all the animals."

At that moment, Dusty chose to return from chasing some creature he had spotted earlier. Trotting over, he sat to the left of Jimmy, watching the rancher.

Nodding at the dog, Douglas said, "They sure like you right back."

Jimmy looked down at the wiry mess of a dog. "He's grown on me," he said, patting Dusty on his head.

"He does that to a man." Douglas looked at Dusty and said, "Ain't that right, Dante?"

Jimmy's head jerked back, and his eyes widened. "What'd you call him?"

"Dante." The dog panted, looking back at the rancher

before lying down. "Our foreman disappeared, gone on three weeks … nearly a month?" His voice raised on the question. "Not exactly sure because I was away from Double Star at the time. No one told me right away, either." He nodded toward the dog. "That there is Lars Nielsen's dog. Aren't you, boy?"

The dog, wagging his tail, barked at that and continued to look at the rancher. Jimmy was looking back and forth between the rancher and his foreman's dog, unable to disguise his surprise.

Scratching his head, he said, "Well, if he disappeared, that explains why Dusty was so scrawny. He looked like hell. Like no one been carin' for him. I suppose that kind of explains why we're having a very similar conversation."

"He doesn't normally follow others. That's why I've had my eye on you. Couldn't quite make out what was going on. Had to make sure you weren't telling stories, either."

"Some others were taunting him. I stood up for him when no one else would." Jimmy knew the rancher was fishing for information, but he wasn't about to give it to him. He stuck with the more obvious point of discussion—Dusty.

"Well, that explains a lot." Elliot's tone was skeptical, as if he knew there was more to Jimmy's story than he was letting on.

"Yeah, but where'd your foreman go? Dusty doesn't seem like the kind of dog who'd leave his master. He was good to him, wasn't he?" Jimmy's eyes narrowed.

"Yup. Dog was always following him pretty close. Didn't really leave his side." He looked down, thinking for a moment, before he raised his head to ask, "Where'd you first see him?"

"The trail that leads to the back way here. A group of us were riding it when I first saw him. Didn't think much of it because he was watching from the trees at first, taking our measure. The others didn't notice him until he came out, trying to get our attention. A couple taunted the poor dog. A few days later, he came running up to me, and I fed him. I was by myself at the time. Told him to go on and git because some of the men I'm with don't treat animals very well." He shook his head. "I don't stand with that."

Douglas Elliot's clean-shaven, tanned face looked thoughtful. His lean figure stood more erect.

"I hear you. I'm just trying to figure out what happened to Lars. He's a responsible man, been with us for years. He wouldn't just up and go." Elliot rubbed the back of his neck. "And even if he did, he certainly wouldn't leave Dante behind."

They stood silent for a few moments before Jimmy said, "Let's ride back to where Dusty met up with us the first time. Maybe we can find some clues as to what happened."

Elliot nodded. "I've scoured the area, but it wouldn't hurt to have a fresh set of eyes looking. Besides, now we've pinpointed a location where we're positive Dante has been for an extended period—and that dog gets around, let me tell you." He gave a wry chuckle, but his lips remained pressed together.

Jimmy watched him for a moment, clearly seeing the sadness in his eyes. "Was he a good friend or just someone who'd been at the ranch for a long time?"

Elliot stood up taller but looked out in the distance instead of directly at Jimmy. "He was my wife's cousin. We weren't exactly close, but he was a good man, nonetheless. He kept to himself and did his job well."

"Did your wife have anything to say that was helpful in your investigation?"

"'Fraid not. She passed on almost two years ago." He drew in a long breath, setting his face into a grim expression before blowing out a long exhale.

"I'm sorry."

"Not your fault. No one's fault. I figure God thought it was time to take her back home."

Jimmy watched the man standing as still as a living creature could. But no matter how still Elliot remained, he couldn't hide the loss in his eyes. They were dry, but held a deep, watery, and obvious sadness. Giving the man some space because he was clearly thinking about his wife, Jimmy played with Dusty's big, floppy ears.

After a few moments, Jimmy asked, "Do you want to backtrack from here to your property or go directly to the spot where Dusty was watching us?"

"Good question. He came up to you on the back trail? Just the once?"

"No, he seemed to be there both times. When we first rode in. Later when I was riding back from town. That's the time he followed me."

"Same place on the trail, though?"

Jimmy paused, making sure because the second time Dusty startled Coal. "Yup, pretty much the exact same place. He ran toward me from behind the second time."

"He's not an aggressive animal, but he's protective. Maybe that's why he waited … or he just wanted to make sure the others weren't with you." Tipping back his hat, he said, "I hate to ask." Elliot squinted at Jimmy as he went on. "Are you good friends with the others?"

"No. They know it, too."

Elliot nodded. "Thought so, but had to hear it from the horse's mouth, so to speak." Exhaling, he added, "Well, I'd sure appreciate it if you rode me back to where Dante found you. I can backtrack from there. The properties abut, and I can see if that's where Lars and Dante headed out from." He nodded. "No one saw them leave, so this makes him even harder to trace."

"As good a place as any to start. Let me saddle up. Be just a minute."

Jimmy strode off to saddle Coal while Dusty trotted over to Elliot for scratches. Elliot certainly knew just what he liked, so Dusty was completely pleased with himself.

* * *

THEY RODE IN SILENCE, looking off the path into the trees and shrubs for anything out of the ordinary. They were also making sure they weren't being followed or watched. Dusty trotted along happily. This time, however, he seemed to sense the importance of this ride and didn't wander off. He kept to the path, sometimes running slightly ahead, sometimes alongside them. It was as if he were riding point for them. When they got to the area where Jimmy had first seen Dusty, Dusty ran off into the shrubbery where he was originally watching them. They waited for a few minutes, but he didn't return.

Dismounting, Elliot and Jimmy took the same path as Dusty, going deeper into the trees and shrubs. That's where they found him, about a half a mile in, sitting next to a mound of recently dug earth. His head was resting on the mound as he watched their approach with mournful eyes and drooping ears.

"I'll be damned." Elliot took off his hat and pushed his hand through his hair. He slapped his hat on his leg in frustration. "Been here the whole time."

"Probably right." Jimmy's eyes didn't leave Dusty.

The dog had been looking for someone who'd follow him here. That's why he was in the same spot. It's also why Dusty kept leaving him for longer periods of time. He was checking on his former owner. Jimmy shook his head.

"Better go back and get a shovel. Need to make sure, so

you have closure." He looked over at Elliot who hadn't taken his eyes off the mound. "Besides, we need to give whoever that is a proper burial."

The thought of digging up someone who'd probably been murdered wasn't high on Jimmy's list of things he wanted to do today—or ever. But he also knew there needed to be an ending so the mind would stop wondering and have some peace.

"You mind if I just sit here a minute? Wait for you?" Staring at the mound, Elliot's entire posture was wilted, not at all like the strong and determined man he had presented.

Jimmy looked around them, scanning the ground. "Doesn't look like anyone's been here for a while. I suppose it'd be all right. I think Dusty should stay with you so you don't get caught off guard. Who knows who did this and if they're watching this spot."

Elliot stared blankly for a moment before nodding. "Much obliged."

Jimmy nodded back at him before turning around. *First Josie, now this. I'll never have time to gather evidence. What is wrong with this town?*

* * *

JIMMY RODE BACK in a black mood. *Who'd murder the foreman and why?* His frustrations were mounting. *Damnit. Just what I need. Another thing to do.* Jimmy sighed heavily. *Poor Dusty, but damn it all to hell. Trouble follows that dog.* All sorts of jumbled thoughts and feelings were tumbling around in Jimmy's head as he leaned forward, riding a little harder back to camp. Coal was happy to have free rein. Clenching his jaw, Jimmy couldn't stand the thought of Dusty waiting for help, and if Elliot's correct, something terrible was going on because Dusty wouldn't have let this happen. This was yet another afternoon dealing with strangers' issues and no closer to helping Josie or himself for that matter. Lying low seemed to be impossible. Dismounting by the trough outside the barn, Jimmy met Van Der Kamp leading his horse out.

Van Der Kamp didn't ride for pleasure or without a specific reason because of his leg. His old war injury tended to act up. Jimmy's eyebrows raised in question. Instead of answering him, Van Der Kamp made a statement of his own.

"Seem to be in a bit of a hurry." He nodded at Coal who was still at the watering trough.

Jimmy blew out a breath. "Neighboring rancher, Douglas Elliot, has been watching me because of Dusty. Wondered why he was with us. His foreman disappeared about three or so weeks ago, and the dog belonged to him." He grimaced.

Van Der Kamp nodded. "Mmhm." His eyes narrowed. "Did we find some more trouble?"

"Yup."

He knocked his hat back, putting his hands on his hips. "In what form does this trouble take?" He quirked an eyebrow, pretty much knowing the answer before he asked the question.

"A body. I came back for a shovel. Rancher's waiting at the mound with the dog."

Van Der Kamp sighed heavily. "Not what I was wanting to hear, but pretty much expected. Need my help?"

"Not sure. Dusty led us to it, pretty sure it's the rancher's foreman. Or was. Better take a tarp, too." Shaking his head, he stepped around Van Der Kamp, grabbing what he needed. "I'm going back to dig him up, and we'll go from there. I don't know if we should alert someone for the rancher. What d'you want me to do? I know we're supposed to be lying low here, and this doesn't fall under that and all."

Van Der Kamp's jaw worked as he thought about it, making a kind of grunting sound while he formulated a plan.

"I was planning on riding into town anyway. See what I could see. I'll go have a word with the sheriff and have him ride out with me. He may be busy, but I'll try to get him out there sooner than later. Never know how Elliot will react, despite their relationship. Kind of wanted to get the lay of the land before I dealt with the sheriff, but there you have it. It's done."

Jimmy knew the sheriff had to be involved but didn't think it would turn out well for anyone, especially from what little information he had cobbled together. It was a hunch on his part. He wasn't sure how to say that, because no one naysaid Van Der Kamp. He was put out of his misery when Van Der Kamp interrupted his thoughts.

"Go on. I can see you have something to say about the matter." His eyes didn't waver from Jimmy.

"I'm just wondering how far we'll get with this sheriff, given what Harold told me." Jimmy frowned because thinking about the sheriff didn't sit well with him. "Besides," he cleared his throat, "maybe you shouldn't be the one to go."

Van Der Kamp nodded before drawing in a long right nostril breath, scrunching up that side of his face. "He won't recognize me. They never do. Have to follow protocol. This is the rancher's issue, and we're just helping."

He was right. Despite being a "notorious bandit," no one had ever really recognized him. The papers painted an inaccurate portrait of his person as well as his appearance. They tended to make bad guys look ugly. However, Van Der Kamp was a very polite, well-spoken, and handsome man. His appearance swayed most people into thinking about him in positive terms. If it wasn't his good-looking and tidy appearance, it was his firm demeanor and strength. He could be quite persuasive—in either realm.

Jimmy told Van Der Kamp where to bring the sheriff as he mounted his horse, and then loaded up Coal with the necessary tools before heading back out. Coal returned to the location without much direction. Jimmy dismounted just as Dusty came trotting out. Gathering his equipment, he followed Dusty back to Elliot and the mound.

He stood watching a defeated Elliot sitting on the ground, not looking at anything in particular, but deep in thought.

"Need a minute?"

"Nope. Let's get this done." Slapping his hands on his thighs, Elliot pushed himself to standing.

Jimmy handed Elliot a shovel. "Van Der Kamp was heading out, and I asked him to bring the sheriff. You need to know what happened, and we need to keep this on the up-and-up."

Douglas Elliot gave Jimmy an odd look. Clearly recognizing the name, he didn't say anything. Jimmy thought it was for the best. For everyone.

They dug in silence, until Jimmy asked, "Have any idea who might've wanted to do this to him?"

Elliot straightened, stretching out his back. "Some."

Jimmy waited, but it didn't seem Elliot was going to say more. He raised his eyebrows at the older man. Jabbing the shovel into the earth and leaning his forearm on it, he waited a moment before asking, "Mind sharing?"

"A bit." Elliot went back to digging, ignoring Jimmy.

Jimmy pulled his shovel out of the dirt and began scooping up more earth and casting it aside. "You might want to give me more than that," Jimmy said, his tone belying his suggestion. Elliot gave him a doubtful look. "I am helping you out, after all."

"Got me there." Releasing a belabored sigh, he wiped the back of his hand on his forehead. "Lars kept to himself. Always had." Looking thoughtful, he turned toward Jimmy, changing tact. "There's no love lost between the Reinhardt spread and my own. I'm not telling you anything you can't find out on your own in town, but I do dislike wagging tongues."

"Your tongue isn't wagging. I asked. I seemed to have stepped into something whether or not you see it that way. I'd like to know what I'm getting into, if you don't mind. I can't help if I'm not informed."

"'Hate to shoot the wrong man' sort of thing?" Elliot's mouth tipped up at the corners, mischief shining in his grief-stricken eyes.

"Pretty much. Now, if you don't mind …"

"Fine. Frederick Reinhardt's father, Otto, was a very kind man. He helped everyone he could, as did his wife. He got along well with everyone, and everyone loved him. He was found murdered one day shortly before the war ended. Never found the murderer, either." He paused, waiting for Jimmy to connect the dots. His eyes narrowed and locked with Jimmy's. "Frederick was supposedly off at war. However, there wasn't evidence he was actually there. He never wrote letters, either. His mom died brokenhearted after the first year."

"Any suspicions?"

"Have you met the Reinhardts yet?"

"Just the women—a Lillian and Nora."

"How'd you find them?"

"Forward."

"Pretty much says it all."

They dug a couple more shovelfuls before Elliot sighed. "Lillian was teasing one of my cow punchers. Kept coming on to him in the most forward of ways. It was disgraceful, her behavior." Jimmy shook his head.

Elliot went on. "Well, her daddy got wind of it, and all hell broke loose. He came riding hell for leather onto our spread, raging at this poor kid from behind, forcing him to turn around to see what was coming at him. Cleaned his clock before anyone could lend a hand. We had to carry him back to the bunkhouse and give him the following day off so he could get his senses back. We all knew Jeb wasn't the usual carousing type. He was flattered that a pretty, young thing paid some attention to him, and he returned the favor. Frederick didn't see it that way."

"Was that the first time something happened between you and him?"

"Nope. Won't be the last, either. Nora's worse in her own way. She's older and sneakier."

"Thanks for that. They're pretty enough, but I don't find them attractive or at all pleasant. They were improper and ill-mannered, and I couldn't get out of the mercantile quick enough. They were disparaging the woman they called JoJo, too. Harold recommended her for alterations, and they weren't having it."

"Oh, that." He spit on the ground. "They just won't let old stories go, those two. They seem to think they had some claim on Frank Odin. He was the most eligible bachelor in the town until Essie allegedly got her hands on him—in reality, he got his hands on her."

"Who's that?"

"The oldest Snyder sister. Frank loves Essie. He dotes on her, in fact. But he loves her money just as much."

"They have money?"

"No secret. The Snyders and Reinhardts were part of the town's founding families."

"Then why does JoJo have to work so hard and practically live alone on that homestead?"

"That's a good question. We've all been wondering that. It's obvious Frank doesn't care a whit for Beth. He seems to like JoJo and all. But he won't take them in. Some say it's because JoJo won't go without her sister. Frank barely tolerates Beth. Some attribute it to nefarious reasons."

"Who's being nefarious?"

"Why, Frank, of course. You didn't think it was the sisters, did you?"

"No." Jimmy's lips tightened. "It just sounds so off, that's all."

"It does. I try not to think about it. I just watch JoJo and make sure she's looking well. Best I can do without interfering in family business. I liked the Snyders all right. I just don't think they did right by Josephine is all. Essie and Beth were treated like princesses—kind of like those Reinhardt women. Those girls were paraded around, and they put up airs. Josephine has a good head on her shoulders and is a natural hard worker. Parents just treated her like she was the help. Sisters followed suit."

Jimmy opened his mouth to ask more questions about Reinhardt but was interrupted by the sound of hoofbeats. Elliot's face went hard at the sound, and Jimmy, gripping the shovel, looked over his shoulder. Dusty's hackles raised until he recognized a distinctive gait coming toward them. He settled, trotting out to meet Van Der Kamp and the sheriff. Happy to see them, his head dipped then tipped upward with a woof of acknowledgement. His muzzle directed upward for an extra moment, as if releasing the sound to the sky for all to hear. Van Der Kamp bent slightly to pat him then continued toward the others.

"Doesn't look like you got very far. What're you doing?" Van Der Kamp eyed Jimmy. Douglas Elliot scrutinized Van Der Kamp as he teased Jimmy.

"I was wondering what I was getting myself into, that's what I was doing." Jimmy gave Van Der Kamp a wry look, which was uncharacteristic for the generally reticent young man.

Van Der Kamp cocked his head at both Jimmy's tone and

his words. He raised his brows and nodded as if to say, "Well played."

"Besides, it's been less than an hour since I set out here. You just happened to be quick, is all."

Elliot cast Jimmy a look as well while the sheriff watched the three of them. His entire head, not just his eyes, moved between the men. It might've been funny if it weren't for the scowl on his face. He stood a little straighter, his brow furrowed.

"What's going on here? And don't get smart with me, either." He grunted, for emphasis.

"Don't get yourself all in a bunch, Colter. They're helping me. Something you haven't been much of the past few days."

"Now don't go takin' that tone with me. I've been busy with the Taylors. They had some rustling up on their spread. I alerted Chester that his family needed him." He nodded at Elliot, passing a look at Van Der Kamp and Jimmy.

Jimmy took it upon himself to redirect the sheriff. He didn't want to be standing around flapping their gums. The man was deflecting, and Jimmy was tired of wasting time.

"Sheriff, Jimmy Stapleton." He nodded, leaning toward the sheriff and holding his hand out. The sheriff looked him over but didn't reciprocate. Instead of retracting it, Jimmy swept the proffered hand around them, indicating the ground. "I don't see any tracks around here, but you may want to take a look for yourself and see if you notice anything, you being the law and all."

Sheriff Colter stood taller, puffing out his chest, which his belly still managed to exceed, and hooking his thumbs in his belt. "Yes, been the law since the town was established."

The sheriff began looking around without any real examination as the others watched him. Jimmy decided to fill him in while they waited for the farce to play out.

"Dusty, I mean Dante, had adopted me earlier. We kept

seeing him off this trail, but I didn't think much of it until Mr. Elliot told me about his foreman going missing."

"What's that damn dog got to do with anything?"

Elliot huffed. "You know darn good and well why Dante has something to do with this! He didn't go anywhere without Lars." He pushed his hat back on his head. "Colter, I'm thinking you need to be retiring sooner than later if you can't remember simple things like that."

"Ach. You know those kinds of things are easily overlooked. I don't see Lars or Dante often enough to make a big stink as to whether or not they're together. Besides, he's just a dang dog."

Everyone looked over at Dante, whose tongue was lolling from the heat. His ears were drawn back from the tension among the men, his face strained. When they continued to stare, Dante pulled his lips back further, looking like he was grimacing. He returned the sheriff's stare without blinking.

"Bah!" Colter flapped his hand at Dante in disgust.

That's when Dante chimed in, barking at him.

"Now you're talking?" Jimmy gave Dante a stern look. "You need to stand up for yourself better." Dante whined and lay back down by the mound.

"Not you, too?" The sheriff huffed at Jimmy, grumbling. "Everyone and that damned dog."

"Leave Jimmy outta this, Colter. Dante adopted him because he has a way with animals. Dante's the one who led us here. Now whaddya going to do about it?"

The sheriff sighed. "Finish digging and see what's under there. We can decide when we see what we're up against."

Jimmy shot Van Der Kamp a look before picking the shovel back up and resuming digging.

In less than fifteen minutes, Elliot and Jimmy finished unearthing the remains of Lars Nielson. They slowed their digging when Elliot hit the body and carefully dug around it.

Their relief was palpable seeing that the body was whole and intact although the smell wasn't pleasant. Someone had unceremoniously dropped the poor man into the hole and tossed dirt over him. At least they had the courtesy to make the hole deep enough so animals wouldn't dig him up. Elliot and Jimmy stood up, leaning away from the hole when they had him uncovered. The sheriff leaned in with his arm over his nose. He peered down at the body then back up at Douglas Elliot. Elliot stared at Lars's earthly remains. His right jaw had a nearly imperceptible tick. Jimmy watched the sheriff take a couple of awkward steps away from the hole.

"Well, you were right, Douglas. Looks like there's been some foul play with Lars."

Elliot's eyes flared while his jaw tick became more pronounced. His knuckles went white, and his hands shook grasping the shovel. Jimmy knew he was exercising extreme restraint—he wouldn't have blamed Elliot for clobbering the man over his head. Even Van Der Kamp scoffed at the sheriff's words, a huffing sound coming from the back of his throat.

The sheriff swiveled his head toward Van Der Kamp. "What? You got something you want to say?"

"Nope." Van Der Kamp crossed his arms, glaring at Sheriff Colter.

"Well, then. Let's get 'im outta that hole and see what's got to him."

Jimmy's eyes met Elliot's. Elliot's eyes narrowed, and he shook his head minutely before reaching down to grab Lars's shoulders. Together they gently lifted the body and placed it on the tarp Jimmy had laid out. Elliot turned the body slightly to the side to examine the back of the head. Colter grunted as he kneeled for a closer look.

"He was hit from behind. Looks like he didn't stand a chance."

Van Der Kamp jumped in to tamp down the insensitivity and thoughtlessness of the so-called sheriff. "Let's let the undertaker, as well as Doc, have a look at him. What do you need from us, sheriff?"

"What I want to know is what Jimmy here is doing. How do we know you weren't part of this and stole the dog?"

"For Christ's sake. Will you get it together, Colter? You're starting to chap my backside." Elliot stood up, brushing off his hands. He pointed at Jimmy. "I've been watching him because he had Dante. Dante goes to no one he doesn't want to. He won't be forced. I knew something had to be up."

"Yeah, he befriended Lars and Dante, then killed Lars." Conviction plastered across his face, Sheriff Colter pointed at Jimmy.

"What the hell for? He's been in town for a handful of days. I told you Lars was missing before they even showed up."

"Could've been scoping the area."

Elliot raised his left eyebrow at the sheriff, while crossing his arms. When Sheriff Colter didn't say anything, Elliot asked, "To what end? Lars didn't ever have anything of value on him. He rarely talked to anyone."

Colter shrugged, and Elliot moved to lunge at him. Jimmy put his arm out just in time. Instead, Elliot pointed his finger at Sheriff Colter.

"You! If you'd do your job instead of setting yourself up for retirement, this might not have happened." Colter tensed, blanching, but Elliot wouldn't let anyone interrupt. "This town is falling down around us, and you're sitting around twiddling your thumbs."

He jerked his arm down and stomped a few steps away before spinning around to face Colter again. He stomped back toward the sheriff, leaning forward with stiff arms and clenched fists. Elliot stood nearly toe to toe with Colter when he stopped. "Whose payroll are you on? *Whose?*" Elliot spat the words out in the sheriff's face, his own face an inferno of fury.

Sheriff Colter stepped back, placating hands held up in defense. His tone was patronizing, much different from his earlier arrogance. "Now Douglas, I know you're upset about your Ingrid's cousin, but don't go taking it out on me. I'm doing the best I can. I'm just low on resources right now. I don't have help. Why, Merritt—"

"Don't give that bull about Merritt. He's left town, and we all know why. You've had plenty of time to replace your deputy as well as get a new assistant deputy. You chose not to. I want to know why. Just what do you think you're up to?"

Van Der Kamp kept a close eye on the sheriff, who ran his hand down his face, looking away from his accuser. Interrogator that he once was, he knew a liar when he saw one, and that sheriff was lying. The man was sweating profusely, and it wasn't from the extra weight around his middle, nor was it from exertion. Douglas Elliot was asking the right questions but going about it the wrong way with this man. Van Der Kamp took a deep breath in, waiting for this to play out. He always held his cards close to his vest.

The sheriff's face sagged as he tugged at his necktie. "Look, Douglas, I'm tired. I'm trying my best. And I'm real sorry about Lars. I really am. Let's just get this done with— take his body to the undertaker and have Doc take a look. At a minimum, we can find out how he died and then go from there."

Colter didn't lie there. He looked weary. What else he was lying about, they had to wait and see.

CHAPTER 16

Jimmy and Van Der Kamp helped the men load Lars's remains on a pack horse. The trees were still, and the air felt close with the lingering smell of decay. They mounted as soon as the sheriff and Douglas Elliot rode away in the opposite direction of their base camp at Old Man Johnson's.

Jimmy had seen plenty of dead bodies riding with the Van Der Kamp gang. Knowing that death was inevitable, especially after witnessing his parents' murders, he'd become hardened to that fact. But that didn't mean he wanted to see or be a part of it. Unless a horse needed putting down, he didn't take any life. Now, he'd just unearthed one taken. Jimmy had distanced himself from what the gang did, especially anything criminal, so this situation was unnerving. It was foul. The injustice of it all roiled Jimmy's pot.

The sheriff and the general atmosphere in this town were fixing his pot to boil over. If Lars was as much of a recluse as Douglas Elliot said he was, then something much larger than rustling or even a dispute between spreads was going on. Jimmy looked around, thoughtful. The air was heavy, and even the animals sensed the gravitas. Dusty stuck close to Jimmy, as if he were afraid to lose another person. Coal minded his manners and didn't nip at or taunt Dusty, like he'd taken to doing. Horse, dog, and man made for a thoughtful procession.

Van Der Kamp interrupted Jimmy's gloomy musings. "Better keep an eye on Colter. Something's not right."

Jimmy nodded, even though Van Der Kamp wasn't looking at him. "I kind of wonder what's between Elliot and Colter—besides Colter being slow to the draw investigating Lars's disappearance." Jimmy continued to look out into the distance. "It feels like bad blood. Did you hear Elliot mention the deputy?"

Van Der Kamp drew in a long inhale, pulling up half his face. "Mmhm. Keep an eye on him, Jimmy. He's not the root, but'll lead you to the source."

Jimmy turned his head toward Van Der Kamp. He glanced at Jimmy, snorting, again. "Little fish." He faced forward. "Swim after him, and he'll bring you to the big catch."

They rode in silence the rest of the way to base camp, but as they approached, Jimmy hesitated. Fidgeting in the saddle, he turned to say something, but Van Der Kamp beat him to it.

"Go on—go check on your girl. It's probably a good idea anyway."

"How'd you—"

"You have the same look on your face that Charlie did with Annabelle. You are brothers, you know. Where you found your sensibilities and common decency, I'm not sure. Not from your father, I can pretty much guarantee that."

Jimmy wore a wide-eyed expression, and not just because he was surprised someone else felt the same way about his father. "I—"

"This town isn't safe. While I know her having grown up here might give her a modicum of protection, by now, someone's already connected the two of you. Best you go see for yourself. Besides, it'd do good for you to familiarize yourself with all the townspeople and their comings and goings. Undertaker might be clear, but see who else is taking sides with different things. Small towns and all. Asking about ranching or water issues might be a good place to start. Mining as well. We don't know how deep Pennington has moved into the territory."

Jimmy nodded before spurring Coal on. Dusty ran after them, not wanting to be left behind, but not before giving Van Der Kamp a quick woof and setting his own fast pace.

Van Der Kamp smiled, shaking his head, as he watched Jimmy and his pack race off.

Ah, Jimmy. You're more like your brother than you know. You're just as smart, strong, and brave. You're also delusional if you think you're just checking on her for "safety's sake." Turning his horse toward the stable, he pulled his right foot out of the stirrup, stretching his bad leg, loosening it to make dismounting easier. *I'm turning maudlin with all this gang dismantling. I'm beginning to act more like the father Jimmy needs than their leader.* He chuckled softly. *Never wanted to kill or take the boys to begin with.* Shaking his head, the humor had left his face as he slid out of the saddle, boots hitting the ground. Scowling, he muttered aloud, "Damned Pennington."

* * *

RELIEF SPREAD through Jimmy's limbs, catching him off guard. He knew checking on Josie was the right thing to do, as well as scouting more of the town, but he couldn't help but think he was feeling something other than relief. He certainly felt lighter, although that could be attributed to having accomplished something helpful and finally having something to do beyond babysitting. He'd been waiting for some sort of news or action. *Thank God Van Der Kamp made it easier for me to go—that he didn't force me to come up with excuses and reasons.* Despite telling himself that, Jimmy was pretty sure that Van Der Kamp made up his own mind about him and Josie. He felt Van Der Kamp pushing him toward her, and oddly enough, he wasn't minding so much right now.

The small pack made good time to town, slowing down as they rode through it. Jimmy wanted to check if he felt watched again. He usually felt it coming into town from Josie's side not theirs. He also didn't want to attract attention by racing off to Josie's, despite his desire to get there quicker. It had taken most of the day to find, uncover, and send off Lars, so not too many people were milling around. It was in that liminal space between dinner and supper. For the shops, it was a slower and lazier time of day. Not as many customers, but more stocking and organizing.

Jimmy and his pack headed toward the blacksmith's. If there were customers there, he'd linger and see what he could pick up. If not, he'd ask the blacksmith about some simple shoes and then be off to check on Josie. Rolling his shoulders back, he sat straighter in his saddle, his impressive build garnering some looks from people passing on the street.

* * *

AFTER PROMISING to bring a pair of horses to Nathan Kitchener, the blacksmith, the following week, Jimmy left. Before he was aware of it, he found himself sitting atop Coal outside Josie's. He watched the house for several minutes. Indecision had never been a problem for him, but right now he was swimming in it. Oddly enough, he was waiting for some sort of sign. It came in the form of movement in one of the upper windows. Jimmy caught Beth peering from between the curtains, glowering down at him. Before he could think twice, he slid off Coal and walked him over to the shade.

Each movement was steady yet wooden—he felt driven by some unseen force. Propelled up the steps without any thinking on his part, just doing. The door swung open right as he raised his fist to knock on it. What he saw wasn't what he was wanting. Beth's flushed face emerged, her eyes blazing at him. She stood between him and his objective—although if he were truly honest with himself, she was between him and the object of his desire—which was making him a little testy. Beth's lips were tight and her face flushed. Why in the world she was so angry was beyond him. All he wanted to do was see Josie and make sure she was doing all right. Beth barred his way with a stiff arm, keeping the door and her body between them.

"What do you want?" Beth hissed in a low voice.

"Why are you whispering?" Jimmy looked beyond her in either direction. "Is everything okay?"

"Of course. At least everything was okay, until you showed up." She was trying to shut the door on him. "You need to go, now." She used her other hand to help this time, pushing harder.

Jimmy had casually stuck his foot out, making it so Beth couldn't shut the door on him, but he wasn't otherwise trying to force his way in or be aggressive. Despite that, for some reason, Beth's gauntlet was making him angry as well as anxious. She was hiding something, that he was sure of.

"Why?"

"You don't belong here."

"I do."

"How so? Are you courting JoJo?" Her eyebrows raised in challenge.

"I'm her protector. Now let me in or send her out. I need to check on her."

"Need to? Why, exactly, are you here?"

Jimmy heaved a sigh. The tension of the day was getting to him. Pulling off his hat, he ran the back of his hand across his brow. He decided to be polite to Beth, leaving his hat off.

"We found Lars Nielsen's body buried between Old Man Johnson's place and the Double Star spread."

Beth's face went white, and her arm shook a little, relaxing her hold on the door. After swallowing hard, she managed to croak out, "What?"

"Look, it's a long story, but the short of it is Douglas Elliot questioned me because I had Lars's dog. The dog was trying to show me where the body was buried, but I didn't realize that until Elliot started asking questions. We dug it up today, and the sheriff took him away to the undertaker."

Beth's hand went to her chest. Falling away from the door, she allowed Jimmy to enter.

Jimmy stepped in and continued, "Look, I don't know what's going on around here, but this town is showing too many shades of wrong. On top of that, Gus and his followers are interested in Josie, and I'm not having it. I saved her from them and told her I'd protect her as long as I was in town. Now, I mean it. I won't let you get in the way of that, you hear?"

Beth just stared at this stranger. It felt like he'd been around enough that he was starting to become familiar, which was an odd thought in and of itself. She didn't know what to make of all this.

Jimmy looked around. "Where's Josie?"

Beth held up her hand. "Wait. How do I know you don't have something to do with Lars's death?"

"We haven't been in town long enough. He's been missing for nearly a month. We just rode in a handful of days ago. I don't know anyone in this town—it's just a place we're passing through."

Beth's face scrunched up in disgust. *Of course, you're only passing through. It's either that or mining. I knew it!*

"Whatever you're thinking, just stop," Jimmy said. Beth pursed her lips at him, narrowing her eyes, but he continued. "You're so ready to think the worst of me. Why don't you wait until I actually do something bad before you judge?"

Beth huffed, heading for the kitchen. Josie was just coming in from collecting eggs as Beth entered it with Jimmy closely following. After a moment of confusion, her face broke into a wide smile before settling itself. She didn't want Beth to get any ideas or start any accidental rumors.

"What's going on? Is everything all right?"

Beth just stared at Jo for a moment before flapping her hand back at Jimmy. "He wanted to check in." The disdain in her voice was clear. "I'm going in the other room, but I can hear what's going on." She stomped out, leaving the stench of her disgust behind.

Josie and Jimmy stared at each other until Jimmy shrugged. "She doesn't care much for me."

That made Josie smile before she whispered, "Don't worry—I don't think she thinks much of me, either."

They shared a smile so familiar that it felt like an embrace before Jimmy cleared his throat and got down to business. He seemed to forget himself around her, which wasn't good.

"I came to check on you, make sure everything's okay." He bent forward so his head was more level with her eyes. "You good?"

Josie's mouth formed an O. It looked like she choked on the rest of her words. "I—"

Jimmy drew in a long breath, stalling for time. His heart

beat like crazy when he was near her. He had to force himself to keep some sort of proper spacing between them as well as keep from reaching out and touching her. "We found Lars Nielsen's body this morning. So far, no one knows why anyone would want to kill him. I was worried and came out to make sure you're okay."

"You think I have something to do with this?" She took a step back. Her eyes were wide with disbelief, welling up.

"No, Josie. I just dug up a man who'd been clearly murdered and, from what Douglas Elliot said, didn't involve himself with anyone—there was no reason to murder him. As soon as the sheriff took his body away, I came here. I'm sorry—I didn't even stop to clean myself up." He ran a hand through his hair, looking down at his dirty boots to collect himself for a moment before looking back at her. "I had to make sure you were okay. I know it's not rational."

Jimmy shook his head. He couldn't believe he was talking about this. With her. He surprised himself with all the feelings coursing through him. He felt jittery and overwhelmed by emotions he thought were long buried. What was clear was how much this murder bothered him and how fast his mind was spinning.

Josie's face softened, and her hand went to her heart. Stepping forward, she gently placed her hand on his shoulder.

"I'm so sorry."

She whispered the words, but they were more powerful than either of them realized. Neither had had someone comfort them in a long time. People felt sorry for them from afar but didn't involve themselves, or so Jimmy and Josie believed. Josie's throat tightened as she shed tears for poor Lars, who'd always been kind to her whenever they crossed paths. In general, he was grumpy but was always friendly to her. Her eyes were also flowing over for this gentle man standing in front of her awash in vulnerability. She didn't know why he was so fiercely protective of her, but she liked it. She liked his protection, and she liked him— a lot.

Coming to that realization was the moment her heart felt warm, and her body relaxed.

"Mmm." The sound came out almost as a sigh. Her voice confirmed what her heart was feeling, and before she knew it, she had wrapped her arms around Jimmy's middle, and he was hugging her back tightly. "I'm okay." She nodded into his chest. "I always feel safe when you're around."

Jimmy thought he might die of pride. Josie made him feel ten feet tall and stronger than an ox. Others described him that way, but for the first time, right now, he truly felt that way. She gave him a purpose that didn't involve anger. He felt some sort of hope when she was around, although he didn't know why. He tried to remind himself that this was only temporary, and he was keeping her safe until he left.

Stepping away, he kept hold of her shoulders as he looked down at her. Smiling, the palm of his hand went to her cheek. He leaned down and was about to kiss her when Beth's shrill voice sounded behind him.

"I hope you're keeping your hands off my sister, Mister Whatever-Your-Name-Is."

Jimmy rolled his eyes, releasing Josie. Putting his hands on his hips, he called out over his shoulder, "Stapleton."

Beth was at the door by this point. "What?"

"Stapleton. My last name is Stapleton, but I'd prefer if you called me Jimmy." He turned toward her.

"Well, I'd prefer if you stay away from my sister. She doesn't have time for passers-through." Holding his gaze in challenge, she waited for his response.

Josie gasped and beat Jimmy to the punch.

"Beth! You apologize right now. Jimmy's been nothing but

kind to me, and I don't appreciate how hostile you're being to him."

"JoJo, when the town gets wind of him," she tossed her head in Jimmy's direction, folding her arms across her chest, "hanging around out here, what d'ya think'll happen?"

Josie's face dropped. She turned to look at Jimmy, whose face was a mask. He was staring down Beth.

Beth added, "Besides, I don't want your behavior ruining my chances at finding a husband." She shook her index finger skyward as she said, "Watch what you're doing because this town is always watching you."

Josie recoiled. Beth's words hit her like a slap across the face. Her head turned toward Jimmy, who wore an equally puzzled look. He pulled his mouth to one side, contorting his face and spoke out of the side of his mouth. "And that's another reason why I've come to check on you. This town ain't right."

CHAPTER 17

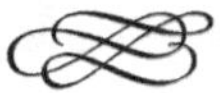

A week later, Josephine was glad for Daisy and that Beth didn't pitch her usual fit about needing the wagon. Not having to walk the couple of miles or so into town felt nice. She'd been working hard on Mrs. Patterson's dress so she could have it in time for the dance. People from the two neighboring towns of Adamsville and Weaver were coming in to see each other, and some of the younger people were hoping to meet their future spouses. It was a big event.

Josie had always been relegated to the serving table with the matrons while Beth and Essie danced the night away. For Essie, the dances were just an excuse to stand close and touch Frank anyway. Everyone knew they were eventually getting married. Well, everyone except Lillian Reinhardt, who seemed to think she had some sort of rights over Frank.

Josephine shrugged as she drove the wagon. Didn't matter now since Essie was the one who up and married him. The Reinhardt women didn't bother her as much as they bothered Beth. They had it out for each other, even more so when Nora returned to town five years ago with a foul taste in her mouth. Nora thought she was free from the

West until her brother, Frederick, tightened her purse strings and recalled her home to look after Lillian because Lillian couldn't seem to be in charge of herself.

Josephine sighed. *So alike, Nora and Beth. Willful and somewhat wild.*

She pulled the wagon behind the livery, looking for some shade. Unhitching Daisy, she walked her to the trough before leading her inside. Karl, the livery owner, never minded that Josephine used the end stall for Daisy when business was slow. Daisy was old, and JoJo took good care of her. That alone endeared JoJo to Karl. "Enough said" is how Karl would've phrased it all—something JoJo really enjoyed. He always told JoJo she was a "good egg," and he didn't want to hear any nonsense that spoke otherwise. He defended against the small jabs made at her.

JoJo popped her head over the stall Karl was working in just to make sure it was okay for Daisy to rest there for a short bit while she ran her errands. He was busy scraping a horse's hoof when she called out. He had his back to her, but he raised his tooled hand and nodded, responding loudly, "Ja, sure! Take yer time, Jo-za-feen."

Josephine smiled. She loved Karl like a father. He was always so good to her. The stark contrast between the two men coupled with the thought of her father made her frown. She couldn't remember a time when her father had stood up to her mother's abusive behavior and her bitterness, nor had he stopped others from taunting or calling her names. He had turned a blind eye to the callous and overly harsh treatment her mother had administered to her and her only. If he disagreed with what was happening, he'd just walk away without saying anything to avoid being the target of his wife's vitriol. Jimmy protected her better than her own father had, come to think of it. *Well, I don't want to think of it. I have work to do. A lot of work, as a matter of fact.*

She picked up her pace as her thoughts wandered back to Jimmy. He was a big brute of a man. The sound of his deep, rumbling voice warmed her. His hands were so large, yet gentle. Ironic that he never once made her fear for her person—even when he manhandled those men. Shaking her head, she kept walking toward Mrs. Patterson's house, the clanking of tools and chattering of people cocooning her in her dream world.

She wanted to arrive before Mr. Patterson came home for his lunch break because his face bore an odd expression every time he looked at her, as though he wanted to say something but wasn't sure if he should. Even more unsettling, she occasionally caught him staring at her, and with such intensity it sent chills down her spine. There was no one she could talk to about it, and there was nothing to be done, anyway. She quickly shook it off, picking up her pace.

Deep in thought, Josephine wasn't watching where she was going. *Jimmy's hair is so dark, the darkness of his waves glint like polished silver. It looks very thick, too, kind of like his eyelashes. Long. And thick. He was—*

Laughter stopped her dead in her tracks. She tensed, knowing exactly who it belonged to before she even met their eyes—*the Reinhardt women*. She adjusted the package in her arms, stalling for time when she heard her name.

"JoJo, what in the world are you smiling about? I'd think someone like you wouldn't have much to smile about. Don't you, Nora?"

"Why now, Lillian, be nice. Everyone can't be as pretty as you are. But JoJo, I am wondering what has you smiling so brightly today?" With a snap of her wrist, she splayed her fan open and fanned herself. East Coast trick. She loved to lord it over the "country bumpkins," as she liked to call the rest of the townsfolk.

"Lovely to see you, Nora. Lillian." Josephine inclined her

head at each woman when she said her name. She spoke more politely than she felt. Everything that had happened the past few days had her feeling unsettled, especially knowing they had met Jimmy. Josephine's stomach was churning, and her jaw clenched.

Nora snapped her fan shut so she could tap Josephine with it. "JoJo, you haven't answered my question. That's rude, you know. I know Mrs. Snyder taught you better than that." Lillian, at Nora's side, tittered, enjoying Josephine's discomfort.

"It's a beautiful day, and I've finished Mrs. Patterson's dress for her."

"I'm sure something else has you smiling, as well. Go on." She leaned toward Josephine, her voice lowering and dragging out her words in a taunt. "Do tell." She raised her brows as if she were completely interested in what Josephine had to say.

Watching Nora look down her nose at her, Josephine didn't trust where this was going. Nora shot a glance at Lillian.

"I do think she's being shy." They burst into unladylike laughter.

Josephine looked on in horror, a little rabbit wanting to run but frozen in fear, until they finally quieted down.

"We know all about your visitor." Nora spoke the word, visitor, as if it were something dirty.

Josephine went beet red at the insinuation, as well as the fact that Jimmy had, indeed, been to her house unchaperoned. Not once, but twice. "I—"

"He's a handsome—and virile-looking—young man. No need to be embarrassed, JoJo."

She was sure she was going to combust from all the blood pumping to her skin, making her flush harder than she had ever had. Josephine thought things couldn't possibly get worse … until they did.

"Did you measure him for new clothes?" They started to cackle this time. Nora looked knowingly at Lillian. "He's no small thing, is he?"

By this point, Josephine's mouth popped open, and it remained like that for a long moment. A passerby slowed his pace to see what all the fuss was about. Mortification didn't begin to describe what Josephine felt. She wished the ground would open and swallow her whole.

Nora gently placed her hand on Josephine's arm, contradicting the next set of words that came out of her mouth. "Just don't go thinking you have any sort of chance with a man like that." She practically hissed her next sentence. "You're just a charity case for him." Her voice returned to its natural tone, apart from when she imitated Jimmy, as she continued to taunt Josephine. "He even said so. Something to the effect of 'It sounds like Josephine needs the work, and it's the Christian thing to do.' Isn't that right, Lill? He told us we weren't being Christian by suggesting he go to the better seamstress, Frannie."

Nora gave a curt nod at that, and Josephine's horror was complete.

A charity case. He didn't come out to make sure I was okay. Now these town gossips know my shame, and they're going to spread it all over town. I just hope they don't spread word that he rode out to our place to get measured for new garments. I hope they don't know he came again. Josephine's hand went to her mouth by its own volition. She hated showing weakness in front of these bloodhounds, but she was unable to stop the trajectory of her hand. She could tell by their smirks that they knew they'd hit their mark.

Making matters worse, Josephine mumbled at them, looking toward the ground. "I have to go now. I'd like to make it to Mrs. Patterson's before her husband comes home for his supper. I wouldn't want to disrupt their routine—or Mr. Patterson's busy day."

She scurried off without waiting for a response but could hear their mocking laughter following her for many steps. Panicked, her breathing became jagged. A flush of heat spread across her skin, burning her flesh, while ice coursed through her veins. Her pace increased. Her shoulders curled in on themselves, keeping her face cast downward. Too busy protecting herself and, once again, not watching where she was going, she ran into the subject of their conversation. Strong arms steadied her, startling her out of her frenzy. Her eyes darted up and met warm, brown eyes with golden specks. *They don't look like pitying eyes.* In a moment of weakness, she paused, but immediately dismissed that thought, replacing it with another. *Some people are just great actors.*

"Excuse me. I'm sorry." Josephine shrugged off Jimmy's hands, skirting around him. Her tone was both sad and bitter, leaving him stunned in her wake. He turned around to watch her retreat as if she were fleeing from a stranger.

* * *

JIMMY GAVE his head a good shake and blinked his eyes as he watched Josie practically run away from him as if her hair were on fire. She didn't look well, either. He moved to go after her, but he felt a hand on his arm. Gritting his teeth, he looked down at the hand then back at the owner of it. Nora. He should've known. Just as he was about to say something, Lillian sidled up to his other side.

These women just don't quit. He stared forward for a moment to gather his patience, which seemed to flee in their presence much like Josie had just left him.

"Mr. Stapleton—Jimmy. How are you?"

"Why, we were just speaking of you, weren't we, Nora?"

Collectively, they bobbed their heads, smiling brightly at him.

"Is that right?" Jimmy's jaw flexed as he created more distance between them and him.

"Oh, but only good things!" Nora spoke and Lillian, bubble head that she was, tittered. A woman passing by gave an annoyed glance at the group for blocking the main thoroughfare.

"Care to join us for a stroll?" Lillian batted her lashes at him.

"I was on an errand—"

Nora waved her closed fan at him. "We know you have some time to spare for your neighbors, being a good Christian and all."

"Where did you—"

"Don't you remember? You were telling us all about it at the mercantile." She half-smiled. "When you chose JoJo over the superior Frannie."

Jimmy saw red. He was pretty sure steam was coming out of his ears, too. They were mocking Josie, that's why she had been in such a hurry to get away.

His voice went low, words slow. "Just what were you saying to Josie back there?"

Nora's eyes widened in surprise. "Josie, is it?" Her voice was full of vinegar. "Now why would you think we were talking to her?"

"Who else would you be talking to about me?" Jimmy's tone remained the same.

"Well, I suppose you're right. It would be very improper of us to discuss you with others you may not have met. JoJo, however ..." Nora snapped her fan open in anger and impatience. "Well, we know you made a special visit to her home —alone."

Lillian nodded emphatically.

Jimmy's nostrils flared. If Nora was part of the gang, he would've roared at her. Instead, he looked around before leaning into her space. "I think you're behaving poorly for a woman who believes she's so finely bred." His look added injury to his insult.

The women's collective intake of breath caused a couple across the way to snap their heads in their direction. The woman clutched her husband's arm tighter, tossing her nose in the air as they walked away.

"I'm sure you aren't making up stories to stir up trouble, are you?" Jimmy said, shaking his head no, speaking very slowly and softly, prompting her to choose her words wisely —much like a mother would speak to a wayward child. His eyebrow raised the tiniest bit. "You aren't like that. Not at all. Or at least you don't want people to think that of you."

He desperately wanted to run after Josie, but that would just add fuel to the fire with these two. It would also look suspicious, and he hated inflicting any further distress on her. The extent of Josie's constant worry over people seeing or just knowing about them being together made more sense after this encounter with the Reinhardt women. The way Jimmy saw it, the issue was more about their brand of shaming and bullying than lack of propriety. This moment was making that crystal clear. Jimmy's cheek flexed while his neck muscles visibly strained.

Exercising some common sense, the Reinhardt women released Jimmy, taking a step away, while shaking their heads "no" in response. He snorted at their temporarily cowed state.

"Seems like you need some strong lessons on being a good Christian along with some etiquette."

He really meant it. Something needed to be done about these women. They needed a setting down.

Nora snapped out of her momentary fear long enough to throw another innuendo at him, "Well, I can think of a few strong things I might need lessons on."

Lillian gasped at her aunt's audacity but didn't look too terribly disturbed by it.

Jimmy straightened while moving away from them. Their very presence disgusted him, and he was angry and had to be careful for Josie's sake. In fact, he needed to walk away before he said something he'd regret. He didn't want to give them any more fodder to throw at Josie.

Pivoting on the ball of his foot, he went back the direction he had come, albeit much faster. He didn't bother with niceties, just marched away.

Nora and Lillian held on to each other's arms and watched Jimmy's broad backside.

"For someone who proclaims to be so charitable and Christian, he sure isn't behaving in a gentlemanly manner, is he?"

"I don't know, Nora. You sure say some racy things. I don't know what he's supposed to say in response. You've even got me thinking."

Neither of them took their eyes off Jimmy. Those eyes were filled with both awe and lust—with a splash of malice. Nora was now positive there was some sort of spark between Jimmy and Josephine, and she was quite sure she was going to do whatever she could to stamp that spark out with her tiny boot heel.

CHAPTER 18

*J*osie's functional and unfashionable boots pounded the dirt, taking her farther and farther away from those detestable women. *Nothing but wolves dressed in finery!* But no matter how fast Josie walked, she could not escape the ache in her heart or the shame that burdened her. Shame followed her like a shadow, forever dogging her. People felt sorry for her, and that was all. She was unfashionable, ugly, and something to be pitied. She thought that she might've escaped that with Jimmy, but it looked like she deceived herself once again.

Finally able to get enough physical distance from people walking and riding down Main Street, Josie slowed her pace as well as her breathing. It wouldn't do to show up at Mrs. Patterson's in a lather. That wouldn't be proper. Josie could hear her mother chiding her, plus she needed Mrs. Patterson's support, not only for the extra income but for backing with the other matrons. Mrs. Patterson's influence was important, as evidenced by Mrs. Cooper's earlier coercion, but so was Josephine's comportment.

Unfortunately, she was struggling to calm her heartbeat.

One would think her heart wouldn't beat at all after the splintering it had taken back there. On top of everything, Frank's repeated hints that she move in with them, as well as the house being too much for her and Beth, had turned into aggressive suggestions and near accusations. He was up to something, but Josie wasn't sure what, so she kept it a secret. It didn't matter, because she couldn't leave Beth, and she didn't want to sell their family home. She would just have to work harder to make sure they could keep living the way they were.

Her pace was still a little quick for propriety, but she was headed in the right direction. She could see the Pattersons' home coming into view. *Calm your heart—this is not the time for sentimentality nor unseemly behavior.*

Brushing the corner of her eye, Josie's finger came away wet. She didn't realize her eyes had been welling up as she drew in a stuttered breath. Apparently, the Reinhardt women had hit their mark hard once again. She was usually free of their vitriol, but Jimmy seemed to be a big attraction for them. She couldn't blame them, not really. *Handsome devil.* She chuckled to herself, thoughts of Jimmy briefly pulling her out of her mood. *He really is.* In her mind, she pictured his shy, boyish smile, causing her to smile briefly.

Her bearings slowly returned to her, and she found herself in front of the Pattersons' home before realizing it. The house seemed quiet, and in response, Josephine let out a sigh, easing some of her tension. No obvious signs of Mr. Patterson. She brushed wisps of hair from her face before gently rapping on the door. It didn't take long for Mrs. Patterson to swing it open.

"Oh, JoJo. Come on in." Mrs. Patterson's face brightened with a youthful smile as she stepped aside, inviting Josephine to enter their beautiful home. Josephine darted a look into the foyer and at the brass hooks above the ornate bench in the entryway before fully entering. There were no hats on the hooks, adding to Josephine's relief.

Most of the families had plainer, practical furniture. The Pattersons had polished and ornate furniture, such as oriental rugs—items shipped after Mr. Patterson was settled and some when Mrs. Patterson came out to join him. It was a luxury most folks couldn't afford. Mr. Patterson, along with the Reinhardts and Snyders, were part of the original towns-people. Mrs. Patterson was the exception. She came out later to marry Mr. Patterson. However, they all came from East Coast money, seeking opportunities to make even more money out West. Miners, ranchers, and soldiers needed goods and services. These were things those with money could provide.

Clasping her hands in front of her ample bosom, Mrs. Patterson exclaimed, "I'm very excited about this dress. The material is so beautiful—I can't wait to wear it!" While generally reserved and refined, she clapped her hands in delight like a child, and not a respectable middle-aged woman, over the package JoJo had in her hands.

Josephine stretched her arms out, extending the package like an offering.

Mrs. Patterson batted a hand at her. "Oh, no, dear. You go on and open it. I want to see you reveal it in all its glory. The light in here will capture the silken threads beautifully. I'll be able to see it better when you hold it up."

Josephine nodded, pulling the string loose on the wrapper. She thought Mrs. Patterson was being somewhat dramatic about the whole thing but supposed the woman was missing society with all the luxury and excitement she was used to having back home. Their town was downright puritanical compared to their two neighboring towns, thanks to JoJo's mother's reign. The other towns had established mines that meant more single men and the saloons and gambling to go along with them. Linden was all about morals and propriety, even though most townsfolk didn't behave the way her mother thought to be "proper." *Interesting, that. Mother was one way at home and another in public. Not sure who was behaving more "improperly."*

Banishing those thoughts, Josephine removed a medium-weight silk dress that whispered as she pulled it out of the wrapper. The dress was as dramatic as Mrs. Patterson. It whooshed and swished when JoJo allowed the extra fabric to unfurl and fall away from its folds. The women stared at the beautiful cerulean blue shot through with silver threads. The gorgeous material was meant to highlight Mrs. Patterson's delicate features and creamy skin and be unlike anything the other women would be wearing. JoJo didn't know how Mrs. Patterson managed to get Harold to order something so fine. She must've paid in full in advance. Judging by the way Mrs. Patterson's face lit up, whatever it had cost was well worth it.

"JoJo …" Mrs. Patterson's whisper held a tinge of awe in it. "You've outdone yourself this time." Reaching out, she placed a reverent hand on the skirt, her fingers running along the silver threads, admiring the feel of the fabric. "You've captured the movement of the fabric so beautifully." Pulling the skirt out so it flared, Mrs. Patterson inhaled slowly and released her breath with a whispered "Oooh." Looking back up at Josie, she added, "I didn't think I could love the fabric any more than I already did." She shook her head. "But here I am loving it even more. Oh, thank you!"

Mrs. Patterson released the skirt and enveloped JoJo in a motherly hug full of warmth and appreciation. JoJo was afraid the woman wasn't going to let go of her, but she was blessedly released when they heard the front door click open. Footsteps followed.

Mrs. Patterson whirled around just as JoJo turned, and they found Mr. Patterson standing in the doorway with the odd look on his face JoJo had expected and feared. "Arthur! Look at the beautiful dress JoJo has created for me. It's just like the pictures I was showing her. And the fabric!"

Mrs. Patterson went on for another minute, unaware that her husband wasn't paying much attention to her. His focus was on Josephine who remained motionless, apprehension enveloping her. Mr. Patterson always had a strange look on his face when they met, and she wasn't sure what it meant or what he was thinking. She never felt comfortable around him. Not because he wasn't polite to her. He was. He was always very proper with her, too. It was more of a feeling than anything else. Like he knew something he wasn't telling her, which spelled trouble in her mind.

Mr. Patterson finally looked at his wife, giving her an indulgent smile that warmed and softened his face. "Why, dear, she did do a beautiful job with your lovely fabric. I'll be proud to have you on my arm when we attend the dance next week." He came closer and patted her on the arm. "I'm in a bit of a hurry today. Do you mind having Mary get started on dinner? I'll see JoJo out for you if you'd like to say your goodbyes now."

Mrs. Patterson clasped JoJo's hands with her own. "Thank you, again, for all your lovely work. I cannot wait to show it off to all the ladies. Goodbye, my dear."

With that, Mrs. Patterson trundled off to commence dinner service while Josephine stood there with Mr. Patterson, who was still watching her intently. Eventually, she gathered up the nerve to drape the dress over the arm of the sofa, folding the wrapping and the string neatly together. Finished, she cleared her throat.

"Well …" JoJo's throat felt dry. "I'll let you get to your dinner. I tried to make it earlier but was waylaid by—"

Mr. Patterson waved away her concerns. "It's no worry, Josephine. My Mabel has it in hand."

"Well, thank you. I'll—"

She was ready to sprint out the door, but Mr. Patterson cut off her words when he put his hand on her arm. He didn't say anything, but the longer his fingers lingered, the tighter they squeezed, and it was beginning to hurt. She tried to pull her arm away but couldn't and began to panic.

"Mr. Patterson." She pushed her hand against his, trying to get him to release her. "Mr. Patterson, that's hurting an awful lot."

He released her arm as if it burned him, clearly not realizing what he had done. Her words seemed to shake him out of his trance.

"Josephine, I'm so sorry. I—" He looked down at his suit jacket while giving it a couple of good tugs. "I'll see you to the door."

Josephine's nerves were on fire, and her stomach was churning. Everything in her body was telling her to run. She felt shaky and hoped it didn't show.

"Did my wife already pay you for your services?"

Josephine shook her head, hoping he wasn't the one who was going to pay her.

"I'll let her know to have the money ready for you the next time you're in town. I hope that will be satisfactory. I wasn't prepared to pay you today, I'm afraid."

Josephine nodded her head vigorously. She tried not to eye the door too wildly. *Just a few more steps. A few more steps.* Arthur placed his hand on the small of her back, leaning into her space while reaching for the latch. This time she knew it was obvious that she tensed up because Mr. Patterson immediately stepped away from her.

"Goodbye, Mr. Patterson. Have a nice dinner." Josephine dashed out the door and rushed up the street trying to shake the nerves that man called up in her. Once again, trying to outrun her fears.

Practically running twice in one day. Josephine could hear her mother's beleaguered voice in her head, berating her. *I wish you were more of a lady. You're always so unladylike.* The voice in her head punctuated the words with the huffing sound her mother always made after scolding JoJo. Josephine shook her head. *I can't wait for this day to be over.* Clutching her elbows to keep from visibly trembling, Josephine slowed her pace, walking back to the livery, anxious to be with Daisy and away from town.

CHAPTER 19

Four weeks earlier …

Standing outside the barn, Lars's beefy shoulders tensed as he heard an unfamiliar set of hooves trotting up behind him. Dante's hackles were raised, and he growled low. He half stood and half crouched, watching the stranger ride up.

"Ho there!" a male voice shouted in greeting.

Lars dropped the mess of reins he was sorting and slowly turned around. He took off his hat and wiped his brow before angling it back on his head so he could better see the stranger. He was stiff from all the bending over and close work he'd been doing. He didn't feel like adding to his discomfort for some stranger who clearly didn't have business with the ranch.

Lars nodded, impatiently waiting for the man to come closer. His hand signal commanded Dante to quiet himself. The dog was a giant beast whose size alone was intimidating. The dog padded over to Lars and sat quietly at his side. Lars was by no means a small man, muscle heavy and tall, but Dante make him look much more average-sized than he was.

Dante's head easily reached Lars's waist—and that's while Dante was sitting.

When the rider saw the dog sit next to Lars, he pulled on his reins and glanced around before stopping short of them.

"Mighty big dog you have there."

Lars nodded, continuing to watch the rider. The rider cleared his throat.

"I was wondering if the foreman was around. I'm looking to see if yer needing some extra hands." Again, he waited for Lars to respond, but he didn't. "Do you know where I could find him?"

Lars moved his hat and scratched his head, all the while watching the man. He drew in a long breath before saying, "Why you asking?"

The man jerked back in surprise as he seemed to think the question was obvious, but he managed to spit out, "Just passing through on my way to California. Needing to earn some money before I can move along."

Lars's eyes hadn't left the unkempt man's face the entire time, and neither had Dante's. Double the eyes on the rider made him shift in his saddle and fiddle with the reins, as if he were reconsidering the entire quest.

"I'm the foreman here."

"Now we're talking." He rubbed his scraggly mustache. "I—"

"But we aren't hiring." Lars turned to go back to the reins he was sorting earlier, but the man's terse words stopped him short.

"Now listen here—"

Lars spun around, cutting the man off with a scowl. "You don't seem to be in the position to be making any demands. I'm busy here, and you need to go."

Dante let out a deep, supportive, startling "woof" that

made both the rider and the horse jump. But they didn't leave.

The rider contemplated his opposition, who looked irritated by the intrusion. The short, stocky man took advantage of his perch over the angry older man and his giant beast of a dog to glower back at them. Turning his mount around to return the way they had come, he shouted over his shoulder, "You'll be sorry you weren't more cooperative. I could've helped you out more than you know."

The rider left a perplexed and annoyed Lars standing in the dust he so rudely kicked up. Lars fanned his hand in front of his face to keep the dust from making him cough and watched to ensure the jackass continued to ride away. He wasn't in the mood to show him off the property physically. Satisfied that he was gone, Lars turned back to the task at hand.

Shaking his head, he patted Dante on the head. "Some people."

He knelt and scooped up the reins.

* * *

THREE MEN WERE HIDING on horseback in the tall trees and the scrub brush just outside the ranch's boundaries. The horses shifted, nickering when they heard a rider coming their way. A scruffy-looking man peered around the tree to see who it was.

"Neil's comin'." He spat on the ground. "That was a little too quick for my liking. I wonder if he got 'er done." Jack's scowl was a permanent fixture.

"Nah, I told you Lars is a tough old coot. He tends to dislike outsiders, especially any waddle." Tack shook his head as he watched Neil's approach. "Doesn't look good."

Neil rode up to them, slapping his hat on his thigh as he

stopped. "Damned old man is crazy. Barely gave me a chance to talk before he was sending me packin'.'"

Jack, Jones, and Tack just stared at him, waiting for more. When Neil didn't say anything, Tack spoke up.

"Did you ask for a job?"

"Of course, I did, you fool!"

"Well?" Tack tugged at his beard. He had been reticent about this venture in the first place. He agreed only because of his cousin, Jack. Jack possessed more temper than the average man and generally went for what he wanted—with force, if needed. Tack had worked the Double Star under Lars, so he knew the ins and outs of the operation. Jack insisted Tack "help" get him get closer to Lars. They needed insider information, and either Tack was going to provide it or get beaten in the process.

Sending Neil to look for a job was the easier way out. Tack knew this was a losing proposition for him no matter what. His cousin lacked common sense, and Lars would beat him senseless if he ever caught wind of what he was being asked to do.

"Said he wasn't hiring and told me to leave."

"Why didn't you teach him a lesson? That's why Draper sent you, you know." Jones looked confused. Neil was constantly bragging about how he'd teach everyone a lesson if they didn't do what he wanted.

"Wasn't that easy. He has a giant beast of a dog that's nearly as big as him that stayed by his side. Was growling and snarling at me the entire time. Lars barely made him stop."

"Stop what?" Jack's fists worked open then closed, warming up to strike.

"Snarling and growling, you idiot. That's what."

"So … you were scared away by a dog?" Jones looked befuddled. He tended to believe Neil's blustering, thinking

Neil was highly capable and not a windbag like some others called him.

"I kind of like not being someone's dinner. That dog was huge."

"Whatever you say, Neil. You were supposed to seal the deal or at least get in the door. Now what?" Jack shook out his hand, glaring at Neil.

"Look, I couldn't very well shoot the dog or the man—the odds were uneven this time. We're going to have to try something else. What else you got on Lars?"

Jones and Jack just looked at each other while Tack proceeded to give Neil the habits or quirks he knew about Lars.

CHAPTER 20

*P*resent day ...

Jimmy was still processing what had happened with Josie in town earlier in the day. He stood by the corral, alone, watching the fiery sun sink below the horizon, but not before it released a riot of colors. Despite the wind whipping around him, bending the trees and blowing dust, it was a time for remembrance as well as solitude. Nature was the solo church he attended every day and the only church he wanted to attend. His shoulders relaxed, and he breathed easier watching the beauty of the evening sky unfold as the pinks and purples slowly took over the fading brightness of the day's sky. Eventually the blazing reds and oranges of the sun drifted off to other parts of the world.

From a distance, he looked contemplative and peaceful, perhaps prayerful, but inside he was burning with the need to act. He was tired of waiting around for Travis and getting sidetracked by the townspeople. Besides, he had given up praying long ago—his childhood pastor as well as his father had cemented his disdain for most forms of authority.

From an early age, the emotional and physical scars of betrayal had been embedded in Jimmy's flesh, left there by those who were supposed to protect their flock, the so-called "authority." Because of it, he wasn't about to forgive hypocrites and bullies easily. Jimmy tensed as he thought about this afternoon. He was caught between the rock of Josie's propriety and the hard place of wanting to help and knowing it would only make things worse for her. He relived the horror on Josie's face followed by the Reinhardt women's malice while discussing her, drudging up another earlier memory of hypocrisy: those who claim to be good Christians.

One Sunday, he had watched the family's pastor push away a beggar on a busy Chicago street just before entering their church to preach Christian kindness. That day forever soured Jimmy. After the service, he had quietly asked the pastor why he hadn't extended Christian kindness to the "sad man." The pastor rained holy hell on him for questioning a man of God. Immediately after, his own father beat him for embarrassing the family and for being a "bad Christian." Jimmy was five. Thereafter, the only time he felt close to God was when man wasn't involved. Animals, yes. Nature, yes. People, no.

Lost in memories, the day darkened without him noticing. His eyes weren't focusing on anything, because the frustration and agitation in his heart were so loud. He wanted to act, and there wasn't any action he could immediately take, aside from forcing himself to head back to the house. But he remained in place. He huffed thinking about the gang and this town. The hypocrisy. The meek. *Here I am, again.* Dusk was generally a melancholy time of day for him. It was suppertime, and he had to leave peace and the animals to put up with some less-than-desirable men.

Worse was that another day had passed where he was free from well-meaning Charlie's coddling and still unable to do anything. It was the trap of impatiently waiting to bring the gang down and find some justice, yet unable to do anything because they're lying low and staying put. Heaving out a breath, he reconciled himself, knowing the sun would rise once again. When it did, he'd have another opportunity to find something, anything to help Travis topple the gang when he eventually returned. And the subsequent justice he needed and wanted would finally bring him peace.

Lying low in this town wasn't helping his information-collecting because there wasn't much activity to catalogue. Van Der Kamp had made a promise to Sheriff O'Donnell when they had left Weaver that they'd lie low. He also made it clear that when they arrived in Linden, that promise would extend to the entire gang. The townspeople, however, were keeping Jimmy busy enough. Shifting his boot on the railing in frustration, he thought about all the meddling townsfolk who needed to start cooperating and let him be. They kept interfering with what he had come to this town to do, the whole reason he had stayed with the gang instead of escaping with his brother, Charlie, and Annabelle, his love. Jimmy's mind drifted off thinking about them. He recalled Annabelle's pealing laughter and Charlie grinning at her antics. Both happy, despite the terrible circumstances that had brought them together. Jimmy shook his head.

I hope Charlie finally realized that he and Annabelle were meant to be together. I also hope they're married before this is over. They love and need each other. Jimmy shook his head again. *If I were Charlie, I wouldn't think twice about keeping all that close.* Of course, Charlie was all about responsibility and following rules, and Jimmy was plain tired of following. It hadn't seemed to get him anywhere anyway.

Letting out a big sigh, Jimmy gave one last hopeful look

into the darkening horizon. The clouds were still backlit despite the dark blues and grays replacing the fierier shades at the horizon point. Another day. His boot slid off the corral rail, hitting the hard ground. Turning on his heel, he headed back to the house toward whatever nonsense was waiting for him there.

CHAPTER 21

Chores completed, relief swept through Jimmy. Now, he could finally ride out to see Josie, using the clothes she was preparing for him as a cover for his return. Still plagued by yesterday's events, Jimmy was anxious to ride out and check on her. The Reinhardt women had been nasty to him, so he could only imagine how they had been with Josie. The Reinhardts' brand of nastiness he could manage. It was the shame, sadness, and hurt on Josie's face that troubled him more, and Jimmy didn't think these women were entirely finished with Josie, either, unfortunately for her.

Coal and Jimmy entered the quiet yard of Josie's house, Coal blowing hard from their run, and kicking up a general ruckus with his prancing and head tossing. Josie, however, didn't flinch, nor did she get up from her garden. She glanced over her shoulder at the pair then returned to pulling weeds. It wasn't her usual shyness, either. She looked resigned and distant. Behaving as if he took offense, Coal snorted and stomped his hooves even more. Jimmy pulled up the reins, forcing Coal to settle before dismounting.

Good thing I left Dusty at Old Man Johnson's. Those two would be a circus right now.

Quietly walking up to the garden, Jimmy tipped his hat. "Afternoon, Josie."

A pale and withdrawn woman looked up at him, not his sweet and vibrant Josie. Something else must've happened, more than just the horrible Reinhardt women. Not wanting to upset her, Jimmy stuck with his original plan and didn't comment on her appearance.

"Any chance my clothing is ready?"

Josie brushed off her hands then wiped them on her apron. She nodded to Jimmy, who extended his hand to help her up. Without a word, she walked off, leaving a stunned Jimmy rooted to his spot. He waited, immobile, until she returned, not wanting to spook her by following.

Her absence was brief. Elbows bent at her sides with her forearms extended, the neatly folded pants rested on the palms of her freshly washed hands. She refused to make eye contact. Arms extended as she looked down, she held the stack directly in front of him.

"Here you go. I hope you like them." When he didn't take them from her hands, she looked up, puzzled. "Oh. Perhaps you'd like to try them on first?"

Arms still extended, she indicated the house with a quick twist of her torso toward it. Her eyes watched him with wariness.

"You could use the parlor to change. I'll close the door for privacy."

Silent, Jimmy watched the varying expressions play across her face, sensing her nerves crackling like an unsure filly. Josie didn't move. When she finally blushed at his scrutiny, he said, "What put you in a mood today? Did Beth do something?"

Her sharp intake of air was obvious even if it was quiet.

"Wh—why no." Josie straightened her posture, even holding her neck rigidly. This time she didn't look away.

"Then what is it? You've barely been able to look at me. Did I do something? Have I somehow become offensive to you?"

He didn't address the Reinhardt issue; instead, he reacted to her moodiness with contrariness. Being with Josie twisted him up, making him forget himself. If things weren't right with Josie, Jimmy couldn't seem to remain calm or rational.

A red flush ran rampant across her face and neck. With small, rapid shakes of her head, words croaked out of her. "Of course not, Jimmy. You're very pleasant company …" The end of her sentence hung in the air.

Jimmy let out a belabored sigh. His hands went to his hips as he hung his head. How could she be so strong yet so fragile? His frustration with all the women got the better of him.

Getting a jump on any excuses Josie was cooking up, he blurted out, "You wonder why no one ever chooses you?" Josie's eyes went wide as her body stiffened. "It's because you choose everyone else over yourself. You never choose yourself, so why should anyone choose you?"

Before he finished speaking, Jimmy knew his choice of words was wrong as he watched Josie's eyes go wide with shock then well up with tears. Inwardly cursing, he desperately searched for a better way to explain himself, but Josie caught him off guard. Dropping the pants, she spun, fleeing as if her hair were on fire and the devil were chasing her. Grunting, he took off after her. Despite her speed, she was no match for Jimmy's long legs and agility. Soon, her skirts tangled with his legs as he wrapped one arm across her chest and the other around her waist, pulling her close. Chest heaving, her hands furiously tried to pry Jimmy's arms away from her. She finally resorted to raising her leg and throwing a backward kick that caught him in the shin.

"Ow! Knock it off, Josie. What the heck!"

"Why do you think you can come around here and boss me around, Jimmy? Why are you even here if you find me so unlikable?"

Unlikeable came out with a sob. Her shoulders began to shake, and reality slapped him across the face—he was the problem, not the others. He was too busy thinking about what Beth and the Reinhardts had done to her that it didn't occur to him that he could be the issue. He was only trying to help. *Unlikeable.* He didn't like that word one bit, especially if she believed that's how he saw her. His body sagged. He relaxed his hold on her, turning her around in his arms.

"Now, Josie—"

"Don't you 'now Josie' me! That's all everyone does around here. You all act as if I can't take care of myself." Catching a deep breath, she yelled, "Well, I have! I've done the best I could for a long time now, no thanks to you!"

Josie had worked herself into a frenzy of tears and labored breathing. She might've fallen to the ground if Jimmy didn't have a firm hold on her. But Jimmy wasn't noticing any of that. He was noticing how soft she felt in his arms. How his hardened heart beat furiously against her gentle curves. How her eyes were warm yet passionate, just like the words that had flown out of her mouth. Well, her words had roared like fire, but he didn't mind that.

She had life and spirit—a quiet kind of grit the other ladies didn't have. She was honest. An ever-burning heat was buried beneath that honesty, and he really, really wanted to kiss her. Badly. But he didn't think she'd appreciate it, given how quickly she had misinterpreted his botched words coupled with her mood. He brushed the back of his hand against her cheek, startling her out of her hysteria. Most of all, he didn't want her to hurt. He wanted to be the one who soothed and comforted her, made things better.

She looked up at him with her large, watery eyes and eventually blinked. Tears ran tracks down her face. Jimmy thumbed them away with his free hand before releasing his other to brush the rest away. Her upturned face was flushed, and her lips were parted. But instead of giving in to the urge to kiss her, he grasped the back of her head, gently cradling it as he guided it to rest on his chest. Wrapping his corded arms around her back, he pulled her even closer to him. And he let her cry it out. Great heaving sobs and rivers of tears soaked his shirt and heated his chest as his embrace was returned. His heart melted when she finally relaxed against him, sighing.

Barely audible, Jimmy whispered, "Ah, Josie. You're more than likable. Much more …" His throat tightened up, corking his unspoken thoughts. He stroked her hair.

They remained like that for quite a few moments. Josie had years of grief and sadness that needed letting loose. Her emotions were like a horse that had been stabled far too long, begging for a good run. He held her while she unleashed heaps of previously unexpressed emotions. He could feel his own sadness calling out to hers, his heart cracking just a little, but he didn't give his sadness any rein. He just held her closer, wanting to help ease her grief. This was about Josie. He was all in—in his heart, there was no halfway with her.

When her sobbing stopped and her sniffling slowed, Josie finally pulled away, swiping the backs of her hands across her face. She kept her face pointed toward the ground, unwilling to make eye contact. After a few moments, Jimmy finally spoke.

"Josie, I think I made a mess of what I was trying to tell you. I also think you misunderstood me." He figured she wouldn't speak, but he gave a brief pause just in case she wanted to. "You keep working so hard for others, and you don't do anything for yourself. People take advantage of that. Since you don't take the time to treat yourself well, others think they don't have to treat you well, either." He stared at the top of her head because she still hadn't looked up. His voice softened. "Josie, you've got to start choosing you."

Josie's head snapped up at that. "Why Jimmy? Why are you even telling me this?" Pulling in a long, stuttering breath and shaking her head, Josie cut him off before he could respond. "I didn't fully realize it until you saved me from Gus that day, that no one in my family—not even my parents—have ever chosen me. Ever. Why should I start choosing me now? Why?"

Jimmy sighed heavily. "Because, Josie, you're worth it. That's why. You are worth it. Forget all the others. They don't count. I'm sorry to speak ill of the dead, especially since they're your parents, but they didn't do anything to deserve you. Parents are supposed to love their children. How they treated you doesn't sound like love to me. It doesn't sound loving, either."

Josie chewed on the inside of her cheek. She didn't know how to respond to that. It was true. And it hurt. It was also something she had avoided thinking about. Deep down, she knew she was the less-favored daughter. Her parents had chosen Essie, Beth, and anyone else over her, including the boys who called her Joseph, taunting her boyish appearance. As if she had asked to be taunted. And if Josephine didn't see it in their actions, their words had certainly expressed their disdain.

They had frequently told her she needed to learn how to care for herself because she probably wouldn't marry. They hadn't invested any time or energy in helping her be more social or even caring about her unless it affected them. Rarely had she gotten to enjoy the big dance or church activities. She had been more of a servant than a participant or even a valued family member. Ignoring her exclusion, the mean and nasty barbs, and how she felt about any of it was how she had managed to keep moving.

Now Jimmy's words had made her feel exposed and vulnerable. How was she supposed to move forward feeling like that? No matter what, family was important to her. Family was supposed to shield, protect, and comfort. At least, that's what she did for hers, despite the way they treated her.

Even in light of all the painful, buried memories and feelings being dredged up, how Jimmy spoke to her touched Josie deeply yet differently. He spoke with such conviction and sincerity that she knew he had to have experienced something similarly hurtful. Jimmy was observant, but observation goes only so far. Besides, he didn't know her or her family. Not really. To speak so deeply on matters such as this had to have come from deep within.

This gentle giant was a paradox to her.

Jimmy could see her mind had gone somewhere else as he watched the myriad emotions play across her face. Wanting to bring her back and avoid going down the dark spiral of family himself, Jimmy playfully tapped Josie's nose with his forefinger, breaking the dark mood. A thoughtful look crossed Josie's face as she tilted her head at Jimmy. His action was out of place, given the heaviness of their conversation, and he wasn't sure what to make of her expression. Part apology and part embarrassment, he gave her a lopsided smile and a half shrug.

Attempting to redirect the conversation, he told her, "Josie, look—I'm surrounded by idiots. Some of them are outright curs. If I give up, well, they win. You can't have the Beths and the Reinhardts of the world winning, can you?"

Josie whispered, "Oh." She hadn't thought of it that way. All she could think of was not wanting to be on the outs with anyone. She was too busy being the "good girl" and trying to make peace to notice she wasn't necessarily the problem. In a roundabout way, she was "aiding and abetting," as the sheriff liked to say about some of the townsmen who didn't point out the disorderly when he asked. At least that's what he used to say before the War of the States.

Josie let out a shaky sigh. She looked burdened, and that wasn't what Jimmy had been aiming at when he had started this whole conversation. He was sure the Reinhardts were weighing heavily on her, too. Jimmy pushed his hat back on his head, letting out a long sigh. They watched each other for a moment before he said, "I didn't say all this to bring you down, Josie. I told you I'd protect you, and here I am. Consider this emotional protection."

Curiosity got the better of her. "What do you mean, 'emotional protection'?"

"Just what I said. There are different kinds of protection, and sometimes it's your feelings that need protecting, and sometimes it's your back." He paused, letting that sink in. "I've had to learn the hard way that, sometimes, they're equally important."

* * *

IT WAS Josie's turn to watch Jimmy go somewhere else in his mind. She knew the feeling of getting lost in memories and emotions, so she waited patiently. For whatever reason, Jimmy provided a fresh outlook as well as a different kind of strength she seemed to lack. His presence eventually shifted her mood before she realized it. And, oddly enough, this stranger made her feel safe. She unwittingly relaxed around him, not realizing she had let down her guard. He didn't feel like a stranger—he felt comfortable, like home should feel. This realization sparked much-needed contentment as she watched him blink a couple of times before clearing his throat.

Josie looked thoughtful for a moment before turning toward the house again. A weight was lifted, replaced with curiosity and a sense of resolve. She looked over her shoulder, beckoning him to follow. And he did, like a docile lamb following its shepherdess. Walking past an indignant Coal, who stamped his hoof at them, they crossed the yard, silently stepping into the darkened house.

Happy they had come to some sort of agreement, Jimmy stood in the doorway, not knowing what to do with himself. This kind of domesticity was out of his realm, but he also had a curious longing for it. Jimmy watched Josie intently as she pulled two glasses off the shelf and set them on the table. Jimmy shifted in slight discomfort. Her movement was fluid and poetic. It created a burning in his heart over the odd intimacy of this scene—one he didn't belong in. She grabbed a pitcher from the counter and began pouring tea. Nodding to the chair, she took the one opposite. They faced each other for a few moments before Josie picked up her glass, putting it to her lips. Jimmy watched the movement of the glass as it reached her mouth, her lips tightening around it, before tearing his eyes away. Feeling feverish, he didn't look back until he heard a gentle thud as the glass settled on the table.

"I've been thinking." Josie inhaled deeply before continuing. "I require an explanation of this emotional protection and what you think I should do."

Jimmy was stunned. Prior to this, Josie had been resisting him at almost every step, and now she seemed almost cooperative. Just a scant bit ago, she was downright sullen and noncommunicative. He looked around the room as if he was going to find some answer—or whomever she was asking—before settling his eyes back on her.

"Yes, you," Josie said. "You seem to be the only other person here. Who'd you think I was talking to?"

"I'm not rightly sure." He shifted again. This time it was from the chair's inability to comfortably accommodate his large frame. "You haven't taken a likin' to any of the suggestions I've had for you, and you didn't particularly care for me escorting you home that first night, either. You were downright prickly about it." He held her eyes until she looked away. "I'm not asking that you obey or anything like that." He held up his hands when her eyes flared.

"Don't get your feathers in a ruffle, I'm just stating facts. I'm trying to help you. Like I said before, I'm not planning on staying in this town. I've got some business to take care of, then I'm riding out. I just don't want to see you fall prey to the others once I leave, that's all."

Josie huffed as she slid her glass in circles, avoiding eye contact. "So, I suppose I'm like one of Mrs. Clarksen's 'pet projects' to you?"

"Hell, no." His response was quick and fierce.

Her eyes widened in shock, making him wince before apologizing in a softer manner. "Uh … sorry. I mean no." Jimmy leaned forward in his chair. "You aren't some sort of project, Josie. Despite your resistance and crabbiness toward me, I actually like you." His ears turned red. "A lot." Pausing, his kind voice shifted to something much harsher and firmer. "However, I also finish what I start. If I can't be here to protect you all the time, the least I could do is teach you how to protect yourself." Punctuating his seriousness, he nodded.

Josie drew back at the vehemence of his words. Jimmy was intense when he wanted to be, and she was unaccustomed to it. People either ignored her or bossed her, so his explanations were altogether new, as was her own engagement. Despite silently worrying and wondering about everything, she hadn't started outwardly questioning people's motives until Frank refused to help her and Beth after being married to Essie almost a year. Unsurprisingly, Essie had done nothing in support. Growing up, Essie had been allowed to do what she wanted because she had been the valuable "beautiful" daughter and firstborn. Josie had never questioned Essie because while mostly sympathetic, she was primarily self-centered. Essie wasn't ever tasked to do anything but be pretty and polite, just the way their mom wanted.

Jimmy broke into her thoughts. "It's a matter of time before someone tries something again." He took a couple of big gulps of tea before continuing. After swiping the back of his hand across his mouth, he said, "Also, you're never going to be free if you keep doing others' bidding."

"I—"

"You do."

Josie crossed her arms over her chest, slumping a little in her chair. The house was still as they waited each other out. Jimmy finally broke the silence.

"Look, about those Reinhardt women—"

Josie paled, but before he could finish speaking, the back door flew open, banging against the wall, and Beth's harpy's shriek rang out. "What are you doing here?"

Jimmy looked at Josie because this was part and parcel of what he was getting at. Remaining seated, he waited for Josie to make the next move. She had jumped when the door banged, rotating her head between an irate Beth and a patient Jimmy. Her brow furrowed, and she bit the inside of her cheek.

"What's going on?" Beth demanded.

"Well ..." Josie started, but Beth's narrowed eyes stopped her. Inhaling deeply, Josie continued. "Jimmy was just here to get his pants, and I offered him some tea. It's a dusty ride."

Her voice was soft and small. Beth's appearance transformed a previously curious Josie into a shell of who she was moments earlier.

Beth nodded at Jimmy's empty glass. "I guess you were on your way, then."

Jimmy didn't move, waiting for Josie to take the lead. Instead, she followed Beth's directives. "Thanks for stopping by Jimmy. I'm afraid I left your pants outside." She cleared her throat, looking at his chest instead of his eyes. "I suppose you can collect them on your way to your mount."

Impassive, Jimmy looked between the sisters before walking to the hook by the still open door and grabbing his hat. "Josie. Beth." He nodded at the women. "Thank you for the tea and for the pants."

Instead of asking her how much he owed, he pulled money from his pocket and set it on the table before snugging his hat on. Whether or not they were aware, he knew that's how the men paid the soiled doves. He hated doing that to Josie, but he also wanted to make a point to both women. He paid his debts, and he meant what he said about emotional support. Thing was, Josie had to choose.

He walked out the door without looking back.

CHAPTER 22

Horses tended to and a good meal tucked into his belly, Jimmy strolled outside and looked around. Everyone was off doing their own thing for the day, making themselves scarce, so he decided he'd settle business with Josie. He didn't feel right leaving things the way they were, on either end—especially after making promises. He wasn't sure what was worse, his actions or her inactions. Ultimately, it didn't matter, because he felt bad about the way things were left and didn't sleep well because of it. Three sleepless nights was his limit, plus he was heartsore. That he was eventually leaving didn't matter because he was becoming attached, and he wanted to see Josie. He also needed to settle the Reinhardt issue.

Dusty and Coal were happy for the excursion, and Jimmy felt better that he was having another go at the whole emotional protection thing. It hadn't started off well. He wanted to talk to her about what had happened on the street but wasn't sure if he really wanted to talk about the nasty Reinhardt women. He knew they were a sore subject, and that Josie was easily embarrassed and ashamed of herself.

Her family must have treated her even more terribly than she had let on with the way she thought of herself. He couldn't think of a thing wrong with her, aside from her self-deprecation. And that was getting tiresome. It made him want to beat some sense into someone for making her feel so unworthy.

How he'd get Josie to understand, he wasn't sure. In general, the whole talking to people thing wasn't going well for him. It wasn't his preference, but Van Der Kamp was pushing him to come out of hiding and take charge. Besides, he and Travis had work to do anyway. Shrugging off his misgivings, he leaped into the saddle and rode toward one of the few places he didn't seem to mind—Josie's. Despite some awkward conversations with the woman, he really didn't mind talking to her, even when she was pushing him away. That alone was surprising to him. It wasn't the challenge of Josie, either. She had some sort of magnetic pull on him. He smiled at the thought of his little forest fairy.

Josie was out in the barn that afternoon mucking stalls and singing sweetly to Daisy. The mare was enjoying herself, her eyes heavy-lidded, head bobbing to the soft tune. The sun angling into the barn illuminated the wispy hair flying free from Josie's braid, forming a halo. Jimmy hated to interrupt. Not only did the moment feel private and the old mare look so peaceful, the combination of Josie's beauty and strength muddled Jimmy, keeping him from calling out. However, to avoid being awkward and inappropriate, he knew he had to call out. Fortunately for Jimmy, Dusty broke the spell. He ran into the barn, aiming for Josie. He kicked up dust and hay while skidding to a halt in front of her and nudged her with his big head as his backside wriggled around, tail wagging wildly.

Surprise and delight lit her up just as Dusty's exuberance knocked her off balance. Laughter and doggy grunts filled the barn as she showered Dusty with pets and scratches, Dusty returning her affection with slobbery kisses. They were so engaged that Josie was startled when she heard Jimmy.

"Hello, Josie."

Josie whirled around, one hand on Dusty, the other resting on her chest.

"Augh, Jimmy." She huffed out a breath. "Sorry, you startled me." Laughter trickled out of her, coupled with a sheepish look, like an embarrassed child getting caught for having fun.

"No, it's my fault. You looked so peaceful that I hated interrupting your old mare's nap there. Dusty beat me to the punch, it seems."

Her smile spread wide across her face like sunshine that began warming and brightening his heart in places that had been cold and dark for so long. It also made him temporarily forget the nature of today's visit. He returned her smile with a dimpled one of his own as he moved toward them. He reached over to scratch Daisy behind her ear, and the old mare groaned in appreciation.

He nodded at the horse. "She's a sweet girl."

"Yeah." It was a soft sound floating out of Josie. She looked fondly at the family horse. "She is. I'm glad we've been able to keep her."

Jimmy tilted his head in question.

"I had to sell my horse a while back. We couldn't afford to feed her anymore and needed the extra money." She mentioned this bit of information offhand, but by the widening of her eyes, it looked as if it had slipped out unintentionally. Clearing her throat, she quickly added, "Beth and I are adjusting since our parents died and Essie married."

Josie flushed, putting her eyes everywhere except on

Jimmy. He understood embarrassment more than most. Despite wondering, he didn't press.

"We don't have to talk about it." Shifting, he rubbed Daisy's flank. "Besides, there's nothing to be embarrassed about."

"Well, I really loved her and didn't want to part with her."

"I understand. Horses are special. And there are special horses, just like people."

His eyebrows shot up, and then he froze. Josie mirrored him. He had no idea where that last sentiment came from. In a rush to cover his tracks, he added, "Anyway, I came to check on you, maybe finish our conversation from the other day. Looks like you could use some help. Where's Beth?"

Josie waved a hand around her. "Who knows. It's easier just to do. Besides, I don't mind doing some chores with Daisy." She turned toward the horse and stroked her nose. "Daisy's a sweet girl, and she's keeping me company."

Jimmy found himself suddenly needing to do something with his hands and glanced around the barn. Anywhere but at Josie's hands and her soft caresses. Besides, he was always happy to help and was practical. A girl like Josie needed a man who had stability. *Might as well be of some use since I rode all the way out here. Josie needs someone to count on besides herself.* "How 'bout I pull down the hay from up there for you and move some feed? It's not quite winter, but I'm not sure how long I'll be around."

While the gesture was sweet, the thought of him leaving was laced with bittersweetness, bringing down the mood. It was obvious when Josie's eyes lit up at the offer of help then dimmed at the mention of him leaving. She was like a flame struggling to stay lit, nodding enthusiastically while avoiding his eyes. Jimmy felt the same sense of disappointment. Reflexively, he reached out, gently tipping her face upward so she would look at him.

"I'm so sorry. I'm just terrible with words. Better with action." He gave her a lopsided smile before climbing the ladder to the loft. Josie's hand rushed to her chest as if it could quiet her rapidly beating heart.

They tackled quite a few chores in companionable silence. It was as if their souls had known each other before and were happy to meet once again. Indeed, they were like an old married couple, although unlike any kind that either of them knew intimately. Both sets of their parents were so much different than this. What they were doing was nice, including the hard work. Neither of them needed words to feel companionable, and they were able to set aside their looming discussion and worries to work together.

A couple of hours later, Josie stretched her back, and Jimmy wiped the sweat from his brow.

"Oh, Jimmy. Thank you so much for all your help. It's quite a relief knowing these chores are taken care of. It lightened my load considerably. I appreciate it."

"It's no problem, Josie. Although that sister of yours—"

"Please. Let it be. I don't want to ruin my euphoria by talking about Beth and her so-called failings."

Jimmy chuckled in agreement. He hadn't come to her to talk about Beth, anyway.

"Care for something to drink and maybe some biscuits and honey?" Jimmy and Dusty perked up, making Josie laugh. "I have some left over from breakfast. Come on."

She walked out of the barn, throwing a bright smile over her shoulder, tilting her head toward the house. His simple gesture of kindness had turned her into sunshine incarnate, making him smile back just as brightly. Her food offering chipped away at his shell since his stomach was always in the mood for food. But to his heart, she unwittingly embodied one of those sirens beckoning sailors to their watery graves in the stories that had been read to him as a child.

Josie held a part of him that felt wild and dangerous—and especially fragile. Something she could easily smash against the rocky shoreline like the sirens did sailors. She uncovered the innermost and tenderest parts of him that he had hidden and avoided, thinking they be best left alone. He tucked away yet another image of what could be, the one of home and family. The one needling him where Josie was concerned. He sent what could be back to where it had lived most of his life, tucked away in his tender heart, safely focusing on the proffered food instead.

Once again, they settled at the kitchen table with a platter of biscuits, honey, and tea. Jimmy's sigh was contentment. To avoid gawking at Josie, he took in his surroundings. *It wasn't the place that made somewhere home; it was the people.* This was a startling realization for him. He had longed for "home" for so long, but his memory of the place where he lived and called "home" was hazy. The problematic edges of his childhood mingled with moments of joy, blurred by time. Home was more snippets of memories, the comfort he took in being with Charlie and the horses. Aside from those warm memories that kept him going was the cold comfort of knowing he'd eventually help bring down the gang. His parents didn't even figure into that equation—neither did their wealthy and privileged lifestyle that had rarely provided the comfort he had needed. He clenched his jaw. *I miss the stable master and the library. That's about it.*

"You doing all right? You look deep in thought."

"I was just thinking about home and what makes a place a home, oddly enough."

"Why is that odd?"

"Well, I can't really remember home, or at least my memories of it are hazy."

Josie put her hand on Jimmy's arm and rubbed it in a soothing gesture. He looked down at her hand then back at her face before placing his hand over hers. She startled when his calloused hand covered hers because she hadn't realized what she'd been doing. Giving her hand a squeeze, he gave her the brief version of his story. He didn't want to scare her away.

"My older brother, Charlie, and I were traveling with our parents to see a half-brother we'd never met. He's the son of our father's first wife. Something to do with some new business deal." He swallowed hard. "Our stagecoach was ambushed by Van Der Kamp's gang. Our parents and the driver were murdered."

Josie's face dropped, paling, both because of the nature of the crime and that she had heard rumors of the Van Der Kamp gang through sensationalized newspaper reports. Ironically, no one knew who Van Der Kamp really was or that he was actually in town. He was more of a sensationalized Robin Hood-type legend than reality.

"Charlie and I were spared, but we've lived a hard life since then."

"Oh, Jimmy!" Josie's voice was a shaky whisper.

Shuddering, she squeezed his arm but let him continue his story. Compassion and curiosity beat out her usual sensibility. Instead of hearing "hardened gang," she saw the lost little boy.

"I was put on horse duty because of my 'gentle' nature. They made us do a lot of chores and other manual labor." He was fiddling with her hand but stopped and looked up at her. "A short while back, they made Charlie rob a mercantile by threatening to kill me if he didn't follow through. He wound up kidnapping the sheriff's daughter trying to save people from a potential shootout." Josie's eyes widened. "Don't worry, he protected her and got her back to her daddy."

"Where's he now?"

"With Annabelle and her father, I'm sure."

"Why aren't you with them?"

Jimmy intertwined his fingers with Josie's, staring down at them for a long while. Finally, he whispered, "It's funny—they're not all bad. Van Der Kamp and Goat have been good to me. But I want justice for all the terrible things some of the men did to Charlie and me … For making Charlie a criminal that he isn't. For the deaths of our parents—and for the others who have been wronged by the gang." Inhaling deeply, Jimmy's breath stuttered on the exhale.

"Wrighty, Van Der Kamp's former right-hand man, beat me senseless when we tried to escape, made Charlie watch when he was begging to take the punishment for attempting it. He kept telling them it had been his idea, but they didn't care. Wrighty took sick pleasure in tormenting us. He tormented Charlie by beating and taunting me." The silence of Jimmy's pause was heavy. "There was nothing I could do … for so long."

Jimmy's voice grew softer and raspier. The sadness in his eyes and slumping shoulders made him look as if he was reliving the past as he spoke. Josie didn't want him dwelling there. She knew from experience that would do him no good. She smoothed her free hand across their clasped hands, leaning toward him, gently interrupting his thoughts.

"How long have you been captive?"

"About nine years, I suppose. I was eleven when they killed our parents. Scrawny and scared." He lifted his eyes to Josie's, and his pain pierced her.

"I held Charlie back. I was afraid and resistant; that's why we were caught. I refused to try again because I was so scared. I constantly felt bad because guilt was eating Charlie up when he couldn't help me—us."

He cleared his throat. Embarrassment for all the emotion was getting to him. Josie waited for him to finish because he looked like there was something else to be said.

"Sorry." He sat straighter, keeping his hand interlocked with Josie's. "My father constantly berated me for being too sensitive. I guess I am because the gang picked up where he left off. It's just that they used their fists as well and that tore Charlie up. My father used only the belt."

Josie had somehow scooted herself closer to Jimmy, angling her body toward him. Her stomach churned and her throat tightened. She was scared for Jimmy and heartbroken for the little boy who had been beaten and tormented, so very frightened, and frightening. Her skin was clammy from just hearing his story, and if he weren't holding her hand so tightly, she'd be shaking like a leaf. Josephine avoided conflict at all costs. That's why everyone walked all over her, and she gave in rather than standing up for herself. Given Jimmy's underlying righteousness, she could just feel where this was going.

Her voice croaked out the question she was afraid to ask but needed an answer to. "How're you going to get justice against an entire gang?" Her eyes widened, and her body went rigid like prey choosing between stillness and flight.

Leaning forward, Jimmy ran his free hand from Josie's shoulder to her elbow, in effect cradling her from elbow to clasped hands, reassuring her.

"Travis is an undercover marshal who helped Charlie and is returning to help me. Don't worry. It'll be all right. People tend to speak freely in front of me, so as soon as I can find enough evidence against them, I'll make things right and help Travis and the authorities."

Instead of allowing her to continue worrying for him, he diverted her attention. Releasing her, he took a biscuit off the platter. Grinning, he held it up before he popped the entire thing in his mouth. A look of pure delight came across his face.

Eschewing manners, he spoke around his chewing. "These are the best biscuits I've ever had. Thank you."

His compliment and complete enjoyment warmed her heart while fighting the icy fear trying to course through the rest of her. A violent shudder went down her spine.

Two men against an entire gang? He seems so convinced. She had no words but understood that Jimmy hid deep pain and sorrow from the world. It was brave and sad. In some ways, he was just as alone as she was.

This time it was Jimmy who interrupted Josie's thoughts. "I didn't share this to make you feel sorry for me." Josie shook her head. "I just want you to understand. I may not have a home anymore, but I have a mission. One I mean to see through."

Josie slowly nodded, eyes unblinking, expression neutral. She didn't know what all that entailed, exactly, but she assumed it wasn't good.

"I don't want any misunderstandings, but I'm also not good at explaining myself—I don't get much opportunity for that. But remember, as long as I'm here, I'll protect you. No matter what. I promise you, and I keep my promises."

Another chill passed through Josie. She shivered. This time, Jimmy ran both his hands up and down her arms as if to ward it off before releasing her. There was something about the word, promises, that sat sideways in her belly. It was overpowering. Shaking off that feeling, she smiled at Jimmy, and he returned it with a sweet dimpled smile of his own. Things seemed settled for him, but they were anything but with her. And this was entirely apart from the issue of the Reinhardt women and the emotional protection he had offered.

Despite her disquiet, their days together settled into an easy rhythm and familiarity. For the time being, that gave her peace of mind, and she was willing to settle for that.

CHAPTER 23

Isaac, the undertaker, prepared the body and laid Lars out in a coffin after Doc had completed his examination and had written his report. They had to wait to transport Lars to the churchyard until word got to Reverend Clarksen, as he was still in Adamsville. When the townsfolk heard where the pastor was, the news was usually met with an eyeroll or two, compressed lips, a heavy sigh, or an occasional grunt. Whether that was for the pastor himself and his alleged "work" or the way his wife carried on about his "work" over there was always the question. Both were suspect. Either way, Clarksen needed to hurry himself along because the warm weather lingered. The body wouldn't keep for much longer. It had already been underground once, and the early fall still burned with some summer heat.

Wiping his brow, Isaac stood up to find Douglas Elliot standing in the doorway watching him. He had an odd look on his face.

"Douglas. Come on in. No need to stand niceties on my account." Isaac waved his hand toward himself, motioning for Douglas Elliot to enter. "What are your plans for Lars?"

Douglas waited a moment, still staring at the open coffin before answering. "As soon as that philanderer rolls into town, I suspect we'll have a brief service and lay poor Lars to rest." He shook his head. "Deserved better than this. Cantankerous fool."

Isaac frowned. "Can't say I knew him real well. He didn't like people getting close to him. That massive wolfhound didn't allow people to get too close, neither. But I agree—no one deserves to be beaten and dumped like that. It's just not right." They were silent for a moment before Isaac added, "This town just isn't the same. Feels like it's falling apart at the seams." He let out a heavy sigh before looking at Douglas. "Okay if I close the lid on him?"

Douglas nodded before turning to walk away.

Isaac called to him before he reached the doorway, and Douglas twisted partially to look at him. "I wouldn't worry none. I think your new friends are hell-bent on finding out who did this. Why, I can't rightly say, but it sure seems that way."

Douglas's eyebrows crowded together, and his forehead wrinkled. The baffled look washed across his face before he turned and walked out the door. Instead of returning to the ranch, he decided to pay the sheriff a visit. Much to his surprise, Van Der Kamp was already there. He stopped, nodding at Van Der Kamp, then at the sheriff.

"Any word on the preacher?" Douglas could barely get the word to fall out of his mouth. That man was useless as far as anything to do with the good Lord. His mouth twisted bitterly.

The sheriff eyed him for a moment before answering. "Sent Harvey out to fetch him. He was more than happy to go. Probably won't see him back for a few days." Van Der Kamp quirked an eyebrow at the sheriff. "Cathouse. They have a right proper one out there."

When he didn't continue, Van Der Kamp asked, "Why isn't there one here?"

Both men looked at him as if he had grown a second head. Douglas responded.

"Guess you don't know much about this town, do you?" Van Der Kamp shook his head. "Well, the Snyders and the Reinhardts came here on the same wagon train. The people on that trip had disagreements on pretty much everything. The wagon master was incompetent anyway, so they made the right choice to lay roots right here. The Snyders had the most money and influence, so they were considered the founding family. The Reinhardts are also considered founders, but they didn't make as big of a deal out of it as the Snyders did."

"Why'd they stop here?"

"Well, there were arguments about inappropriate behavior. One family of females ended up not being an actual family, but a cat wagon."

"Couldn't they have seen that for themselves when they set out?"

"Probably, but these women remained hidden until after they were hundreds of miles into the trip. That's when all the trouble started."

Van Der Kamp remained expressionless waiting for Douglas to get on with his story.

"The women started soliciting. A lot of single men were heading out to seek their fortunes in California and any other place that looked good along the way. They were getting bored and antsy."

"Hmm."

"Yeah, well, Mrs. Snyder was a real stickler for the Lord, goodly behavior and all. She was also an insufferable snob when it came to social stations. She's the one who raised Cain, and a couple of the louder folks followed suit. Most of the others didn't like it but were willing to look the other way for the most part. I think it was less about her god and more that she just didn't want to be associated with those kinds of women."

"Most women don't. It's easy to pick up stink by association—intended or not."

"Agreed, but she was extra odious about the whole affair. It seems the wagon master was planning on setting up a whorehouse at the end of the line, and she was incensed with a kind of hell-fire fury of her own. From what I heard, she was extra awful to anyone sympathetic to these women who had no one to go to and no other way to make money. To say it caused problems was an understatement."

"So, the Snyders put a stop to it and jumped ship here?"

"Pretty much. If you ask me, I think they were 'bout ready to get kicked off the train anyway. This group in particular just wanted to start a new life somewhere else—there were a lot of immigrants, and they didn't want trouble. She was trouble."

"So, no devil's addition in this town, then?"

"Correct. It was a pretty regular town for a long time. We've always had a saloon and drifters, deserters, and solo travelers, but no trouble until recently. Isn't that right, Sheriff?" Douglas's tone went flinty as he turned to face the sheriff, who had been quiet the entire time.

"Come on, Elliot. Why are you busting my backside again?"

"You know full well why. But first, what's going on with that pathetic excuse of a preacher we have? Lars won't hold up much more. He should've been in the ground immediately after the autopsy."

"You know, tending the flock without a shepherd—"

"That's a load and you know it."

Douglas turned back to Van Der Kamp, pointing his

finger in the direction of Adamsville. "That's where the cathouse is, in case you're wondering. Where 'the flock without a shepherd' resides." His voice went sharp with the mention of the "flock."

He huffed in disgust before knocking his hat back and putting his hands on his hips. His nostrils flared, waiting for a response he knew wouldn't be coming.

"Settle yerself, Elliot. You're getting all riled up over nothing. That man's harmless." He leaned back in his chair, placing his hands over his belly. Douglas grunted at *harmless*.

"Don't you go getting all comfortable there, Colter. You have a job to do, Sheriff. You aren't retired yet." Douglas kicked the chair he was sitting on, moving it slightly.

"What the hell, Elliot? Remember, I'm the law."

"Then start acting like it."

Van Der Kamp hid a smirk behind his fist as he watched the two men battle. There was something else going on beneath the banter, something old and unresolved. He'd have to get Jimmy on that, too. Van Der Kamp straightened up in his chair, making ready to leave.

"Well, I think you men need to hash a few things out. I might as well hightail it back to Old Man Johnson's. When the preacher arrives, I'm sure Jimmy will want to attend the services."

He tipped his hat at the sheriff and nodded to Elliot before leaving the office. He took in a long breath as soon as he was outside then looked up and down the street to get the lay of the land. It felt good to be away from whatever was digging at those two. He mentally added another person for Jimmy to look after: Douglas Elliot.

* * *

"WHAT? NO." Jimmy shook his head at Van Der Kamp. He even went so far as to narrow his eyes at him. "Uh-uh."

"Now don't be like that, Jimmy, and remember that I'm not asking." Van Der Kamp's tone held some mild humor to it. Jimmy had never naysaid him before. This was an interesting turn of events.

"You know how I feel about preachers, sir. I don't like being around them. This one's especially oily. I know it without having laid eyes on him."

He nodded at Jimmy in understanding. "There's always a reason, Jimmy. I'm just asking you to find out what it is."

"Why me?"

"It's what you'll do with the information once you find it. You're the only one I trust to efficiently do what I've asked and keep it to yourself. I know I can count on you."

Jimmy swallowed past the lump in his throat. This was the second time this week he was forced between a rock and a hard place. First Josie, now Van Der Kamp. He really didn't like lying, especially to those who treated him well. Of course, "well" was a relative term with Van Der Kamp. He had never treated Jimmy poorly, but he wasn't exactly a free man, either. Interesting thing—Van Der Kamp wasn't for killing him and his brother Charlie, and he wasn't for kidnapping them, either. It was curious. Then, he let Travis and Charlie go after Annabelle without any questions asked. Van Der Kamp was certainly up to something, but what was anyone's guess. Everyone was a pawn in his game.

Van Der Kamp interrupted his thoughts. "Look here, Jimmy. You already broke the dam, so to speak, when you handed Gus and his cronies their backsides. Word spreads fast, and I'm not talking about the hens we run with, either. The town knows you helped Douglas Elliot as much as they know you've drawn a line with your own. And don't think they haven't been speculating about us. It's a matter of time before they really figure out that you're the one to bet on. It's not speculation. It's fact. You're the one to bet on." Van Der Kamp punctuated his words by tapping his finger on the table as he spoke. "I've already been betting on you."

Van Der Kamp flicked the ashes off his cigarillo before nodding his head. He watched Jimmy as he took another long drag, blowing the smoke up to the rafters. Jimmy's jaw was tight from indecision and clenching his teeth.

"I can hear the gears turning in your head. I know you want to stay behind the scenes, but I already made you my second-in-command, and there's no going back. That is"—he leaned forward, putting his elbow on his knee, using his smoking hand for emphasis—"unless you want to constantly be fighting for some basic peace and quiet. These aren't going to let you alone." He sniffed curtly. "Take charge and get what you want."

You have no idea. Jimmy shook his head. Van Der Kamp was canny, but he couldn't have figured out his plan with Travis. He barely had time to dig for evidence against the gang on top of the fact that they hadn't done anything since Charlie and Travis rode after Wrighty, and the gang left Weaver.

"Fine. I'll go to the funeral. I'm not making a bunch of small talk, and I can promise only to try to be nice to that false prophet of a preacher."

Van Der Kamp guffawed. "I knew you had it in you, Jimmy. I expect no less from you."

Jimmy heaved a sigh while dropping into the chair across from Van Der Kamp. "So, what's the plan?"

Van Der Kamp chuckled. This was a new side of Jimmy that he could get used to. He was in total support of these fresh behaviors. Change is good, and that's what he'd been aiming for, even with the gang. Even more so with his dear old friend, Mack Pennington.

CHAPTER 24

Watkins strolled into the sheriff's office with the calm of a man going to a friendly meal, his boots thumping on the hardwood floors. However, the hardness in his eyes told a different story. He stopped in front of the sheriff's desk as Colter looked up from his papers and narrowed his eyes. Putting his hands on his belt buckle, Watkins leaned back, his chest puffing out, as if he were readying to draw. Instead of drawing a gun, he drew in a long breath, releasing it as his shoulders relaxed. He stood there while their eyes remained locked, waiting for the other to speak first.

After a drawn-out stare down, the sheriff tilted his head to the side. "What can I do you for?"

"Good question, Sheriff. How's business?"

"What do you mean 'business'?" His eyes, remarkably, narrowed further.

"You know what I mean." Watkins kicked out the chair, seating himself in front of the sheriff's desk, making himself comfortable. "Business. The things you do around here day to day."

Sheriff Colter snorted at the man as if he had been in the sun too long. "What kind of question is that? You stupid or what?"

"Stupid enough to tell you I've been watching and am seeing some things that the townsfolk won't like." He waited for that bit to sink in as he cocked his head.

Colter waved his hand side to side between them as if clearing the air, dismissing the very idea, although a bead of sweat was beginning to form on his brow.

"Don't know what you're talking about. Do you have some sort of real business to tend to, or are you here just to make crazy pronouncements?"

"I see how you're going to be."

Watkins paused, allowing Colter to stew in his own juices. He knew the man knew—for a sheriff, he didn't have much of a poker face. It almost made him laugh, but he wasn't feeling too humored that he was forced into this confrontation. Timelines had changed.

"Well, in that case—" he started to get up, but Colter interrupted him.

"Wait. I'm still not sure what you're doing here and what you want. Especially since you're on the wrong side of the law and all." The bead of sweat was making its way down Colter's temple and lingering near his cheek. "Just cut to the chase, man, or I might have to arrest you."

That made Watkins laugh. Not a jolly or happy laugh but a bitter one. "That's the best you got, Sheriff? I haven't done anything you can get me on. Even if I did, I wouldn't let you lock me up."

Colter swallowed hard. He tempted fate and failed, again. "Just tell me what you're here for. I don't have time for this nonsense."

Watkins looked around the jail then back at Colter.

"Looks like you've got nothing but time, Sheriff. You're just biding it until you can retire."

Colter's eyes grew wide for a moment before he sat up straighter and became indignant. "Now you look here—"

Watkins took the wind out of his sails. "Who you getting money from? Where ya siphoning it from?"

Colter's indignation died in its tracks. Before Colter could counter, Watkins slowly rose from his chair.

"You don't have to tell me anything right now. But I know you're in cahoots with Draper, somehow. I also know that rancher won't take kindly to it when he finds out. What you're taking money for is what I aim to find out, unless you decide to come clean with me. Take some time to mull that one over. If you don't, I have some things to tell your townspeople that they really won't want to hear."

Watkins returned to the door with the same purposeful stroll as when he had come in. Turning around, he tipped his hat at the sheriff. "Don't you worry none. I have my eye on you, and I'll most certainly be back to continue this fine conversation." Nodding, he added, "Pleasure, Sheriff."

Out the door he went, into the blinding sunshine of the high noon, leaving a gaping sheriff scrambling to figure out what had happened.

* * *

THE MINUTE GEORGE WATKINS LEFT, the sheriff threw his coffee tin across the room. "Damnit!" Clenching his fists, he blew out a huff of air before releasing them. He continued to shake his head while staring blankly at the wall. Finally, he hung his head for a moment before getting up to fetch the tin. When he picked it up, he noticed the dent from throwing it so hard against the wall. "Grrrhah!" He slammed the tin on the desk.

Knowing it was a bad idea, he grabbed his hat and marched out of the jail and down the street to the saloon. He didn't really care if Watkins was watching because he knew he wouldn't be able to talk or shoot his way out of this bind. Watkins was right about Douglas Elliot. That man already had his hairy eye on him, and he couldn't afford a big screw-up like this. Especially so close to retirement.

Mrs. Clarksen's progression interrupted his march. It was too late to duck into the livery or cross over to the mercantile. He was in her sights and had the misfortune to lock eyes with her. Trying not to grimace, he kept walking toward her until they met. He tipped his hat at her. "Morning, Mrs. Clarksen." He didn't want to engage her, so he kept his words polite but somewhat clipped. That didn't deter her.

"Why, Sheriff! You must be so busy. It's already after noon." She flapped her hand at him. "Are you heading out for a bite or doing your rounds?"

Sighing inwardly, he felt bad. He wanted to get moving, but Mrs. Clarksen was genuinely interested and was probably a little lonely for male interaction. Her husband seemed to pay all the lady parishioners a lot of attention and his own wife very little. On top of that, he knew Draper was sending a willing Mr. Clarksen to Adamsville under the guise of "tending the flock without a shepherd" while in actuality using him as a messenger. It also gave him the perfect opportunity and cover to visit the whorehouse over there, "guiding" and "tending." He huffed to himself as he thought about the situation. *The only tending that hypocrite does is to his own needs and coffer. Here I am having my chops busted for a little watch money, and he's a philandering, bilking, and general pastoral sham.*

"Are you all right, Sheriff? You went a little red there. And silent."

Poor Mrs. Clarksen's brow was creased and her eyes

searching. Her hand was on his arm, and she was peering at him as if he were actually unwell. He shook off his irritation before he responded.

"Sorry, there, Lettie. I had some things on my mind. I wasn't meaning to be rude to you. Where are you heading?"

"I'm making courtesy calls. Mr. Clarksen was heading out to Adamsville, and I thought to make the parishioners' rounds on his behalf. Poor dear, he works so hard traveling between two towns and two flocks. I thought I'd try to lighten his load in whatever way I could."

Her smile was bright and shiny, like a woman who was pleased with what she was doing. Someone who had a purpose and didn't mind doing it. His stomach reacted by turning sour, and his face showed it. It went a shade paler and the corners of his mouth turned down making him look like he ate something bad.

"Sheriff, honestly, I think you should step into the shade and sit down a spell. I hate to admit it, but you really aren't looking too well. May I run into a shop and procure you a glass of water, perhaps?"

Damn you, Clarksen. You should be here with your wife. Not with a bunch of fawning whores. "Lettie," his voice gentled as he patted the hand resting on his arm, "you're a gem. I'm just gonna go down to Draper's and sit a spell there in the dark. I'm sure he'll give me something to whet my whistle." He grinned at her to take the bite out of rejecting her help. She thrived on helping, but it just bordered on nosiness that grated on his nerves.

"I'm not so sure that's—"

"It'll be okay. I appreciate your kindness, I really do. I know there are others who could benefit from your visits today, and I don't want to take you away from them." He smiled at her because it was at least partially true. Some townsfolks needed her sunshine and nonstop conversational skills to keep them company. He just wasn't one of them. "Go on. I'll be all right. Thank you, Lettie."

He watched her walk on and made shooing motions with his hands when she hesitated, turning back around to watch him. Eventually, she kept walking, and he headed over to the saloon. He needed a little more than something to whet his whistle, and the darkness wasn't going to solve his burgeoning problems.

CHAPTER 25

The lingering summer roasted their heads and shoulders while a gentle wind tried to mitigate the heat. A preacher stood, Bible in hand, at the top of a grave surrounded by a crowd of ranchers and a smattering of curious townspeople. Lars hadn't been a sociable man, and in his later years had kept primarily to himself. The town had slowly decayed as the elders of the founding families died—starting with the untimely death and suspected murder of Otto Reinhardt, Frederick Reinhardt's father. Everyone loved Otto. Afterward, suspicious characters had trickled into town—a shift Lars hadn't stood for.

Douglas Elliot was sure that some clash with an outsider had cost Lars his life. Elliot darted glances to his left then his right. The problem was he couldn't figure out who or why. Otto Reinhardt's murder remained unsolved, and Lars had barely ever left Double Star. Those nagging thoughts gave over to his curiosity at Jimmy's presence, but he figured it had a lot to do with his boss, Van Der Kamp. Elliot couldn't figure that one out either. He knew they were outlaws, but their behavior didn't match the others who had come to hide. Elliot made a sound from the back of his throat like a mirthless laugh, primarily because they weren't hiding very well. Rolling his shoulders, he let it go as Reverend Clarksen was clearing his throat.

"My fellow townspeople." Mr. Clarksen looked around at those gathered. "Let us bow our heads and pray."

Elliot's face hardened at the hypocrisy of some of these people. His head was bowed, but his eyes continued to search for suspicious behavior. The regular servants of good were present: Mrs. Clarksen; Edna, the baker's wife; Martha, the blacksmith's wife, as well as JoJo, who was always so kind-hearted to everyone, even when they weren't so kindhearted back.

Lars had kept a soft spot for the girl, too. He had seen how her hypocritical mother had treated her, her vain sisters following suit. Her father had been such a pushover that whatever Mrs. Snyder said went. He had rarely objected even at the expense of his own daughter. Lars, who had made a point not to comment on anything the townspeople did, had broken that rule because of the Snyders' behavior. That's how self-righteous and odious those people were.

When Elliot lifted his head to look around again, he met Jimmy's eyes, which were hardened and dark, something unreadable to even the most astute. Elliot figured Jimmy had his own demons he was waging war with, but when Jimmy nodded at him, he knew he was an ally. Jimmy imperceptibly tilted his head toward Elliot's blind spot, almost directly behind him. Blinking acknowledgement, he pretended to stretch his neck, rolling it, so he could see what Jimmy was indicating.

Standing apart from the rest of the crowd was Terrance Draper, surveying the crowd like a man surveying his people. His head wasn't bowed like everyone else's, nor did he try to look mournful or contrite. Not that Elliot expected him to.

As far as he knew, Draper had only known of Lars. They had had no reason to interact. The town had already been sliding sideways by the time he had arrived. He had just been the first nail in the proverbial coffin. Elliot shook his head. Mildly inappropriate comparison, but he knew Lars wouldn't mind him making it. He might've made it himself were he alive. Rueful, Elliot dropped his head so he was staring at the tips of his boots.

This shouldn't be his funeral.

* * *

Draper was a recent addition to the town. He had arrived a couple of years ago, shortly before Mr. and Mrs. Snyder caught the influenza and later died. For some reason, the timing stuck in Elliot's craw. Rolling his shoulders then bowing his head again, he tucked away Draper's smug image for a more private moment. Spoiling food would smell sooner than later, and he was prepared to wait that out. Draper was up to something, and it wasn't his saloon or the speculating he had initially come here for. Inhaling deeply, he caught Jimmy's eye again, giving him a curt nod. They'd be having a chat later.

As the mourners were leaving the graveside to go to the potluck, Essie and her husband, Frank, caught up to Josephine. Josephine was carrying a platter of fried chicken that still smelled fresh out of the frying pan. Frank lifted the napkin covering it, leaning in to have a better sniff.

"Sure smells good, JoJo. Can't wait to eat. I'm hungry."

"Frank, keep your hands to yourself. You can wait like all the others. Come on, JoJo, let's go put out our platters and help finish with the setup."

Essie turned, gracefully walking off toward the long tables that were arranged outside the church. Frank watched his wife's hips as they swayed, carrying her away from him, but when Josephine turned to follow her older sister, Frank's grasp on her upper arm prevented her. Fumbling with the platter to keep it from falling, she turned her head in confusion to look at him.

"Hold up, JoJo. We need to talk."

JoJo's face went expressionless, but she bobbed her head slowly in acknowledgement while remaining otherwise still. Frank's eyes had hardened, creating a churning pit of fear in her stomach. This either meant a lecture or a threat. She drew in a long, long breath as slowly as she could, holding it, as she waited to see which it'd be. These days, neither was good.

"Have you made any decisions, JoJo?"

She cocked her head, not understanding. She slowly motioned no, not taking her eyes off him. She didn't dare make a sudden movement.

"You can't keep goin' on like you are. You're working yourself to the bone, and Beth's no help. Besides, it doesn't look good having you scrabble around for work like a common laborer."

Her eyes narrowed a fraction as she started to speak, but he cut her off before she could get her words out.

"I can find you a good husband. You should be doing all that hard work for your own man, Josephine, not to keep that old house and your sister."

"I—"

"I know you love that house. Maybe I can find a man who'll want to move in there. It's a ways from town, but it's still a nice house. One you can fill with a lot of children."

JoJo looked aghast. What was unseemly was having this conversation out in the open for all to hear. At a funeral, no less. She could hear her mother's chiding tone about the inappropriateness of it all. True, Frank was kind of her guardian since he had married Essie and was the only male in their family. But he had taken all their money along with Essie and never did anything remotely guardian-like before all this marriage talk. It was ironic that he had started pushing hard right before Jimmy had arrived.

Frank was intently watching over JoJo's shoulder. Curious, she turned her head to see a man heading their direction. She couldn't quite make out who he was because his hat was low, covering his face, and he was coming around the opposite side of the church. When she turned back, Frank was watching her. Her lips compressed before she turned to walk off. Once again, he held her back.

"In fact," Frank continued in a tight tone, as if he hadn't been interrupted, "the perfect man for you is heading toward us right now." With the look of the cat who had eaten the canary, so full of himself, his voice had a sharp and false cheerfulness to it. "Isn't that fortuitous?"

JoJo, however, did not look pleased. She looked madder than a wet cat. Frank thought she was going to hiss at him, but instead, she lowered her voice so others wouldn't hear. Despite what her mother liked to say, she had manners. However, the harsh whispers would've raised eyebrows if anyone was close enough to hear them.

"There's nothing fortuitous about this at all—you planned this. Why are you so set on me marrying? And suddenly marrying? Beth is the one who should be next. She's the middle sister." Frank's features hardened. "Besides, if you remember correctly, I'm not one of the 'pretty Snyder sisters'—Essie and Beth are. No one's supposed to want me." Her last sentence had an uncharacteristic edge to it, throwing Frank off.

While he wasn't expecting such a fuss from the docile Snyder sister, he was quick with a comeback. "All the more reason to help you first." He stood straighter, pleased with his quick comeback. Lifting his hand in greeting, he called out to the mystery man. "Carter! Come meet my sister-in-law."

Under his breath, he spoke to Josephine with gritted teeth. "Don't you dare move away or think about objecting. I'm doing you a favor." To cement his point, he grasped Josephine's shoulder, giving it a squeeze. From afar it might've looked like a familiar gesture, but it was nothing of the sort. It was painful and controlling. It took effort for her not to wince.

Josephine didn't dare disobey Frank and his temper. Instead, she shifted the platter in her hands, plastering a smile on her face.

Carter strode up to them, picking up the pace as soon as he spotted Josephine's smile. A bright, responsive smile stretched across his pleasant features.

"Hey, now—that's looking a little heavy. Here, let me help." He reached out to take the platter of chicken from Josephine's hands just as Frank slapped him on the back.

"Good to see you. This here is Essie's youngest sister, JoJo."

"Nice to meet you, Miss JoJo." Tipping his hat with his free hand, he smiled brightly once again. His friendly demeanor caught Josephine off guard, as everyone in town had been surly and suspicious of late.

Frank nudged her with his elbow, causing her to stumble forward just a bit.

"Ah, I— Sorry, you've caught me off guard. It's a pleasure to meet you, Mister ..."

"Carter Bass. Please call me Carter."

"You'd best stay close to that platter—our JoJo is a mighty fine cook. I'd start with that dish if I were you." He nodded at the dish before looking toward the food table. "I see Essie has her things set out and is looking for me. I better head off before she thinks I've run off on her." He laughed before shaking Carter's hand. "Good to see you, Carter."

Frank put his face close to JoJo, his tone lowered in warning. "We'll talk some more on this."

The pair watched Frank lope off to Essie, her face brightening when she noticed him heading toward her.

Shrugging his shoulders, Carter asked, "Shall we?"

Josephine slowly nodded, unsure of what was going on. This wasn't proper being left alone with him even though they were with a crowd. She didn't know the man. Holding out his arm for her, she took it as they walked toward the tables, joining the others.

The rest of the mourners had begun to gather closer to the tables and weren't paying attention to this exchange. Murmuring voices and soft conversation floated in the air, becoming more distinct as they drew closer. But from afar, three sets of eyes were watching. Beth stood closer to the crowd, keeping an eye on JoJo while Jimmy and Douglas Elliot remained closer to the gravesite. However, it was Jimmy's pair of brown eyes with flecks of gold that were once again darkening; he couldn't take his eyes off Josephine or get them to stop seeing red.

CHAPTER 26

The following day, Jimmy stood with his arms across his chest, legs braced apart, watching men gather mounts so they could head out. The controlled chaos raised dust at the corral, but Jimmy stood stoic and still. Van Der Kamp had assigned a few of the men who knew how to keep their heads cool and remain unseen some scouting jobs around the neighboring towns, specifically Adamsville, as it was so lawless. No one would take notice of them, and they could find out what the Reverend Clarksen was doing. He had left almost immediately after the service to go back to his "other flock," to the sadness of his wife and the dismay of his own parishioners. Van Der Kamp didn't stand for injustice, and that held extra weight being in his old friend's home. Watching the goings-on in this town didn't sit well with him. It was ironic that his firm belief in being just and fair had led him to become an outlaw.

"And feel free to spend some quality time in the cathouse, as long as you can keep your ears open and your wits about you, that is." Comically, Van Der Kamp had rolled his eyes when he gave that command to Jaems and Buford. Although he did add with a measure of seriousness, "Keep your ears open for talk about ranching and mining. There's some connection with Clarksen that we're not seeing just yet."

Jaems and Buford saluted before setting their heels to their horse's flanks, kicking up dust with their departure. Given what Van Der Kamp had heard about the situation, he didn't believe a word that came out of the reverend's mouth, or anyone associated with him, although the jury was still out regarding Mrs. Clarksen. She was an anomaly.

Van Der Kamp stretched before walking toward Jimmy, who was in a low mood for someone who normally maintained a neutral expression. He stopped and looked at the riders still saddling up.

"What're you thinking?"

Jimmy continued to watch the field with a frown, looking like he had eaten something sour. "That was a sad funeral Lars was given." Van Der Kamp cocked his head and waited. "He's no reverend. He's just a Bible puncher."

Van Der Kamp's lip twitched. "Care to elaborate?"

"He wasn't spiritual or holy," Jimmy's words came out harsher. "Just spat out flat words from the Bible. I'm sure he doesn't live it."

Van Der Kamp made a noncommittal sound.

"Even his prayer was lamer than Old Man Johnson's horse," he spat out, disgust clear in his tone.

That made Van Der Kamp chuckle because Goat could probably outrun Old Man Johnson's ornery horse on a bad day. He shook his head. Jimmy's words put quite a picture in his mind that'd take a while to shake.

"Well, I suppose we'll find out just what he's up to then, won't we? Jaems is pretty darn good about getting news without looking like he's digging for it. Mmhm. What're your thoughts on Mrs. Clarksen?"

"I think she believes the lies he tells her." Jimmy blew out a long breath of frustration. "Or at least she chooses to believe, because the alternative is just too painful. If she believes, then maybe everyone else will, too. She's the town busybody. Either way, she can't afford not to. It'd look bad for her."

"You like her?"

Jimmy snorted, giving Van Der Kamp a scoffing look. "That's a stretch. I don't believe she's purposely mean, although that woman has a tongue on her that cuts like a surgeon."

"Mmmhmm. Heard that, too. She friends with anyone in particular?"

"Not really, but she's friendly with everyone. She really does like to help, even when it's unwanted."

The last of the riders were long gone by that point. Jimmy watched the horizon as if he were waiting for something or someone to show up. Curiosity and motivation for moving his plans forward got the better of Van Der Kamp. He wanted to know how things were going with Josephine. She was Jimmy's best chance for a better life. Van Der Kamp had heard word about her solid character and kindness through gossip and carefully placed questions, and knew she was a perfect partner for Jimmy.

"Tell me what you're thinking."

Jimmy flinched before turning to look at him.

"Don't look so surprised. Ever since we got here, you've worn your emotions like a bad poker player. Started with Dobbin and his stupid stunt."

Jimmy snorted. "You would've, too, if you'd seen sweet Winnie hobbling with her ears pinned back. He's lucky he still has his head on his shoulders—I wanted to knock it off. Return the favor for Winnie."

"I'm sure you'll still have a chance at that. He's up to something, and I intend to find out."

Jimmy nodded. "He's been a little twitchy, lately. Keeps looking over his shoulder."

They stood quietly for a few moments before Van Der Kamp finally asked what he wanted Jimmy to answer on his own. "How about that woman of yours?"

Jimmy raised his eyebrows at him. "Don't have a woman."

"You do. Josie. Isn't that what you're calling her now?" He gave a half smirk in a "gotcha" fashion.

"She's a complication I don't need right now."

"You need her all right. You just don't know it."

"I need a complication like I need a hole in the head."

"You need this girl and a boot to the backside."

"I'll take the boot."

"You'll take the girl and like it. You already like her. You just don't realize it right now."

Van Der Kamp looked squarely at Jimmy before nodding. "You get what you need and not what you think you want." Snorting, he added, "But I'd be happy to oblige if you're still wanting the boot." He gave a rare grin, taking the bite out the offer.

With that, Van Der Kamp limped away in no apparent hurry. "Trust me," he shot over his shoulder. He shook his head without looking back. He already knew Jimmy was giving him that same thin-lipped look his father had. If only Jimmy knew.

CHAPTER 27

With Mrs. Patterson's dress completed and delivered, it was time to find some more work after the next stop, delivering eggs to the inn. JoJo entered the front door, glancing around then looking up the stairs for any activity. Craning her neck and not seeing anyone, she headed toward the office but stopped when she overheard Bridget, the innkeeper's wife, talking to her husband. Bridget wasn't trying to keep her voice down. It was sharp, tinged with disapproval.

"But she relies on these extra little sales to support herself." There was a thumping noise, like a palm hitting the desk.

The innkeeper's low, indistinct rumble was all JoJo could hear. Even with straining, she couldn't make out any specific words. She felt guilty for her invasiveness and impropriety, but this was important, as she was pretty sure they were talking about her and the income she desperately needed.

"Are you sure?" Long pause.

They must be looking at each other. Josephine's entire body tensed, and her eyes squeezed tight. Internally, she begged,

Please, please, please. The handle on her basket threatened to break from her unconscious squeezing.

An exacerbated and scoffing sound whooshed out of Bridget. "I don't want to be the one to tell her. I don't know why you're putting up with that bully. With everything else happening—"

More low male sounds.

"No." Bridget's voice was clipped. "I'll tell her because I like her too much to have to face you. I, myself, barely want to face you right now." Strained silence. "Know that I understand why you're doing this. I just don't agree. I'm telling her as much."

Josephine's eyes flew open, and she hurried to move away from the hallway leading down to the office. She brushed off some dust from her skirt, pretending that she had just walked in. Feigning surprise, Josephine looked up from her concentrated efforts on her skirt.

"Oh, Bridget! Good morning."

Josephine smiled as brightly as she could, given what she had just overheard. Bridget was a less-successful actress. Her face was mottled and pinched. After a silent, curt nod, she swept her arm toward the kitchen.

That's when true panic began to set in. "Bridget, what's wrong? Are you okay?"

Honestly, Bridget did not look well. She looked both feverish and peptic, a terrible combination of upset and ill. Josephine thought speaking might choke her or cause her to expel.

"No, I'm not." She let out a sigh as she brushed an imaginary lock of hair from her face. "There's no beating around the bush with this one. I have some bad news for you that I really don't want to deliver."

Josephine's face and stomach dropped, especially since she knew what was coming.

"Conor just told me that we can no longer purchase your extra eggs."

"I—"

Bridget held up her hand. "I wanted no part in this, but apparently it has to do with some business arrangement that he already had with Terrance Draper. How this relates to you, I do not know. I do not care. But know I do not like it." Despite her steely tone, her lips quivered, and her eyes were watery.

She paused and said, "I'm so very proud of you holding up the household like you do. I realize that it's none of my business, but I think Frank and Essie have done you and Beth a disservice. I'd also add that it goes without saying that Beth is of no help whatsoever." Bridget harrumphed with a curt nod. She watched Josephine's crestfallen look closely.

Leaning forward, she placed a hand on Josephine's arm, whispering, "Have you tried the mercantile, yet? Perhaps Harold could sell some eggs and whatnot for you?"

Josephine nodded then glanced at the basket on her arm. Looking up at Bridget, she opened her mouth to speak, but no words came out.

Bridget shook her head sadly. "I'm afraid not. The deal starts now, or so I'm told."

Josephine nodded. Really, she understood Bridget's predicament. She was beholden to her husband's dictates, no matter how much work she managed and directed at their inn. What she didn't understand was Mr. Draper's interference or why.

Bridget interrupted Josephine's musings. "Wait a moment, please."

She stepped away from Josephine, who was still in shock, despite her eavesdropping. An icy sensation washed through Josephine along with a wave of overwhelm. Deep inside she was immobile, but her muscles were agitated—her body was at war, wanting to do two different things. Bridget returned with a package that she gently tucked into the basket of eggs, being careful not to break or disturb them.

Considerably calmed, Bridget's voice was softer and lower. "It's a little bit of cheese and ham. Conor won't miss it, and it'll feed you and Beth for a couple of meals. I'm afraid that's all I can do for you right now."

She leaned in, giving Josephine a quick hug before shooing her out the front door. She knew Conor would be listening to make sure she didn't give JoJo any false hope. She wouldn't do that to her, anyway. That girl had sustained herself on so much false hope that she could have built her own castle with it. Shaking her head, Bridget plodded back to the pantry to count the eggs they had left from JoJo's last delivery.

* * *

JOSEPHINE SHUFFLED MORE THAN WALKED. Moving away from people and situations was a habit, but this current setback warranted moving as far away as she could. She was confused and mortified. The sun felt extra bright to her, even though she was wearing her sturdier bonnet. She couldn't say what her plan was, but she knew she needed to get one together—and fast. She also needed to pass off the eggs in her basket to someone.

Since Bridget suggested she ask Harold, JoJo decided to pay him a visit. Again, habit. Rule follower. At any rate, she didn't have a better idea, which reinforced her resolve. Blowing out a breath, she straightened, picking up her feet and walking with a lot more confidence than she felt.

Melodic tinkling announced her arrival as she pushed the mercantile door open, making her very glad that the store was empty. Hopefully, she'd be able to sell the eggs to Harold and make some sort of standing arrangement, perhaps for store credit. Wringing the basket handle with both hands, JoJo relaxed when Harold came out from between the shelving, wiping his hands on a cloth. His kindness meant a lot to her.

"Good morning, JoJo! How're you?"

"I'm well, Harold. How're you?"

"Good, good. Looks like you have your hands full there." He nodded to the basket with Bridget's packet sticking out the top of it.

"Yes, I do. Say … I have some extra eggs. Are you in need of any?" She held up her basket. Her heart was thumping so hard she considered hiding it with the basket.

Harold looked thoughtful for a moment before nodding. "I do believe we could use some. How many do you have?"

As they discussed the particulars, the tension Josephine had carried from the inn to the mercantile rushed out of her, along with a lot of perspiration. She had felt feverish walking in, and now she was able to release a thankful breath. This was better than she had thought. She could do this.

"Thank you so much, Harold. I really appreciate your help. And thank you for sending Jimmy my way. I'm almost done with his clothing. The extra work helps so very much."

Harold's smile broadened. "Well, that Jimmy sure seems to be a nice fellow." He chuckled. "He stood up to those Reinhardt women. They were insisting he go see their friend, Frannie. He insisted right back at them that he was going to see you."

Josephine's face drained of all its color before flushing bright red. She swallowed hard when Harold assessed her expression.

"Something happened." Josephine shook her head vigorously, but Harold persisted with a firmer tone. "Yes. What happened?"

Josephine's eyes went round like saucers. Her day kept getting worse and worse, and just when she thought things were looking up.

"I'm trying to help, Josephine." Harold enunciated every syllable of her name.

Oh, oh. The full name.

She couldn't face him and tell the story, but she couldn't not tell him, either. He'd eventually find out, anyway. Shaking her head and looking down at the ground, she relayed the story in a small voice.

"I saw the Reinhardts." She sniffed, and Harold nodded encouragement despite her downcast look. "They said I was just a charity case …" Her voice dropped to a whisper. "They implied that something inappropriate was going on with him coming out to see me."

A concoction of guilt and embarrassment washed over her. She felt like her outsides were burning up, and her insides were icy. *While some of my thoughts about Jimmy may be inappropriate, our actions have been nothing but proper. Besides, he's just trying to help me. Do his good Christian deed.*

Harold's hand slapped the counter. Josephine startled, looking ready to jump out of her skin.

"Sorry m'dear. Those women make my blood boil. They were here when Jimmy arrived. Made him uncomfortable the minute they clapped eyes on him." He was shaking his head, talking less to Josephine and grumbling to himself. "Forward women." Snapping out of it, he realized Josephine was increasingly anxious. "Don't you worry yourself about this." He patted her hand. "I have a good feeling about Jimmy. He'll do you right. Don't you worry."

All Josephine was able to do was slowly nod her head yes, which was most interesting. She never had anyone she could unconditionally rely on, including herself. She tended to cave to others' needs first. But, for some reason, she did feel as if she could rely on Jimmy, and that realization made her feel a whole lot better. Lighter, even. All this despite the devilin' seed the Reinhardt women planted in her head.

"Thank you, Harold. And thank you for helping with the eggs. Please let me know if there's anything I can do to help you, too. I'll be back in a week to check in."

Harold nodded at her, watching her retreat from the store. The relief was short-lived, however. Frank was watching her leave as well and took that opportunity to make himself known.

* * *

FRANK MOVED AWAY from the shade of the bakery toward the mercantile. JoJo was looking a little lost, which made him feel better. He picked up the pace, but not too much, so he wouldn't look like he was chasing her down in broad daylight.

"Ah, JoJo!" Frank casually called out to her after looking around to see who was watching.

Tensing, Josephine looked back to see Frank coming from across the street. *From bad to worse,* her mind taunted as she watched Frank pick up his pace, closing the distance between the two of them.

"What're you doing out?"

"Well, I had some errands to take care of, Frank. Why are you asking?"

Taken aback by her tone, Frank's neck stiffened. "I'm concerned, that's why."

Josephine's eyes narrowed at him, as his "concern" was generally self-serving. Like abandoning Beth. "Concerned how?" She spoke sweetly, tilting her head while searching his face. Her examination belied her tone.

Frank balked at her scrutiny. She'd never been so sassy

before. He was unaccustomed to that and intended to put her in her place. He stood straighter, tugging on his shirtsleeves.

"JoJo, what sort of errands are you doing? You aren't trying to get work, are you?"

Josephine had had it with this day, and it wasn't even halfway over. "I'm not sure it's your concern. Excuse me. I have business to take care of."

Frank reached out, grabbing her elbow as he steered her toward the saloon. "Your business is my business. Didn't I make that clear at the funeral?"

Josephine tried tugging her arm. "Frank, you're hurting me. Let go."

"I'm not letting go until you listen to reason, JoJo. You need to start behaving. That starts with doing as I say."

Josephine's mouth opened partway before she snapped it shut, clenching her jaw. Drawing in a deep breath, she chased it with clearly enunciated words. "I am not your wife. You cannot boss me like this, Frank."

"I can and I will. You need to be taken in hand. It's about time you started paying attention to your behavior and settling down. You're acting like a beggar on the street or some drifter running around, looking to make a quick coin."

Josephine tried her best to slow their progress, digging her heels into the ground, but it served only to infuriate Frank even more. Instead of yelling, as he was wont to do, he stopped and gave her a good shake with the hand that was still digging into the space between the muscle and bone of her upper arm. He wanted her to feel the pressure as much as possible. Leaning down, he put his face directly in front of hers. His voice was sharp and loud despite lowering it.

"You will stop making a scene and calmly walk with me to the saloon. We have business to take care of."

Josephine had enough sense to cooperate with his demands, even if she was vehemently opposed to the saloon and its owner, Terrance Draper. For whatever reason, she feared Mr. Draper more than she feared Frank. She didn't think Frank would hurt her, because he'd hate to displease Essie. Despite Essie's lack of help or even communication, Josephine knew Essie didn't wish her or Beth harm. Mr. Draper was a different story. Him, Josephine wasn't so sure about. She also wasn't sure what the two of them had in the works, but she was certain they had something.

CHAPTER 28

Jimmy went to the saloon to make sure Gus and his bootlickers were behaving. Huffing, he pushed at the doors leading into it. Babysitting—he hated this part of his tasks. A few men were scattered around the saloon, sitting at various tables. Those who bothered to look up did so more because they were daring the sunlight to leave rather than having any interest in who had entered. Among those men happened to be Gus, Harry, and Cy. Jimmy's eyes searched for Ned while remaining still as a couple of the strangers sized him up. Ned was at the bar flirting with a drink gal. Jimmy narrowed his eyes at Ned, who did a double take. Jimmy jerked his head over to the table, clenching his jaw. Ned sighed and sauntered back to the table.

"Come on, Jimmy. I finally got Flora over there to talk to me, and you run me off her."

"You're not supposed to be here."

He looked directly at each of the four men. Harry was the only one who had the grace to look contrite before looking away.

Gus smirked and looked over at Cy, but Jimmy put a stop to that. "What part of lying low don't you understand?"

He bent his six-foot-four frame in half to bring himself into their collective space. Ironically, he sounded just like Van Der Kamp with his low tone and slow articulation. Icy and unhurried in his fury. Blank looks and silence were all they could deliver.

"Thought as much." He straightened. "Sometimes, I feel like you were served up short. At least use what God gave you."

The comment missed the immediate mark, as they were slow to get Jimmy's gist. As he watched realization slowly dawn on their faces, one by one, he leaned his torso back so he could look down at them more effectively.

"If you make this a regular habit, our fists will be having an intimate conversation. Go home." When they didn't immediately move, he barked out, "Now!"

Between Jimmy's tone and the harsh scraping of chair legs against the floor, the men gawked in their direction, especially at the bossy giant. Just as quickly as they turned to look, they turned back to what they were doing. For most of them, it wasn't much.

Hating to be ordered around or one-upped, Gus made sure he got in a parting remark. "You think you're smarter than the rest of us. That's why you're acting all bossy."

"No. I just think all of you are stupider than you realize."

A stranger behind Jimmy guffawed. Gus scowled at him, then Jimmy, before turning on his heel to leave.

Jimmy watched them walk out. He started to follow but stopped when he felt a hand on his arm. The cloying perfume assaulted him before he felt the hand, but he chose to ignore it.

"Mister," the sultry voice purred. "You sure can stay. I'd rather be talking to you, anyway."

Jimmy had to force himself not to roll his eyes. *This town!* He pried the small hand from his forearm and released it.

"Can't. Your time's better spent with one of the other men, but thanks."

He nodded politely to her before heading back out into the sunshine where he liked to be.

Squinting at the sun, Jimmy stopped outside the saloon door, giving his eyes a moment to adjust. He hadn't been inside for long, but he also wasn't accustomed to the relative dark during daylight hours. As he looked down to avoid the searing sun, Jimmy felt the hairs on his neck raise. Slowly lifting his head, he angled it to look over his left shoulder.

A group of men were milling around, but only one was looking directly at him. Jimmy narrowed his eyes at him, and their eyes met. The older man looked to be sauced, with bloodshot eyes and a bulbous red nose. Deeming him unthreatening, Jimmy nodded, walking away. However, the man sounded sober when he called out to Jimmy, bringing him to a halt.

"Be sure to tell old Van Der Kamp that George sends his regards."

Jimmy paused before casually looking over his shoulder again.

"And who might that be?"

George pointed his index finger at his chest twice. It was a deliberate, measured movement of his arm jabbing at his own chest without releasing eye contact.

Fully turning around, Jimmy put his hands on his hips. "George …" Jimmy left the question hanging in the air.

"He knows. But just so's you know, it's George Watkins."

Jimmy nodded and turned to leave. He'd had enough nonsense for the day.

George called after him in a sing-song tone, "Don't you forget, now!"

Jimmy raised his arm in the air, flicking his wrist so his flat hand gave a curt wave. Adrenaline became his friend again, coursing through his veins, belying his externally dismissive attitude.

Now, I finally have something to work with.

* * *

IRRITATED THAT HE might have a situation on his hands if Gus, Ned, Harry, and Cy didn't move out quickly enough, Jimmy picked up his own pace without looking like he was rushing. Despite his plans with Travis, Jimmy's reflexive defense of Van Der Kamp and his loyalty to the man wasn't surprising. Jimmy defended Van Der Kamp because Van Der Kamp kept Jimmy sheltered from the hard-core gang activity, aside from the most recent developments. He also showed more concern for Jimmy and Charlie than their own father had done. Besides, Jimmy wasn't about to back down from a challenge thrown Van Der Kamp's way, despite his conflicting and complicated entanglement with the gang. It didn't matter that he had initially been held against his will. Jimmy still had loyalty as well as no place to go. He shook his head—loyalty until he could figure out how to get justice for those wronged by the gang.

Rounding the corner to the shaded hitching post, an unusual movement out of the corner of his eye forced Jimmy to retrace his steps. At the other end of the street, he could see Josie being manhandled by someone a few years older than her. He was dressed nicely, and they seemed familiar with each other, but the whole situation wasn't sitting well with him. They were too far away for him to hear their conversation, so changing tack, he headed in her direction.

They were keeping their voices respectably lowered, but as Jimmy drew closer, he could hear snippets of their conversation drifting in the wind. "Taken in hand" was the bit that struck him hard, moving him immediately into their space.

"Josie!" His voice echoed loud enough that passersby looked in their direction.

Josephine startled, looking away from Frank's snarling face. "Jimmy!"

Her face lit up, but her voice pitched too high. Jimmy's heart clenched. He looked down at Frank's hand then back up to his face. His eyes went dark as his hand shot out swiftly for a handshake—so quickly that Frank flinched, lurching partially forward to protect his gut.

"Jimmy Stapleton."

Frank eyed him for a moment before reaching out to clasp Jimmy's hand. "Frank Odin. JoJo's guardian." He shot a look at Josephine, daring her to naysay him.

She briefly paused, lips compressed, before turning an open palm in Frank's direction. "Frank is married to my older sister, Essie. He's my brother-in-law." *In-law*, harshly intonated.

Frank's eyes briefly narrowed at JoJo, but he addressed Jimmy with an overtly friendly tone. "Which also makes me the head of the family, as their parents are deceased."

Despite the lighter tone he tried to strike, the tightness around his mouth gave away his annoyance. His eyes remained sharp, piercing Jimmy with their intensity. Jimmy acknowledged Frank's words with a slight nod but gave his full attention to Josie.

"I was wondering if you could add another shirt to my order. I could go pick up more material from Harold. I may need something lighter weight than what I have." He looked skyward. "Seems to be getting mighty hot out these past couple of days."

Josie barely suppressed a smile at Jimmy's stalling. Besides, fall was in the air, not a heat wave. Unfortunately, the Reinhardt women's words flooded her mind with negativity. *He probably doesn't even want it and is messing with Frank with this weather nonsense.* Regardless, she chose to play along with Jimmy since it was irritating Frank who was irritating her. She also grasped at the reblooming hope that had returned after listening to Harold, despite her fears of being a charity project.

"Yes, I'll do that for you. I finished Mrs. Patterson's dress, and I'm almost done with your shirt—"

"What?" Frank interrupted, his eyes flaring at Josephine.

"I'm working on some clothes for Jimmy. Harold didn't have anything that fit him, so he sent him my way. I—"

"I need to talk to Harold. He was out of line. I told you, no working. You're getting married, remember?"

"No, Frank. I'm not."

"We're not having this discussion out in public." He paused, giving Jimmy the stink eye before glaring at JoJo. "Or in front of strangers."

Jimmy subtly straightened to his full height as a reminder of who had the upper hand if push were to come to shove. Frank didn't flinch this time. He, too, stood straighter, stepping toe-to-toe with Jimmy. "Nice making your acquaintance; however, we need to be leaving."

Jimmy looked over at Josie who was pale and a little unsteady on her feet.

"Josie?"

"It's all right, Jimmy. Frank wants to show me something. I'll have the remainder of your clothes finished in four or five days."

Frank all but dragged her down the road. Jimmy suppressed the urge to wrap his hands around the man's throat. He didn't want to embarrass Josie any more than she looked, so he satisfied himself with watching them walk toward the saloon. They stopped, and he could see Frank waving his arms around at Josie before looking back down the street at Jimmy watching them. Scowling, Frank pulled Josie out of Jimmy's line of sight.

By sheer force, Jimmy remained in his spot, once again holding himself back from running after her. Instead, he decided he'd ride out to her house just before suppertime to make sure she made it back and was doing okay. Something in his gut told him she was in trouble again.

* * *

FRANK YANKED Josie's arm hard, steering her to the back side of the tavern where eyes wouldn't wander in their direction.

"Remember when I said you're getting married? It wasn't a suggestion, JoJo. You can barely make it on your own. You need a man to tend to and someone to take care of you. Once you're married, there'll be no more working outside the home."

"Frank, I—"

"No." The word sliced through the air with a sickening finality to it. Josie's stomach filled with dread. "You are going to go back to the livery. Get Daisy. Take her and the wagon back to your house." Josie leaned away from Frank. This was the fiercer side of him that she didn't like. "Do you understand me?"

Josie nodded vigorously, but Frank grabbed her arm again, lifting her slightly as he shook her. "I need the words, Josie." His voice no longer sounded like Frank, and it sent a chill down her entire back and arms, creating goose flesh.

"Yes. Yes, I understand you. I'm going to go home now."

This time, she waited for permission to leave. Frank's eyes searched Josephine's, looking for any hint of deceit. When he was satisfied that she wasn't going to run to that giant, Jimmy, he gave her the rest of her instructions.

"You're going to put on a nicer dress and wait for me to come pick you up. You're having supper with Essie and me." His jaw worked as he scrutinized her. "And do something with yourself for a change. I know it's hard, but try to make yourself look good." He dismissively flung his arm in her direction, his lips pulled back, derision plastered across his face.

Josephine's eyes welled up at that last comment. It sent her right back to childhood with her mother admonishing her to try to make herself look "prettier" even though she wasn't pretty to start with.

I realize you weren't blessed with natural beauty like your sisters, but do try to enhance yourself, Josephine. I feel like you make yourself homely just to embarrass and irritate the rest of us. Why must you be so vexing?

That was always followed by a sympathetic look from Essie and cackling laughter from their mother. Much later, that cackling included Beth. She never knew why Beth took such a turn on her during their middling teen years. As JoJo focused on Frank again, her mouth parted, and her brow furrowed. She didn't know if she was going to cry or gasp for air. Panicked, she could barely keep herself from running away from him. She might have, if she didn't know better. He'd have no problem chasing her down the street and disciplining her in front of God and everybody. Her heart set to racing just thinking about it.

Frank knew he had hit the mark. He'd heard these kinds of stories from Essie all the time and had seen it in action. No further prodding was necessary on his part to get JoJo to comply. She'd go home and be ready. All he had to do was invite Carter to dinner, and things would take their natural course. Carter Bass wanted the deal his cousin Terrance Draper was offering him, and he seemed to be smitten with

JoJo, the timid waif. The sooner he got JoJo out of that house, the better.

"Well, off you go." He made a shooing motion with his hands and watched her walk away, practically curling in on herself. Defeated.

He called out louder to taunt her. "Don't make me wait, you hear?"

Flinching, she picked up the pace. Frank had to chuckle at that. *Always the obedient one even when she tries to rebel.*

CHAPTER 29

Jimmy restrained himself until late afternoon. When the sun began dropping lower in the sky, he took Coal out and cantered toward Josie's house. The air was cool, and the light breeze soothed his overheated skin. His normally calm demeanor was now a flush of anxiousness and low-level fear. He'd tucked these feelings away years ago because they only served to get him beat. He didn't want to think too much about their reappearance.

Dusty interrupted his train of thought by joining him but was running a jagged path both on and off the trail, occasionally dashing under Coal. This went on the entire way, mirroring the emotions churning inside Jimmy. Sometimes Dusty would bark at Coal, who tossed his head and whinnied right back at the spry dog. They had developed such a routine that Coal no longer took issue with Dusty's antics—even the crouching dashes that brushed his underbelly. Coal joined in by nipping at Dusty like a game of tag. Huffing out pent-up energy, Jimmy eased the grip on the reins when the Snyder house came into view, especially since someone was clearly at home. His shoulders relaxed, and his breath eased. Seeing Josie is what he imagined coming home felt like. That errant thought both shocked him and had him suppressing a lopsided grin.

He tied Coal to his usual tree, patting him on the neck before walking away. Dusty flopped down next to him, panting. He was worn out from running circles around Coal. Jimmy ran up the stairs to the porch and knocked vigorously, his worry mingled with excitement about seeing Josie. But instead of being greeted by her sweet face, framed with her halo of flyaway hair, her sister—the harridan—greeted him with a scowl as she threw open the door.

"What do you want?"

"Not you."

"Well, Jo's not here."

"Where is she?"

"Why should I tell you?"

Jimmy's eyes narrowed. Beth's bitter look was masking something. Her lips were turned down and twisted to the side. He realized she looked worried, her face a reflection of his without being aware of it.

He frowned. "I think she's in some sort of trouble."

Beth's face registered surprise for a split second before going back to scowling. "Why do you say that? I think you're the only trouble she's encountered." Her words were clipped, like Dusty's yipping when he was annoyed with Coal.

"I met Frank today."

Beth's expression dropped. She stood in the doorway for a moment longer before she stepped back, allowing Jimmy in without inviting him. Inviting him would just be too much for her and her pride.

Jimmy snorted at her concession to him and took off his hat before entering.

"Well, aren't you the gentleman?" Beth slammed the door shut behind him.

"More so than you give me credit for. Now, where's Josie?"

"With Frank."

"What for?"

"Who do you think you are? Why do you think you can come here and just start taking charge of her?"

Jimmy jabbed his finger toward the floor as he spoke. "Look here—you all take advantage of that poor girl. It's as plain as day. I don't know why you feel you can treat her the way you do, but that's not the way you treat family. Especially nice family." His eyes held her.

"Why are you even around here? What's she got that you want so bad?" Pursing her lips, her other facial features followed suit. "She's not that way, you know?"

"Stop talking about your sister like that. She's a good, kind person. You, of all people, should know that."

"Yeah, yeah. The entire town seems to be reminding me of that lately." Beth flicked the back of her hand at him. "So why are you here?" She crossed her arms over her chest while shifting her weight to one leg.

"I saved her from Gus, and I mean to keep protecting her while we're in town. I don't trust him or his so-called friends."

Beth looked like she was ready to be nasty again, but Jimmy held up his hand. "And I don't trust you. None of you have her best interests in mind."

Huffing at him, she asked, "And you do?" She rolled her eyes at him.

Jimmy was beginning to lose his patience once again. "I do. I don't like seeing people mistreated. When I do, I stand up for them—no matter how long it takes to get justice."

Beth's eyes widened at *justice* because it had held extra

heat laced with venom contrary to his normally even speech and intonation. Even his drawl disappeared. It chilled her, despite standing in the warm part of the house during the late afternoon. She watched him, waiting for his expression to change, but it didn't. His eyes were dark, and his face looked like thunder might rip out of it at any moment.

Ugh. She decided her dislike of Frank was stronger than her dislike of Jimmy. Perhaps it was less dislike of Jimmy and more a jealousy of Jo for having the attention of the likes of him. He was something she would've wanted for herself—tall, strong, and fierce, for starters. Fiercely loyal, from the looks of it, and completely protective. Something she sorely missed. When he wasn't glaring at her or demanding she help Josie, he was an extremely handsome man in a rugged, quiet way. He had a square jaw dotted with stubble, assessing eyes that didn't miss anything, and a gentle way about him despite his enormity and assertiveness. *Yup. I could get used to someone like that.* She wished she had all that following her around.

Jimmy kept his face neutral as Beth was assessing him because he needed Beth to open up so he could find Josie. Things weren't right. She should be at home. He cleared his throat. At least Beth had the decency to blush, unlike the Reinhardt women.

"Ah, sorry. Got lost in thinking about how much I dislike Frank."

Jimmy's eyebrow shot up, but he didn't call her out on her lie. Instead, he angled his head forward, waiting patiently.

"She went into town today to take eggs to the inn. I know she returned because the wagon was here when I got back to the house."

"Where were you?"

"None of your business. Do you want to hear about JoJo or not?"

Beth was back to being snippy, so Jimmy bit his tongue. The muscles in his forearms bulged as he crossed them in front of him, giving her a curt nod.

For some reason, his shirt sleeves were rolled up, which seemed odd to Beth and distracted her before she answered.

"I think she's over at Frank and Essie's. When I was in town, I overheard a couple of ladies in passing mentioning how Frank looked angry and was taking JoJo away. That's when I rushed home, only to find the wagon and Daisy but no Jo."

"Why weren't you invited?"

"Ach." This time, she flapped both her hands at him. "Frank hates me. Don't you know that by now? You've been hanging around long enough. It's common knowledge."

"No, I don't gossip and rarely talk to others unless I have to."

Beth's raised eyebrows and downturned mouth challenged that statement.

"It's better that way."

"Fine." Beth swept her arm from her front to her side. "I don't know what's got into Frank, but he was talking to JoJo for quite a while at the funeral. I'm sure you noticed that."

Jimmy nodded. He thought it was quite odd as well but didn't say anything. He had been barely able to contain his anger when he had seen Frank leave Josie with another man. Talking about it wouldn't make anything better. It rarely did in his world.

"He's up to no good. Always has been."

Jimmy sighed in exasperation, dropping his arms to his sides.

"No, hear me out. I'm only telling you this because I hate him, and you're the lesser of two evils." Scowling and crossing her arms, she snapped at him. "Don't go thinking I'm being nice to you or anything."

Jimmy finally allowed himself to roll his eyes. They'd been begging to do that the entire time he'd been in this town.

"Get on with it. I need to go get her."

"Just hold on, Romeo." She held up her hand. "You should listen. Frank has always loved Essie. It was no secret they were going to marry, and our parents gave their blessing for this. He's the most eligible man in town. At least, he was." She made a frustrated dismissive gesture before recrossing her arms. "Anyway, our parents die, and he marries Essie, making her think he'll help all of us, then doesn't let her have anything to do with us. Not that she tries incredibly hard." She huffed in annoyance.

Jimmy's lips flattened and his eyes narrowed as he continued to watch Beth for lies. He still didn't trust this self-serving woman.

"He took nearly all the money from the bank—our parents' money—and said it was Essie's. Told us we could continue to live in the house. We live in the house, but we have no money."

Jimmy was getting angrier by the minute. "So, Josie has to go out and earn money to support the two of you?"

Beth flushed an ugly shade of red. This was her forever shame, and while she was lazy, she still hadn't completely reconciled herself to leaving all the work to Josie. In her mind, she was doing the difficult job, and trying very hard at it, to get married. No thanks to Frank.

"Don't have to answer that—go on."

Her lips pressed tight. "Lately, he's been pressuring JoJo to go live with them, 'cept I'm not allowed to come. He's forcing her to choose between them and me."

"What have you done to them?"

"Nothing."

Jimmy quirked a brow at her.

"Honest, nothing. He just doesn't like the fact I'm trying hard to find a man to marry. Says I'm being too forward."

Jimmy looked like he was about to agree when Beth jabbed a finger in his direction.

"Don't go answering that. We do what we have to do."

They stood there like two bulls in a field facing off. Finally, Jimmy huffed at her. "Get on with it. I'm starting to grow roots. You're telling a tale too long for daylight hours."

"You're impossible, just like all the other men in this town. The bottom line is I don't trust the sheriff, and JoJo doesn't trust Draper. I hate Frank and know he's up to no good, even though he seems to treat that ignorant sister of ours like a queen. She stays out of our business because Frank tells her to. And he tells all of us he's 'the head of the household.'" She imitated his imperious voice, which made Jimmy chuckle, earning her look of scorn.

"What? That was spot-on." He shrugged at her, making him look sweet and younger than his twenty years.

Beth tried and failed to look upset about his comment, a slight smile sneaking out from her gruff exterior as she looked at him sideways. They waited in a comfortable silence, each in their own thoughts.

Finally, Jimmy slapped his hands together. "Well, we know Frank is up to no good."

Beth shot him a look like he was off his rocker. "Obviously. Anything else brilliant you'd like to add?"

Jimmy's eyes narrowed at her again. "No, you're the one adding to this. What else? She was introduced to someone at the funeral—who was that?"

"Oh, him." Her tone held an edge of dismissal. "I think JoJo said his name is Carter." She shrugged.

Jimmy stuck out his arm, flapping impatient fingers toward his open palm in a "give me" motion.

"She didn't say much beyond that, but then again, I think

she's hiding something, too." She threw up her hand to block the objection he was about to throw her way. "I don't know what, so I don't ask. I've been busy here."

Jimmy's lips stretched like a line across his face. "You can't be serious."

"Told you. Marriage. Has to be done."

"Fine. I'm going over there." He ignored Beth's look of genuine horror. "Where do they live?"

"You can't."

"I am."

"No! Frank'll take it out on JoJo." She threw her arm out to the side. "If you go there, you're going to ruin whatever he has planned, and she's the one who'll be hurt, not any of the rest of us."

"Well, I can't just stand here with you."

"Go home. You don't belong here." She paused a minute, deciding to rub salt on the wound. "You're not planning on staying anyway, and you'll just hurt JoJo."

"I'm not going to hurt her."

"Pfft. You probably already have and don't even know it." She said that more to herself than him, which made him pause. It sounded like she was talking about her own situation more than Josie's. Beth walked to the door and opened it. When Jimmy didn't move, she made an ushering movement with her arm indicating the exit.

* * *

BETH WAS PEEVED BEYOND BELIEF. *Jimmy was going to stir the pot and make a bad situation even worse, despite his good intentions. Humph! Do gooders.*

Crossing her arms over her chest, she leaned against the door in an attempt to slow her breath as well as the panic that was filling her. She had no idea what Frank ultimately had in mind for Jo, but from what she could gather from the gossips and in passing, he was angry and determined. She was fairly positive Frank planned to push Carter on JoJo. But she couldn't understand why Carter. Frank didn't do anything that didn't serve him, and she intended to find out what his plans were and stop him. She owed JoJo that much.

Guilt washed over her about her middling teen years and how she had treated Jo. She couldn't do anything to fix that, but she certainly could help her now and get back at Frank in the process. Heaving a big sigh, she pushed herself off the door just as she heard noise outside. Startled, she ran to the closest window and peered out, but didn't see anything

Thwack. Thwack. Thwack. The sound was slow, steady, and insistent. Curious but not afraid, she hurried to the kitchen window, looked out, and shook her head. She watched Jimmy raising the axe over his shoulder to bring it arching down at the wood he was chopping. His shoulders tensed, and his arms flexed while his rhythm was steady and easy. Jimmy made everything look so easy—even when he was ready to ride to Josie's rescue without a plan. Stupid, but undeterred. Josie had asked her to chop a few pieces from the wood stack so they could slowly build stock for the winter without having to wear themselves out in the process. Josie— always the planner and caretaker.

Deciding there was nothing to be done with Jimmy, she let him work out his need to help as well as his anxiety over not being allowed to. She had her own plans to figure out.

* * *

AFTER WORKING out his frustrations and helping in the only way he could in the moment, Jimmy rode back to base camp, mulling over Beth's change in attitude. While she wasn't necessarily friendly, she wasn't as hostile as she normally was, either. He shook his head. None of this was making any sense. While he'd like to go charging in and rescue Josie, did he really know that she wasn't safe? Beth seemed convinced that Frank would take things out on her. He certainly didn't want to make her situation worse, by any means. Charlie tended to do that inadvertently. He meant well, but things didn't always seem to pan out that way.

Coal moved along at an even pace because Jimmy's head wasn't with him. That horse sensed Jimmy's moods as if they were connected by an invisible string. He knew Jimmy was thinking and thinking hard. Dusty, however, seemed to be fine with Jimmy being deep in thought. He had critters to chase and birds to flush, and he was having a ball. When he became bored, he returned to nip at Coal's legs to irritate the horse. Then he'd dash underneath and circle around him. Coal snapped and snorted at the dog, occasionally breaking his gait to stomp his hooves. Jimmy finally had enough of their shenanigans, and his piercing whistle called a halt to their play. Duly chastised, they hung their heads and fell in line but continued to toss each other looks.

Indecision gnawed at Jimmy's gut. What he couldn't figure out was Beth. She had an odd relationship with Josie. *She clearly uses her, but then she's protective of her, too. Was she just protective because she didn't want to lose her cash cow?* Jimmy chewed on that for a few minutes before shaking his head. *No, it's more than just that. Beth's hiding something, too.* Where Van Der Kamp could smell a lie, Jimmy could sense it. He sensed something today, and it was playing with what he knew in his mind.

The rhythm of Coal's gait was soothing and helpful. It settled the frayed edges of Jimmy's nerves while he tried to piece together what was happening, and why he suddenly felt so drawn into this drama. He couldn't leave it well enough alone. *Darn it, this town.* He avoided people at most turns, and here he was riding straight into the proverbial crowd of them. Women, no less. Jimmy snorted, and Coal responded with a snort of his own as he kept moving steadily. *Clomp-click, clomp-click, clomp-click, clomp-click.*

Maybe I'm overthinking this. Maybe it's just a family dispute. All families are different. That thought made him notice the ride was quieter than normal. Jimmy straightened in his saddle, widening his vision. They were closing in on the edge of town, which is where he had felt like he was being watched the last time he had come from Josie's. Before he could think too much about it, he heard a commotion by the livery echoing down the street. He saw a group of men circling a pair of horses and raising a ruckus. Without hesitation, he jabbed his heels into Coal and rode hell for leather, which left a surprised Dusty sneezing at the dust they had kicked up before he followed.

Riding closer, Jimmy saw the taller of the men yank hard on the gelding's reins, causing him to rear up, pawing at the air and shrieking at the man. A shorter, bulkier man took a whip to the side of the horse and made him scream. The mare being held next to the gelding was frantically pulling, trying to move away, earning her a lash across her rump for her efforts. The pair continued in a frenzy, rearing and screaming, eyes rolling in fear. The three men quit beating the horses long enough to yell at Karl, the livery owner, when he came back out shaking a pitchfork at them. He was beet red, yelling at them in German while trying to separate the men from the horses without getting trampled or whipped.

Jimmy leaned over Coal, spurring him on, riding in hot. He jumped off Coal while Coal barely slowed down. All four men stared in surprise as Jimmy looked like something out of a trick riding show. His appearance was even more spectacular since he was no little man pulling stunts most regular-sized men barely tried. His eyes narrowed as his body seemed to grow taller and broader before their eyes. The angles and planes of his face became harsher. He was filled with fury, like an avenging archangel, and it was a sight to behold.

Snatching the whip out of the man's hand, Jimmy pushed him down to the ground, securing him foot to chest. Rotating, whip in hand, he faced the other two abusers. They stopped, hands up in the air. Even Karl stopped yelling and jabbing, and quickly gaining some sense, he moved to calm the terrified horses. The horses knew him well enough to trust they weren't in danger with him.

The men remained frozen with their hands held chest high in front of them. The lanky man with dingy hair and a droopy mustache spoke first. "Hey now, mister. We mean no harm. We're just teaching our horses some lessons. Just let up Neil, and we'll be on our way."

Jimmy didn't say anything but did press harder with his boot. Neil squealed at the pressure, even though Jimmy really wasn't pressing that hard. He continued to watch them all closely because he felt on the edge of being out of control. His nerves were jumpy, and he wanted to take care of business, but thought he might give them worse than he gave Gus and friends if he didn't hold for a minute. Like an enraged bull—his height and bulk filling the space—he looked dangerous with nostrils flaring and broad chest heaving. Even the ragged and labored sounds coming out of him were angry and impressive. Yet, he didn't move to harm, only to subdue.

Tack, the taller of the three, started toward Jimmy, until Jimmy raised the whip. "Don't." When he saw the man reconsidering, he said, "I'm in no mood."

By this time, Karl had moved the horses out of the way. It didn't stop Lanky Mustache, however, from trying to make a break for it. He turned and ran for the mare but didn't get far. Jimmy uncoiled and snapped the whip, catching him around one of his legs, pulling him to the ground, eliciting a high-pitched scream. Unfortunately, that action released pressure on Neil and allowed him to gain enough leverage to grab Jimmy's ankle. Yanking hard, he brought Jimmy down like a felled tree. His fall sprayed a large cloud of dust, temporarily blinding Neil, who was still on the ground. His hands went to his face as he hollered.

Coughing, Jimmy jumped up as Tack lurched toward him. He landed a good punch before Jimmy grabbed Tack's arm and swung him around. Jimmy cocked his arm back and threw a punch dead center to the man's face, forcing him to stagger back a few steps. Jimmy pulled back to hit him again, but Lanky Mustache, who tried to make a break for the mare, grabbed Jimmy's arm.

As Lanky struggled to twist it behind his back, Jimmy roared and pulled his arm straight down, taking Lanky with it. Twisting, he pulled Lanky toward him, reared his head back, and smashed his forehead into Lanky Mustache's face. Blood splattered everywhere, and Lanky increased his screeching and wailing, which were pitiful, ear-splitting sounds. By now, a crowd had gathered, and someone had run to get the sheriff. Jimmy had hit Lanky so hard that he was laid flat. Lanky and Tack weren't much for fighting, anyway, but the angry blow made Jimmy's head reel, forcing him to pause. Neil, the professed fighter of the group and first man down, had regained his vision. He stumbled behind Jimmy, getting in a hard kick to Jimmy's kidney.

Jimmy's back arched as he bellowed in pain. His torso curved forward, the surprise and pain of the kick pitching him toward the ground. Jimmy saved himself from eating dirt by landing on his hands. Thinking he had the advantage, Neil jumped on Jimmy's back. Instead, Jimmy rolled, using his weight to press the squat man into the ground. Neil had ahold of Jimmy's arms, but Jimmy broke free and pivoted to throw a punch to his gut. Although Neil curled protectively in on himself when he landed, Jimmy continued to hit him where he was exposed. The head, the shoulders, then his back when he rolled to his side. He let loose on the man.

Tack regained his senses and was staggering toward Jimmy when the thunderous sound of paws distracted him. He turned just in time to see a blur of wiry fur and a wide-open maw, teeth bared, leaping toward him and snarling. It was the last thing Tack saw before he hit the ground hard and unconscious. Jimmy was too busy with Neil to pay attention.

Karl was worried Jimmy was going to kill these no-accounts. After securing the horses in the livery, he ran up to Jimmy, grabbing him by the shoulders, shouting at him. Dusty watched Karl closely but didn't move from his post with Tack.

"Schtahp. Halt. He'z naht vurt it. No." Karl was shaking Jimmy's arm with all his might. The violence to the horses had unleashed pent-up fury and anger, annihilating the stagnant frustration and fear from years of abuse. Strong didn't begin to describe the power Jimmy exhibited. His strength appeared unearthly and was deadly.

Karl's voice somehow pierced his rage because Jimmy eventually stopped and sat down, his hands on his thighs. His breathing was labored from fighting but also from the emotions coursing through him. Karl patted his back trying to get him to calm down and snap out of the fury Jimmy had disappeared into. "Eets okay. Yer okay. Za horses are safe now."

Jimmy was mortified at the mess he'd made. He looked around and saw a small crowd had gathered, and three men were lying prone on the ground, Dusty watching over two of them. Jimmy hung his head, shaking it, before looking up to the sky. He blew out a breath.

We're supposed to be lying low. This is not lying low.

He got up just as Sheriff Colter came jogging up to them, his belly jumping up and down as he pressed his gun holster against his leg to keep it from flopping around. The sheriff was more out of breath from running down the street than Jimmy was after bringing down three men, with one assist from Dusty, all while running through an emotional maze. He held his arms out to either side away from his body. He didn't want to hold them up, because he wasn't a criminal, but he didn't want to look any more threatening than he already did.

"What in tarnation is going on here?" Colter managed to bellow even though he was a little wheezy from all the exertion.

Sheriff Colter looked around, his hand remaining on the butt of his holstered gun. Jimmy wondered when the sheriff had last fired the thing. Everything about this sheriff was just a little off and certainly disorganized—Jimmy hoped the gun had been cleaned recently if Colter was planning on firing it. Last thing he needed was guilt on his hands for whatever the incompetent sheriff was about to do, even if it included doing the town a favor by putting himself out of commission. Jimmy mentally shook his head. Colter's incompetence was clear. He wasn't just mentally retired. Things were amiss.

First off, Colter didn't bother to secure Jimmy, which, as Jimmy was the last man standing in a fracas, was odd. Colter had only met him once and under suspicious circumstances. He had previously accused Jimmy of foul deeds, so Colter's inaction didn't make any sense. Jimmy lowered his arms, his eyes following Colter's movements as he went over to each man, looking down at them while giving Dusty the side-eye, before looking at Karl.

"Karl, what the hell happened here?"

"Oh, Sheriff, zeese men ver beating za horzes. He"—Karl nodded toward Jimmy—"saved zem."

Colter turned around and pointed a finger at Jimmy, who hadn't moved. "What is with you, anyway?" His lips twitched in and out of grimace as if they couldn't decide what to do. "Are you some sort of do-gooder or something?"

Sheriff Colter squinted at Jimmy. He spat out *do-gooder* like it was a cuss word or something foul. Normally, Jimmy would've kept quiet, but between a passel of yahoos who beat horses and a sheriff who behaved as if "good" was the wrong thing to be, he'd had it. Members of Van Der Kamp's gang were looking like saints compared to these fools.

"You'd think being on the right side of the law, you'd appreciate such a thing."

"Oh, yer a funny man, too." He took out his handkerchief to wipe the sweat from his brow. "You can't just run around doing what you think is right, now."

The side of Jimmy's mouth ticked up but stopped before it could form an actual smirk or half-smile. "Isn't that what your Bible-thumper tells you all to do? 'Do what's right'?"

Sheriff Colter's face pulled tight, flushing, before he jabbed a finger in Jimmy's direction. "Keep your smart remarks and blas-phee-ming to yourself. I'm 'bout ready to haul you down the street and lock you up."

Jimmy just stood there waiting for Colter's next move. His arms had dropped long ago.

The sheriff's words caused a collective intake of breath in the small crowd. Most of them stood apart because Neil and the George Watkins gang that he ran with were known to be dangerous, even if Jimmy had laid them all out. The prevailing sentiment whispered among the crowd was many were rooting for this young man who had his own brand of Western justice and were simultaneously fearful for him. If

Colter didn't haul him off, George's gang would eventually come after him. Karl stood opposite the crowd watching Colter intently.

Colter glared at Jimmy, weighing his options. He didn't have time for this. He was too close to retiring to mess that up with some Easterner who was hell-bent on doing good around this place. Despite evidence to the contrary, he was convinced that Jimmy was an Easterner newly arrived and thinking he could "manage" things. Jimmy was strong, had no fear of working, and didn't have any airs or notions about him. This was a prejudice Colter held strongly because he hated those coming from the East trying to do things their way and change the people who were already established out West. Draper's interference was bad enough. Now this.

Shaking his head, he finally announced to the crowd, "Show's over, folks. Go back to what you were doing."

Hands on hips, Colter waited for them to disperse. There was an air of disappointment as well as relief as they lingered. When they didn't move fast enough, Colter started to make sweeping motions with his arms to move them along. Finally, people walked away—some quicker than others, and a few turning their heads to look over their shoulders one last time before going about their business. Jimmy, Dusty, and Karl remained where they were, waiting for Colter to make up his mind. They were also unwilling to let the fallen men out of their sight, despite their collective incapacitated state. If any of them moved, Dusty made sure to growl at the source.

Exhausted and irritated beyond patience, Jimmy shifted his stance, trying hard to remain cooperative. He was feeling indignant like Coal and angry like Dusty, but also anxious to get back to base. Throughout the mayhem, Josie had skirted through his thoughts. Still undecided about her and perplexed by Beth's behavior, he had more thinking to do. He wanted to get on that and away from all these people. Swiping his hand through his hair and looking down at the ground, he released a big sigh.

Get on with it, Sheriff. He shifted his feet again, casting an exasperated side-glance at Sheriff Colter. *How that man ever became sheriff is beyond me.*

Colter pursed his lips, looking between Karl and Jimmy. He spat on the ground and sauntered over to Jimmy, going toe to toe with him. The heat of his threat was lost when he had to tilt his head back at a ridiculous angle to look Jimmy in the eye, even more so when he jumped after Dusty's warning bark.

"You and me are gonna walk nicely down to my office. You're going to have a little cooling off time in a cell until I can figure out what I'm going to do about you, Mr. Goody Two-Shoes." Colter jabbed his index finger between the two of them. "And do something about Lars's damned dog."

"Dusty." Jimmy snapped his fingers, pointing toward Old Man Johnson's, "base" as they called it. "Go home."

Dusty jerked his head toward Jimmy, incredulous. His eyes widened before tilting his head in both directions at Jimmy. The heavy panting kicked in.

Jimmy cleared his throat. He didn't like doing this to Dusty, but he hardened his tone, this time jabbing his finger toward base. "Go on, git."

Dusty whined, dropping his head, and turned to leave but not before he threw a decisive woof and snort at Sheriff Colter.

Affronted by the idea of cooling off, but wanting to keep the peace, the giant went along with the middling man and his paunch—middling in height, talent, and intellect. He cast a look over to Karl, who shook his head.

"Don't wuree. Yer horse will have goot care. I won't charge you." Now that the bedlam had settled down, Karl's accent had relaxed its tight grip. His consonants and vowels came out more rounded, and his demeanor was more relaxed.

Jimmy smiled ruefully and nodded a curt thanks before his face set as he turned to walk toward the jail. A puffed-up Colter followed him, overly confident, as usual. For whatever reason, Colter didn't bother with the three men on the ground. They weren't in a tremendous hurry to get moving either.

CHAPTER 30

ravis Henderson was tired and saddlesore. The undercover marshal had been riding hard to get back to the Van Der Kamp gang. Wrighty's extradition, trial, and eventual hanging were finally finished. Wrighty didn't get nearly what he deserved, but at least he was no longer a menace to society—more specifically, a life-threatening danger to women. He had taken out his anger and sick pleasure on them for far too long. Travis's face flared with anger and disgust whenever he thought of that useless son of a gun. *See you in hell, scourge.* He might've spit with anger, but he had no spit to give. He was too dehydrated from being on the trail for so long.

Travis finally relaxed when he saw the small spread in the distance. From what limited information Van Der Kamp had given him, this had to be their new hideout. The place belonged to Van Der Kamp's friend, whom he affectionately referred to as "Old Man Johnson." Straightening in the saddle and stretching his arms, he prepared his body for the painful dismount. He had been in such a hurry to catch up with the gang that his body had locked up on him while riding. He was feeling every single one of his twenty-nine years. He was thankful Wrighty's trial was quick, especially given the nature of his crimes coupled with the collective outrage. People didn't stand for that kind of behavior against innocents, especially when they were related to influential ranchers.

Unfortunately, the expeditious nature of recent events made it feel like he'd been in the saddle for weeks on end without ever dismounting. Beyond tiring. He was sure there wasn't a word strong enough to describe how he felt. If he included cleaning up after Wrighty, this entire case was turning out to be much more than the government had realized or he had expected. Mack Pennington was a complex character with many friends in high and low places, requiring some careful unraveling. Even Van Der Kamp wasn't what the government expected him to be. Wrighty was just one knot in an already overly tangled situation.

Exhaustion weighed on Travis, and he was ready for a short break and some sleep before working with Jimmy on their plan. That way, they could at least wrap up the Van Der Kamp gang portion of his task. It would provide some closure and agency that would go a long way in healing Jimmy's wounds of being sheltered, teased, as well as beaten for the exact characteristics that were his strengths—being kind, gentle, and caring. It'd also set Jimmy free to do whatever he wanted with his life. Travis still had high hopes Jimmy would turn to law. He was calm, patient, and fair. Just what was needed in many of these situations.

Sliding out of the saddle with a groan, Travis put his hands on his lower back, stretching himself out as a yawn escaped him. He started to walk Sassafras to the stable when he heard a familiar baritone rumbling at his back.

"Keep that up, and everyone'll think you're as old as me."

Van Der Kamp's voice was lighthearted, but the limp

seemed a little more pronounced. His limp had improved before Travis left, and it wasn't just the forced rest and stand-still caused by early monsoons. Things were more relaxed and peaceful, despite Annabelle's initially disruptive presence and Wrighty's attempts to undermine the gang. But now, they were both gone. *Hell, I wonder what's been happening around here for him to look like that.*

"Yeah, well, this whole Wrighty thing and all the miles I've ridden is making me feel as old as you." Travis clapped Van Der Kamp on the back. "How have things been around here? Everyone behaving?"

His question was meant in a teasing manner, but the grim set of Van Der Kamp's mouth indicated something was amiss. He drew in a long breath and sighed. His lips lifted on one side, but it wasn't a happy look. Van Der Kamp put his hands on his hips while continuing to watch Travis.

"That bad?"

Van Der Kamp drew in another prolonged breath, scrunching up half his face while doing so. "Jimmy's in the hoosegow."

"What?" Travis's brow furrowed and his tone incredulous.

"George Watkins just happens to be in town, too." Van Der Kamp watched Travis's eyes momentarily flicker. "Jimmy caught some of Watkins' men beating their horses and taught them a lesson."

Travis's eyes narrowed. "What do you mean 'lesson'?" Travis drew out the word *lesson.* He looked fit to be tied as well as incredulous.

"It seems our Jimmy has grown up and realized he has size on his side, and he can use it. He's been teaching a lot of *lessons* lately." Van Der Kamp imitated Travis's pronunciation of *lesson.* Travis frowned. "He provides these yahoos fair warning, but if they choose not to listen, he unleashes right-eous fury on them." Van Der Kamp made a clicking sound from the side of his mouth. "That kid has a lot of pent-up anger. Seems to be letting it loose on those who are less than kind to others, those who can't or won't defend themselves."

Van Der Kamp let that sink in for a moment. "Jimmy's a good kid—kind, gentle, and all that." He hooked his thumbs under his belt buckle. "He's just sorting some things out for himself."

"Sorting some things out?" Travis asked incredulously.

"Yup. He's my right-hand man now. Until he sorts himself out and gets out of here."

"What do you mean by that?"

"Exactly what I mean. You want the same for him; otherwise, you wouldn't have been helping him and Charlie. You probably wouldn't have come back here so quickly if you weren't worried about Jimmy or wanting to give him a hand or something." Van Der Kamp raised his eyebrows at Travis and angled his head. "You usually stay away much longer."

Travis retained his poker face, but he knew the jig was up. Van Der Kamp was always too canny, so Travis decided to run down the middle with this one.

"Jimmy was dealt a bad hand. He doesn't deserve to be here anymore than Charlie and Annabelle did. They got out. Jimmy was just too scared to leave."

Van Der Kamp watched Travis with icy blue, appraising eyes. Gone was the congeniality. He pointed a finger at Travis.

"Quit storytelling. We both know why you're here and that I've been allowing it. I'm not as witless as Mack makes me out to be, nor the cold-hearted killer the press paints. That's their story to make themselves feel better." He drew in a quick sniff, pulling up the right side of his face. "They're all part of the problem that I have issues with." His face went flat with that while his unreadable eyes remained locked on Travis.

Travis's pause felt like an eternity before he finally nodded his head. He admired Van Der Kamp for his moral code and principles. The other marshals and his superiors struggled to understand how he felt about Van Der Kamp. Yes, he was a criminal, but his robberies were aimed at the government and the business tycoons who profited from war and government contracts. They all used people and harmed others—especially relating to the War Between the States. Van Der Kamp was a disgruntled vet who unlawfully and forcefully made his point, unlike Mack Pennington, who twisted the law and officials for personal advantage and monetary gain.

The way Van Der Kamp saw the situation, it was economic gain for those already in power and no help for those in need. When vets returned to nothing, his disgruntlement grew, coupled with the strong discomfort with how the regular man and now newly freed man were treated as disposable. In his mind, the war resolved nothing. It had only created death, destruction, and broken families—and made some of the already rich richer. In many ways, Mack was the true criminal in this scenario. Bringing down Mack was the end goal for everyone, Jimmy included. Jimmy just didn't fully realize that yet.

Travis sighed. "Tell me what's going on with Jimmy." Van Der Kamp grinned, but Travis held up his hand. "Start there first."

Van Der Kamp rolled his eyes at Travis, which made Travis chuckle, feigning a cough behind his fist. Things must be bad for Van Der Kamp to be this open rather than his usual impassive self.

"It's a long story that you'll need catching up on, but things aren't right in this town. There're foul goings-on here. I don't know if the sheriff is in on it, or if he's just a lazy or incompetent pawn. Keep an eye on that one. He's locked up

Jimmy. Thom rode back to tell me. He saw the whole thing go down."

"He didn't help Jimmy?"

The corners of Van Der Kamp's mouth turned up slightly, and his eyes sparkled with humor.

"You've missed a lot while you were gone. No one 'helps' Jimmy. They either do what he 'asks,' or they get their backsides handed to them."

Van Der Kamp laughed loudly at Travis's slack expression. It took a lot to surprise Travis.

"Holy hell." He scrubbed a hand down his face. "Didn't expect that. He's the calm one. He watches and stands apart."

"Mmhm. Like I told you, he's working out some things for himself, and we just need to leave him to it. But right now, we need to get him out, and you need to be the one to do it."

"Me? What am I going to say?"

Van Der Kamp widened his eyes as his lips went into a straight seam. "Really?"

Travis didn't want to be in this standoff. Jimmy reminded him of a younger version of himself. He felt both an obligation and a connection to the lost little boy who was now a behemoth of a man. Apparently, a threatening man. He'd have to deal with Jimmy and his expectations of justice and revenge after he sprung him. Travis thought about it, realizing he had a better chance of that working with Van Der Kamp than trying to bring him down, too. He'd have to alter his plan some way, especially since he was being forced to show his cards.

"I can hear you thinking clear over here. Look—we both have the common goal of taking down Pennington's operation. He's as crooked as the day is long. He's hurt too many good people, the kind of people that I'm rooting for. Look what he did to Charlie and Jimmy. How about Sheriff

O'Donnell and Annabelle? Think about what he's planning to do or at least capable of doing." Van Der Kamp watched Travis's face. "If you were really part of my gang, I'd just tell you to do something, and you'd do it. Let's stop pretending about your undercover status, Marshal. I've known for a while. I'm pretty sure you know it, too."

Travis's lips tightened, eyes locked with Van Der Kamp's. Van Der Kamp pulled up his right cheek and nostril, breathing in deeply, again.

"Why you didn't leave me when you knew your cover wasn't safe, I don't know. Despite being a U.S. Marshal, you've been good to me. Be good to Jimmy and spring him. Deep down, I'm pretty sure you know what I'm planning. We can either do this together or work against each other." Van Der Kamp let that sink in before going in for the kill. "Be far more rewarding for us—Jimmy included—if we do this together."

He turned and limped toward the house, leaving a shocked Travis in his wake. Stunned and rooted to his spot, Travis continued looking where Van Der Kamp had disappeared into the house. How long he stood there he wasn't sure. It was Sassafras's nickering that snapped him out of his stupor. The mare nudged his shoulder just as he turned his head.

"Right."

He needed a minute for his eyes to focus and his mind to clear. He looked at sweet Sassy until she stamped her foot in a huff. She was ready for oats, water, and a rub down.

"Sorry, I know I promised. But we have one more place to go."

She sighed in exasperation and shook her head as he mounted, and they headed toward town. Sassy could have some water while he had some words. He was hoping that was the only thing he was going to have.

* * *

"Sheriff."

Travis nodded his head to the man sitting behind the desk. He wasn't necessarily old but looked like he was riding toward retirement. Probably more so because of the beleaguered look about him.

Sheriff Colter sat up in his chair, putting on his stern face. Yet another new face in this town that had become filled with all sorts of unfamiliar faces. However, this face was serious. While Travis's voice was warm and friendly, the sharp planes of his face, square jaw, and lean sinewy body told a different story. He was a "friendly until he's not" type.

"What can I do you for?"

Travis jerked his head over to the cell where Jimmy sat silently. "I'm here for that one."

"Well, I—"

"What, exactly, is he in for?" Travis heavily emphasized every syllable of *ex-act-ly*.

"There was a public disturbance. I—"

Travis sighed, jamming his hands on his hips.

"Did he cause it?"

Colter was dumbfounded by the question. Maybe it was Travis's earnestness. Maybe it was the way Travis edged into his space when he leaned over the desk, asking. Thinking back, Colter supposed he didn't really know who had actually caused the ruckus, but he could make a darned-good guess who it was, and it wasn't Jimmy. After the fact, Colter just wanted them all to quiet down so Terrance Draper or George Watkins wouldn't come running and causing him more trouble. Instead, the townspeople came to witness the debacle, gawking. A town of men hiding, women gossiping, and no one doing anything about anything except complaining. This town was turning into more trouble than it was worth.

"I don't suppose he did, come to think of it."

"Then why on God's green earth is he the one locked up?" Travis looked around. "Where are the other combatants?"

Colter's brow furrowed as he scratched his head. "I didn't have anyone to carry them here. Figured they'd sort themselves out when they came to."

Travis's eyes blazed. Colter thought they might burn a hole in his face the way fire was jumping out of them. He scooted back, just in case.

Travis swept a frustrated hand in front of him.

"Get up. I don't know what you were thinking not securing the entire scene." He pitched a thumb toward Jimmy. "That one isn't your problem, in case you're rethinking your decision."

Colter gripped the cell key. He really didn't know what to make of this new stranger other than he didn't want to cross his path again. Travis's eyebrows raised. Colter swallowed hard and gave a nod before standing. He scurried over to the cell and released Jimmy.

He waved Jimmy out of the cell, closing the door behind him. Silence ensued as Travis and Jimmy walked out of the building.

Aside from the three of them, no one was ever the wiser as to how Travis sprung Jimmy, but sprung he was.

Silence was their third wheel. After the fracas, the streets were quiet. They were too. Travis didn't say a word or even look at Jimmy. Down to the trough, unhitching Sassafras, then heading toward the livery, they followed a similar, comfortable routine from before Travis's departure. However, this time they watched each other from the corner of their eyes and waited. Their standoff was interrupted when Karl saw Jimmy enter the stables, his voice raised enthusiastically.

"Hallo! I'm zo glad you are free." He clapped Jimmy on the back with such zeal it caught him off guard but brought a smile to his face for the first time, well, since he had last seen Josie.

Jimmy flushed. Having someone care about him with kindness—a stranger no less—was odd.

"Thank you for protecting the horses." He stuck his hand out. "Jimmy Stapleton." He looked over his shoulder at Travis. "And this here's—"

"Travis. Travis Henderson." Travis interrupted because he

knew Jimmy wasn't sure what his status was nor how to properly introduce him. They hadn't planned that far.

Karl enthusiastically shook both men's hands. He looked between the two of them before cocking his head. "Are you za uncle?"

Karl wasn't wrong to ask. Their features flirted with being similar, but it was their bearing, stance, and general presence that stood in solidarity. Jimmy's six-foot-four, broad, solid frame was like a lumberjack, warrior, or some sort of demigod—especially when he flew into action, like with Josie and the horses. His brown eyes brightened when he laughed or was happy but could just as easily go black and flinty with anger. He'd been a simmering pot these past few weeks, so it was a toss-up as to what people would see. It was either calm waters or raging storms with him since coming to town, no in-between.

Travis's energy was subterranean. Hidden from others but no less powerful, just more controlled. His build was rangy and slender compared to Jimmy's, with a leaner, sleeker muscularity. If Jimmy was a bull, Travis was a stealthy mountain lion. Their faces held similar expressions of watchfulness, yet they were both ruggedly handsome with friendliness that made others feel safe. Square jaws, strong noses—nothing was soft about either of them until they smiled. Then their faces held a captivating and boyish charm. When this happened, they were mirror reflections of each other.

Eyes widening, Travis and Jimmy turned to look the other over. Making their appraisals from head to toe, they shrugged at each other with a look of "maybe." Karl laughed at them.

"Don't be insulted. Eez a compliment."

They laughed, and no further explanation was necessary. Another round of handshakes, and they were off.

* * *

WHEN THEY WERE a good pace from town, Travis finally prodded Jimmy.

"What in the hell is going on around here?"

He didn't need to look at Jimmy to know he was frowning. They rode a stretch more in silence before Jimmy cleared his throat.

"They were beating their horses something fierce. Karl was yelling at them to 'schtaahp,' but they weren't listening." He snorted a breath of annoyance. "You should've heard the screaming and felt the panic. It was awful." He whispered the last bit as if it came more from some memory of his own past than from the events from earlier.

A kind wind whispered gently, and the lulling, rhythmic sounds of hooves patiently kept them company while they rode with their thoughts. Travis knew well the pain Jimmy was reliving—he'd seen him go through some of it. He could only imagine the rest, having seen just a tiny sampling of what Jimmy and his brother, Charlie, had suffered. Some of the knowing came from his own personal experience at a similar age. Travis exhaled heavily, waiting to see if Jimmy had anything else to add. When he didn't say anything, Travis did.

"I hate to do this to you right now, but we may not have a good time later. Or much privacy." He darted a glance at Jimmy's profile. "Give me as much information as you can."

For the first time ever, Travis saw Jimmy slump in his saddle. Not even after a thorough pummeling did Jimmy slump or show defeat. So the heavy sigh accompanying it surprised him nearly as much as the weary posture did.

"Here we are, supposedly lying low, and I've done nothing but make a mockery of that, along with Gus, Ned, Cy, and

Harry." He shook his head. "They were harassing a young woman and didn't take kindly to my request to leave her alone." He cleared his throat. "My fists might've helped them have a better understanding. That's when Van Der Kamp decided I was going to be his second in command, so to speak."

He looked at Travis, whose gaze was steady. His previous hesitation was overtaken by a cataloguing of the rest of his misadventures, albeit somewhat generically.

"Let's see." He ticked them off with his fingers. "A giant hunting dog adopted me. I seem to have befriended the neighboring rancher and then found the body of his missing foreman. I don't even know where to begin with Josie." He flung his hands to either side when he mentioned her. A giving-up gesture from a man who did not give up.

Travis raised an eyebrow at him. *That's a lot to shovel through.*

"She's beautiful."

Jimmy didn't seem to be telling Travis that—it came out more as a whispered breath and a realization. It was as if Jimmy was seeing this woman and not Travis. Snapped out of his trance, Jimmy faced forward, ending their talk. Travis figured he'd have to wait on the Van Der Kamp portion of their discussion. He stifled a chuckle. Perhaps when they went together to check on this beautiful Josie. He let it slide for now because Jimmy was acting completely out of character, and he didn't think the jail time caused it.

I suppose that's what infatuation'll do to you. Or young love. We'll see which it is when I assess this for myself. Wonder if she's anything like Annabelle.

This time, he chuckled. The comedy behind that thought sustained Travis until they reached base. Annabelle was a spitfire who, through no small feat of her own, managed to run the camp as a captive—or "guest," depending on who was talking—but like a little general. She had Charlie, her abductor, wrapped around her little finger. Charlie had no idea what had hit him. Travis's rumbling stomach brought him back to the present. Jimmy had fallen back into his sullen mood, a mood that permeated the air, reminding Travis that he was flat-out exhausted. Instead of engaging with anyone, he went in search of a place to rest.

* * *

THE FOLLOWING MORNING, Goat was banging around in the kitchen, still unwilling to adjust his outdoor cooking methods to the enclosed, indoor space. He was loud and unapologetic about it. He also sounded like a bull in a china shop, except for the off-key singing and the occasional howling and yammering of his newly found cooking partner. Engrossed in his cooking, he spun around, reaching for a platter, belatedly realizing he had an audience.

"Augggh! God Almighty, Travis. You'll give a man heart failure sneaking around like that."

Goat clutched his chest, leaning forward slightly. Dusty trotted to him and nudged Goat's free hand before licking it. "Ahhh," his breath huffed out before he straightened.

"When'd you get in?"

"Yesterday. Had some business in town to take care of and then a lot of rest to catch up on." Travis rocked on his heels, adding wryly, "I could've used a tad more sleep ..." as Goat picked up the platter.

Goat hurled one of the biscuits he was piling on the platter at Travis. For an old man who liked to pretend he had all sorts of aches and pains, he had quite the aim as well as reflexes. He was ornery as all get out, which masked his agility. Travis caught the biscuit midair and tore off a bite with an exaggerated head jerk.

Goat guffawed, "Animal." He canted his head toward the coffee. "Help yourself. You ain't getting none of that fancy service from me, ya hear?"

Travis had just settled himself into a chair when Van Der Kamp silently joined him. No one spoke, but the silence wasn't uncomfortable. It was early enough that the others hadn't found their way to the big house, so it was peaceful, despite a sullen Jimmy striding into the kitchen. He glanced around the room, scowling, then made for a cup of coffee before plunking himself down with Van Der Kamp and Travis on either side of him. Dusty immediately put his head in Jimmy's lap and waited for his morning greeting.

Van Der Kamp shook his head, chuckling. Travis, a slight smile to his face, watched Jimmy petting the dog. "That the dog who adopted you?"

"Yup."

He brought the hot beverage to his mouth before jerking it away. Still too hot. He knew everyone was watching him, and he didn't know what to do with himself, so he brought the mug right back to his lips, burning them again. Between being watched like a hawk and his own bad behavior, he was feeling like a trapped animal and couldn't seem to help himself.

"You're a slow study today."

Van Der Kamp glanced at his mug. Snorting, he crossed his arms over his chest, leaning back in the chair. His eyes settled on Jimmy.

Sighing, Jimmy set the cup down a little too hard, hot coffee sloshing over the rim, burning him, once again. His lips compressed, but he didn't say anything as he shook hot coffee off his stinging hand. The others laughed at him. Goat put the biscuits on the table, followed by a platter of sausages and eggs.

Grabbing a sausage barehanded, Travis took a bite and talked around the food in his mouth.

"Thought you weren't going to be doing any fancy service for me."

"Nope. And yer still eating like an animal. Did you go feral on the trail? Knock it off."

Goat playfully smacked Travis on the back of his head before grabbing his own coffee. Travis shoved the remaining sausage into his mouth with exaggerated emphasis at Goat's back. Goat didn't bother turning around. He raised his index finger in the air and said, "I saw that."

That was enough of an ice breaker to get Jimmy out of his unusual and foul mood. At least the scowl melted off his face. They needed to talk before the rest of the gang decided they were hungry.

Travis finished chewing, darting a look at Van Der Kamp, who nodded.

"Look, Jimmy. What we talked about before—there's been a change in plans."

Jimmy's mouth dropped open. He was wearing all his emotions on his face today. Travis made an upward scooping motion with his index and middle fingers, indicating Jimmy should close his mouth. He snapped his mouth shut and just stared.

Wrapping his hand around his mug then leaning forward, Travis said, "Van Der Kamp and I had a little chat—before and after I sprung you. I'm up to speed, but you aren't."

Jimmy's brow furrowed and his face darkened. Travis extended his forearm across the table with a partially upward-tilting palm as he said, "Look, we're going to do right by you."

Jimmy looked between Travis and Van Der Kamp, who hadn't moved from his relaxed position.

"I'm not understanding."

"Mack Pennington is the final target. He's the root source of all the problems we here at the table are fighting." With a sweeping gesture, he indicated the three of them. When Jimmy didn't move or respond, Travis went on. "We get him, and ultimately you get the revenge and closure you need. It also helps Charlie, Annabelle, and Sheriff O'Donnell. You know what Mack's done to them. We're thinking he's going to focus more on Annabelle right now, and we need to work on this before he can do any more terrible damage."

Jimmy huffed at Travis before turning toward Van Der Kamp. "What do you get out of this?"

Van Der Kamp's eyes narrowed a fraction before he cleared his throat. Time to lay his cards on the table, but he wasn't going to make this easy for the kid. "Look, here." He tapped his finger on the kitchen table before flexing it in Jimmy's direction. "Have you ever wondered why I even took you and Charlie in?" He gave Jimmy the side-eye.

"Didn't think so. I only ever do things that are right or that make a point. The slaughter that happened that day wasn't right, despite your father deserving it with his underhanded and double-crossing ways. You and Charlie? You didn't deserve punishment for the sins of your father."

"You're saying you somehow saved us?"

"Yes and no. You didn't deserve to die, and Goat threw me a bone by saying he wanted you for help. In warfare like that, there tends to be no survivors. Want to know why everyone —including women and children—are historically killed?"

Jimmy shook his head. He didn't think that way or about those kinds of things.

"Survivors seek revenge, Jimmy." Van Der Kamp doubled tapped the table with his index finger. "Revenge."

He eased himself out of his chair. Nodding to everyone, he refilled his mug then left them in silence. Goat followed a minute later to give Travis and Jimmy some privacy, but not without adding his two cents.

He patted Jimmy's shoulder before giving it a gentle squeeze. "Burns yer biscuits, don't it?"

Jimmy cradled his head with his hands. He wasn't in the mood for this. At all.

Travis leaned forward and hissed at Jimmy, "He knows who I am. Why do you think he sent me to spring you?"

Jimmy looked around, making sure this wasn't a joke and that no one was listening. "Have you bumped your head? What do you mean?"

"I mean, he's canny. I suspected he might've known, especially when Charlie and I went after Wrighty and Annabelle, but when I came back, he pretty much told me to stop pretending and work with him." Travis threw himself against the back of the chair, huffing with exasperation.

Jimmy looked at the ceiling and sighed. "All right. Tell me again why he's so set on getting back at Mack. It's not just because of me and Charlie."

Travis waved his hand around in front of his face as if he were clearing smoke from the air.

"Mack Pennington was just a means to an end, as far as we know. Van Der Kamp needed a filler job to make ends meet. He doesn't rob for personal gain, that's for making points—that we do know. He works to earn his keep. He made it clear to Mack taking out your father was a one-time deal. True to form with Mack, he made everything much more convoluted and entangled—he's sticky like a web." Travis stopped and studied Jimmy.

"The information Pennington gave him was purposefully false, so there couldn't be any survivors. He wanted your entire family killed. Thanks to Wrighty, the situation got out of hand quickly. Van Der Kamp would've had your father killed and let the driver go, but an entire family who could point the finger at him? No way." He shook his head, mouth turned downward.

Jimmy swallowed hard and then said in a tight voice, "So, he doesn't kill children. What of it?"

"He had your mother shot only so Wrighty didn't act on any crazy ideas and to put her out of her misery. By that point, everyone had seen enough, whether you remember any of it or not. You two? He's setting you both against Mack, paving the way for when he can come in and bring him down. Why do you think he was so happy Charlie kidnapped Annabelle?"

"Accidentally kidnapped," Jimmy snapped at Travis.

The fact they coerced Charlie into robbing a mercantile by threatening Jimmy's life still sat sore with him. Charlie was the furthest thing from a criminal.

"Yes, accidentally." Travis's voice was gentle. He knew the problems that incident had caused between the brothers.

Crossing his arms tightly across his chest, Jimmy waited for Travis to go on.

"Annabelle's just another tool Mack'll use against O'Donnell. Mack still seems to be trying to get back at him. Van Der Kamp just let Mack's granddaughter go—without telling him he had her. Wasn't supposed to even have Charlie, but he let him go, too. Pretty sure it's just a matter of time before Van Der Kamp ropes Sheriff O'Donnell further into this mess."

"Why would he go against his own father?"

"Because O'Donnell hates Mack as much as Van Der Kamp does. Why do you think he has a different last name?"

Jimmy shrugged.

"He took his mother's maiden name to create even more distance from Pennington—an Irish surname, no less—on top of refusing to run his mine. Chose to be the law instead. The solid kind."

He tilted his forehead forward. Jimmy nodded slowly in return.

"Besides," Travis said, "when O'Donnell finds out the extent of Pennington's mis-dealings and crime, he's going to want to take him down for that alone. Forget any of the shared history they have as a so-called family."

"Hmm." Lost in thought, Jimmy took a swig of the now-cooled coffee. "I always thought it was kind of strange that Van Der Kamp let Charlie go so easily. I know he liked Annabelle and all … and thought that her and Charlie should be together, but still—"

"He's setting up his takedown, Jimmy. Van Der Kamp's strategic. Very strategic. Nobody underestimates him, and for good reason. We agreed Van Der Kamp was acting awfully strange after Annabelle's handoff. Remember? He wasn't in any hurry to move out, but we didn't have time to think about that. We had to save Annabelle from Wrighty."

Jimmy huffed in agreement while Travis continued.

"That's why the government's been tiptoeing around him. They can't seem to get to him without some sort of loss on their part. As for Mack, one of his defenders or lackeys always seem to be at the ready waiting to 'help' him out. He's got people everywhere, and a lot of people are beholden to him. I'm just stockpiling information right now—that's all. They don't want me acting … for whatever reason."

Grabbing another biscuit, Travis tore it in half but took his time to butter it. When he was finished, he pierced Jimmy with a hard stare.

"I know I told you I'd help you get revenge. I keep my promises, Jimmy." He took a bite of the biscuit, chewing slowly. "Just be prepared that justice and revenge may not look the way you want it to."

Jimmy sat on that for a moment. He twisted his mug back and forth between his hands, watching the coffee slosh around. Running his finger around the rim, he spoke without looking away from the coffee. When he spoke, he sounded more like a petulant child than a grown adult.

"I finish what I start."

"I hear you, Jimmy. I just want you to be prepared. We don't have the full story, and Van Der Kamp reveals things only on a need-to-know-basis." He drank some coffee slowly. "We both know that."

They ate in silence for a few minutes, more picking at the food because it was there than to satisfy an appetite. Their appetites had fled earlier in the conversation. Deciding Jimmy had enough time, Travis doled out more information.

"Van Der Kamp is already two steps ahead of us, if not more." Jimmy looked up from his plate. "Think about it—he sent Charlie away, and now he's with Annabelle and O'Donnell. He's using you as his extra set of eyes and ears here. Doesn't that strike you as strange?"

"Yes, but I thought it was more to do with Gus being a problem and me handling it than anything else."

"Your actions were the spark and the logical point for him to start implementing you in his game. He knows you're ready for what he has set out for you."

Jimmy gave him an incredulous look. Travis wasn't deterred.

"What else has Van Der Kamp done that's out of the ordinary?"

Jimmy had a blank look on his face, but then realization blazed. Sitting up straighter, he cocked his head. "You know, he keeps telling me that Josie's my woman."

"Clearly."

"What do you mean by that?"

"Your face—it goes soft when you think about her. You mentioned she was beautiful without me asking about her."

Red rushed across the tips of Jimmy's ears, making Travis smile. "Maybe you found your own Annabelle?"

In answer, Jimmy tucked into his breakfast with a gusto he hadn't had have a few minutes prior. Fortunately for him, Dusty had finally had enough of being ignored. He let out a lusty bark, requesting some breakfast of his own. Jimmy smiled and rubbed his head.

"Have you always been this pushy and opinionated?"

CHAPTER 32

About a month ago ...

The giant wolfhound trotted happily to his resting corner. Dante liked to lay there watching the road that ran between town and the ranch. He liked strangers about as much as Lars did, which was not much at all. They were a well-matched pair. But before he could reach his favorite spot, he stopped, raising his nose in the air and sniffing. He caught scent of something unusual and ran off in search of it.

Standing downwind, two men were watching from an upper pasture, camouflaged by the herd. They had rubbed themselves against some of the more docile beef, trying to avoid being scented. When Dante left the area, they moved closer. One threw a large chunk of poisoned beef in Dante's domain before running toward the tree line to wait.

Not finding what he originally smelled, Dante trotted back to his spot. Comically, his face morphed from being disappointed in not locating his scent to his mouth and eyes widening with delight when he spotted the treat that had been left. His tongue lolling, drooling with anticipation, he loped over to the meat and gulped it in one bite.

The men were astounded that a large piece of meat like that could be swallowed whole, but Dante was no small dog. On his hindquarters, he stood taller than the average man. Dante trotted back to his resting spot, circling six or seven times before plopping down hard on the ground. He blew out a contented sigh and blinked a few times before settling in for his afternoon nap.

The men continued to watch, waiting for his breath to slow down and eventually stop, but Jack became impatient.

"We should go now." He started to move, but Tack grabbed his arm.

"No, he's still breathing—look at him." Tack pointed at the dog who looked like he was napping.

"The longer we stay here, the more is we 'r' gettin' caught. Can't go back to the hoosegow." Jack spit tobacco juice on the ground and wiped his mouth with the back of his hand. "Won't go back." He bent toward Tack, sneering.

"Who said we're gonna? We're bein' safe is all. Those cowpunchers catch us, it's over."

Their eyes remained locked until Jack finally ground out, "Fine."

He jerked his arm away from Tack, and there they sat for another twenty minutes. Waiting. The dog hadn't moved, but they couldn't tell if he was breathing, either. He looked dead, but he hadn't convulsed or vomited. If they were honest with themselves, they didn't know what they were doing or even expecting to see. They hadn't really thought this plan out. They just knew they needed to get past the beast to get to the man. A message needed to be sent.

Jack increased his fidgeting and twitching, enough to irritate Tack. Tack shot Jack an impatient look after he shifted for what felt like an uncountable number of times. Glaring at each other, this time Tack finally sighed.

"Fine."

They got up and slowly approached the dog. Pure stupidity had them so sure Dante was dead that Jack reached out to shake him … just as Dante simultaneously lifted his groggy head and released a god-awful warning sound. Tack was smart enough to jump away from the yowling Dante. Jack was too stupid to realize what was going on that not only did he not retract his hand, he continued to move forward to smack the dog.

That move cost him a big chunk of flesh. Dante lunged his head forward, maw open. He clamped down on Jack's forearm as Jack howled just as loudly as Dante had less than a minute prior. Dante shook his head, bringing Jack's arm with him.

That was about the time Lars came around the corner to find these two in a reluctant tango of teeth and skin.

"Dante, leave it!"

Dante's eyes rolled toward Lars, and his tail lethargically thumped, but he wouldn't let go.

"Dante—" Lars stretched out Dante's name in a low, scolding tone.

Dante gave his prize another firm shake for good measure before releasing it. Jack had been caterwauling and pulling so hard that he flew backward with a cry as Tack pulled a gun on Lars. Lars's hands slowly went up into the air.

"What in God's green earth do you boys think yer doin'? What have you done to my dog?"

"Apparently, not enough," said Tack. Using his gun, he motioned for Lars to move away from the barn. While keeping the gun trained on him, Tack barked, "Move away from that damned beast. Go."

Dante watched Lars take measured steps away from him and the barn until he could no longer keep his eyes open. His head made a thudding sound on the ground.

"'Bout time." Jack held his bleeding arm across his body while watching the dog on the ground. He looked torn between staying where he was and kicking the dog.

"Leave him. We're going." Tack jerked his head toward the thicket of trees. "Yer coming with us," he told Lars.

Lars nodded, giving Dante a passing look before heading toward the trees. That was the last time he'd see Dante, or anyone he remotely liked, again.

CHAPTER 33

*P*resent day

Lost in thought, Jimmy rhythmically brushed Coal. In turn, Coal nickered encouragement, occasionally flapping his lips at Jimmy and bobbing his head. Yesterday had given Jimmy a lot of fat to chew on. His head felt like one of those tops children played with, spinning around and around in a blur of colors. Today made everything worse. It was like spitting into a windstorm and having it come back at you after already spinning out of control.

Animals and mindless work put Jimmy at ease. Although he didn't think it was mindless, it allowed him to think better and gave him peace. Despite working his muscles, the brushing helped Jimmy's muscles relax. At least, they relaxed until he heard a familiar voice behind him making him tense all over again.

"You can't keep avoiding me." Travis walked up to Coal's stall and leaned against the wall. "I let you off easy yesterday."

"Hmmph." Jimmy didn't bother looking back at Travis, continuing to brush his horse.

"Everyone's inside eating." Leaning forward, he slid his

boot on the bottom slat of the gate resting his arms on the upper one. "Talk to me."

"What do you want me to say, Travis?"

"Start with what's been going on around here and then go from there. Unless you want to talk about your little anger problem—we'll eventually have to get to that—then by all means."

He slapped the gate to get Jimmy's attention but not hard enough to startle Coal. Coal was unbothered until Jimmy stopped paying attention to him, which he called out with a snort.

"Ach." It was a noncommittal sound that came from the back of his throat. Twisting, he pointed the horse brush at Travis. "I don't have anger problems. The gang has listening problems." He twisted back to Coal.

Travis laughed. "True, they have some problems with their ears." He waited Jimmy out on the rest of the information, knowing he was a sensible man.

"Fine." He tossed the brush behind him and patted a protesting Coal. "It started with Dobbin bringing back Winnie lame. I was so worried we'd have to put her down." A hostile huff blew out of him. "It's just gone downhill from there."

"What do you mean?"

"Gus, Cy, and Ned drug Harry along for more fooling around. They're supposed to be staying close to base. Instead, they've been disruptive and drawing attention—getting drunk and causing fights. They're the ones who harassed Josie on the street. I saw her home, and Van Der Kamp has had me checking in on her since."

"Really?" Travis said the word nice and slow, clearly unconvinced. His lips pulled to one side.

"Yes, really. Said she was my responsibility."

"All right."

After pausing long enough to give him time to change his tune, Travis said, "How about telling me the whole truth? Time's running fast on us here."

Jimmy's eyes narrowed, but he continued. "She was all shrunk in on herself when I first saw her. I feel protective of her. She's out on this big piece of land all alone on the outskirts of town. Her family's using her, and she's working so hard—no one's helping her." Smoothing his hand down Coal's flank, he grimaced. "They're all treating her terribly on top of it."

Travis took in a deep breath. Jimmy's pain for this woman as well as the profound empathy he had was palpable. It was like another entity sharing the stall with them. He gave a firm nod.

"I hear you, Jimmy. There's no shame in that. What about this is bothering you?" He held up his hand to Jimmy's coming protest. "Aside from the injustice of it all?"

"She needs a man to help her out and look after her."

His face remained impassive until Travis's eyes narrowed, and he nodded at him to go on.

"I like her. I like her a lot—and she doesn't deserve all this." He shook his head then slapped his thigh. "I'm just not stable. I can't offer her or myself any future. Heck, I can't even get any evidence against this gang."

"Well, if the gang's lying low, that means no one's doing much of anything, so there's that. Besides, things have changed. Don't borrow worry."

"Travis, I don't even have a bucket to piss in. I can't afford to borrow anything, and I'm certainly not stealing it."

Travis clasped Jimmy's shoulder and gave it a squeeze. "You were dealt a bad hand, but things aren't going to stay that way. We're still going to make this situation work to our advantage, despite what Van Der Kamp knows or thinks he knows. Now, finish catching me up."

* * *

WHILE TRAVIS MIGHT HAVE SMOOTHED over some apprehensions Jimmy had at that moment, the following day, Jimmy felt a different kind of murderous rage building up within him. It had been simmering for a few days and was ready to boil over. His brief stay in the jail cell had added fuel to an already raging inner inferno. Agitation thrummed through his body, the energy looking for an escape route. Feeling a familiar heat running down the length of his arms, Jimmy shook them out, flapping his hands at the wrists for extra measure. He had to avoid making a fist. If he didn't get these feelings under control, he might find himself taking it out on Gus or Cy. Or maybe both. At the same time.

He shot a glare over his shoulder to make sure the horses were being treated nicely. Really, he was looking for an excuse to hit someone. *Yup. From bad to worse, Jimmy. Bad to worse.* Jimmy shook his head. He was becoming just as bad as the rest of them. His mouth turned downward in disgust. He'd spent too much time with these men.

With perfect timing, Travis sauntered up behind Jimmy. "Walk away, Jimmy. You're skirting trouble again."

Jimmy heaved a big sigh. "Can't seem to help myself these days. I'm not sure what that is." He rolled his neck.

"Deep down you do."

Shoulder to shoulder, they watched the men saddle up. Some of them were going to the neighboring town of Weaver to see what was happening with the mines. Speculation was on the increase as were some other shady dealings. Word was that someone with a large hand from the East was buying up parcels, but there were also threats, scuffles, and more mishaps than usual. Van Der Kamp had some ideas and wanted to get feelers out.

The other group was going to the neighboring town,

Adamsville, in the opposite direction. Linden had the dubious distinction of being the epicenter of mishaps in the most recent year or so. It was nestled between the two towns, and crime would leave one town to hide in Linden. It didn't used to be this way. It started life as a tight-knit, peaceful community and had flipped too close in the other direction. Lawlessness ran this town. And it was looking like the sheriff may have some part in that—and not by way of his ineptitude, oddly enough. Frederick Reinhardt, from one of the founding families of the town, and his crooked cowboys, were part of it—somehow. Everyone was so afraid of Frederick that not only did they not gainsay him, but they seemed to go out of their way to avoid him. Not even mention his name. The Reinhardt women were a different story altogether. They were a plain nuisance. Sensible people avoided those two for other reasons.

Jimmy looked up to the sky. "Smells like rain again." His head moved around, looking for the clouds. "Rolled in quickly. We need it, but this might be bad timing."

"If they're smart, it'll be good. Wash away their tracks. If they're dumb …" Travis just shrugged. No sense wasting words on those who should know better.

CHAPTER 34

Checking in on Colter was a good idea. But not too profitable. The man had no idea what he was doing or what he was up against. That he was on someone's payroll was obvious after he left the buffoons from the brawl out on the street. He was clearly afraid of something. Or someone. It was who rather than what that Van Der Kamp was leaning toward. He didn't think Draper had enough pull, although he certainly seemed to have the funds. Frederick Reinhardt, Douglas Elliot's rival rancher, seemed to be a good possibility, but he needed some better evidence tying them together.

That wasn't something he was going to get jawing with the sheriff. Sheriff Colter reeked of lies. He just had to figure out their source. Grunting as he pushed against the door, he left the jail and slowly made his way down the main thoroughfare.

The rain started to come down heavier as Van Der Kamp returned to the livery. He had put his Thunder up for this very reason—he wanted his old coot of a horse to be comfortable, not cantankerous. It looked like this trip was going to take longer than expected, and being in a stall went a long way to mitigate Thunder's potential testiness. And his tendency to bite those he didn't like. The other reason was walking his way.

"What do you think you're trying to do, John?" George Watkins's face was poised in a smirk, smug and self-congratulatory. "Did yer lackey give you my message?" He gloated, thinking he had bested Van Der Kamp out the gate.

Van Der Kamp no longer flinched when someone called him by his first name. That was history. He stopped, forcing Watkins to come to him and, while waiting, pulled in a curt sniff, scrunching half his face in the process.

Without blinking, he asked, "What're you doing so far from the hornet's nest, Watkins?"

Huffing, Watkins responded, "Always thought you were so clever, didn't ya, John?"

He moved closer to Van Der Kamp, sizing him up like a smaller dog might size up Dusty. Or scrawny Ned would Jimmy. Van Der Kamp neither moved nor responded as Watkins reached out and pulled on his vest.

"Just what do you think you're doing here? Huh, John?" Watkins leaned forward, his mouth twisted and breath foul.

It wasn't always his violent nature that had others backing away from him; sometimes, it was the alcohol fumes and the stench of his breath. But now, instead of stepping back like Watkins was expecting, Van Der Kamp stood taller, pushing Watkins back with his forefinger, features unmoving.

"Not your business." He leaned over Watkins as he had the advantage of height. "The only person who called me that is dead." He leaned into Watkins's space. "Remind me why you're here."

"Well, Mr. Know-It-All, I'll tell you. Since you need a refresher and all."

Watkins waited for a response that he was disappointed not to receive. He frowned and finally continued.

"Pennington sent me. You're not doing your job."

The rain continued to pelt them. The tapping of the raindrops made the silence louder.

"Well, what're you doing? Pennington's waiting on you." Watkins's tone was strangled as it pitched higher. Van Der Kamp's cool façade wasn't cracking.

"We took care of Stapleton. Job's done." Van Der Kamp's tone was slow and dismissive.

He shifted and began to move around Watkins because the conversation wasn't moving fast enough for him, but Watkins grabbed Van Der Kamp's arm. Van Der Kamp looked down at Watkins's hand and back to his face. His brows were knit together, and his eyes were icy. He rotated to face Watkins head on.

"That's all I agreed to, and he knows that. Why I need to explain it to you is beyond me."

Just then, the rain let up. Van Der Kamp glanced up, sighing. The icy edge in his tone melted, replaced with exasperation.

"Why you here, Watkins? I have real work to do. Save us all the trouble and either tell me or leave."

"Come on, you can't be that stupid, John. Pennington knows you're up to something. Knows you holed up in the abandoned Weaver mines when you normally would've kept going, especially since you finished off those pesky prospectors for him." Watkins leered, showing off tobacco-stained teeth that were crooked and mismatched.

"Don't go getting all self-righteous on me, too, George."

"Doesn't explain why you stayed in the camp for so long. Pennington's been a-wonderin', that's all."

"He can wonder all he wants. I don't work for him, and it's just a matter of time before he goes down. You know how hard the mighty fall." Van Der Kamp's face was impassive, as was his tone. He shifted his bum leg, widening his stance. "He'll find out soon enough what I've been up to, and then he'll be sorry he asked." Van Der Kamp looked George Watkins up and down. "And he'll be real sorry he sent you."

"He's probably sorry that he didn't hire me in the first place." Watkins's chest puffed up, putting on the airs that he had convinced himself to be true. "Besides, he's fallen before and got right back in the saddle. What makes this so different?" His tone was dismissive.

"His cards are starting to show, and he refuses to fold, the arrogant bastard that he is. He's ruled by greed and arrogance. Getting sloppy."

"What? You all of a sudden some sort of expert on Pennington?"

Van Der Kamp grunted. "I'm no fool. I keep my cards close to the vest. You sat at the table. Now, decide if you're in or you're out. I don't have patience for jawing or Pennington's foolishness."

"You don't know nothing." Watkins spat on the ground and wiped the back of his hand across his face. "Yer bluffing, and we both know it."

"I don't bluff." His voice sliced through Watkins's bluster with a razor's edge. "I don't have time for that, and Pennington knows it." He slowly extended a finger in Watkins's direction. "He's screwed up sending you, thinking there's something to straighten out."

Watkins's eyes widened as he drew his head back.

Van Der Kamp pulled in a deep breath. "Before you go throwing stones, don't think I don't know about you and Shirleen."

Horror-stricken, the normally fearless George Watkins looked drained of his life's blood. Even his bulbous red nose had paled. Usually, he did things as a signal to others so that they knew he'd been there, and he didn't care they knew. But this revelation? That was a secret that was supposed to go to his grave, and Pennington knew it. That's why Pennington had such a stranglehold over him. When Pennington called, he came. Pennington was the only person who had that kind of power over him. The only person. Well, him and Shirleen's husband who he was sure would kill him if he ever found out about his terrible secret.

Little beads of sweat formed around his hairline. Starting at the brim of his hat, a fat droplet slowly ran down the middle of his face, dangling on the end of his veiny, red, bulbous nose before slowly falling to its demise in the puddle at his feet. Watkins visibly swallowed with Van Der Kamp watching his Adam's apple bob up then down. Van Der Kamp's facial expression didn't change, but Watkins's certainly did. He was also singing a completely different tune called backtracking when he should've sung some humble instead.

"Now look here Van Der Kamp, don't go gettin' all high and mighty on me. We're in this together, aren't we? We're both Pennington's pawns. Don't go believing everything you hear, now."

"I don't."

Van Der Kamp nodded at Watkins before turning his back to him. Under normal circumstances that might've been a deadly move. Watkins had a terrible temper and was a horrible drunk. He also fought dirty. That didn't bother Van Der Kamp a whit, because he had played his trump card and won. For now.

CHAPTER 35

The thrum of raindrops was Josephine's only company as she looked out the front window. The sound was heavy on the roof, just like the emotions rattling around inside her. They weighted her, holding her immobile. She'd been counting on Jimmy's arrival. So predictable and steadfast in his comings and goings, she could set a clock to him. It was unnerving realizing she had set her clock to Jimmy's presence. Worse, that she was gladdened by it. While it had been only a few weeks, it felt like their schedule had always been regular.

He's hours late.

Sighing, she dropped the curtain and walked away from the window. Standing dead center in the living room, she crossed her arms and looked around. A sharp pain of reality hit her—this place no longer felt like home. It was just one sliver of reality she'd been avoiding for quite some time. The other she'd have to address soon was Frank's insistence on Carter. She shook her head, putting that thought aside.

Walking over to the bookshelf, she picked up a vase her maternal grandmother had brought over from Germany. She stared at it for a moment, studying it as if the vase held some sort of answer for her. She brought it face level before turning it this way and that. Frowning, she set it back on the shelf. Her body remained rooted, but her head slowly rotated as she looked around the room, taking everything in. Her eyes absorbed every detail. Placing her hands on her hips, she gave the room another once-over before she heaved an even bigger sigh.

Overcome with warring emotions, weighed down and weary, she moved toward the sofa and plopped down on the edge. With another glance around the room, she splayed against the back of the sofa, tipping her face up to the ceiling while sighing loudly.

Nothing in this room felt like it belonged to her. *I love this home, but it doesn't feel the same. Why?* Josephine's legs were outstretched, and she moved her left foot back and forth like a metronome to her thoughts. *Is it just the devil I know, or is it actual love?* Left, right, left, right went her foot. She looked down at the movement with unseeing eyes. *What's changed? Why do things feel so wrong?* She waited for an answer to come, but an excuse barged in. *It's just the rain. The weather is getting me down.* That didn't feel right either.

Finally, her heart overrode her sensible side, the side she relied on to get her through so many difficult years. Years of painful neglect and verbal abuse. Years of feeling simultaneously like a servant and a burden. *It's Jimmy. Jimmy has made everything different, you little fool. Follow me, for once,* her heart whispered. *Jimmy knows you, your family doesn't.*

Exhaustion overcame her. Josie shivered, drew her legs against her chest, and laid her cheek on her knees. Her eyelids fluttered, and eventually she rolled to her side, curled up on the sofa like a kitten. Tired beyond belief, she tucked her hands under her head like a pillow before her thoughts lost the grip they had on her, their strength fading away.

Odd, her last thoughts were a mixture of Frank's and Jimmy's comments on the house and not what she felt about it.

* * *

IT WAS a bad idea to head out. The rain was coming down so hard it was nearly impossible to see more than a few feet ahead. Rain pummeled the roof. The thunderous sounds were making some of the horses nervous, and they were stamping their hooves and neighing to each other. But everything, including the suspect roof, seemed to be okay when Jimmy looked in on them. Running across the yard in the deluge made walking into the enveloping warmth of the kitchen feel both comforting and stifling. He stamped his boots before entering.

Dinner had come and gone, but Goat was baking loaves of bread and some sort of dessert. Sweetness filled the air, and the cinnamon and sugar kept drawing the remaining men back into the kitchen with excuses of some sort of "business" or other or needing "something" they couldn't quite remember once they had gotten there. Goat had effectively run them all out, except for Jimmy, who felt like family. Jimmy shook off the rainwater and hung his hat on a hook.

When the gang had first kidnapped Jimmy, he spent most of his time helping Goat with meals before they realized he had a knack with the horses. Goat took both Jimmy and Charlie under his wing, as did Van Der Kamp, only Van Der Kamp did it discreetly and from afar. No one really knew what Van Der Kamp was up to, as with most of what he did. Goat, however, was more direct, threatening to take a wooden spoon to those who messed with "them boys" when he was around. Unfortunately for Jimmy, Goat couldn't always be around, and Jimmy wouldn't fight back. Goat knew and felt bad about it, but he also couldn't coddle him and make Jimmy's situation worse.

Years of holding in anger as well as forgoing retaliation for the abuse was itching to burst out of the gentle giant. It would serve the recipients of his ire right, those who tormented a newly orphaned, shy, and scrawny preteen. Jimmy hadn't been his usual calm and quiet self since Charlie had left—and his discontent was growing worse after being in this unlawful and unsettled town.

Jimmy paced back and forth in the kitchen, periodically stopping to look out the window before returning to his pacing. Goat glanced over his stiff shoulder at him and watched for a moment.

"Coffee ain't chewy yet." He nodded to the brew still on the stove. "Git yerself some. Warm up."

Goat returned to the dough. He figured he'd make extra today since they were all stuck inside. When Jimmy didn't move, Goat shook his head. He started to smack the loaves to get Jimmy's attention. Jimmy shook himself out of his reverie, wondering at the crazy Goat was making.

Jimmy cleared his throat. "Ah, do you need some help, Goat? I can wash up and help you."

Goat shook his floury open hand at Jimmy. "What I need you to do is to stop pacing."

Jimmy was taken aback by the outburst but didn't say anything.

"What? Cat got yer tongue?" He held Jimmy's eyes for a minute before adding, "Why don't you just brave the weather and git on over to see your woman?"

Jimmy froze mid-stride, eyes wide. Goat would've laughed if he weren't so irritated with the pacing in his kitchen.

"Yer wearing a hole in my kitchen floor." He slapped the bread, again, for good measure. When Jimmy still didn't respond, Goat raised his voice. "I know you want to go, so go on—git!" He made a brushing motion in the air, trying to move him on out.

Jimmy blinked and moved it on out.

* * *

THE RAIN HAD LET UP, but the roads were a flooded mess from the late monsoon. Now the rain was more of a steady caress than its earlier liquid assault. Not ideal traveling conditions, but fortunately Jimmy wasn't going far. The tight ball that had been growing in his chest let up, relaxing incrementally as he neared Josie's home. *No. Not home. House.* Jimmy's eyes narrowed, focusing on the horizon. *Not sure why she ever called that place a home. I suppose that's all she's known, so to her it's a home.* Jimmy rolled that around in his mind for a bit. He made a sucking sound with his teeth. *I suppose that's why she defends it so hardily. She doesn't have anywhere else to go, it seems. From what I've seen and heard of Frank, he's not an option, either.*

Coal acted put out that Dusty hadn't joined them. Such a dramatic horse. His standard gait was one of a warrior. Right now, his head was low, and he was dragging himself along, pouting. Most likely jealous that Dusty was with Goat, eating sweets and staying dry. Jimmy chuckled and patted Coal's glistening coat a couple of times before brushing off the water beading up on it. Coal blew and bobbed his head as he picked up the pace toward the tree he was usually tied under. Jimmy slid off. Coal shook his head, dousing Jimmy even more.

"Easy there. You'll be dry, and I'll get you some treats when we get back. Just hang tight."

After a pat to Coal's hindquarter, Jimmy strode toward the house, his long legs eating up the distance. It wasn't rain he was avoiding by rushing. It was the woman inside the house he was headed toward.

*   *   *

PERSISTENT KNOCKING on the door startled Josie awake. Blinking, unsure of what time it was or even where she was, Josie realized she had fallen asleep. Scurrying to the window, she peered out and saw a sullen Coal hanging his head, standing in his usual spot under the sheltering tree. Coal made her chuckle. Apprehension flew out the window, and anticipation danced into its place. Carelessly, she flung open the door.

Shaking the rain off his coat and pulling his hat off, Jimmy stepped into the house. "You didn't even check to see who it was, Josie. You need to be more careful."

Crossing her arms, she huffed. "Jimmy, I saw Coal standing out there under the tree. It could only be you."

"Or it could be some horse thief riding Coal."

He smirked at her to lighten the seriousness of his statement. He meant what he said despite knowing Coal would bite someone else if they tried to ride him, if he didn't kick them first.

"Jimmy!" Admonishing him, she scanned the front yard before closing the door and brightening her tone. "Care for some coffee and a sticky bun? I made some fresh."

The rain had darkened the room, but Jimmy's smile lit it up—gleaming white teeth and sunshine beaming from his eyes. "Yes, ma'am. You don't have to ask me twice."

He followed her into the kitchen like Dusty begging for an extra helping. Jimmy was always enthusiastic about Josie's cooking, and today, he seemed even more so. He was like a little boy being offered sweets. While Josie began heating water for the coffee, Jimmy took a deep breath in, and his chest expanded along with a palpable joy.

"Smells so good in here, and I know it'll taste even better. You're the best cook I've known. You make the place seem homier, too."

The broad smile Josie held quickly dropped when he mentioned homier.

"What'd I say? Are you okay?"

Josie's lips twisted as she thought about what she was going to say to him. Compelled by honesty and the connection she felt to Jimmy, but stifled by her upbringing and current situation, she remained silent and shuttered her expression.

How can I talk about something so delicate with a person who's practically a stranger yet knows me better than my own family? And a man, no less.

Jimmy pulled out a chair for her and helped her sit. He pulled the neighboring chair close to hers as he sat and then waited patiently for her to talk.

"It's just the rain." Josie sat ramrod in her chair and looked uncomfortable, and not just from her posture.

Jimmy cocked his head at her, watching her closely. He scrutinized her tired eyes and her peaked complexion. "Hmm. Might've set off something, but it's not the rain itself."

Josie twisted the apron she forgot to take off earlier, watching her hands as they created even more wrinkles in the fabric. Jimmy laid his large, calloused hand over hers and rubbed the side of her hand with his thumb. The intimacy of the gesture was intensified when he leaned in and spoke softly.

"I won't judge. I'm in no position to."

The melancholy smile he gave her nearly did her in. She

felt their shared sadness as well as the hysteria that crawled out of her stomach and up her throat, squeezing a tight path along the way. How this stranger—who knew her better than anyone else—had come into her life, she would never know. It felt like providence, but it couldn't be because she had given up on that years ago. She shook her head at the thought of both providence and ever having it in her life. Not that she would willingly admit it to anyone or dare give breath to that personal defect. Then there was Frank lurking in the back of her mind. A pit formed in her stomach as it began to churn.

"I can wait. In fact, you think on that while I make the coffee."

He patted her hand as he stood. His touch created a fire in her heart and a warmth in her belly that she'd never felt before. An odd combination of love, desire, and wanting swept over her, elevating her temperature even with the coolness of the day. Shivering, she turned to watch Jimmy make his way around her kitchen as if he'd always been a part of this house. Her heart had already welcomed Jimmy as part of it. Her mind just needed to catch up.

He seemed to sense her watching him because he spoke to her without turning around. "Go on—I'm listening. It may be easier for you to speak if I'm not looking at you. At least at first. I'll give you a minute."

True to his word, he slowed down his actions in a nearly exaggerated manner to pantomime his earnestness. He even stopped the coffee preparations to stretch his back, making Josie smile. Her hand automatically went to cover it. *Don't smile so much, it's inappropriate.* Her mother's voice cut through the happy moment, throwing her back into her own pit of conflict and worry. She looked down at her lap and back up at Jimmy who was now pouring a bit of cold water over the brewed coffee to sink the grounds. He put his hands on his hips, and he waited both her and the coffee out.

Making a tiny throat-clearing sound, she spit out what was on her mind but missed the mark. "I got to looking around the parlor. Looking at things…"

"Mmhm."

"I realized that I… I suppose I… well—"

"Go on, Josie." Jimmy reached for the mugs while keeping his face forward. "Not judging, remember?"

"Right." She blew out a breath. "Not judging." She gave a curt nod mostly to encourage herself. "I got to thinking about some different things you've said to me. About me. About the house. I— well, I… I suppose you're right. I don't really belong here."

Jimmy glanced over his shoulder at her. Josie met his gaze with owlish eyes and downturned lips. Slouched, she shrugged one shoulder in a gesture of defeat, trying hard to keep the tears at bay. It was painful to admit she had a house but no home despite how hard she had tried to keep a home. She was back at twisting her apron as if she would tear it in half, but quickly smoothing it out before she tried. Jimmy's eyes softened. He picked up the mugs and gently set them on the table. She tilted her head up to look at him and saw Jimmy was watching her intently.

Reaching out, he brushed the flyaway strands of hair away from her face with his palm. He continued to run his hand over the top her head, cupping the back of it as he leaned down, gently kissing her on her forehead, then the bridge of her nose. His mouth moved toward hers as she sucked in a shaky breath and leaned forward.

But just as their lips were about to collide, they seemed to remember the stories they had told themselves as well as each other. Pausing midair, the magic disappeared when realization hit. Sheepishly, they drew their heads back.

Clearing his throat and remembering her distress with Frank and that he was here to check on her, not add to her troubles, Jimmy released her as he sat down. Covering his embarrassment at taking advantage of the moment, he nudged Josie's coffee toward her. "Drink, it's getting cold."

Josie was flushed, and her hand was shaking. Jimmy saw a haunted look in her eyes. Her voice was even softer than before. "I'm sorry I shared that with you. That wasn't appropriate, and I shouldn't have—"

"Josie, I'm sorry." Jimmy's heart sank. This wasn't what he was going for, and he felt to blame. "That was inappropriate of me. There's no need for you to be sorry. You can tell me anything. We seem to have struck an unconventional friendship. I hope that doesn't cause any problems for you. I know your brother-in-law didn't seem to like it."

"No, he doesn't. He doesn't like me working, and he doesn't like me being unmarried either." She picked up the coffee mug and set it back down slightly to the right, adjusting it. Her eyes remained fixed on it. "He doesn't seem to like much these days, aside from Essie and their respectability."

Jimmy waited to see if she'd continue. She kept picking up the mug and setting it down in a precise manner, as if her actions were of extreme importance and somehow kept her tethered to the room.

"Beth's not married, and she's older. Why's he getting so uptight about you?"

"For starters, he doesn't like her. He's never really said what she did to deserve his treatment of her. He just started treating her mighty awful one day and hasn't let up. Also, she was engaged." That slipped out unawares. Josie flushed, dropping her voice. "Then rumors started spreading."

"What do you mean, *was*?"

"Well, her and Matthew were close, and then he suddenly left town. No one knows why."

"Did she give him reason?"

"No. He wouldn't leave her like that."

"But he did."

"Yes."

"The rumors?"

She looked up at him and shrugged one shoulder. "The usual. She's the one who was pushing marriage and not him. He left because he wasn't really in love with her. She's just looking for someone to tie down."

"Well," he cleared his throat, his ears tinged red. "She is, isn't she?"

Josie swallowed, staring at Jimmy. Beth was complicated. Even she didn't completely understand what was in Beth's heart and mind. She sorted her thoughts before she responded.

"Beth and I were close when we were little. There was a period where she wasn't very nice to me. In fact, she wasn't really very nice to others, either." One hand fell back to her lap, plucking at the apron. "But when they were courting, Beth was really nice—nicer than she was for a couple of years there—to me and everyone else." Josie looked from her apron to Jimmy.

"They really were in love. Everyone knew they were to be married and by both of their wills, not just Beth digging around for a husband. But one day he was here; the next he was gone. Vanished." Josie's voice trailed off, and she stared at nothing. "She hasn't been the same, since."

"Was he a good man?" His question brought Josie back into the room.

"Yes." She nodded enthusiastically, smiling. "Really, the best. He was nice to everyone and followed all the rules. The town was better when he was around." She tilted her head at Jimmy. "He was the deputy. Deputy Merritt. Everyone seemed to love him. Except maybe the sheriff. That's why Beth's so against the sheriff. She doesn't trust him. She thinks he's up to no good. She's convinced he ran Matthew out of town." Josie's eyes widened. "She's not the only one."

"What about you? Do you trust him?"

"Not really." Jimmy watched her until she felt obligated to add, "I don't trust Mr. Draper, either."

He nodded, digesting that bit of information. Out of the mouths of babes, really. She didn't realize how much he was able to piece together with this little bit of insight. He was happy to help her get what she was worrying about off her chest, but he also needed to make sure she was okay after their encounter on the street with Frank. That's really what had brought him here.

He watched Josie biting the inside of her cheek, wringing her apron, yet again, like someone wringing a chicken's neck, except she did it repeatedly. Squeeze, twist. Squeeze, twist. Like she was trying to kill something in her mind but acting it out with her hands. They were looking red and somewhat swollen from the repeated action.

"Josie?"

She nodded but didn't look up. She blew out a stuttered breath but still nothing.

"About the other day—is everything all right? You seemed distressed and Frank looked angry. I came by to check on you, but you weren't here … Beth was."

Josie finally stopped twisting her apron and looked up, aghast. She started to say something, but her mouth opened partway without words. She snapped it shut, redirecting her words just like she needed to redirect this conversation.

"Everything's fine. Frank is just overbearing. Likes to assert his position in the family, especially since there's been troubles between him and Beth."

Doubt was etched on Jimmy's face as he watched her. She nodded vigorously, a tell on her part.

"It's true. He's much easier to handle if you just nod and comply."

Jimmy's face went flat. "What if you don't want to do what he says?"

"Ahh …"

"Is there something else?"

"No, Jimmy. You've been real helpful, as always."

He waited, knowing she was hiding something. She tended to be skittish, so he didn't want to press his luck. That's when she hit him with the unexpected.

"Jimmy, I really do enjoy your visits. I like you, a lot."

He raised his brows, worried about what was to come.

"Perhaps you should stay away … just a little. I don't want the townspeople to talk. You've been out here a lot, and not just to pick up clothing." Jimmy looked about to protest, but she sat up straighter, cutting him off. "Not that I don't appreciate the work—or your help …"

"It's just that Frank doesn't want me around?"

"Um …"

Jimmy rolled his neck. He'd been enjoying the visits more than he'd like to admit. Gave him some purpose beyond waiting to serve up some justice with Travis or babysitting nitwits for Van Der Kamp. It also felt like coming home when he was around her. Like a frozen part of his heart had been melted by her warmth and goodness. But he wasn't here to make her life harder than it already was, that's for sure. He also had to remind himself just as much as he reminded Josie and the other townspeople that he wasn't long for this town. *Just passing through because I no longer belong anywhere*. Putting his palms on his knees, he pushed up to standing.

"Thank you for your fine company and the coffee, Josie. I'm glad to see you're all right. I don't want to cause you any extra harm, so I'll be on my way."

His tone was even, but it was tinged with sadness and regret. Regret that he had caused Josie harm. Sadness that he enjoyed her company so much and had to leave. For the best, anyway. As much as he tried to tell himself that, his heart wouldn't believe it. The squeezing sensation in his chest was calling him out on his lies.

Josie slowly rose, her eyes watery. Her lips were pressed together, and her head made the tiniest of nods. "Jimmy, I—"

"It's okay, Josie. I understand. More than you know."

Unable to stop himself, he placed his rough palm on her soft cheek. Her eyes drifted closed as she leaned into his hand. Smoothing down her hair with his other palm, he gave her a lingering, sweet kiss on her temple before leaving the kitchen. This time, Josie couldn't bring herself to follow social etiquette. She didn't show him out but remained standing where she was, tears streaming down her face.

* * *

THE ENTIRE RIDE back to base, Jimmy's mind was blank. He made it home by memory—primarily Coal's. His stomach was on fire, and sharp pains continued to plague his chest. He'd done the right thing, but the right thing felt awful. All that was shoved aside when Jimmy returned to Old Man Johnson's and saw Van Der Kamp watching Dobbin mess with the horses.

Jimmy's heart rate accelerated, and his entire body tightened. His hands went immediately into fists. He didn't want Dobbin near any of the horses, and everyone knew it. He was about to let his fury loose when Van Der Kamp chuckled and pointed at Dobbin with a cigarillo between his fingers.

Jimmy's head swiveled to see what Van Der Kamp was laughing at. Chester kept putting his head over Dobbin's head. Dobbin kept pushing the gelding's head away, and

Chester kept returning to his former position. He was about to take a fist to Chester when Van Der Kamp called out to him.

"He doesn't respect you."

"What?"

Dobbin looked flummoxed. He wasn't the sharpest tool in the shed to begin with, but his clear confusion between Van Der Kamp and Chester had him squinting and moving his mouth so his already bucked teeth jutted out, looking more the fool.

"Huh?"

Van Der Kamp didn't bother to respond. Instead, he turned toward Jimmy, who was nearly upon him. Jimmy opened his mouth, but Van Der Kamp cut him off.

"Don't worry about that fool. He won't be harming any more horses. Chester has him in hand, if the mud doesn't do him in first."

Jimmy turned to look and nearly bust a seam at the scene in front of him. Chester kept bobbing his head over Dobbin's, and it was all Dobbin could do to keep his calm. The more agitated he became, the less Chester respected him. Chester then took to nudging Dobbin on the shoulder, causing Dobbin to lose his footing. Furious, Dobbin grabbed Chester's reins and yanked hard on them. Chester snorted and pulled back but allowed Dobbin to put his foot in the stirrup and mount him. Dobbin had a smug look when he noticed Jimmy had arrived. Jimmy glowered, his eyes boring holes into Dobbin.

Van Der Kamp shook his head at Jimmy. "Just let him go. He's going to learn his lesson this time. I can smell it coming."

Jimmy raised an eyebrow but didn't naysay him as Dobbin rode off. Van Der Kamp put his boot and an elbow on the fence slats, leaning forward.

"Looks like you learned something new. Let's have it."

Jimmy incrementally widened his eyes but shared his news about Beth, Colter, and Frank. He was able to set aside the sting caused by Josie's declaration because he was caught off guard by Dobbin and Van Der Kamp. By the time they finished sharing and discussing, Chester had trotted back to the yard with Dobbin barely keeping his seat. He was pale, and his arm was twisted oddly. They ran toward Chester. Van Der Kamp held the reins while Jimmy pulled Dobbin out of the saddle. He was as limp and as pale as an overcooked noodle and groaning in pain. Van Der Kamp smirked, but Jimmy kept his face neutral.

"What fool thing did you do, Dobbin?"

"Nothing. I didn't do a thing." He wailed like a small child while Jimmy held him upright. "Damned horse tried to scrape me off on a tree."

"You shouldn't have taken Chester out. Like Van Der Kamp said, he doesn't respect you." Jimmy's eyes narrowed. "Besides, you have to start treating the horses nicer and look where you're riding."

Dobbin managed a contrite look, but his derisive snort contradicted it.

"For crying out loud." He was so disgusted with Dobbin. Dobbin looked like he was about to retort, but Jimmy waved him off.

A warning rumble came from the back of his throat. "Start learning some lessons. This could've been so much worse." Jimmy released Dobbin, leaving him to fend for himself.

Chester happily followed Jimmy without a care, swishing his tail at Dobbin in annoyance when he passed in front of him. Just before Chester entered the barn, he threw a glance back at Dobbin with a firm bob of his head and an "I told you so" snort.

CHAPTER 36

Frank Odin was perched at the saloon's bar. Terrance Draper was behind it pouring him a drink. He slid it over to Frank but didn't release the glass. Frank eyed him.

"We've waited long enough. You need to get your part done."

"I've been working on it. Beth's the problem. JoJo is easy. She likes to cooperate. It's that Beth who doesn't." He spat out *Beth* like it was a nasty taste in his mouth.

"That's because you keep antagonizing her. Then you went and spread all those awful rumors. If you had just went with my original plan—"

"No." He glared at Draper. "Essie'd never forgive me if they had to go through something like that. JoJo doesn't deserve that."

Draper lifted an eyebrow at him. "Yet here you are." He spread his hands in front of him, palms up. "You marry Essie, take all their family money, leaving Beth and JoJo to scrabble for a living. Then you decimate Beth's reputation after Colter runs her intended out of town. You've poured salt on their wounds, my friend."

Frank's eyes hardened as Draper puckered his lips, observing him. Nonchalantly curling his fingers over his palm, Draper examined his nails.

"Ever occur to you that I might've liked Beth for myself? Hmm?" He looked up at Frank's now contorted face. "She has more of a womanly figure than Essie, by far."

Frank stood up so fast the barstool toppled, skidding behind him. His fists and jaw were clenched. Reaching across the bar at Draper, he opened his mouth to speak, but was pulled back by Carter, who had just walked in. Carter continued holding him by the back of his jacket while he looked between the two of them like they were some sort of curiosity at a sideshow.

"What're we up to, fellas?"

Cheerfully, he looked at his cousin first then at Frank. Frank jerked away from him as Carter released his grip. He bent down to pick up the stool and set it down with a mighty huff.

"Ask him." He threw his arm in Draper's direction before sitting back down.

Carter cocked his head at his cousin, who shook his own. "Disagreement is all. Nothing that can't be settled by you marrying JoJo and getting your hands on that house."

A broad smile spread across Carter's face, which helped bring down the heat of the moment. Pleasure radiated from him.

"I sure wouldn't mind that. She's a pretty gal and a good cook. I wouldn't mind waking up to that every morning—not to mention going to bed with her every night, too."

Carter winked at Frank followed by Draper and Carter's guffawing. Frank remained sullen.

"Don't be talking about my sister-in-law like that. She's

an innocent who needs to be treated well." He shifted on the stool. "Besides, that house is like gold to us right now, as is the location."

"How's the weather up there on your high horse, white knight?" Draper gave Frank a smug look that had him tensing up all over again.

"Look." Frank pointed his finger at Draper. "I think your scheme is a good one. I just don't want to be hearing about JoJo like that is all. And don't you dare sully my wife's name again with that foul mouth of yours, Draper."

Draper held up his hands in surrender, but not before casting Carter a side glance.

"When are we having a wedding?"

Frank snorted, pulling himself out of his pout. "I figure shortly after the dance. The dance is usually where couples from the sister towns meet, and a lot of marriages are arranged, if not announced. If things go well—"

"You mean if Beth cooperates."

Frank ignored Draper. "If things go well, then we might be able to announce her engagement at the dance. JoJo won't cause a scene, especially if we surprise her with this news."

"Notwithstanding Carter's obvious enthusiasm for this venture, I have Watkins breathing down my back. The sooner the better. I don't want Pennington coming in here and thinking he needs a piece of our investment as well."

This was one of the few things they could all agree on, despite Frank and Carter being in the dark about Mack Pennington's true nature and stronghold on Terrance Draper. There was a round of head-nodding, and Draper poured Carter a beer as he joined Frank at the bar.

* * *

Beth was hurrying back from Old Jenny's house. It was her one selfless act, and the townspeople wondered about it. Old Jenny was Deputy Merritt's gram, and Beth still did weekly check-ins with her. They were close. So close that when Matthew disappeared, Beth tried to return Gram's wedding ring, but Jenny told her to keep it. Old Jenny knew there was more to her grandson Matthew's absence than was being told. In her bones, Jenny knew he'd come back. He wouldn't just leave Beth.

The fallout from all this was poor Beth's reputation. Jenny refused to pay heed to any of it and told others as much. Especially that busybody Mrs. Clarksen. Beth loved Jenny even more for her unwavering support—and she already loved her a lot. It was unconditional. It was also more than she received from Essie and even her own mother. Her mother's love was completely conditional. That's partly why she had turned on JoJo those couple of years—to save her own hide from her mother's never-ending wrath. The only one who hadn't suffered their mother's wrath was Essie. She could do no wrong.

Trying to shave off travel time, Beth cut behind the saloon's outhouse off the main street. It was a risky move, especially given her recently tattered reputation. She still didn't have proof for who was to blame. The only people who had come to mind were the Reinhardt women and Frank. Her money was on Frank; however, the Reinhardt women certainly had fed the fire. Just the thought of it made her want to scream, but she crept along quietly so as not to draw attention. Draper had a couple of new girls shipped in who were serving drinks, but many suspected they were serving their personal wares off duty. She couldn't be too careful.

When she heard voices coming her way, her hand touched the side of the outhouse to steady herself. Panic bubbled up, tremors coursing through her. Despite her bravado, she really didn't enjoy being the town's harridan. She froze when the two men kept talking, but neither made a move to go into the outhouse.

"Didjaw hear 'em a-talkin'?"

"Naw, they argue all the time. What's it this time?"

"Sounds like the cathouse is going to open sooner than later."

Beth flinched. She leaned forward a tiny bit, not wanting to miss any gossip.

"Yup. Out at the ol' Snyder place—"

Beth's gasp was audible. She slapped her hand across her mouth, clamping down hard.

"Didjaw hear that?"

"Naw, ye ole coot. Tell more. These new drink girls are teases. And I'm tired of riding clear over to Adamsville to get me sum."

She could hear chuckling and one man slapping the other on the back.

"Yup. That's 'bout right. Draper's cousin's gonna marry that quiet Snyder girl, and they'll turn the house 'round for business." Belching loudly, he pounded his chest. "Think I best head on home. Had 'nuff."

"'Kay."

The remaining man went into the outhouse. As soon as the door shut, Beth hightailed it over to the only person who would help her combat prostitution and wielded a strange sort of power—Mrs. Clarksen. She rolled her eyes heavenward. God help her.

* * *

BETH WAS HUFFING and puffing by the time she reached the Clarksens' house. Bent over with her hands on her knees, she gulped in as much air as her lungs would allow, and it still felt like they were on fire, and she was going to die. Her dress was sticking to her back, sweaty with panic and exertion. Hunched over as she was, she had a sudden attack of empathy for JoJo and all the walking she had made her do. When Beth was finally able to breathe somewhat normally, she smoothed out her skirt and patted her hair. Adjusting her posture and dabbing her damp hairline, she marched herself to the front door and banged on it in the polite yet demanding way that only Beth would do.

A lamp was lit in the front room, and she could hear light, clicking footsteps make their way to the front door. The curtains swished as Mrs. Clarksen peered out to see who was coming so close to the supper hour. Fortunately for Beth, Mrs. Clarksen was alone. She threw open the door with her standard hysteria.

"Beth! Is Josephine all right?" Mrs. Clarksen looked past Beth and around her, for what, Beth had no idea.

Biting down on her retort of "I'm fine, thank you for asking," as it wouldn't earn her any points and would only slow her down, Beth swallowed hard.

"I—Mrs. Clarksen, I really need to talk to you. May I come in?"

Mrs. Clarksen looked taken aback, as they'd had an especially contentious relationship ever since Deputy Merritt had disappeared, and had been hit and miss even before that. Mrs. Clarksen had naturally blamed it on Beth, choosing to believe the rumors, especially since she was a supporter of "poor Josephine." The irony that she didn't do much to mitigate Josephine's suffering despite her lip service was entirely lost on Mrs. Clarksen—but not on Beth. In fact, her husband, the self-righteous reverend, had a lot to do with her inaction. Mrs. Clarksen's hand flew to her chest, but she quickly recovered her manners with a less-than-dainty huff. She stepped away from the portal with a slight tilt of her head so Beth could enter.

Mrs. Clarksen was quick to close the door behind her and wasted no time interrogating Beth.

"You haven't gotten into some trouble, have you?" Self-righteously, she jutted her chin up.

"Oh, no, Mrs. Clarksen. I overheard something, and it's very important. I need help."

"Well, I can't help you with your male problems …"

Beth flushed. "I don't have male problems, Mrs. Clarksen," she hissed before regulating her tone. "This is more about JoJo and our house."

"Beth, I'm not understanding you. You aren't making any sense."

"Please." Desperation edged in. "May we sit down so I can explain?"

Mrs. Clarksen's arm swept toward the living room. Beth entered and waited for Mrs. Clarksen to seat herself first. She had no idea how to begin, especially since she hated the idea of needing Mrs. Clarksen's help. So, when she sat down, she folded her hands in her lap, staring at them without immediately speaking despite her earlier urgency. Her head was bowed as Mrs. Clarksen observed her with a kind of morbid curiosity.

"Go on, child. Daylight's a burnin'."

Beth sighed. "I didn't know who to go to."

Mrs. Clarksen's lips thinned, and she pointed her nose upward. It wasn't a good look.

Beth's tone became urgent. "It's just that I know you'll support me on this. I overheard that they're trying to bring a cathouse to our town."

Mrs. Clarksen's eyes went comically wide, and she nearly shrieked, "What?" Her hands gripped the arm rests as if she was trying to keep herself from flying out of the chair.

"I was leaving Old Jenny's. I wanted to get home quickly, so I cut behind the saloon's outhouse—"

"Harrumph." Mrs. Clarksen glared at her. She began to open her mouth, but Beth cut her off.

"I had to get home. Frank's been badgering JoJo to get married, but he's also been on her to move in with him and Essie."

She held up her hand to stop the interruption. Mrs. Clarksen looked indignant but didn't say anything.

"He threatens her. He threatens to take away the house. He uses her love for me against her."

Mrs. Clarksen gave her the gimlet eye. Beth ignored the piercing look.

"Mrs. Clarksen, please. I really am begging you. This is serious." Beth gulped air. "I wouldn't have come otherwise."

Mrs. Clarksen's eyes softened but remained watchful for signs of lies. "Just who did you hear talking? It's a place where drinking occurs. It could've been wishful thinking by lustful men, Elizabeth."

Beth sighed. She hadn't been called *Elizabeth* for years.

"Don't you go sighing at me either. These are serious accusations. What would you have me do about it? And what do Frank and Josephine have to do with a"—Mrs. Clarksen fanned herself—"house such as that?" She whispered the last part as if her sensibilities couldn't handle the very words coming from her own lips.

Beth was too panicked about the prospect of being home-less to be annoyed with Mrs. Clarksen's sensibilities as she normally would. Beth's hands worried her skirt, just like Jo was prone to do, surprising her. She released the fabric and smoothed her skirt.

"I think that Frank has some sort of plan to take the house away from us and marry JoJo off. If he does that, our house would become the—" She changed her verbiage because of Mrs. Clarksen's stricken look. "The—place."

"This doesn't make any sense. Why would he do that?"

"I can only tell you what I heard. I heard the men talking about 'them' arguing. That 'the quiet Snyder girl' was getting married soon, and that the Snyder home would become *the place*." She whispered the last part.

Mrs. Clarksen covered her mouth, eyes watering. Her head continued to move from side to side. Whether she was telling Beth no or she was in disbelief about the whole story was unclear. These two had a history.

Finally, Beth asked her, "What are we going to do? We can't let this happen." Her voice had a remarkable upward tick.

Mrs. Clarksen finally gathered her wits, sitting up straighter. "There's nothing we can do right now. We'll have to keep our eyes and ears open. Have you talked to Josephine? Is she aware of this?"

Beth shook her head. "I just found out. Besides, Jo is hiding something from me. I think she's trying to protect everyone. I'm sure it has something to do with Frank. She also has a healthy dislike of Mr. Draper. She's voiced it more than once, even though she tries to not speak ill of anyone. So, I wouldn't doubt that this rumor is true.

"Protect everyone?"

"Me, she's always trying to protect me."

Mrs. Clarksen gave her a pickled look, flapping the back of her hand in Beth's direction. Her words came out sharp.

"And look how you repay her."

Beth's expression wilted, and her eyes welled up. She chose to ignore the biting remark and stay on task.

"I'm sure she likes Jimmy Stapleton and is afraid to admit it. He certainly likes her and won't say anything. Frank doesn't like any of it. I heard that around town."

"You seem to be doing a lot of eavesdropping of late." Mrs. Clarksen mulled that over. "I'll let the Jimmy Stapleton comment rest for the moment." She tapped her finger on her lips before sighing. "I suppose if Frank is really trying to marry her off, he'd do something at the dance. We should keep an eye out for Josephine and her would-be suitor."

Beth nodded.

The softer, thinking expression dropped, and Mrs. Clarksen's features returned to their sharp edges. She pointed her finger at Beth, shaking it. "You best not be playing me for a fool, young lady. Or be fibbing."

Beth slumped in her chair. "No, ma'am. I wouldn't do that." She shook her head. "I may do things to rattle your cage, but I'd never lie about something as important as this." She swallowed hard, her voice tight. "That house is real important to JoJo."

Shaking that sadness off, her lips moved to one side as she resisted making the next comment while simultaneously feeling compelled to. "Despite all my poking, I have yet to lie to you." She nodded, standing up, surprising Mrs. Clarksen.

For a moment she sat there looking sullen, and she watched Beth and rolled the question around in her mind that she had wondered about for several years. Using a soft voice she hadn't used for quite some time, she went ahead and asked.

"Beth, whatever happened to the sweet girl from a few years ago?" She cocked her head. "You changed and became bitter. What did I ever do to you?"

Stunned, Beth remained immobile. No one had ever truly confronted her about her behavior. Well, Jimmy had, but that was different. He was looking out for Jo. Mrs. Clarksen was wondering what she had done to deserve such nasty treatment. It was humbling as well as humiliating. Those were a painful pair of years she'd like to forget.

Despite the memories, her face relaxed because for the first time in a long while she wasn't preparing to do a battle of wits with Mrs. Clarksen. Neither was she waiting for the personal jabs and attacks to come. She was contrite, but guilt made her stomach sour.

"I promise I'll tell you, but it'll have to wait for another time. JoJo's more important right now."

Beth gave a rueful smile, and Mrs. Clarksen's eyes watered. She pulled out her handkerchief, dabbing at the corners of her eyes. She put her hand on Beth's arm with a gentle touch and a pat.

"I'm going to hold you to that, now. I really do want to know, my dear." She sniffed. "I really do."

They shared a brief smile and a temporary truce until they could figure out what was happening to their JoJo and this town.

* * *

BETH MADE it home in time for dinner. She scurried up the stairs to wash up before she was caught. It was for naught, as JoJo wasn't paying her any mind. Jo's mind was swimming with all sorts of dreadful possibilities. She was sure she had heard Frank correctly and didn't know what to do about it. She wasn't going to marry Carter, and she wasn't going to move closer to Frank and Essie. While Carter seemed nice and very interested in her, she still couldn't figure out why. Frank must've promised him something in return for pawning off the "undesirable" Snyder sister.

She really needed to talk to Beth to find out what had happened between her and Frank. She was worried that if Frank got his way, Beth would be left out on the street. Carter had to be of the same mind as Frank; otherwise, there'd be no reason for them to associate. He didn't seem to be bringing a lot of money with him and didn't have a trade Frank could profit from. She knew nothing about this mystery man who coincidentally happened upon poor Lars's funeral.

She shook her head. JoJo still couldn't get over that. The old curmudgeon was one of the few people who had been unconditionally nice to her. Besides, she had liked him on his own merits. He had stood his ground without being mean.

Melancholy and nostalgia washed over her. She was longing for the days when life was simpler, and she wasn't trying to hold a family together—especially one who fought her every step of the way. Of course, there was the alternative where she was always wrong and was forced to hear the endless lists of her personal faults. That wasn't fun, either. *False nostalgia. Ha.* She was sure Jimmy would have something to say about that. Hearing Beth's footsteps, she turned to look at her.

"Are you all right? You look a little peaked." JoJo frowned at Beth's complexion. She really didn't look well. "Is Old Jenny ill? Is she doing okay?"

Beth started to shake as she lowered herself into a chair. JoJo rushed over, placing her hand on her forehead.

"You feel a little clammy. Are you sure you're well? Do you need to go have a lie down?"

"No, Jo. Thanks." Beth croaked.

"Honestly, Beth. You're giving me a little fright."

"I was going to ask if you were doing all right. You seem a little washed out yourself."

Beth didn't use any heat with her words, which made them feel more like concern and less like an insult. Jo sat next to Beth and held her hand. They were both lost in thought for a few moments before they simultaneously tried to speak.

"I was—"

"Jo—"

Laughing, Beth said, "Go ahead."

JoJo searched Beth's face. "Do you think Essie might be expecting?"

Beth's eyes widened. "Well, that's out of nowhere. It's possible, but you know I've not been able to speak with Essie because of Frank."

"Mmm." Jo struggled to pick a line to follow. She decided on the one more directly related to Beth. "About that. What happened between you and Frank?"

Beth stiffened and pulled her hand back. "Why do you ask?"

"Frank's up to something." Josephine searched Beth's eyes. "I'm worried for you. For me."

Beth rounded her lips and blew out a long breath. "I think he had something to do with Matthew's disappearance. Frank started treating me differently after that." She paused, looking surprised. "Come to think of it, it started the day he disappeared. Frank was watching me and acting strange. It wasn't normal for him to want to be around me, but that day, he kept up with excuses of Essie 'needing' this or that. He wasn't nice about it either. Not that he was exactly wonderful to either of us while he was still here. Why?"

Josephine visibly swallowed, and the color drained from her face. She whispered, "You know Carter, right?" Beth nodded. "Frank wants me to marry him."

Beth swayed in the chair until Josephine reached out to steady her. "Did he say that?"

Jo nodded, her lips trembling. "It doesn't look good. What do we even know about him? I'm going along with Frank right now to keep the peace, but what will you do if he forces me to? Where will you live?"

"I—" Beth shook her head, steeling herself. "We'll have to cross that bridge later, JoJo. But I don't want you to marry because Frank says so. I want you to marry because you want to. Don't give in to him, and not just because of me."

Beth was gripping JoJo's hand and giving it little shakes. JoJo finally covered Beth's hand with her other hand, patting it and making shushing sounds. Beth was becoming overly worked up about her news, which was surprising. Beth had been so focused on getting married herself that Josephine didn't think ...

"Beth," Josephine spoke barely above a whisper, as she was unsure how her words were going to be received. "I know you still love him. That's okay, you know?" She gave a rueful smile. "He wouldn't have just left you. The people who are important know this. You don't—"

The bubbling pot on the stove interrupted them. Josephine jumped up to tend to it, and Beth sat there worrying her lip. This was becoming much more real by the minute.

CHAPTER 37

Gus and his cronies had ridden into town for some supplies with the express rule to avoid the saloon at all costs. It was a final test, of sorts. Jimmy was surprised they were back so quickly and turned to look over his shoulder at them, pitchfork in mid-jab. The smirks on their faces spelled trouble, so Jimmy stood up and stretched his back. They dismounted when they got closer and began speaking overly loudly.

"Saw pretty Jo-sa-phine on the boardwalk this morning." Gus called to Ned.

Ned picked up from there. "Mm-hm." He shook his head with the syllables, his scar shimmering silver in the sunlight. "She was lookin' real fine. Wasn't she, Cy?"

"Well, I was more noticing that she wasn't alone. She had some fella on her arm. He was looking mighty pleased with himself, I might add. Like a struttin' rooster ruling the hen house." Cy nodded, running his fingers down his mustache before turning his head in Jimmy's direction.

Jimmy's nostril's flared, and his eyes darkened. He clutched the handle of the pitchfork to keep from yanking the men away from their mounts. His knuckles whitened, and his jaw flexed, but he didn't say anything. He continued to watch them smirking, collectively looking like the cat that had swallowed the canary as they dismounted. He was familiar with the look, as they had used it on him before his big growth spurt when they had pushed him around and roughed him up.

Gus sauntered over to Jimmy, shifting his girth. "Ah, Jimmy. Did ya catch some feelings while you were 'protecting' her?" Snickering, he nudged Ned who also had moved closer.

"Do I detect love?" He clasped his meaty hands and batted his bloodshot eyes as he leaned forward in a mockingly feminine manner.

Jimmy blinked before scoffing. He turned back to the hay, pitching it over his shoulder onto Gus and Ned. Instead of getting angry, like usual, they started making kissy noises until he whirled around with his pitchfork at the ready.

"Knock it off, already."

His grip tightened even more, much to their delight. They knew he wasn't going to hit them. He was trying too hard to control himself. Laughter ensued. Cy pointed his finger at Jimmy.

"Looks like the monk is venturing from his monastery." He slapped his knee. "Guess it just took a sweet piece of calico to do it—too highbrow for the soiled doves we make do with."

Cy straightened, broadening his shoulders and pursing his lips, mimicking a high-brow gentleman, twitching mustache and all.

Gus added salt to Jimmy's wound. "Hope you don't mind sharing. Your Josie was lookin' mighty cozy with her new man."

Jimmy threw down the pitchfork and left the area.

Breathing heavily, he was resisting the powerful urge to pummel them. The control he exerted over his anger caused them to laugh even more. Jimmy couldn't even see straight by the time he reached the house. Blind fury was guiding him.

Jimmy slammed the door and stomped up the stairs. With his size, his footfall sounded like a herd just moments before a stampede. Add to that the banging around Jimmy did while washing up and changing clothes. *Damn that Frank. Damn him.* Mind made up, Jimmy was going to see Josie. It was irrational, and he knew better than to be goaded by Gus, Ned, or Cy, especially after Josie had told him to stay away. At least Harry had learned his lesson in town and was keeping a low profile, especially since he hadn't been chosen to ride out. Harry was pouting like a child, but at least he was behaving. Jimmy huffed. One less person to keep track of, even though he was failing at keeping track of himself. The door's slamming was proof of that.

* * *

On Jimmy's way through town, Harold waylaid him. He happened to be sweeping in front of his shop when he flagged Jimmy down. It was a frenetic waving disguised as a greeting. One he couldn't ignore. Dismounting, Jimmy tipped his hat.

"Morning Harold. Everything okay?"

"Jimmy!" His voice was tight and ringing of false cheerfulness. Perhaps something he'd use with the Reinhardt women when he couldn't be outright rude with them. "Come inside, Jimmy. I have that package you were waiting for." He jerked his head back toward the store as if Jimmy might refuse him.

Jimmy nodded, casually looking around before following.

Once inside, Harold got straight to the point. "I saw JoJo this morning. She wasn't looking too pleased."

Jimmy blew out a breath of selfish relief chased by concern. His brow furrowed, but before he could collect his thoughts, Harold went on.

"She was with Terrance Draper's cousin, Carter Bass. He had her on his arm and was looking like the cat that had eaten the canary. She looked like the canary that was facing down the cat, if you know what I mean. Tense and nervous. She smiled and was friendly, but it wasn't our JoJo who was with him, if'n you know what I mean."

"I was just going to check on her. I heard she was in town with someone—wanted to make sure she was okay."

"I'm glad someone's able to go out there and see her." Blowing out a breath, the tension in his face and shoulders relaxed. A cheeky smile spread in its wake. "It's okay to admit yer sweet on her." Jimmy's ears turned red when Harold winked at him, laughing. "Go on—you looked like you were on a mission when I saw you. Just wanted to make sure you knew. Now that I know where you were headed, it all makes sense."

"I—"

"You're remarkably in tune with our JoJo, or you're just really good at keeping watch." Harold's expression turned thoughtful as he nodded his head. "I'm thinking it's both."

Jimmy stood there not knowing what to say. Harold gave him a little nudge.

"Well, go on. You better get out there and see for yourself. Keep me posted. Frank's really been keeping an eye on her as well. Gave me what for the other day for trying to help her out. Frank?" He shook his head. "Well, I do not trust him. Does right by Essie but not the other girls."

Jimmy nodded and turned for the door. He looked back over his shoulder with his hand on the latch. "Thanks,

Harold. I'm glad she has some good friends in town to watch over her."

With that, he was out the door and back in the saddle quicker than Harold could blink.

* * *

JOSIE WAS in the kitchen brewing some coffee when she heard a knock on the door. Carter held up his hand for her to stay.

"Don't worry, I'll get it."

"I don't think—"

"No one should be dropping by this far out, JoJo."

Josie gritted her teeth. The insufferable man had made himself at home. They'd had two dinners together with Frank and Essie—one forced and the other by happenstance—and then he'd attached himself to her in town this morning, escorting her back home. Completely unnecessary and most definitely Frank's doing. Now, he was making himself at home without care to propriety. She was sure Frank was trying to ruin her reputation, so she'd be forced to marry Carter.

Boots clomped heavily on the wood floors, and a flushed but stone-faced Jimmy stood in the doorway.

"Jimmy—" Josie's smile dropped when Carter came in behind him.

"Hello, Josie. How're you doing?" Jimmy had his hat in his hand and was searching her face for any clues. He was also memorizing it because something about this cozy situation felt final. His gut churned at the thought of being replaced. He thought he knew Josie, but maybe he didn't. Good things get ruined, just like everything else.

"You can see she's doing fine. Now, you really should

leave. Frank wouldn't like to hear of some strange man in his sister's house."

"Sister-in-law."

"Splitting hairs, mister."

"And why would he be fine with you here?"

"I'm courting JoJo." He smiled brightly, looking over at a stricken Josephine. "With Frank's approval."

"Do you have Josie's approval?"

Josie was shaking her head furiously, alarm on her face. The men ignored her.

"I have Frank's, and that's enough for now. The rest will come."

Carter went to reach for Jimmy's elbow to usher him out, but Jimmy shook him off. Jimmy turned toward Josephine, clinging to what was.

"I was wondering if you had time to finish my extra shirt."

Josie nodded, her face brightening and voice cheerful as she said, "I'll go fetch it. Excuse me."

She scurried out of the kitchen, happy to be away from a room filled with men and the tension they brought. Alone, Jimmy took up a lot of space, but Carter wasn't a small man either. As soon as Josie was out of earshot, Carter casually turned and faced Jimmy. Leaning against the counter, he crossed his arms.

"I didn't realize what a prize I was offered. Too bad for you, cowboy."

"Don't fool yourself. You haven't won anything, yet."

They had edged toward each other, their bodies leaning forward so their faces were inches apart. This is what Josie came back to, stopping her in her tracks. She clutched the folded shirt in front of her chest as if that would protect her. Jimmy was the first to step away, but only to calm Josie. He shot a look at Carter saying as much.

"Thank you, Josie. I appreciate your hard work. This will

come in handy. I was needing some extra clothes." He reached into his pocket to pay her, but she stilled his hand.

"Please, let's settle this later."

She smiled to soften the blow, and Jimmy couldn't help but return her sweet smile. She kept her hand on his arm as Jimmy leaned toward her, their magnetic pull an easy thing between them. Carter stiffened, clearing his throat, looking like he felt it, too. He threw his arm in the direction of the front door.

"I'll see you out now. Looks like your business is done."

Jimmy's eyes found Josie's. She nodded and gave a small reassuring smile. He nodded before turning to leave.

At the door, Carter's demeanor changed. Sneering at Jimmy, he dared poke him in the chest. Fortunately for Carter, Jimmy's calm had shifted back into place.

"Don't come by anymore. JoJo has me to watch over her. She will no longer be taking in sewing either, so don't ask."

Jimmy's face was unreadable, but inside he was churning.

"Don't think I won't be watching you. Best take good care of her."

Jimmy had broadened his chest and stood taller in a manner that even the more hardened took note of. He was like a stone wall when he did that. Carter huffed weakly at him.

Jimmy turned on his heel and headed to Coal, who stamped his hoof impatiently while snorting. And just because the horse was feeling extra ornery, he bared his teeth for good measure.

CHAPTER 38

The last interaction at Josie's didn't sit well with Jimmy. He was trying to let the dust settle, which was already more difficult than he had expected, but the townspeople kept coming to him about rumors of Josie and Carter. Apparently, Frank had been hard at work talking up his "suspicions" of those two. Increasingly apparent was the town's growing dislike of Frank Odin's airs and his association with Terrance Draper. Even Mrs. Clarksen had approached Jimmy about both those points, as well as concern for her JoJo.

Keeping his anger in check and using the guise of collecting the pants Josie had made, he rode at a brisk pace out of town. He'd purposefully not asked about them on the last visit, and Josie was smart enough to not mention them. Their conversation was brief but to the point, confirming what he had heard in town.

"Please, Jimmy, don't." Josie placed her palm on his cheek. "You don't need to do this. I'll be fine."

Jimmy's jaw flexed. "I do. This is a slight that can't go unpunished. No one messes with you. They were warned and chose not to listen. They don't get a second chance. People who need second chances walk all over others. This ends now." Jimmy jabbed his finger toward the ground as he said *now*. Jimmy headed toward Coal as Josie scurried after him talking to his back.

"They're just rumors spread by a lonely Mrs. Clarksen. Even if Frank was telling the blacksmith something about Carter and me, I'm sure he's doing it for some other selfish reason of his own. We don't know what his true plans are, Jimmy. Jimmy!"

Jimmy reached Coal as Josie grabbed his arm. Her pleading look almost did him in. "Just don't use the business end of your Colt, okay?"

"Where did you hear that?" Jimmy's agitation burst into flames.

"Wha-what?"

"That phrase." Jimmy voice went low as he leaned toward Josie.

"I ..."

Jimmy straightened, crossing his arms over his chest, willing her to speak.

"The other day."

He quirked his eyebrow at her, telling her she wasn't finished explaining.

"I went to take a cake to Essie ..." Her voice dropped lower. "And I overheard Frank talking to someone—not Essie, someone else. A man."

"Who?"

"I don't know. I couldn't hear his voice, and I knocked on the door, hard, so I wouldn't see him if I just walked in."

"Why, Josie?"

"Well ... ah—because."

She nodded as if that made it better, then startled when she realized Jimmy was still scowling.

Sighing, she added, "Frank's up to something, and I don't want to find out." She whispered that last part.

"Why's that?"

"Because if I know something, I'll have to tell Essie, and she won't hear me. Then I'll worry. If I worry, I'll pester Essie—Frank'll eventually find out. If he finds out—"

She stopped when he blew out a breath like a mad bull. Her eyes widened before she let the final words slowly fall from her mouth.

"Then he'll know that I know." She cleared her throat, and he nodded. "Then he'll try to force me to do something I don't want to do."

"What would that be?"

"Marry Carter."

"I thought he was saying that to get my goat."

Swirling feelings of hurt, anger, and protectiveness waged war inside Jimmy. Heart and fists clenched, his face went red, and the veins on his temples throbbed. His nostrils flared as his body tried to get more air into his system and back to his brain because his fists were trying to take over. Jimmy was ready to beat sense into someone and everyone. Particularly Frank. Carter immediately afterward.

"I'm going to—"

"Jimmy, no! If you say or do something, then they'll know. I'm not talking about the rumors, either. They'll either think you have something to do with it or realize that I know."

"What, exactly, is it that you know?"

For the first time ever, Jimmy moved into Josie's space in an invasive way. Instead of making her heart flutter, his proximity created an erratic tattoo that had her feeling slightly panicky and on the verge of unsafe, even though she felt in her bones that he'd never, ever hurt her. Ever.

She was fearful about sharing the painful truth. That truth made her feel unsafe. Josie's voice came out strangled.

Her throat constricted from fear, having never spoken the words aloud before.

"I think that Frank is somehow involved with Terrance Draper."

She nearly winced saying the man's name. She'd always felt there was something a little off in that man but could never tell anyone why.

Jimmy released a breath, edging away from her border of discomfort, giving her space where she could relax despite having shared one of her many fears. Wringing her apron, she watched Jimmy process a series of thoughts. She could practically hear the wheels turning, he was thinking so hard and fast.

"You think or you know?" Jimmy dipped his head forward, locking eyes with her.

"I—well, uh—"

"I knew it. That son of a gun." He slapped his hat on his thigh while shaking his head. "I need to go, Josie."

"Wait! What're you going to do?"

He let out a hissing sigh. "I have to talk to Van Der Kamp. He needs to know." Josie looked ready to object. Jimmy held up his hand. "Don't you worry. I won't do anything. Yet."

"Jim—"

He stopped her with a kiss. When she sighed into his mouth, he grabbed the back of her head pulling her closer to him, deepening the kiss. Just as suddenly as the kiss started, he released her.

Josie was too stunned—first by the kiss then by the intensity of it. Her hand went to her mouth. She stood still with flushed cheeks until Coal snorted, bringing her back to reality.

Shocked by her revelations and then Jimmy's kiss, all she could do was watch him ride away.

Fit to be tied, Jimmy drove Coal hard. It wasn't just sense

he wanted to beat into Carter; it was a show of possession. For whatever reason, Josie was his. He didn't understand these feelings at all. Neither did he understand the loss of his self-control and calm demeanor. Those characteristics flew the coop with his arrival in this darned town.

* * *

TRAVIS AND JIMMY sat across from Van Der Kamp in his dark office. The curtains were drawn, the lamp low. Jimmy was fidgeting, and Van Der Kamp cast him a dark look.

"You're like an overgrown four-year-old. What's got into you?"

Jimmy stilled, looking between the two men before squirming again.

"Sit still!" Van Der Kamp barked.

Jimmy sat up and did what he was told. It didn't help that these chairs weren't made for a man his size, but he refrained as much as he could. His mind, however, was still tripping over itself.

"For God's sake, Jimmy. I can practically hear your mind churning from here." Travis leaned back in his chair.

"That lamp's smoking. Can we open the window a crack?"

"No!" Both Van Der Kamp and Travis had had enough of Jimmy's restlessness.

Ignoring their annoyance with him, Jimmy launched into some of what he'd gathered.

"Something's going on between Frank Odin and Terrance Draper. Josie nearly walked in on their conversation. Did we find out anything from the scouts?"

Van Der Kamp's eyes narrowed. "What would that be?"

"She said she's not sure and is afraid to find out. I'm sure she's aware of Frank and Draper working together. Heard men's voices behind closed doors. Frank has her on a short lead. Takes pleasure in bossing her even though he doesn't help them. She's afraid he'll find out she heard him talking, so we'll have to be careful about how we handle him."

"He'll immediately blame her?"

"More like take it out on her. Some of the townspeople have seen him get angry with her out in public when he thinks no one is looking. He certainly doesn't want her working—heard that from the horse's ass himself and Carter." Jimmy whined Carter's name like an annoyed teenager and continued the tone. "He's made himself at home with Josie."

Crossing his arms, Jimmy leaned back in the chair as much as he could. The chair creaked in protest when Jimmy leaned back at an awkward angle.

Travis and Van Der Kamp exchanged glances.

"Thom told us that Carter Bass is Draper's cousin. We're still not clear where he comes from. Seems his arrival coincides with Lars's funeral." Travis looked at Van Der Kamp.

"Yup. Jaems watched him ride in the day prior. Said he seemed familiar with the town. Thought he had either lived here and was returning or visited previously. Hard to say. Rode directly to the saloon. Buford was already inside. Watched him walk straight into Draper's office. He didn't mingle or acknowledge anyone. They both thought his behavior was odd. Seems he was expected."

Van Der Kamp eased back in his chair, watching Jimmy work his jaw. Van Der Kamp's elbow went to the armrest, and he raised his fist to rest over his mouth. His eyes darted to Travis, who just shrugged. They waited Jimmy out.

"What do the two of them have to do with each other?" Jimmy huffed. "Draper isn't necessarily well-liked in town. He's the so-called outsider, the bossy Easterner. Frank wants to be the man of the town. Josie says respectability is very important to him. That's allegedly why he has such a problem with Beth, but he's the one who's caused that problem to begin with."

"You mean Beth's 'loose' ways?"

Jimmy looked surprised that Travis was already aware of that. *The town must hate her, and I'm not sure she deserves all that.* Jimmy recognized her bravado after their odd talk, which earned Beth some of his hard-won respect. *She puts up a good front.*

"I heard it from a Mrs. Clarksen. She managed to wrangle an introduction out of the shopkeeper at the mercantile when I stopped in for some supplies." Travis's lips twitched with a humorous expression. "She has the pulse on everything around here. Not much gets past her."

"Except the fact that her husband is a liar and a cheat?" Jimmy frowned.

"What did the riders bring back about the reverend?" Travis asked.

For some reason, Van Der Kamp and Travis found Jimmy's distaste for preachers funny. Jimmy did not. He threw them a squinty, annoyed look even though they were unaware of his history with preachers.

Van Der Kamp updated them. "Buford and Jaems returned from Adamsville. Yes, there's a cathouse there that Clarksen visits." They nodded, and Van Der Kamp leaned forward, piquing their interest. "Seems whores aren't his only problem." He looked from one to the other. "He has a family over there, too."

The clock continued to tick, resonating in the silence that filled the room. Jimmy broke it.

"How's that even possible?"

Their heads swiveled toward Jimmy.

"Really? Do we have to explain how families are made?" Travis's face was filled with mirth despite the news.

"You know what I mean. Do they know about Mrs. Clarksen? *Our* Mrs. Clarksen?"

Travis stifled a chuckle. "Bet it killed you to say that." Jimmy responded with only a glare.

Van Der Kamp smiled, but his tone turned serious. "Thing is, he's not the Reverend David Clarksen. He's the Reverend Daniel Cooke. Mmhmm."

"Holy smokes. He's craftier than I gave him credit for." Jimmy's eyes widened.

"What else does he have going on over there? Or here for that matter?" Travis asked.

"He's barely been in town since we've been here. He returned for Lars's funeral and turned around the same day, back to Adamsville. To say Mrs. Clarksen wasn't pleased is an understatement. I saw her after the funeral having a discussion with her"—Jimmy cleared his throat, his face looking sour—"so-called husband. Didn't think much of him then. I feel downright hostile about him, now."

"Apparently, the other wife, Mrs. Cooke, is a mousey woman. She doesn't stand up to anyone, especially her husband. Whether or not she believes him no one really knows. She doesn't talk to anyone and rarely goes out. She's a young, timid thing. He's straddled her with a couple of young children, baby included. I'm sure he doesn't really care." Jimmy tensed, but Van Der Kamp kept talking. "It's Mrs. Clarksen that's the harder sell. Not sure how he's gotten past her."

"I don't think she wants to believe ill of him." Jimmy made a sucking sound through his teeth. "Despite her meddling, she means well."

"I'm surprised you're standing up for her, Jimmy."

Jimmy chuckled. "Me, too. She's really not bad, just irritating. I can't shake the stink that the men in this town are a bunch of dogs, aside from a couple of very good exceptions.

The women 'round here have the short end of the stick." He grunted thinking about Harold's mention of Mrs. Reinhardt. "And sometimes, they feel that end as well." Jimmy's lips turned downward, and his eyes took on a faraway look.

Travis could see Jimmy drinking from the cup of melancholy, so he redirected.

"What else do we have on Clarksen? Is he really a reverend?"

Van Der Kamp double jabbed the air at Travis with his fore and middle fingers pressed together. "Good call, Marshal. He's not."

Travis whistled. "Maybe that's why Mrs. Clarksen chooses to ignore his behavior. Her father was a pastor. She's very proud of it—told me all about it."

Jimmy's jaw looked like it was about to break from clenching his teeth so hard.

"Hold your horses, Jimmy. Let's get a plan of attack together." Van Der Kamp gave him a slow "sit down" motion with his hand. Jimmy grimaced.

"Anything else?" Travis hadn't met Reverend Clarksen but already had a type in mind. He wanted confirmation.

"Like a dog with a bone, Trav."

Travis chuckled.

"Draper's the one who figured out his double life. He hired Clarksen to run between towns with messages and do some of his dirty work long-distance. He holds his double life over him, threatening to share the news with Mrs. Clarksen, then the town. Heard that from Buford. He was in a dark corner when Draper was badmouthing Clarksen to Carter after Carter asked where he was."

"Gotcha. That fits his profile. He's kind of a snake oil salesman, with the Lord, so to speak."

"Funny thing is no one particularly believes him anyway. Draper doesn't have one on the town like he thinks. They're smarter than that. You should've heard tell of his pathetic sermon at Lars's funeral." Van Der Kamp rolled his eyes.

"It's true!" Jimmy flashed a look at him and raised his voice. "Add that to the fact he could barely wait to leave town. There was a poor woman been waiting for a christening, and he left her high and dry again. Could've left that afternoon or early the next morning. But no. She looked crushed, and her husband was fit to be tied. Clarksen made some weak excuse about another deathbed he had to go to."

"I think it's been the same deathbed for the past month."

Van Der Kamp smirked, and Jimmy's eyes narrowed. Travis watched the exchange. It was like a father teasing his son.

"Well, now what do we do?" Jimmy asked.

"About Clarksen? Not much we can do right now. He hasn't done anything to us personally." Van Der Kamp pointed his finger at Jimmy. "We've got other things to deal with first." Jimmy gritted his teeth.

"Well, I have news."

Travis was reluctant to bring this up because of Jimmy's current state, but it needed to be taken care of and corresponded with what Josie had told Jimmy.

"I was in the saloon yesterday afternoon. Our friends Draper, Frank, and Carter were in there having a little chat about your friend Josephine."

Jimmy tensed up, nearly lifting himself out of his seat. Travis shook his head at him. "I'll continue only if you settle yourself. Otherwise, leave, and I share without you."

Glaring at Travis, Jimmy paused but finally gave a curt nod while lowering himself back into his uncomfortable seat. Travis waited a beat to make sure Jimmy was good on his word.

"Apparently, Carter is supposed to be marrying Josephine so he can gain control of their house." Jimmy's hands curled over the armrests. "After he marries her, the three of them are going to turn her home into a cathouse."

Jimmy's breathing was audible, a jagged rushing in and out.

"When's this alleged wedding supposed to take place, and does Miss Josie know about it?" Van Der Kamp asked.

Jimmy cut off Travis before he could respond. "She's smart. She suspects. Frank's been on her about getting married, and Carter's been sniffing around her skirts for a bit. In fact, he's the one Frank introduced Josie to at the funeral. I just didn't know who he was until later."

Travis nodded. "There was talk of surprising her at the dance this weekend. Carter seems eager to wed Jose—" Travis gave Jimmy the side-eye to make sure he continued behaving because Jimmy looked ready to bolt. "—phine and people from the neighboring towns are coming to celebrate and intermingle. It'll be a real organizational nightmare. Hard to keep track of people."

"You mean Watkins? Already taken care of. Don't worry about him. May want to watch out for some of his lackeys. They're a bunch of amateurs."

Travis opened his mouth to comment, but Van Der Kamp cut him off and continued. "Don't ask. Won't tell you anyway." Travis furrowed his brow. "Need to know, remember?" Van Der Kamp grinned. "Need to know. And you don't need to know."

Van Der Kamp just repeated what the gang always said about him and communication. Some of them didn't think he knew, but he did. He was very aware of what went on around him.

Van Der Kamp scrunched up half his face pulling in more air through one nostril. "Jimmy, you go to the dance and be with Josie."

"Can't. Carter's laid claim on her, and she's essentially

sent me away because of Frank. I'll protect from a distance. She doesn't want Frank to know that we know."

"When has that ever stopped you?" He quirked an eyebrow at him.

"I need to stay away from her. I'm just causing her more trouble than she already has. She doesn't need more."

"You went back, didn't you? I believe twice, after you were told to stay away. Besides, like you said, she has plenty, and you're going to help her with it. I'm pretty sure she's counting on you to help, anyway. You made a promise, or did you forget?" Van Der Kamp was needling him.

Travis joined in. "And you keep your promises."

They both smiled broadly, which made Jimmy finally crawl incrementally out of his sulk. He knew he'd been had.

"Fine."

CHAPTER 39

$\mathcal{D}$oc pushed his glasses farther up on his nose. He stood in front of the window, shaking his head as he watched the stranger leave. He's odd, and his story didn't pass muster. *Despite the swelling and the gangrene setting in, his injury looked like a dog bite. A very large dog. It's difficult to tell the difference between a dog and wolf bite. However, a lone wolf wouldn't attack a human, and a pack would kill him outright.* Doc shook his head. "That man didn't use the smarts God gave him. No matter what, he wouldn't stand a chance."

The man's friend was holding the horse's reins while he mounted. He was still watching out the window when it came to him: *Dog bite. Dante.* He drummed his fingers on the windowsill until he made his decision. Heaving a heavy sigh, he whispered, "Lars, we're getting you justice."

He had to tell Douglas Elliot but wanted to run this by Arthur Patterson first. He needed to make sure they were thinking similar thoughts about the evidence and the sheriff before he went stepping on all sorts of toes. Sheriff Colter was beginning to wear out his welcome, especially since he botched Lars's case so badly.

* * *

IT WAS an odd grouping of men—Jimmy, Van Der Kamp, Travis, Doc, and Mr. Patterson. Mr. Patterson had convinced Doc they should tell Jimmy first because Douglas would immediately hunt down those yahoos, and Jimmy had shown reason when finding Lars. In terms of practicality, Jimmy had the needed backup since they knew Sheriff Colter wouldn't provide any. They were standing in a semicircle near the corral. It was the only private place at the moment. The gang tended to steer clear of the area anyway because they feared this new version of Jimmy might put them to work.

Van Der Kamp pulled in a long inhale, scrunching up half his face before knuckling his hat back. His eyes shifted toward Jimmy who, nodded back at him. Jimmy was the lead for this.

"Who was the man?"

"Didn't recognize him. He came to me in a lot of pain, but the pain wasn't what was making him stupid." Doc shook his head. "He was born that way."

"Was he alone?"

"No. Another man was holding their horses like he was the getaway. Nondescript. Regular cowboy. Average height."

"Can you describe the patient?"

"He was scrawny and dingy. His hair might've been blond, but he was a mite dirty, so it's hard to tell. Lanky, ungroomed mustache." He shook his finger. "Now that one was shifty. Very impatient for me to give him something for the pain and to patch him up 'like new.'"

Jimmy's face went taut, and words ground out of his clenched teeth. "Those were the men from the livery."

"The horse beaters?" Travis rubbed his knuckles against his jaw. "Not surprising."

Doc and Mr. Patterson quickly glanced at each other then back toward Jimmy.

"Gentlemen, I think we have a problem." Mr. Patterson looked stricken, pulling at his collar, hand trembling. "They're part of George Watkins' gang. They've been milling around here for a few weeks now. I can't speak to who arrived first—your …" He cleared his throat. "You or them." Removing his handkerchief from his pocket, he dabbed his brow.

Van Der Kamp nodded. "We're not here to do harm. Never the plan."

Mr. Patterson sighed in relief then eyed Doc.

Doc spoke up. "We have no reason to trust or mistrust you fellahs. But here's the thing—you've done right by Elliot here, and that means a lot. Lars, too. He was a good man. Didn't deserve what happened to him. But as sure as the air I breathe, I'm convinced Draper had something to do with Lars's murder."

Van Der Kamp raised his eyebrow at Doc. Doc held up his hand.

"Now hear me out, if'n you will. Lars has been dead or at least missing longer than you all've been in town. Draper's been here the entire time."

A round of nodding from solemn faces encouraged Doc to go on.

"Lars took issue with Draper. Didn't trust him as far as he could throw him. Do you know why he came here in the first place?" He glanced around the group. "Sure wasn't to run a saloon. He just found that to be more profitable. He came here because some big bug sent him to secure mining interests and to speculate. Only he was not on the up-and-up. Made a few folks mad, including Elliot."

Travis shifted. "Sounds about right. Wouldn't happen to know who that big bug would be, would you?"

"Nope. Elliot might, though. Lars did. Made it his business to find out what Draper was up to. I'm thinking that's what got him killed. I'm sure he had something on Draper and was planning on telling Elliot, only Elliot was out of town. Who else would want Lars dead?" Narrowing his eyes, Doc jabbed his pointer finger upward. "No one. That's who. Not even Reinhardt. He's a loner and likes it that way. He also didn't have any money to speak of—"

Mr. Patterson cleared his throat loudly. "Well, about that …"

* * *

THUNDERING hooves in the distance stopped Douglas Elliot mid mending. He stood up, tipping his hat back to get a better look. Watching the five riders heading in their direction, he handed the wire to the ranch hand helping him before wiping his brow. He blew out a long breath as he waited for them to arrive.

Jimmy rode point and slowed Coal early enough to mitigate the dust as they stopped. Raising a hand in greeting, he gave a half-smile when Elliot returned it. He slid off Coal easily, extending his hand.

"Afternoon." Jimmy nodded to the ranch hand, who was now standing behind Douglas before he looked back at Elliot. "Mind if we have a moment? Learned some things that you'll want to know about."

Without turning around, Elliot called over his shoulder. "Joe, ride on out with Buck to the next section. Keep mending until you're either done with the pasture or I catch up to you. Whichever comes first." Elliot's lips pressed tight, and his eyes glinted.

"Sure thing, boss."

The men watched Joe gather the supplies and him and Buck ride well out of earshot before Elliot nodded to them.

Doc spoke up first. "Elliot, I think we've found your man. Came in with an injury he was trying to pass of as a wolf bite. Gangrene is setting in because the fool didn't take proper care of it right away. His story doesn't add up. He'd be worse off if something wild had attacked him."

Elliot's face was impassive, his body still. All eyes were on him because they weren't sure what he was going to do.

"Who is he?"

"One of Watkins's gang, but I'm pretty sure Draper hired him before Watkins arrived. You know all the trouble Draper's been stirring up." Elliot exhaled slowly. "Lars was on to him. He had something he wanted to talk to you about but didn't get a chance. Couldn't talk to Colter because of the Reinhardt incident."

Doc tilted his head toward Patterson.

"He's right. Lars came to see me about a will—"

Elliot leaned forward, but Patterson impatiently brushed the air with his hand before continuing. "I'll get to that in a minute. It's also very important." He smoothed his hands down the front of his jacket to the hem, tugging it twice before continuing.

"Lars knew that Draper was trying to secure a bank loan, and he came to warn me. Draper was salting mines, among other things. He didn't want me to fall for something and told me he'd update me after he talked to you. That's about the time he disappeared—although I didn't know he had disappeared until you found him. I'd grown accustomed to not seeing Lars very often."

A muscle in Elliot's cheek twitched. "What's the other thing I need to know?"

Mr. Patterson cleared his throat then looked around. He shifted his feet and tugged at his jacket again. "Understand that I'm telling you this because of Lars. Normally I'd have to be more discreet. I can't—"

"Spit it out!" Elliot barked. "I'm getting a little twitchy here. I'm also feeling a spate of justice coming on, so if you don't want me rounding up my ranch hands and finding these folk on my own, you better get talking"—he huffed, jabbing his fists onto his hips—"quick like."

"Okay, well …"

Elliot raised his brows at Patterson, who spit the next bit out. "Lars left everything to Josephine Snyder. He also created a special account for her before she was born."

Mr. Patterson's normally meticulous moustache was drooping on the left side, and the wind was trying its best to move it. Everyone stood rooted in stunned silence, and after taking a deep breath, he began to get this story completely out.

"I'm going to speak plainly as the involved parties are deceased, notwithstanding our JoJo. Lars Nielson and Lena Kraus are JoJo's natural parents, not Maria and Georg Snyder."

The wind picked up, fluttering their clothing and making the horses blow and snort behind them. No one's mouth seemed to be working. Only the quiet whistle of the wind blew between them. Mr. Patterson looked directly at Elliot.

"Don't you remember when Lars was courting Lena, but Maria wouldn't have any of it? She said Lars was beneath them socially."

"Vaguely. Hmm. That's about the time Lars stopped going to town or being friendly." Shaking his head, Elliot ran a hand down his face. "I'll be damned."

"Well, Maria wanted Lena's portion of the family money she was set to inherit, as their parents had passed shortly after their arrival out West. She didn't want Lena to get married because she wouldn't be able to get her hands on it, but Lena was already enceinte."

"No one knew." Elliot's voice was small and tight.

Doc interjected. "Maria made sure of it. Wanted to make the baby look like it was hers. Forced Lena to stay in the house to 'convalesce,' telling everyone Lena was ill. Shortly after, Maria went into 'confinement.' I delivered JoJo but returned to care for Lena because she took a turn for the worse after delivery. I got on Maria for not taking care of Lena. Lena's the one who told me their story—she knew she was dying and wanted someone to know."

"What'd she tell you?" Travis asked.

"Georg began courting overtures with Lena back East, but Maria was jealous because it was always a competition with her. Maria cried to their parents about the unfairness and 'impropriety' of the younger sister's accepting suitors before the elder was married, demanding Georg be allowed to court her, not Lena. Their parents, being very traditional German immigrants, did just that—no one was getting married unless it was Maria. Then they forced Lena to go with them to help Maria when Georg wanted to lay stakes out West."

Doc reflected for a moment. "Personally, I don't think Maria ever forgave Lena for having Georg's attentions first, and Georg was too weak and swayed by the Kraus's influence and money to care which daughter he got."

Travis brought the conversation back to the important person, Josephine. "So, what you're saying is Josephine is a very rich woman thanks to Lars and Lena?"

"That's what I'm saying, but I can't tell her because Frank has been in the bank so many times trying to get that house from her and Elizabeth. Who knows what he'll do when he finds out she has money of her own. He's been harassing that poor girl something fierce, and she always caves when it comes to family."

Doc gave Jimmy a knowing look, tilting his head in his direction. "Although she's been much braver and bolder since a certain young man has come to her aid."

Jimmy had been clenching his fists during the conversation, but Doc's expression had Jimmy starting for the horses. "I'm going to talk to Frank."

Travis gripped Jimmy's arm and pulled at him.

"No. You will not." Tossing Jimmy's arm away, Travis jabbed his finger at him. "There's a time and a place for everything. We have even bigger issues now and some still-missing pieces. If you go running roughshod, you'll ruin any progress we've made here. We need to get as many of these thieves as we can and do it by the book."

Van Der Kamp rolled his eyes. "Travis, let it rest. He's staying put, if he knows what's good for him and his woman."

"Not my woman." Jimmy nearly shouted.

Doc and Mr. Patterson recoiled at Jimmy's vehemence. He crossed his arms.

"She pushed me away."

"And why was that?" Van Der Kamp's voice rose with sarcasm.

"Because of Frank." Jimmy quietly answered, cowed for the first time since they came to this town.

"Exactly." He jabbed his finger at Jimmy. "That's why we need to be more methodical, as Travis so kindly reminded us."

Van Der Kamp snorted when Travis shot him a dirty look.

CHAPTER 40

The shops and businesses were bustling with activity, everyone too busy to notice the two scrubby men at the end of the street huddled behind their horses. One cradled an injured arm as the other leaned forward, emphatically shaking his finger at him. Their voices were low and harsh.

"Look, Jack, I've told you. We need to leave. Watkins ain't right. He's not taking care of Draper; he's focused on that Van Der Kamp. Let's just collect for the rustling from Reinhardt and hit the trail. Besides, we don't need Watkins finding out we did any side jobs. We can hook up with Thompson's gang—cut our losses. They're just over in Adamsville."

"Are you nuts? Watkins has been promising us the big payday. We've put up with that drunk and Neil for far too long just to quit. Besides, I didn't get bit by no mangy dog for nothin'. We wouldn't be in this stupid town if'n it weren't for him and his obsession with Van Der Kamp."

Jack shook his head. "You and Jones can rustle a few more beef while we're waiting and then cash out. Reinhardt won't stand for funny business, and he pays. I'm not leaving until we get all that's owed us. From everyone. Then we can leave Watkins before he's the wiser."

Jack's hair and shirt clung to him. He had worked himself into a fury, his dirty, droopy mustache flapping along with his anger and rivulets of sweat running down his body.

Jones looked at Jack's arm. Just like Jack, it was angry. It was red and swollen and beginning to putrefy. Jack was smelling as bad as he looked. He was sweating and swaying on his feet.

"I have a really bad feeling about this, Jack. Really bad."

* * *

DOBBIN RODE over to the Rocking W, the Reinhardt spread. His arm was in a sling, and he could barely manage his mount. Still fuming about having been made fun of as well as having been bested by a horse, he was going to get his payout before Van Der Kamp or Jimmy did something he wouldn't like. He knew he'd been testing Jimmy with the horse issues but hadn't realized how much Van Der Kamp was on to him. That he hadn't gotten to ride out on the last recon rubbed him the wrong way. Figured he better get while the gettin' was still good. He was determined to collect all he could.

The sun was lowering, and it was about suppertime, the perfect time to catch Reinhardt and not have to ride all over to find him. Besides, Dobbin's arm was hurting something fierce. Spotting him standing with a ranch hand, Dobbin shifted in the saddle and made his way toward him. Reinhardt scowled when he spotted the rider.

"What the hell you doing here?"

"I came for my payment."

"What payment?"

Reinhard glowered, and his hands dropped to his belt

buckle. Talking to the hand he was with, Reinhardt tossed his head in the direction of the big house. "Go on and get some chow. I'll be along shortly. This won't take long." Narrowing his eyes at Dobbin, Reinhardt asked, "Will it?"

"I don't suppose so."

The hand looked between Reinhardt and Dobbin before saying, "Yes, sir," and walking away. No one worried about Reinhardt holding his own. A brute, he was mean and as wily as a snake. Clumsy and awkward Dobbin had his arm in a sling and an unsteady seat. He didn't belong on a ranch or even on his own. There was no comparing the two men.

"What do you think you're doing, showing up here in front of my hands telling me things like that?"

"I—"

"And what, exactly, do you think you're getting paid for anyway? You didn't finish with the Taylor herd. Barely scratched the surface." Reinhardt moved into Dobbin's space, causing him to shift in the saddle. Docile Millicent stood her ground.

"I thought I could get paid for what I've done and—"

"That wasn't the deal. You get paid when all the head have been moved to the Mountain View Valley."

"But you told us to only move a few beef at a time—that could take weeks!"

"What's changed between then and now?" Reinhardt's brows raised. He walked the handful of steps toward the barn and reached around the door for his rifle. "I don't want this traced back to me. That hasn't changed."

"The other men aren't doing what they're supposed to—Jack, Jones, and Gordon. Gordon says he's waiting on Jack and Jones, but I haven't heard from them." Dobbin's tone took on a grating whine.

"That's your problem." Animosity rolled off Reinhardt like rain out of storm clouds.

"It's your problem if I don't get paid." Dobbin's face flushed more with irritation and bluster than anything else. His words lost their bite with his shifting mount and Reinhardt retracing his steps.

"Turn around and ride on back where you came from." He pointed a finger at Dobbin. "Figure this out, or you don't get paid. All the beef or nothing—for any of you jackasses."

He cocked the hammer back, but kept his shotgun lowered.

Dobbin awkwardly turned Millicent around. Chester be damned because Millicent minded. It took so long for him to regain his seat from the simple maneuver and get her pointed in the right direction that his bravado and stupidity kicked up a notch. He put Millicent at a slow trot but shot off his mouth without thinking.

"If you don't pay me, I might have to let someone know what you've been up to." He shouted over his shoulder.

"Poor choice," Reinhardt growled. His patience was gone.

Dobbin never saw it coming.

Reinhardt raised the shotgun and took aim. Millicent shifted into a sudden hurry with her newly dead weight.

CHAPTER 41

oJo slid the final pies into the oven while Beth wiped the counter. When JoJo turned around, their eyes met.

She rubbed the back of her neck, brow furrowed. "I hate to say it."

"Then don't." Frowning, Beth watched JoJo's expression. "But I'm surprised, too."

"Carter—"

"We don't know what Frank's doing or what's he's told Carter. Let's just be happy that Carter's not here to boss you around in Frank's stead. I didn't like finding that nasty surprise when I came home last time."

JoJo shook her head. "Carter didn't make it easy for any of us, especially Jimmy. I'm worried about tonight. I just don't like not doing anything …"

"Don't fret. We need to act like we don't suspect anything." Beth squeezed JoJo's arm before leaving the kitchen.

Josephine gripped her apron. *That's the problem. I know too much, and it makes me worry even more.* Her hand went to her stomach. It was churning sour as well as firing up a burning urge to fix things. Her hands smoothed her apron before she twisted it with vigor as her mind ran rampant with thoughts of Jimmy.

What they had was a strange dance of deep connection mixed with resistance and outright avoidance. She realized that no matter what happened, she was inextricably bound to Jimmy and he to her. There was a companionability that made it feel like they'd known each other much longer than they had. She couldn't deny that he made her feel safe and loved even while she barely knew him.

Despite sending Jimmy away more than once, he still returned and rode around her property to make sure everything was in order; he just didn't go to her door or try to talk to her. If he noticed any outdoor chores that needed to be done, he'd quickly do them and leave. No more fighting with Beth about helping her. No more insisting she keep safe. No more listening to her or just being a companionable presence during her day.

Josephine rubbed her aching chest as a more recent memory popped into her head. She was watching Jimmy pretend not to see her at the window, following him with her eyes, unable to stop the tears from rolling down her face. The pain in her chest was palpable, one that she couldn't smooth away. She'd finally found something she treasured, that was just hers apart from the family, yet ruined by family. Even if it was just a friendship, Jimmy had somehow chosen her and made her feel special. Contrary to her own desires, she pushed him away to keep peace and everyone safe. What wasn't safe was her heart and her happiness. She had finally found those things only to have them taken away and broken.

Shaking off the racing thoughts and bracing herself, Josephine went to get ready for the dance before tending to the last of the pies.

Closer to suppertime, Beth and JoJo packed up a meal for themselves and the refreshments for the dance then loaded the wagon. Jo had spent extra time taming her hair and pressing her dress in hopes of seeing Jimmy but worrying it would encourage Carter. She ran her hands down her skirt while Beth read her heart.

"Don't worry, you look pretty. Jimmy'll notice, and so will the other men. Try to ignore Carter as best you can and stick to the serving table. It won't look like you're being defiant, because you always work the table." Josephine was cautiously watching, waiting for the rude remark that usually followed. Her least favorite was, "You might as well do all the chores because you'll have to do them yourself when you're all alone and unmarried."

Beth sensed her discomfort. She put a hand on Josephine's arm and smiled warmly. "It's going to be okay. I promise. Mrs. Clarksen will be there, and she won't let anyone bother you, unless you want them to."

Beth winked at her while taking the basket from her hands and placing it in the wagon. Josephine didn't know whether to be shocked or to laugh, as Beth was being a little outrageous with her.

* * *

The Carlson spread turned into an impressive sight with the arrival of a steady stream of wagons and horses coming in either direction from Adamsville and Weaver during the late afternoon. Some people had set up camp just outside town while others rode in directly closer to the supper hour. The dance was scheduled to begin shortly thereafter, so the little ones could have some fun romping around the open field.

Even after sunset, the evening's natural light provided varying levels of illumination for a few more hours. The women had set up tables for light refreshments, and the men were distributing lanterns and bringing in some extra chairs for the elders so they could sit and watch. The dance was a big to-do held at the Carlson's winter barn, being a midway point to the three towns and easily cleared, as it was just prior to fall harvest. It held quite a few people and had plenty of space for overflow. Families came to see old friends, while others hoped to find a mate for either themselves or their children. Differences were set aside, and everyone relaxed. Excitement and anticipation were in the air, as were laughter and squeals of joy from the children.

Josephine felt the excitement and the anticipation thrumming through her, too—she was hoping to see Jimmy, and that made her skin flush and her heart beat extra fast. Despite what she had told him, she still wanted him around. But there was also a foreboding dread and fear. Impropriety had passed. This fear was something deeper and more frightening than being a social outcast. She felt shaky, and her stomach was still churning and burning like hellfire. Frank would be there watching her—and Carter with him. Ironically, no one commented when Jimmy helped her or stood up for her, but everyone took notice with Carter. She wasn't sure how she felt about that or what it all meant.

Josephine's insides were a quivering mess, and her hands slightly tremored, but she continued to set out her pies and arrange the table with jars of cut flowers. Anything to keep her hands busy.

The fiddlers started their set with a lively tune, garnering a responding cheer. Initially, Josephine startled, clapping her hand to her chest, but that quickly morphed into a bright smile and laughter. People scrambled to find their partners or were quick to grab the hand of someone nearby. Others rushed in from outside. She swayed to the music and hummed along, at ease. Then she saw Jimmy.

He looked from left to right before turning his head in her direction at the far end of the barn. The corners of his mouth started to lift in a small, secret smile as he propelled himself toward Josie. His legs ate up the distance, and her heart ratcheted up, but two pairs of hands reached out, grabbing him from either side. Josephine frowned. The Reinhardt women.

As quickly as her heart had raced, it iced over. Josephine sullenly watched the women fawning over Jimmy, inappropriately touching his arms and reaching toward his face and even his chest as he tried to dodge their caresses. Josephine's blood boiled, and her face flushed when Nora had the audacity to throw her a coy side smirk, tilting her head and laughing right at her as she did it. The pair of women managed to steer Jimmy in the opposite direction as they walked toward Nora's brother and Lillian's father, Frederick Reinhardt.

Frederick's appearance jolted Josephine out of her misery soup. He hadn't been around in ages, and she wondered at his presence. A horribly angry and nasty man, he despised most people in town as well as social events. Rooted, she watched the four of them standing together, the women talking as Jimmy and Frederick stood immobile. Despite the men's lack of engagement, watching was still painful and self-flagellating. Josephine thought to look away but couldn't help herself. Her eyes remained glued to the foursome.

Her frown grew deeper with each look Nora and Lillian cast in her direction. Lillian was especially clingy, practically hanging on Jimmy's arm even as her father glared at her. They made him look like a stud bull presented at auction—

buyers trying to get Frederick's approval for this "purchase" or for Jimmy's services. As soon as she felt the onset of tears prickling at the back of her eyes, she turned away. It was more than JoJo could take. She didn't need to publicly cry on top of it all. With fortunate timing, Mrs. Clarksen sidled up to her.

She wrapped a motherly arm around Josie's shoulder and gave her a firm shake, bussing her on the cheek. Josephine turned so they were face to face. She blinked with curiosity. Mrs. Clarksen wasn't usually this demonstrative or gentle. At least she hadn't been for a good decade. Josephine had often wondered at that.

"It's all right my dear. Those harridans will get their comeuppance one day. What comes around goes around. It always does." She brushed a strand of hair from Josie's face. "Fortune's wheel spins round, and when you reach the top, you must inevitably fall to the bottom. It may feel like you're at the bottom right now, but I can most assuredly tell you that's not a place someone like you stays." She tapped Josephine's nose with her finger. "This, too, shall pass."

Releasing her grip on Josephine, she went about straightening everyone else's hard work before scurrying off to intervene in a discussion between, oddly enough, Martha and Mary. Mrs. Clarksen's busybody nature made her smile today instead of gritting her teeth or feeling pitiful because she had managed to kindly point out some flaw or other that Josephine had. When Martha and Mary solicited Lettie Clarksen's help, their faces carried an element of relief as well as wide-eyed enthusiasm for their own points of view. Josephine giggled to herself as she watched it play out.

"You should do that more often."

A chill ran down Josie's spine before she whirled around to confirm who the speaker was.

Draper stood there examining her face for a long

moment before his roving eyes ran up and down her body. He always made her feel dirty and her skin crawl. Shuddering, she wrapped her arms around herself. The half-smile on his face was more of self-pleasure than one of humor or warmth. He raised his brows before speaking.

"I can see why Carter has taken such a shine to you. You really are a pretty gal. But you're so quiet, and your sisters are always front and center. I've never taken the time to really review your charms."

Josephine's horrified gasp didn't prevent him from reaching out, grabbing a strand of her hair, and twirling it between his fingertips. She was about to say something when she saw Carter coming up behind Draper. Her fear of Mr. Draper made her extraordinarily happy to see Carter, as much as she hated to admit it. In fact, her face lit up with joy, and she gave him a wide smile of relief and pleasure. Unfortunately for Carter, her pleasure was in knowing he wouldn't take kindly to his cousin manhandling her and that she'd soon be free of Mr. Draper.

To Carter's credit, he really did take pleasure in Josephine. He responded with an even brighter smile of his own.

"JoJo!"

Draper didn't release her hair. In fact, he began taunting Carter with it, raising it as if he were planning on smelling the lock. Carter's face went dark, and a muscle at the side of his face ticked. He growled his words in a low tone and nudged Draper aside.

"Let her go. Don't be touching my woman, Terrance."

Draper released her hair and said, "See?" He tilted his head toward Carter but addressed Josephine. "He really has taken a shine to you. Even more so than I realized. I like that. Very healthy for a new relationship." Turning toward Carter, he added, "I'll let you at it. You'll be wanting to make the rounds with your announcement. Wouldn't want any other man to get any ideas, especially since that's the purpose of this dance. Isn't it?" His voice rose at the end in a falsely teasing manner.

He started to walk away but took only two steps before he turned around with mock innocence.

"Carter? I'm so glad our mothers made us share everything. It'll make this new arrangement so much more fun, won't it?"

His laughter trailed him as he walked away with long, carefree strides, looking about him as if he were the belle of the ball. Carter was throwing darts from his eyes at Draper's back while gripping Josephine's arm as if she'd disappear if he didn't. Josephine patted his arm with her free hand to gain his attention.

"Carter?" She patted again. "Carter." Sharper that time. She shook his arm slightly. "Carter, whatever does Mr. Draper mean?"

That managed to shift Carter's intensity, his face softening as he searched her eyes. He put his hand to her cheek before answering. Too shaken by Draper's odd behavior, she didn't flinch. Her eyes remained locked with his.

"Don't pay him no never mind. He's full of crazy notions and childhood nonsense."

Josephine stared, not understanding. Carter was debating about how honest to be with her. Draper could be dangerous when he wanted something, and his tastes ran toward the unusual. He seemed to have found Josephine suddenly interesting. Carter wondered if it was just because he had her, and Draper usually wanted what he had, or that Draper was just now starting to pay attention to her on his own. Josephine always strove not to call attention to herself.

"Ah, he tends to want what I have. It's a bad habit of his."

Although his voice was cheerful, his words left Josephine

feeling anything but cheery. Another chill ran down her spine. She already mistrusted Draper, and she had issues with Frank's arrangement with Carter, whatever that was exactly. She felt it entailed more than just marriage, but she was resistant to finding out. The devil-you-know sort of thing.

Carter grabbed a cup of punch from the table they were standing in front of and handed it to Josephine.

"Here you go. You work too hard. Let's enjoy this evening, shall we?"

Hesitating, Josephine looked from the cup to Carter's face, unsure of what she should do. She could see Carter didn't intend for her to work the tables, and right now her and Beth's plan was already veering wildly off track. A sense of foreboding crawled across her skin, creating gooseflesh. Her plan certainly didn't include an encounter with creepy Mr. Draper either. She was at a loss as to what to do.

Turned out it didn't matter. The decision was made for her. Carter was already dragging her off to parade around. He wanted everyone to know JoJo was with him. He preened with her on his arm, standing taller and beaming with pride, whereas Josephine wanted to hide. While Draper created an icy fear in her, she knew Carter's tender kindness and male pride was leading to someplace no less scary—just a different version of it.

* * *

JIMMY FINALLY MANAGED to extricate his limbs from the Reinhardt women while not being rude in front of Frederick Reinhardt, a cold man devoid of emotion. Nora and Lillian were trying hard to sell him on Jimmy's horsemanship, strength, and good looks, and Frederick wasn't biting. He kept looking around the room instead of paying attention to the people he was with. He'd nod at the appropriate moments, but the interaction lacked attention and connection. Reinhardt finally grunted, acknowledging someone across the room whom Jimmy hadn't seen before. The scruffy, shorter man had peered around cautiously before catching Reinhardt's eye.

"Excuse me. My man has brought me a message. Something might be going on at the ranch, Stapleton."

Reinhardt nodded at Jimmy but did not say a word to his sister or daughter. Jimmy was about to make his own excuses when he heard a voice behind him.

"Hello, Jimmy. Care to dance?"

Jimmy spun around. Beth smiled sweetly, a nice alternative to her contrived smile or her bitter one. The corner of his lip went up as his brow raised. He had a humored expression belying the situation at hand.

"Why I—"

Lillian shrieked and grabbed Jimmy's arm. "He's with me, Beth." She tried to yank him close to her, but he was immovable. "Go peddle your used goods with someone else."

"Tsk, tsk, Lil. Wasn't it you who got Jeb knocked out by your daddy? Leading him on like that. You ran out of men to flirt with, so you had to sashay over to the Double Star to find someone new. At least I was engaged."

Lillian's face twisted in rage, looking like she was ready to spit nails. Nora put a hand on her arm to steady her and addressed Beth.

"Well, at least no one has disappeared on Lillian like Deputy Merritt did with you." She straightened and put a tight smile on her face. "Shameful that you're trying so hard to pin some man down in marriage. You drove the poor deputy away. And him liking his job and all."

Beth was stone-faced, but Jimmy could tell it cost her. He'd been there. He'd bet dollars that her stomach was churning, and guilt, helplessness, and rampant self-doubt were running amok in there. He took her hand, placing it on his forearm, pulling her closer. Frowning at the Reinhardts, he walked Beth away.

"Thanks for coming to my rescue, Beth. You're my hero."

They smiled brightly at besting the Reinhardt women together and were patting themselves on the back as they managed their escape. The tension lightened, and leaving that pair wordless was the icing on the cake—it never tasted so good.

Jimmy calmly led Beth to the dance floor even though a lively tune was playing. They were able to slip in, find their footing, and talk without missing a beat. They did a couple rotations before Beth remarked, "For such a big man, you sure dance well. Where'd you learn?"

Jimmy's lips pressed together as they did a twirl. He grumbled before answering. "Dance lessons as a boy."

Frowning, he misstepped before getting back into the rhythm. To avoid giving her a fuller explanation when she looked like she was about to ask another question, he deflected, asking her one of his own.

"How'd you know I needed help?"

"Ugh. Those women. They've made it their life's mission to make our family's life miserable, which usually means me and JoJo. Everyone else they just make miserable by being who they are—nasty shrews."

Jimmy laughed. "Well, I really do appreciate your help."

They circled around a few times before he continued. "I had the oddest encounter with Lillian's father."

"Yeah, I'd steer clear of him if I were you. He's bad news. If you think the Reinhardt women are trouble, well, Frederick is a completely different trouble than them. He's frightening." Beth's eyes showed worry. "Wouldn't want to be left alone with him. Not sure what he'd do, but just being near him feels dangerous."

Jimmy nodded, remembering his earlier conversation with Harold at the mercantile. "I can see that. He certainly wasn't very nice to his sister or daughter. I found that odd. They were trying their darnedest to get his attention while throwing me into the arena. He was preoccupied with something."

"Mmm. I'm sure they were selling you to him. He's also trying to marry Lil off. Seems to be going around."

Jimmy's face shifted from contemplative to sad. The thought of being married off made him think of Josie, and just as he did, they danced past her. Josie managed to look up at the same time Jimmy looked over. Their gazes locked only a moment, but it was just enough time for Carter to notice. He pulled Josie closer and placed a gentle kiss on her cheek. Carter smirked at Jimmy when he flinched. As quickly as they whirled by each other, they had whirled away.

"Look away. He's just baiting you. He thinks he's won. JoJo doesn't want him, and you know it. Now quit that. You're just giving him fuel for the fire."

Jimmy looked down at Beth like she'd grown another head. "What's got into you? Suddenly you're siding with me?" Beth flushed. "Or am I just the lesser of two evils?" Her face held open shock, rendering her speechless. He laughed bitterly. "That's it, isn't it?"

He looked up to the ceiling but kept dancing until the end of the song. When it ended, he led her off the dance floor.

"Thank you, Beth, for saving me." He turned to walk away, but Beth touched his shoulder.

"Wait."

After he slowly turned around, Beth saw the wounded little boy who was tormented by the preacher, berated by his father, and pitied by others standing in front of her. The sensitive boy who was too kind, too gentle, and not "man" enough. Jimmy was feeling duped and more than a little angry about it.

"What, Beth? I'm not understanding your game."

Beth looked around. "No game. I need to talk to you—privately."

"Forgive me if I don't."

Beth's whisper was strained. "Frank is headed this way. I must talk to you about JoJo. Very. Important."

She was gritting her teeth, and a sheen sprouted across her forehead. The closer Frank got, the wilder and more pleading her eyes became. They were both aware Frank would try to send them packing and publicly humiliate them.

Jimmy saw Beth glancing at Frank and relented, but only because he knew Frank's type and how horrible he could be. Give the man a small amount of power or authority, and he'd manage to derail the train just because he could. Jimmy held out his arm for Beth, and they headed for the barn doors at a leisurely pace because Frank was still watching. But as soon as they were outside, Beth guided him deftly through the crowd, picking up their pace. Once they were around the corner, she kicked up her heels, hightailing it to the tree line despite the possibility of there being lovers out there. They could manage better there, and most likely, the lovers wouldn't care what they were talking about anyway. Jimmy looked around warily before following.

"Beth, what are we doing out here? You shouldn't be out here alone with me."

"Not important right now. Besides, you heard the Reinhardt women. My reputation is in tatters already."

"Hurry up, then. Let's not create more problems for you. Lord knows you don't need any more."

"Honestly, Jimmy. You sure know how to hit where it hurts."

"You know I didn't mean it like that. You've got a lot going on, and you don't need me adding to it. Now spill. We don't have much time. Besides, I don't want Josie thinking about how I'm out here doing things with you that I won't do with her."

"What do you mean by that? Don't you like her?"

"Of course I like her. Why are you yelling at me?"

"I'm not yelling at you, I'm whispering."

"It's not whispering if everyone can clearly hear what you're saying."

Beth went rigid and put her hands on her hips. She raised a finger to begin scolding him, but he grabbed it.

"Talk. We don't have much time. Frank's been watching you and Josie like a hawk."

"He's going to marry your Josie off to Carter, and she doesn't want to marry him. I also overheard that he wants to turn our house into—"

"Shh." His voice gentled. "I know."

Beth was taken aback. "But—"

"Your town is full of dirty little secrets. Buford happened on that one the other day in the saloon."

"Who's—never mind. Who are you, anyway?" She leaned back, scrutinizing him.

"It doesn't matter. Just know that I don't like bullies or people who get away with doing terrible things. It's too much to explain right now. I promised that I'd watch over Josie, and I will keep that promise even though she keeps trying to run me away. Trust me on this. We don't want to attract Frank or anyone else's suspicion. We have to go back and act natural."

Beth nodded, and Jimmy took a moment to really look at her in the moonlight. While there was a family resemblance between Beth and Josie, they didn't look like sisters. Not really. He had noticed it before but hadn't paid much attention. Beth's behavior had always been his focus. Initially, she'd been incredibly angry, nasty, and ugly before shifting to oddly accommodating. He hadn't noticed anything else.

Their beauty was of a different quality. Beth was fair in more of an icy, Nordic sort of way. Josie was fair in an earthier, warmer way. And she was lithe, spry, and strong like a forest fairy with delicate features and coloring that shifted with the sunlight. Whereas Beth was robust and curvy, a woman built for long winters—the stereotypical build for childbearing and lusty men's gazes.

Curiosity got the better of Jimmy.

"I don't know if it's the moonlight or what, but if I didn't know you and Josie, I'd think you were cousins, not sisters."

Beth tensed, pressing her lips together tightly. It was an unusual response to an offhand observation. He noticed she had paled, and looked somewhat ill, too.

"JoJo got that a lot growing up. People were pretty mean about it, and Mother didn't do anything to lessen the cruelty. Sometimes, she joined in and laughed along. Jo's real sensitive about that." She swallowed hard, lowering her voice even more. "I wouldn't say anything to her about that, you know?"

Jimmy nodded. Being the black sheep of his own family, he knew cruelty all too well.

"Go back first. But don't go straight in. Zig zag and mingle outside for a while. I'll wait about ten minutes before I return. I'm going to go directly to Josie and say hello."

Beth opened her mouth to object, but he countered her.

"Just to check in. Nothing more. Whatever happens, there'll be a good reason."

Beth's nostrils flared, but Jimmy held up his hand.

"Everything I do is to help." He watched her for a moment then nodded. "Her best interest."

She returned the nod and was off in a flash. For a woman carrying a large bosom, she was especially quick. It was a lot to rein in, and he didn't find it as attractive as many men did. That's because his mind kept returning to his forest nymph with a splash of freckles across her nose and flyaway hair that couldn't decide if it was blonde, brown, or red. Indecisive hair. He chuckled at that, smiling for a while before he returned to the dance.

CHAPTER 42

Carter's eyes followed Beth and Jimmy's brazen path to the front of the barn. He purposely put his arm around Josephine and rotated so she'd see the same thing.

"I was hoping to catch Beth before we start making some serious rounds. Make sure she stays in check. I see Frank coming our way. Do you see Beth?"

He looked the other direction pretending not to see her. Josephine's crestfallen expression almost had him changing his tact—almost. Personal interest wouldn't allow that kindness. Josephine watched them leave and continued to look their direction even after they had disappeared. She was blinking owlishly when Carter gently, lightly ran his hand down her arm.

"JoJo, honey. Are you okay?"

He turned her to face him, smiling down at her. He really did like JoJo and was willing to play dirty for her and his share of the profits when he finally got hold of the Snyder house. Her face was slack, but she nodded, looking washed out and anything but okay. She didn't seem to be seeing him, but merely looking in his direction. Her lower lip trembled imperceptibly.

"Do you happen to know where your sister is or who she's with?"

Josephine froze. She stood silently for a moment. "I just saw her leave. She's outside … somewhere."

"Oh? By herself?"

"No." She whispered so quietly that Carter needed to lean toward her to hear. "With Jimmy."

He straightened up, feigning surprise.

"Really, now? Well, that's something. He seemed to move on quickly, or maybe Beth has managed to make another attack."

He chuckled at his joke until he noticed Josephine glaring at him. Despite what Carter thought he knew about her and how she felt, Josephine surprised him by turning white-hot at criticism thrown at Beth.

"She's not some sort of man-eater like everyone would have you believe."

"It's all right, JoJo. Her behavior won't be held against you." Noticing an older couple standing within earshot, he purposely spoke louder. "Especially after we get married."

Smiling, the pair turned toward the "happy" couple. Martha broke away from her husband, and he followed.

"Oh, Josephine! I didn't mean to eavesdrop. Did I just hear that you're getting married?" Martha pulled her into a hug. "Congratulations!"

Mr. Smith turned toward Carter and held out his hand. "I don't think we've had the pleasure. John Smith and my wife, Martha."

Martha, still holding Josephine by her forearms, smiled at Carter.

Carter was all smiles. Their plan was going better than anticipated. He stuck his hand out.

"Carter Bass. I'm Terrance Draper's cousin—our moms are sisters. Nice to meet you."

Martha chimed in, "Our Josephine is a lovely lady. Many blessings to you."

John looked at Josephine, who was still pale from the surprise of Beth and Jimmy's departure and the multiplicity of Carter's betrayal. He watched her with a stern face because she didn't look like a happy bride-to-be. Josephine's behavior belied what Frank had told him. Frank had been strutting about town telling everyone who would listen how he had finally, found the perfect match for JoJo. Carter Bass seemed nice enough, but he did not seem like the perfect match for JoJo. In fact, she looked quite ill about the whole prospect.

* * *

MEANWHILE, Josephine was churning over her own stupidity. *I should've known that Beth's kindness was too good to be true.* It hurt her even worse this time because it felt so real, like she had turned a new leaf and was the kind sister she used to be. Wanting to cry but not wanting to be inappropriate, her smile became lopsided and stuck. Her face refused to move from this awkward half-smile. It was the best she could manage.

True to Carter's word, they made the rounds among the crowd. She had refused to acknowledge their engagement was becoming a reality and the announcement tonight was his plan all along. More the fool she was. All the things she didn't want to happen were slowly coming true, and she felt more alone than she ever had, this time surrounded by well-intentioned people.

* * *

JIMMY HAD RETURNED to the barn and stopped in the entryway. Beth was nowhere to be found, but he saw Josie talking to Frank and Essie. Carter's arm was around her shoulders. She looked wan and disengaged. Resisting his urge to charge over there to make sure she was okay, he stood to the side, watching them. Frank and Carter were deep in conversation. Frank seemed pleased by what he was hearing, occasionally nodding, smiling broadly. Carter was facing away from him so Jimmy couldn't properly assess him. He had a possessive grip on Josie, and surprisingly, she wasn't stiff or leaning away from him.

Essie looked patiently happy. Her smile was neither enthusiastic nor warming and gave her a somewhat bland look for such a pretty woman. The smile reached her eyes, but it was more of a settled smile. One a tired mother would bestow upon her children when she was satisfied by what she was witnessing but not necessarily engaged with what was going on. Indulgent. She let everyone do what they did without interfering. By all accounts, Essie wasn't a simpleton, but she certainly skirted that with her innocuous, immovable facial expression.

Now I understand why Josie's in the predicament she's in. That sister wouldn't raise a finger to help even if she could take the time to figure out her sisters needed her.

Eying the rest of the guests, Jimmy bided his time. There was a brief musician switch that happened so quickly it felt like an intake of breath—seamless and natural—the music continued, and the dancing didn't falter. Despite his size, he was able to blend in and not attract much attention. He faded into the walls as he noticed Mr. and Mrs. Patterson walk over to Josie's group.

Mrs. Patterson was ebulliently showing off the gown Josie had made for her. After giving Josie another hug, she took Essie's arm and walked away with her. Mr. Patterson followed them, deep in conversation with Frank. They walked erect and stone-faced, looking ahead and not at each other.

Jimmy was slowly moving in Carter and Josie's direction when Draper rushed up to them, as much as Draper ever rushed, being the dandy that he was. He said something close to Carter's ear, and Carter nodded in response. One on either side of Josie, they walked her over to the tables where she had been standing when Jimmy first arrived, and they left her with Mrs. Clarksen. Carter squeezed Josephine's arm before they rushed off, faces strained.

The women watched them leave, looking away when they were out of sight. That's when Josie noticed Jimmy heading toward her. Stiffening, Mrs. Clarksen grasped Josephine's hand in support.

"Mrs. Clarksen." Jimmy nodded. "Josie."

His voice softened as he gave her a tentative smile. Her heart reacted by clenching. She resisted the urge to rub her chest—the pain was acute. Waiting Jimmy out as he searched her face, she knew he was waiting for a reply, but she was angry and unyielding.

"I—" Darting a glance at Mrs. Clarksen then back to Josie, he asked, "Do you think I can talk to you for a moment … privately?"

"What you have to say to Josephine can be said in front of me. Right now, she's under my protection."

Jimmy gave Mrs. Clarksen a droll look while leaning away from her and tucking his chin and shaking his head. "I'm not the one she needs protecting from."

The color drained from the women's faces for differing shades of the same reason. He leaned toward them, lowering his voice.

"I talked to Beth—"

"I saw you go outside with her. How could you?" If Josie stiffened any more, she'd crack.

"What? No! Josie—"

"Don't you Josie me. Everyone's been Josephine-ing me. I'm sick of it. Everyone behaves as if I'm fragile and don't know things. I—"

"I don't doubt that. But this time, I don't think you know the things you think you do. We really need to talk. What Beth told me matches what the ga—" He threw a look at Mrs. Clarksen. "—group has dug up. We need to talk."

At this, Mrs. Clarksen was suddenly busy straightening the table and looking anywhere but at them. She had released JoJo at the mention of Beth and was trying to subtly move away from them, hoping Jimmy would just talk. Jimmy cocked his head in the older lady's direction while keeping his eyes on Josie. Josie turned to Mrs. Clarksen.

"Mrs. Clarksen?" She continued to straighten, so Josie called out again. "Mrs. Clarksen, you seem suddenly reticent, whereas before you were my defender. Are you aware of this?"

"Aware of what, dear?" She pasted on a tremulous smile.

Josie's lips pursed as she looked between the two of them. "Tell me what's going on besides my surprise marriage announcement? And by surprise, I mean surprise to me." She spoke firmly, bordering on anger, her jaw still set, as she had yet to relax.

Her words, however, were like a punch in the face to Jimmy. It took him a minute to register their meaning and for his breath to return. He shouldn't have been surprised, because he knew what Frank and Carter were planning. However, hearing it from her lips was a different story, making it more real. Reality stung.

"I think you should let Mr. Stapleton explain this to you."

Turning to Jimmy, she asked, "I take it Beth explained what she had overheard?"

Her tone was tremulous yet hopeful, and she looked uncertain about the content's explanation. The poor girl had already had a lot dumped on her tonight. He nodded, face grim.

Glancing around to make sure they weren't being watched, Mrs. Clarksen made a slight shooing motion with her hands close to her skirt. She was trying her best to be covert.

"Go, quickly—skedaddle—and hurry back! Josephine, you need to hear what Mr. Stapleton has to say. I'm not sure what can be done about this, this whole—" Mrs. Clarksen flapped her hand about in front of her as if she were clearing the air, clearly flustered.

Reaching out, Jimmy grabbed Josie's hand and pulled her toward the makeshift dance floor. He moved her across the floor, bobbing in and out of the dancers until they'd made it to the barn doors. He slowly backed them out because now the barn was extremely crowded with both dancers and spectators. No one took notice of them.

As soon as they were clear of the doorway, Jimmy grasped her hand and pulled her along the darker perimeter. Josie's small feet scrambled to keep up with his long, easy strides.

CHAPTER 43

_J_immy guided Josie along the same path Beth had taken him on earlier. When they were in the shadows, and he was sure no one was around, Jimmy turned around and gently grasped Josephine by her shoulders. She stiffened until he began gently caressing her shoulders, and she involuntarily relaxed into his hands. He looked long and deep into her eyes before bringing himself back to the urgency of the moment.

"We don't have much time. It's very important that you listen to all I have to say before you ask questions—no matter how difficult. Got it?"

Jimmy bent forward to make sure he could read Josie's expression. Chewing the inside of her cheek, wary, she hesitated before nodding. Jimmy was in mission mode much like the first time they had met—all seriousness and business, but still maintaining a soft edge despite looking fierce. His brow was knitted together and face set, whereas his hands and voice were soft.

Jimmy's hands moved further up and down Josie's upper arms in a calming motion as he tried to figure out the best course of explanation without insulting her or her sensibilities.

"Beth must've found out the same information we came across. It seems Mrs. Clarksen is aware as well. Frank, Draper, and Carter are trying to take your house from you."

Jimmy looked deeper into Josie's eyes despite the darkness enveloping them. When she didn't react, he went ahead and told her.

"They want to turn it into a … a … devil's addition …"

Josie cocked her head at him.

"A house of ill repute."

As she gasped, understanding washed over her face.

"Yeah, … well … I know that Carter is sweet on you and all, but from the looks of it, he's not going to let you keep your house. You were right about Frank and Draper. They're in on it too. I wanted to let you know so you can be aware and stay safe. Beth, Mrs. Clarksen, and the gang all know. So does Doc, Mr. Patterson, and Douglas Elliot."

"Oh, this—" Josie's voice cracked. "This is so humiliating. The entire town knows my business, and here Frank is being so harsh on Beth about respectability."

Jimmy couldn't help but chuckle. Josie mimicked Frank the same way Beth had. They were good at it. He was glad she didn't notice.

"How will we ever live this down—even if I manage to keep the house from them?"

"Josie." He captured her hands, bending to her height. "Josie, you're going to do fine. We're going to make this right. There are a lot of things that aren't right around here. They're most likely connected, but please, just trust me. Trust us."

Josephine shuddered as she struggled to inhale. Lips turned down, she gave a curt nod in a controlled effort at keeping her emotions contained. Jimmy could see she was trying hard to keep herself together—in part for him, like she always did for others. She maintained eye contact for a second longer before sagging her shoulders and dropping her head. Forlorn, she looked much smaller and fragile.

Pulling her into a tight embrace, Jimmy's hands rubbed her back with soothing patterns while resting his cheek on the top of her head. That's when her silent tears and unspoken sadness broke open until they had soaked Jimmy's shirt. At first, her breath was uneven, making her breasts pulse into his chest. Eventually, it evened out as did her overall storm under Jimmy's ministrations.

I wish we had met under different circumstances. Where I got to keep you safe and happy, and you'd always be home for me—no matter what.

He held her close, feeling her heartbeat and savoring the sensation of her slender form nestled against him before releasing her. He smoothed the flyaway hair from her temples before bending down to touch his lips to hers. Their kiss was soft and delicate, like her, but turned fiery and bold, like him. Quickly, they broke apart, as if they were repelled by some force, gasping for breath.

As they watched each other, breathing hard, Jimmy managed to say, "I need to get you back."

"But what should I do?" Josie's voice pitched higher. "Frank will know something's happening. He always does. And Beth—"

"Beth'll be fine. We've got this. Behave like you normally do, nothing unusual. Beth or I will let you know if something changes. Even Mrs. Clarksen. She won't steer you wrong. Just try not to be alone with Frank or Carter if you can. Don't panic if you are."

Jimmy didn't give her a chance to respond. He grabbed her hand and moved through the dark with the grace of a predator on the prowl. When they were closer to the barn, he released her hand. Still in the shadows, he whispered to her.

"Go on ahead. Go back to Mrs. Clarksen. If someone questions your whereabouts—well, you were … heeding the call of nature."

Josie blushed and Jimmy shrugged. Not a total lie, they did kiss. But no one needed to know that, and they most certainly didn't need to hear about her alleged trip to the outhouse, either. He gave her a gentle push with both hands, and off she went. He went in the other direction, just in case.

CHAPTER 44

Three days prior to the dance, Jaems and Buford rode to Adamsville while Thom and Grant rode in the opposite direction to Weaver, gathering reinforcements for the final shakedown and roundup using Travis's connections. Van Der Kamp brought the forces to help all the parties involved, but mostly himself. He smelled trouble, and he was pretty sure it had Mack Pennington written all over it. He took it upon himself to help not only Josephine with her house issue and Douglas Elliot with the death of his foreman, Lars, but also the town's general well-being. Van Der Kamp could not let injustices against the innocent go unpunished. That's what had started his crime streak a few years earlier—the strong drive to right the wrongs, even if he had to unlawfully punish the wrongdoers in the process.

Regarding Terrance Draper, Douglas Elliot had a legitimate complaint and enough information to start a government investigation on Draper's mining speculation even though he had slowed down selling and coercing others to sell their land to him. Elliot had been able to get a couple of the other ranchers who were involved to talk to Travis privately. Travis wanted to make sure they had enough information to make charges stick and keep Draper locked up—or at least financially burdened.

If Draper was involved with Mack Pennington as Travis and Van Der Kamp suspected, then he'd most likely find himself on his own. It all came down to the almighty dollar and which way the chips fell for Mack. However, he had plenty of friends in high places who owed him favors if he had to bail out Terrance Draper.

Travis and Van Der Kamp were waiting at base for the motley crew of help to roll in. Nearly the entire town was getting ready for the dance or already out at the Carlson barn, including some of their men, so it was quiet. The stars were beginning to twinkle as the sky darkened, oblivious to the air of anticipation. In this liminal time of day, the sun had set, but the sky wasn't yet dark—an odd brightness held back and lit the world. It was the last reminder that soon the night would be completely dark, so see whatever was important before the day perished.

Van Der Kamp usually smoked on the front porch this time of day. Sometimes he watched the sun set. But mostly, he liked this odd light show that held both day and night—the brightness before the dark. It was beautiful and unsettling, the time of day he felt most at home and relaxed.

He had just leaned back in his chair, legs extended, blowing smoke upward and watching it dissipate. While other commanders might pace or worry about orders being followed, Van Der Kamp enjoyed his favorite time of day instead. He wasn't one to borrow worry. He raised a glass holding a finger of whiskey but stopped halfway to his mouth when the sound of thunderous hoofbeats came from the direction of the Reinhardt spread.

Van Der Kamp retracted his outstretched legs and jumped up to look in that direction. Sure enough, Millicent, a roan, was heading his way with a rider caught in the stirrup.

"Travis!"

Van Der Kamp ran in front of her, holding up his hands in an effort to slow the terrified mare and grab the reins.

"Whoa, girl. Steady."

Millicent danced around Van Der Kamp a few minutes trying to head to the corral, continuously rearing up and shaking her head. She was lathered, and her eyes were rolling because of the burden she'd carried for miles. Others were pouring in from varying directions, but Travis was the one who eventually caught the reins. Then Van Der Kamp took them and steadied her. Hollow, shaking his head, unhooked the man's foot from the stirrup.

"It's Dobbin."

Van Der Kamp handed the reins to Harry. "Take care of her."

Harry shot a glance toward the corpse, shuddering. Dobbin was a bloody mess. Who knew how far he had been dragged? Millicent was jittery and prancy but managed to follow Harry to the barn. He secured her in a stall and stood watching from afar, arms crossed as if trying to comfort himself.

Van Der Kamp bent down to check out the dusty body before rolling him over. Among the wounds, Dobbin's back was torn open from buckshot. Van Der Kamp pulled in a long breath and looked over at Travis. "Close range. Had to know the shooter."

Travis scratched his head. "Confirms he was up to something. Why would he be coming from the Rocking W? Isn't that Reinhardt's ranch? What did he have to do with them?"

Travis looked around at the men who were watching. Most of them looked just as surprised as he did. Gus and Cy, however, looked indifferent, shrugged, and left to go back to their cards.

"I thought Reinhardt wasn't friendly. Why'd he go over there?"

Grant scratched his beard. "He ain't friendly. Usually shoots at those who are too stupid not to know." Grant was the philosophical one who had everyone nodding their heads in agreement.

Travis pointed at Dobbin's body. "But he's been shot from behind."

"Maybe he was caught stealing." Joe spoke up from behind the group.

"Stealing what? He can't bring anything here. He'd get caught."

"That family with the small ranch was having problems with rustlers. Only a few head would disappear at a time. Sheriff didn't do anything about it. Said there wasn't anything to do, that they'd probably just wandered off." Joe offered up.

Hollow threw his arm in Joe's direction. "That's right. They were right angry too. Blamed Reinhardt and his 'crooked cowboys.' Sheriff went red in the face when the foreman said it, too."

"How d'you know that?"

"Foreman rode all the way into town because Colter refused to go out there." He chuckled. "Kind of funny. That wiry foreman got in his face and gave him what for. He was so mad he was spitting and shaking his fist. The sheriff wasn't looking so great after that. Thought his heart might stop right then and there."

Van Der Kamp narrowed his eyes. "Grant and Joe"—he pointed at two of the larger men closest to the body—"take Dobbin out back to the smoke shack. But for God's sake, don't leave him on the food table. Make sure to cover his body and shut the door tight behind you."

Harry walked up as they carried the body away, and the others were dispersing.

"Van Der Kamp, sir. I need to tell you something." Harry still felt the sting of the outhouse incident, but what he needed to share was too important to continue hiding from their leader because of his own foolishness.

"Dobbin had dealings with Reinhardt somehow. For sure with the one of the crooked cowboys they call Cash. Them and a couple of Watkins's guys were rustling for Reinhardt— I'm guessing the Taylors' small herd. I overheard them talking behind the saloon one day about taking a few beeves and easy money but didn't think much of it until now. Dobbin rides for shit. Doesn't know much about horses let alone moving beef. You know what I mean? I thought he was all bluster."

Harry's lips twisted as he waited for the blow. He was trying to take it like a man but found himself quaking. He was still a young kid in many ways, barely seventeen and thin as a rail. Van Der Kamp eyed Harry for a moment. He made a sucking sound through his teeth, then scrunched his face while pulling a quick inhale. He spread his feet, putting his hands on his hips, as he exhaled.

"How long?"

"What?"

"How long have you kept this bit from me?"

"I didn't really keep it from you, sir. I didn't think much of it, 's'all. I didn't realize it was an issue until I saw him lying there. He was always about quick money and big talking but never did anything to make it."

Van Der Kamp watched Harry to see if he'd alter his story or add anything. Harry was steady and didn't flinch. But he was still thinking he would get hit or beat somehow even though Van Der Kamp had yet to hit anyone in front of him. The threat was almost worse.

"All right. If you think of anything else you feel is important, best let me know sooner than later, you hear?"

"Yessir."

"Oh, and Harry?"

Harry froze.

"Yes?" His voice had a slight tremor.

"Thank you for sharing that. It was mighty helpful."

Van Der Kamp nodded at a stunned Harry, who was still waiting for the blow that wasn't coming. He almost chuckled at the poor kid but gave him a break and walked away instead. Now he really needed that finger of whiskey. He might add another to the glass for good measure.

CHAPTER 45

Jaems and Buford followed Draper and Carter out of the barn and watched them huddle with Frank. Frank went back into the barn as Draper headed to the surrounding trees. Carter got his horse, Buford following him. Good luck had Jaems passing Doc as he pretended to check on his horse.

Jaems slowed his approach and whispered, "Send for the gang. Something's going down at the Snyder place."

Doc nodded, pivoting back toward his horse and keeping his head down so he wouldn't make eye contact and be forced to stop and chat.

*　*　*

MEANWHILE, Frank walked up to Essie and took her by the arm. "Darling, I'm going to ask you to remain with Mr. and Mrs. Patterson until I return. I won't be long."

He kissed her on the cheek then led her toward the Pattersons.

"Can't I just remain with my sisters? I haven't had much of an opportunity to visit with them."

"You know I don't want you picking up Beth's taint, and JoJo is safe with Mrs. Clarksen." He patted her arm that was resting on his. "You'll be better off with the Pattersons, trust me."

Frank smiled brightly despite the churning in his stomach. He had his suspicions about Draper, but the money was too easy. Now he had some cleaning up to do before they could move forward. His jaw clenched, and Essie gave him a concerned look.

"Are you sure everything is all right? You're tense. We're supposed to be having fun, Frank."

"Sorry, my dear. There are some troublemakers lurking about, and I'm going to help take care of them. Don't fret. It's still early, and I'll be back in plenty of time so we can have some more fun." He stood a little taller and puffed out his chest.

Essie tilted her head, holding his eyes. "Just be careful. I love you."

For the first time since Draper propositioned him about the cathouse, Frank was having some doubt and a heaping dose of guilt. He knew JoJo lived for that house. It was the only thing she had to cling to, and now he was ripping it away from her. Of course, he justified it, and he was sure Carter would take good care of her.

Notwithstanding, it was the look of love in Essie's eyes that pierced his justification barrier. Essie blindly trusted him, loved him, and assumed he was always doing the right thing. He'd loved Essie before he started loving money so much, and he loved Essie a whole lot. He didn't want to lose her or any of her honest loving. Good thing he had it all figured out. Draper and Carter were taking the fall for the cathouse. He had that all planned.

* * *

MRS. CLARKSEN and Josie watched Frank escort Essie to the Pattersons before hurrying away. They looked at each other before Josie announced her decision.

"I'm going. He's up to no good."

Mrs. Clarksen gasped, grabbing her arm with strength that belied her normally delicate sensibilities.

"You are not. This is dangerous—I can feel it."

"Frank's not going to hurt me. I'm just going to follow him."

She was looking around for Jimmy but couldn't find him. Spotting Beth, she said, "I'm taking Beth with me."

"Have you lost your mind? What are two women going to do?"

"We're going to spy and get to the bottom of this." She lowered her voice. "He cannot take that house from me. That and Beth are all I have and all I've ever known. He's already taken Essie and won't share. I can't live like this. I need to know. I'm tired of living in the shadows, Mrs. Clarksen. This is important to me."

Mrs. Clarksen looked like she was about to cry and go into protective mode. She shook the arm she was still holding as her eyes filled with tears.

"Be careful, dear. I'll let Jimmy or one of his companions know if I see them. I'll tell Carter that you went with Frank, if he asks."

Josie's eyes went wide.

"I won't really be lying then, will I?"

Patting Josie's arm, Mrs. Clarksen laughed. "Be careful." Her eyes welled up again, so she turned to busy herself with the table.

Something had shifted in Mrs. Clarksen, but Josie wasn't sure what. She seemed more at ease with everyone, kind of like her old self had returned. Josie watched her pretend she wasn't on the verge of tears before going to find Beth.

Jimmy came up to the table and got a drink. As he raised it to his lips, he asked Mrs. Clarksen, "What does Josie think she's doing?"

Casually glancing around, Mrs. Clarksen said, "She's going to follow Frank, and she's taking Beth." She held up her hand. "Girl is set on that silly house. It means so much to her, and Frank's betrayal cut her. She isn't having it. She said she was going to watch from a distance."

Jimmy nodded, setting down the cup. "Mighty fine punch. Thank you, Mrs. Clarksen." Lowering his voice, he added, "I'm getting Clyde to detain those two while I ride after Frank. I'm itching to have a little chat with him myself."

"You're quite welcome. I hope you're having fun." A look of alarm crossed her face. She hissed at him, "Hurry, the Reinhardt women are heading this way. I'll hold them off."

Jimmy hightailed it out of there looking for Clyde. He didn't have the time or the patience for those women. His long legs meant there was no way they could ever catch up, and no amount of calling could entice him to stop, no matter the looks he was receiving for ignoring them.

CHAPTER 46

Frank, Draper, and Carter stood in the shadows watching Jack and Tack mosey up to the Snyder house. They were taking their sweet time, but they were brazen and stupidly riding in the open. The bright moonlight illuminated the pair, showing they were being followed by a group of men a short distance behind them, but Jack and Tack didn't seem to notice or care. The smirks on their faces made them look even dumber than they were.

"Who's behind them?" Carter leaned forward, squinting. They were shaded by the large trees planted close to the house.

"Can't quite see yet. Looks like a bunch of cowboys, but the one riding point is dressed nicer." Frank squinted into the night.

"Wait—that's Reinhardt. What's he doing out here?" Draper hissed.

Impulsively, Frank stepped into the moonlight, holding up his hand to Jack and Tack. "Stop there. Who's following you?"

The pair looked behind them and cursed their luck.

"Looking like Reinhardt and his crew. Don't know why they'd be following us. Must be here to see you." Jack scowled at Draper.

"Our business isn't with him. It's with you, Draper. Don't think you'll be wanting to discuss it in front of your fancy friend here. Do you?" Tack leered at Draper, who stiffened.

Frank, Draper, and Carter looked among themselves trying to decide how to handle Reinhardt and these two. After receiving a cryptic message about the Snyder house, they rushed out without having formulated a solid plan. Draper had just wanted to get them out of his proverbial hair. Now they seemed to be knotted up with Reinhardt and his violence.

"Might as well wait for him and see what or who he wants. We're outnumbered anyway," Carter reasoned.

True enough, Reinhardt had brought eight men with him. All of them looking a little rough around the edges—the fabled crooked cowboys. All of them heavily armed.

Reinhardt pulled up in front of Frank, Draper, and Carter, looking down at them. His men kept their distance but were alert.

"Might've known you'd be behind all this, Draper. What's your story this time?" He leaned forward in the saddle as if he were eager to hear. "Go on, I'm listening."

"Hold with your sarcasm, Reinhardt. I have no issue with you."

"Well, I have issue with you, but that's not why I'm here."

"Then why are you here?"

Reinhardt nodded toward Jack and Tack.

"What're they to you?"

"None of your business, that's what."

"Why are they with you?"

"I could ask the same of you."

Reinhardt straightened, releasing a long breath to end the exchange. He threw his thumb toward the house.

"Then I say we go inside and have ourselves a little chat. At least one of us is going to take care of business tonight, and we'll have to see who that is."

Frank was out of his element, but he interjected anyway. "We can go inside, but just us." His finger circled the immediate group standing around. "Not them." He canted his head at the crew behind them.

"Fair enough." Reinhardt shifted his eyes from Frank to Draper as he called, "Michael, handle my mount while I take care of business."

He slid off his horse, handing the reins to Michael, who had broken from the group. Fortunately for Jack and Tack, they wisely kept their mouths shut until they heard another rider coming up on them. Everyone turned to see who it was.

"Shoot."

"Tarnation." Jack and Tack said simultaneously.

"Can't find him when we need him, and now he shows up."

Draper was fit to be tied. This was not working out as planned. "What are you doing out here, George?"

"I was kind of wondering what my men are doing out here, Draper. Are they moonlighting for the likes of you?"

George Watkins turned to Jack. "And what did we do to our arm, Jack?" He leaned forward, feigning sympathy. "Looks mighty serious there. Mmhm."

Jack went red in the face. "A wolf got me."

The men burst into laughter that made Jack even angrier. He clutched his arm.

Someone else shouted, "More like that hellhound got you!"

Word had spread about how the gang had named Dusty the "hellhound." Even more laughter ensued because everyone had seen Dusty with both Lars and Jimmy, and he was protective as all get out. Dusty didn't suffer fools, and Jack was a fool.

Frank paused, remembering that large wolfhound following Jimmy around. The pieces were starting to come together. He glanced at Draper, whose face looked set in stone.

"Did that wolfhound get you?" Frank raised his brow at Jack.

Jack's face went pale, and Tack shifted in his saddle.

Reinhardt had had enough of those two. Everyone knew where this was leading because everyone wondered about Dante and Lars. Even Reinhardt hadn't wanted Lars dead, despite disliking the man. Lars had kept to himself, doing what was right, and hadn't interfered with his dealings. Reinhardt's facial muscles were taut, aside from one cheek muscle that flexed from his jaw being clenched so hard. His own stupidity over hiring those two morons to rustle the Taylors' herd was becoming clearer and clearer.

"Off your horses, now!"

Jack and Tack startled but did as Reinhardt commanded. A couple of the cowboys came to take their horses. Reinhardt jabbed his finger toward the house.

"Inside."

Looking around, he snarled, "All of you." He drew out *all*.

The men filed in while the cowboys waited by the horses. Frank lit a lamp and shook out the match. He took it to find his way to other lamps and began illuminating the room. When he was finished, he extended his arm toward the parlor.

"Let's go inside and sit, at least. Sounds like we have a lot to cover."

They filed into the parlor, which was large enough for all seven of them. Reinhardt was the last to take a seat, and he glowered at everyone before he did. They sat in a silent face-off of sorts for a couple of awkward moments before Tack spoke up.

"Alls we want is our money. We've been doing a lot of work and not getting paid."

He nodded at Jack, who was still put out about being made fun of. He rolled his eyes.

"We aren't doing you dirty. We earned it." Jack's voice pitched higher into a near whine.

"What did you do to earn your money?" Frank asked. He was probably the most confused of all of them. He had no idea the depths he had entered when making a deal with Terrance Draper.

A slight sheen formed on Draper's normally congenial face. He was a smooth talker, and his pleasant features normally tricked people into trusting him. That's why Pennington had hired him for the mine speculation. Things went awry when he got greedy, tried to do too many things at once, and became careless.

Jack and Tack fidgeted, but this time, Jack spoke. He nodded, indicating Draper.

"He hired us to get close to Lars, didn't say why other than he had done him wrong. But Lars wouldn't hire Neil, so we went back and took care of him."

Watkins gritted his teeth at the mention of Neil. That one caused him more trouble than he was worth. Neil's actions were what had outed him to Van Der Kamp.

"What do you mean, 'took care of him'?" Carter asked.

"We disappeared him." He looked at Carter as if he was the simpleton.

"Did he ask you to do that?"

"He—"

Draper cut him off. "I asked them to get close and bring me information. That's all."

Jumping out of his seat, Jack shouted, "That's not what you told us!" He pointed at Draper. "You told us to either get hired or kill him."

"Enough!" Reinhardt roared. His palms slapped the chair's armrests as he stood. "Don't think you two are in the clear, either." He whirled on Draper. "What the hell were you thinking? Lars didn't do anything to harm anybody. What's your game, because I'm already on the verge of taking care of you myself."

Draper's eyes flared with indignation. "Why are you defending old Lars? We all know there's no love lost between you and Elliot."

"That's not the point, is it? He's blameless. You? I don't even know where to start. We all blame you. And for your own sake, your mining ways better pay off. Your watery drinks in the saloon don't help your cause either."

Tack and Jack snickered. Reinhardt glared at them before jabbing a finger in Draper's direction.

"As for the murder, you know very well who the first person of interest would be—me." He jabbed his thumb toward his chest, leaning into the room with his feet braced. "I won't stand for that."

Reinhardt's voice thundered. He wasn't shouting but might as well have been. It had the same effect.

Draper leaned back in his chair. While he wasn't a small man by any means, he also wasn't a fighter. He was a border-line dandy, a soft Easterner. He didn't do hard labor or dirty work but was surrounded by those who did. Outnumbered, he tried to talk his way out of it, something he did do regularly.

"Frederick, there's no need for that. No one's going to blame you for murdering Lars. You said yourself that you wouldn't do it. Clearly there are other, more suspicious" —he glanced at Jack and Tack—"people to blame other than yourself."

"Yes, suspicious people who could finger anyone at any moment." He frowned at Draper.

Draper swallowed, tugging at his collar before brushing his hand through the air in front of him. "Who's going to believe these two?"

Everyone turned to look at the unlikely pair then back at Draper. Draper pointed at Jack.

"That one wants us to believe he was bitten by a wolf, and that one," he said, pointing at Tack, "wants us to pay him for things we allegedly asked him to do. They're fools who are out to get what they 'deserve.' Can't you see their game for what it is?"

Draper was convincing, even though everyone knew the evidence pointed to something else entirely. That had always worked in his favor, but he didn't get the opportunity to see if his words worked their magic, because raised voices outside interrupted him.

Frank ran to the front room to look out the window. The others followed. Turning back to them, he growled, "It's Jimmy! He's brought others with him."

Everyone pushed around him, trying to get a good look out the window, which caught Jimmy's eye. His face turned dark, scowling at the faces pressed against the window peering out at him, especially at the man in the center—Frank Odin. His eyes narrowed, and his shoulders stiffened before he bounded up the stairs and threw open the door.

"For the love of Pete. This is never-ending," Frank said to nobody in particular. He sighed while turning in the direction of the front door that was nearly ripped off its hinges when Jimmy filled the entryway.

CHAPTER 47

"You!" Jimmy bellowed as he came into the room, his voice bouncing off the walls. He pointed at Frank. "You have some explaining to do."

"I will do nothing of the sort. You're the one who doesn't belong here—neither does the gang you associate with."

Outside, there were shouts and some tussling, the occasional horse neighing and screeching because of the increasing hostility tossed around. Believing that noise somehow proved his point, Frank smirked at Jimmy. He crossed his arms, taunting the giant.

"Why are you here, anyway? Josephine is promised to Carter. You don't have business with any of us."

"I told Josie I'd protect her as long as I was in town. I'm still here."

"She's got family. She doesn't need you, cowboy."

"You've done her wrong. None of you have been treating her like family—for years. She doesn't need or want your help, Frank. And don't pretend that what you're doing is helping."

"You're wrong. I'll have a little talk with her. She's just

confused with you crowding her. Very inappropriately, I might add."

Jimmy's jaw clenched; otherwise, his face remained still. While debating whether to pummel some sense into the man, Frank interrupted his thoughts.

"You and your friends ought to leave right now. We're having a business meeting, and you're interrupting."

"At this time of night? During the dance?" Jimmy scoffed.

Looking around, he saw Lanky Moustache and friend from Doc's description—the very same from the stable fight. The pieces were starting to fall into place.

"You might want to include my friend, Douglas Elliot, in your little meeting here."

He nodded at Jack and Tack, who gaped at him. They remembered him from the stable, too. They weren't willing to go toe-to-toe again.

"Well, looks like you gentlemen have bigger things to discuss than we do. We'll catch you another time."

Jack and Tack started to move, but Reinhardt blocked their exit.

"We're not done with you, yet."

Scowling, Reinhardt nodded at Jimmy to go on.

"Posses from the sister towns are heading this direction. You might as well tell Reinhardt and me what happened to Lars and why before they get here. Save them some time." Jimmy shifted his feet and crossed his arms. "Marshal is coming with the posse from Adamsville."

No sooner were the words out of Jimmy's mouth than Draper made a break for the back door, knocking over the lantern Frank had lit. Watkins took off after him, moving deftly around the broken glass and flames. Jimmy started after them, but Jack took that opportunity to throw a left hook at him as Carter jumped him from behind.

Tack went after Reinhardt. He was at a distinct disadvantage, as Reinhardt was angry and violent, and Tack had a weak arm from the infected dog bite. Reinhardt threw Tack backward without breaking a sweat. When Tack rocked the table, he knocked over a lamp.

The glass shattered, and kerosene went everywhere, the flames chasing after it. Reinhardt punched Tack a couple more times to subdue him before stamping out the flames crawling toward him. It was too little too late; flames spread across the freshly waxed table and floor, igniting the curtains in their path before climbing the walls. The room quickly filled with harsh, acrid smoke that permeated the air and burned their lungs. Wracked with violent coughing, Tack headed for the door.

Reinhardt focused his efforts on prying Carter off Jimmy's back. Within minutes, the flames found kinship in another lantern and the wall sconces, exploding when they met. Skirting Jimmy and the other two, Frank ran out of the house. Jimmy threw Jack from his chokehold toward the door. He twisted while jabbing Carter in his side as Reinhardt and Carter struggled against each other in an odd embrace.

Jimmy moved upward, punching Carter in the jaw and the temple before Carter's head drooped.

"Enough—get outside!" Reinhardt shoved at Jimmy to distract him from continuing the fight. They had only seconds to leave before being burned. Bending his knees slightly, Reinhardt hoisted Carter over his shoulders and carried him to fresh air. Jimmy had knocked the snuff out of the man with three punches. Reinhardt shook his head, impressed.

Outside was just as chaotic without the pyrotechnics. The posses had arrived one after the other from opposite directions. Horses shrieked and men shouted. Bits of char were floating in the smoke-filled air. Van Der Kamp was shouting directives, and the crooked cowboys were being surrounded. A shot rang out from the back of the house, slicing through the rest of the noise. A few men raced behind the house to investigate the shots.

Meanwhile, the parlor was engulfed before anyone found enough buckets and organized a water brigade. Everyone had waited a beat too long, and that's all it took. Fortunately, the horses had been moved as far away from the house as possible. Unfortunately, their shrieking, men hollering, and smoke filled the air.

Sheriff O'Donnell had come from Weaver to lead their posse. When he heard the shots, he wasted no time riding around the house and the ensuing chaos. As with everything else that night, he just wasn't quick enough.

atkins followed Draper through the kitchen and out the back door into the animal yard. He had nearly reached the barn before Watkins pulled his gun and shouted for him to stop. Draper stopped, turning slowly.

"You know I don't carry. I'm not holding my hands up like some sort of common criminal."

"Do what pleases you until I tell you to stop. You may think you're no common criminal, Draper, but you're no better than the rest of us."

Watkins sauntered toward him, motioning with his gun to indicate which direction to go. They walked around the barn before Watkins said, "Stop."

He didn't lower his gun, and he wasn't swaying like the drunk that he was. Draper could smell the whiskey from where he stood. He was surprised George was as functional as he appeared, particularly with the bulbous red nose and sallow appearance of one who hit the bottle first thing in the morning. Draper relaxed somewhat while waiting for the next directive, falsely assuming George was too pickled to do much of anything.

"You know why Pennington sent me here. What I'm wondering is what you had against this Lars fellow. Did he know you were salting the mines? Did he figure out you were inflating share values? Double selling parcels? Hmm?" Watkins wiped his mouth with the back of his hand. "Well, what was it?"

"What's it to you, Watkins? The reason is unimportant. I took care of a problem, and I'm doing what Pennington's asked. Why are you interrogating me about the way I run my business?"

Watkins sniffed. "Well, the way I'm seeing it right now is you've been using and abusing my men. Why'd you drag them all the way out here? This ain't even your place yet, and you're doing what you want."

"Word gets 'round in this town, and I don't think we have Mrs. Clarksen to thank for this one."

"I've been watching that giant. He's sweet on that quiet gal, and you're interfering. Don't think he's going to take too kindly to that when he figures out it's been your idea all along to take that house she loves so much from her."

Watkins shook his gun at Draper a couple of times. Draper flinched, afraid the gun would accidently fire. He looked at Watkins's eyes and realized that he wasn't drunk. Worse than drunk, Watkins wasn't right. His eyes were glazed and empty. A chill went up Draper's spine.

"He's loyal. Loyal to her and loyal to Van Der Kamp. Was thinking 'bout asking him to join up with me, but he's too loyal for that." He spat on the ground and raised his voice. "I'd kill for some loyalty like that, Draper. Do you understand loyalty?"

"Why I—"

"No. Talking." He blew out a breath. "You used three of

my men. One's out concussed, and one was stupid enough to mess with that damned hellhound. He's probably gonna lose that arm if Reinhardt don't kill him first."

"George, I don't know what you're getting at. You're talking nonsense. Please." Draper motioned back to the house. "Let's go back and discuss this like the reasonable men that we are."

"Nope. You're not reasonable, and Pennington's going to have me killed anyway because you've made such a mess of this that there's no fixin' it. If'n I can't fix it, that means I'm done. If I'm done, so are you."

Draper's eyes went wide as he gulped in what would be his last breath. Watkins aimed the gun he'd been swinging around and shot Draper dead center in his chest. That was the first shot everyone heard. The second was when Watkins put the gun to his own head. In this, he knew much better than Draper.

Draper had always been an opportunist as well as an optimist. He had been optimistic that he was always going to come out on top. Watkins had been a realist as well as pragmatic. He knew that men who looked and acted like him rarely came out on top, unless everything went according to plan. Since the original plan in this case hadn't gone well, he had taken matters into his own hands. There had been no way he'd have let Mack Pennington have satisfaction this time. With that last action, he had finally sided with Van Der Kamp.

Sheriff O'Donnell arrived too late to save anyone with his own brand of reasonableness. He shook his head when he found the two bodies behind the barn and dismounted as three of his posse rode in behind him. They had just cleared the area when they heard another rider coming around the barn from the other direction. O'Donnell pulled his gun but lowered it when recognition hit. His lips went thin for a split second, but his eyes began to crinkle and sparkle, and he broke into a broad smile.

"You didn't make it far." His tone was wry.

Van Der Kamp chuckled for the first time in days. "Guess you can say I didn't, did I?"

"What part of 'lyin' low' did you misinterpret? Do you need me to do some explaining to you?" O'Donnell pushed his hat back and put his hands on his hips.

Van Der Kamp scrunched his face, drawing in a snorting breath. "Nope. Found some things needing takin' care of here."

The sheriff swung his arm around, indicating the all-around disaster. "You didn't cause any of this?" He quirked one eyebrow.

"Not this time. Sorry." He flashed O'Donnell a toothy grin before sliding out of the saddle. "You may want to hang around for a bit while we process everyone. There's another marshal in the mix somewhere, and there's someone I think you'll want to meet. Maybe take back with you if everyone's agreeable to it."

"Let's get this mess wrapped up. It's starting to get late. You can explain the other in your own time. We're camping out here anyway, but still." He uncharacteristically knocked his elbow into Van Der Kamp's side. "You need your beauty sleep."

Van Der Kamp's face dropped in shock at the joke, then he threw his head back, roaring in laughter because of it. O'Donnell shook his head and smiled. Their situations made it so that they weren't meant to be friendly with each other, but everyone be damned, they were. Barring side-taking and alliances, they were both for doing the right thing. They just went about doing the "right" thing differently.

The house was smoldering, and men were separated in

groups by the time they made it out front. Travis nodded at O'Donnell, extending his hand in greeting.

"Sheriff, good to see you. How are Charlie and Annabelle?"

"They're off on their honeymoon and doing real fine."

He shot Van Der Kamp a knowing look that Travis caught. Van Der Kamp had suggested to the sheriff that if his daughter and Charlie hadn't already married, they should get on it. And take a long honeymoon while they were at it.

Travis leaned in, lowering his voice so only the three of them could hear. "I knew you were a softy."

Van Der Kamp narrowed his eyes at Travis but didn't respond. O'Donnell coughed to stifle a chuckle. That's when they heard women's voices coming up the lane.

* * *

"DEAR LORD, WHAT HAS HAPPENED?" Beth gaped as they stopped.

Beth and Clyde grasped Josephine's arms from either side. Her head swiveled back and forth, tears pouring out of her eyes as she struggled to break free from the pair. Clyde had been fighting these women all the way out to the property, and he was exhausted. Josie's panic made her extraordinarily strong. She first slipped Beth's grip then stomped on Clyde's instep with her heel to get him to release her other arm.

"Ow!" He bent over and clasped his foot as Beth ran after Jo.

Josephine bolted toward the smoldering remains of the house, calling for Jimmy the entire time.

"Jimmy!" Looking around, she spun in the other direction, screaming louder. "Jimmy!" She didn't see him and became more desperate. Fear was propelling her.

None of the men knew what to make of this spectacle. Most of them didn't know who she was. Of those who did, Carter was laid out; Frank was detained; and the remaining didn't know her well enough to approach her in that state. Coughing, hacking, and heaving, Jimmy was bent over trying to catch his breath. When he finally stood up gasping for a breath between coughs, he heard her.

"Josie!" Jimmy rasped, stopping her in her tracks.

He ran toward her, sweeping her into the circle of his arms, pressing her tightly against him. She burst into racking sobs, clutching him, burrowing her head into his sooty and sweaty neck.

She was so beside herself that she started to hyperventilate. Jimmy frowned, stroking her back, rocking her. He thought she was distraught over the house, as did the rest of the men. Nothing would be salvageable after that fire. Frank had lit enough lamps for a dinner party, unaware of what would become of the prize he had meant to steal from JoJo.

He carried her over to the old animal yard, and they sat down on the stack of wood he had chopped for her during their "breakup." Holding her face with both hands, he watched her intently. She was heaving sobs and gulping air. He was sure she wasn't seeing him with hysteria driving her cart.

He gently shook her head and spoke softly to her. "Josie. Josie, honey." She sniffled, her eyes refocusing. "It's going to be okay. We'll build you a new house. I'll find help, and we'll raise it before the winter comes."

Her mouth dropped open, which he thought was shock, so the words that came out took him by surprise.

"I— don't— care 'bout the house." Stuttering breaths and more tears. "Jimmy— I-I thought y-you were in the house. I d-didn't see you. I didn't see—"

Her voice wavered as words battled strangled emotions.

She looked around wildly and finally whispered, "Was Frank in the house?"

"No. No one was hurt from the fire. I'm afraid your house took the brunt of it, though."

Josie collapsed in relief against Jimmy's chest, and his arms cradled her. They were in their own comfortable cocoon. Their breathing had synchronized, and they didn't speak for a long while. The men returned to their various discussions, leaving the pair to themselves.

Finally, Josie murmured, "Jimmy, I know you don't want to hear this, but I love you. For the first time ever, I have a sense of peace and calm and belonging—with you. You made me think about my life differently when you burst into it, but after I finally managed to push you away, I was sad. I was brokenhearted watching from the window as you continued to do the chores you'd always done to help us out, even when I told you to leave."

She stopped, and Jimmy thought she would start crying again. But she said, "I couldn't tell you how much you meant to me. And I couldn't tell you that I was terrified for you and Beth because of Frank. I didn't know what he was capable of, especially after I realized he was dealing with Draper. And Draper—" She shuddered. "He frightens me."

"You don't have to worry about Draper any more ... or Frank. Everything will take care of itself. I promise."

Jimmy brushed the wispy hairs from her face before thumbing away the tears. He planted a sweet kiss on her lips, lingering for only a moment because what he had to share was more important now. They'd have plenty of time for kissing, in private, later.

"The thing is, Josie, you make me think of things like home. Something I barely remember. Something I thought I'd never have again. What I do remember is that home is where the people who love you are, and you love them right back. Not because of what they have or who they are, but because of the people they are inside."

Jimmy swallowed hard. "I hated being with the gang and would cry because Charlie desperately wanted to help but couldn't because of my fear and resistance. Even then, I loved him not because he's my brother but because he's a good person and always had my best interests in his heart."

He took her hands in his. "Josie, you're that for me. You're always so good and kind to others, even when they only give you the worst of what they have. But for me?" Jimmy thumped his chest with his fist. "You've always given me the best. You're home for me, Josie. No matter where that may be."

Josie was sobbing by the time Jimmy finished talking, and a crowd, once again, began to gather around them.

Van Der Kamp strolled up and watched them, suppressing a smile.

"Well," he drawled, "I suppose that means you'll be leaving us soon. You've got your woman to care for and a home to build, wherever that may be."

Josie blushed to the roots of her hair and felt like she was going to catch fire. It didn't matter that the moonlight cast shadows on her. Their relationship was now official, and she didn't know how to proceed. She wasn't used to being in the forefront.

"Listen, let's round up your sister and get you to Mrs. Clarksen. She'll take you in for the night. You and Jimmy can talk in the morning. People should still be at the dance. Mmmhmm."

Van Der Kamp walked away, giving them a few moments. If people didn't know him better, they would swear he had a tiny smile.

"He always like that?"

Jimmy watched Van Der Kamp's retreating back. He

shook his head. "Not really. Especially with the others. Funny thing? He's more like a father to me than my own father was." His face scrunched in deep thought. "He's always had Charlie's and my best interests in mind." His eyes were still locked on Van Der Kamp's slow progression away from them. "As a matter of fact, Van Der Kamp is a lot like home, too." Jimmy's eyes widened. "Huh. Never thought of that until now. Darndest thing."

Beth watched Jimmy cling to Josephine like she was his lifeline. A wistful smile crossed her face, then her eyes misted over. *JoJo deserves it. Jimmy is a good man.* Turning away to give them some privacy, a familiar figure among a group facing Frank caught her attention. He looked to be interrogating Frank, and Frank didn't look too pleased about it. Beth's feet automatically trudged in their direction. Her body was leaden while her heart pounded wildly, as if it, not her legs, were the driving force. She crossed the yard by sheer willpower. Her blood felt icy as it coursed through her veins and a light sheen of sweat spread across her skin, forcing a shiver.

Frank glanced over the man's shoulder, and his eyebrows raised in such alarm that his hairline rose, too. The man looked over his shoulder to see what was scaring Frank. His face registered shock as Beth halted abruptly. A shaky hand flew to her mouth, and tears ran rivers down her face as her knees began shaking and started to buckle.

"Matthew." His name barely made it past her tight throat. He was the only one who heard her say it.

"Beth!"

He ran toward her, arms open, and caught her as she slumped to the ground.

"Beth." Her name came out with his breath, like a whispered prayer.

He cradled her in his burly arms, holding her like she was a priceless treasure. Beth's body shook with her sobbing, and she was unable to speak, unable to ask all the questions that had been running through her mind. *Are you okay? Where have you been? Why did you leave? Why didn't you return for me?*

"Beth. Beth. Beth."

As he spoke softly, Matthew stroked her hair, soothing her. Her eyes fluttered closed.

"Sweetheart, you're going to make yourself sick with crying. Shhh. I'm here. And I'm not leaving you again."

He held her tighter for a few more minutes and rocked her until her tears subsided.

"Why? Where'd you go?"

Her eyes searched his face for answers. He looked well, albeit tired. That's when she spied Frank leering over Matthew's shoulder.

Frank's face twisted in anger, pinning her with his hatred. He spat his words at her. "You stupid bitch. This is all your fault."

Beth gasped and was ready to fly at Frank, but Matthew beat her to the punch. Somehow, he managed to roll to his feet and set Beth aside without dumping her then grab Frank by his lapels. Being a large man with arms like a blacksmith's, he lifted Frank off his feet and held him there.

"Don't you *ever* talk to my fiancé like that again. Ever. Do you hear me? This whole mess is partly your doing, and I'm going to see that you pay for your actions."

In his fury, Matthew's veins in his already thick neck were bulging, and he shook Frank like a predator shakes its prey. Fortunately for Frank, Matthew dropped him before he did any serious damage. Unfortunately for Frank, no one came to his defense. His fellow citizens were tired of his airs, and from what they were piecing together, no one was happy about how he had been treating the Snyder sisters.

Sheriff Colter had come up behind Matthew while he was berating Frank and was watching the entire incident. In the moment of silence when Frank hit the ground, Elliot and one of his hands commented on Colter's arrival.

"Oh, now you decide to show up."

"Perfect timing, Sheriff. As usual." Elliot huffed in disgust.

Sheriff Colter turned red and was about to lose his cool when Reinhardt walked up to him.

"Sheriff. My boys and I are going to head out. We've helped as best we could. You know where to find us."

Colter nodded to Reinhardt. Travis and Marshal Harvey, who had come from Adamsville, watched him walk off. They knew they couldn't hold him on anything, and Colter was technically in charge, despite having only just arrived. However, Douglas Elliot wasn't about to hold his tongue. He pointed at Colter.

"Now hold on a moment. You're just going to let him go?"

"He didn't do anything, and he isn't going anywhere either." Colter stood straighter, hands on his hips.

"At least we know whose payroll you're on." Elliot pursed his lips so hard they went white around the edges. He was resisting a powerful urge to lay the man out. Before Colter could respond, Van Der Kamp spoke up.

"What about Dobbin?"

"Your man? Who knows who shot him? You're the one who said he might be rustling."

"Yes, rustling under Reinhardt's direction."

"Just because his horse returned from the direction of

Reinhardt's spread doesn't mean that he had anything to do with it. You're grasping at straws."

"Kind of like I was with Lars?" Elliot huffed.

"I'm not guessing. Your two men over there are saying it's so—the same men you failed to detain," Van Der Kamp said evenly.

Everyone turned their heads to look at the miserable pair of misfits, Lanky Mustache and friend, or Jack and Tack.

"Pfft. They're just trying to get out of murder charges."

Travis spoke up. "They aren't. They know they're hanging. They're just mad because none of this would've happened if they had been paid for the jobs they did. They're fingering Draper, Reinhardt, and Watkins. Unfortunately, two of the three are dead. They're pretty sure Reinhardt was here to kill them, too."

"Why would they think that?"

"Dobbin worked with them, and he's dead, too."

"Yer making up stories there."

"We'll see."

"You know who's making up stories, Sheriff?" Venom laced Matthew's words. "You. You drove me out of town when I tried to get out to the Double Star to resolve trouble before Reinhardt rode out there. You knew he would, too. Then you didn't even give me a chance to say goodbye or make any provisions for my loved ones."

Matthew took a step toward Colter. "Ran me out like a criminal for doing the right thing and threatened me if I ever showed my face. You knew Reinhardt was in the wrong that time. His daughter's a tease and a troublemaker."

"You ran when things got hard. Beth was trying to tie you down."

This time, Beth was quicker than Matthew. Her hand connected with the sheriff's cheek faster than he realized he'd been hit. The sound echoed, silencing everyone. Even the crickets stopped their noises.

"I knew there was something wrong with you." Her outstretched arm and raised palm looked if she were warding him away, her scolding scorching Colter's ego, burning a ring around them. "JoJo and I have suffered because of you. Mr. Elliot has suffered. You made Matthew out to be the villain when it was you all along."

Her voice raised as she leaned forward. "Look around you, Sheriff. Men from other towns had to get this mess under control. Where were you? Where?"

Holding her by her shoulders, Matthew drew her away from Colter. She continued to singe Colter with her glare, but he said nothing in his defense.

In a small but barely controlled voice, she added, "You and Frank ruined our reputations, wasting precious time we could've spent together. We did nothing to any of you. Nothing." She stood taller and pointed as she finished with, "You're the one who should've left town."

Turning, she pressed her face against Matthew's chest, threading her arms around him. Matthew held Beth in his arms and Colter with his narrowed eyes.

Van Der Kamp broke the silence.

"Merritt, you go on with Jimmy and Miss Josie and take Miss Beth to Mrs. Clarksen's. She'll take the women in for the night. We can clear things up in the morning. Travis and Harvey will secure things here.

CHAPTER 50

After the night they had, Beth and JoJo chose to share a bedroom, protected in each other's hugs like they had done when they were little girls during one of their mother's tirades. They had cried so much that they felt as if there were no more tears to be shed. That is, until Beth's eyes began to water again thinking about what she needed to tell JoJo.

JoJo slowly roused, her eyes fluttering open.

"Beth? You okay?"

Beth's lips were pressed together. She nodded but looked pale, even in the room's dim light.

Concerned, Jo sat up. She touched Beth's forehead with the back of her hand.

"You sure? You're looking pale. Maybe I should ask Mrs. Clarksen for—"

Beth grabbed Jo's hand. She gave it a gentle pat before shaking her head. Drawing in a tremulous breath, she looked at Jo with a weak smile and watery eyes.

"JoJo. I haven't been so nice to you these handful of years." She sniffed.

"I understand. You were so sad about Matthew and then—"

"No excuses, Jo. I hope you don't hate me after I tell you this, but I want you to know that I've always loved you … and, and … maybe was a little jealous of you." She sniffed again, and her voice wavered. "But when I was about sixteen, I found a box of Mother's letters—and I read them."

"That's no—"

"Jo." Beth's voice became raspy. "This is hard. So hard to say." She nodded her head as more tears fell. Dabbing her face, she went on.

"The thing is—" She drew in a deep breath. "I found out why Mother was so terrible to you. She … she's not your mother. She's your aunt."

The color drained from Josephine's face as she slumped back into the bed. Beth's sobs came back stronger until Jo clasped her hand.

"What else did you find out?"

Beth shook her head. "Your mother's name is Lena. She's Mother's sister. Our mother—my mother—she's an awful woman. She said terrible things about Lena. She said terrible things to you. I said terrible things."

Her entire body shook with her anguish. Josephine mechanically rubbed Beth's back as she hunched over, covering her face.

"I was so afraid that Mother was going to turn on me because Essie was the beautiful girl. The one with the best manners. Essie this and Essie that."

She stifled a sob and shook her head. JoJo waited, torn about wanting to know more.

"When I found out about your birth mother, I sided with Mother to save myself from her wrath. I was terrified I was going to be next. Essie was going to find a wonderful husband because of how she looked and acted. You were efficient and resourceful despite all the horrible things she said to you. What did I have? I wasn't as pretty or resourceful. Mother reminded me of that constantly." Beth blew her nose. "JoJo, I'm so sorry. I'm so very sorry that I was so awful to you."

"But why didn't you tell me what you found?"

"Would it have made you feel any better? Would it have changed how she treated you?"

Jo's brow wrinkled, and after a moment, she shook her head.

"If I had told you, you'd have had this burden to carry and no recourse. As is, I'm sorry I found out, because I used it to 'protect' myself from Mother, and it was wrong." She looked deep into JoJo's eyes. "So very wrong." Her face went back into her hands.

"Beth, please don't cry anymore. We've cried enough in the last twelve hours to last us a lifetime."

Beth continued to cry.

"Besides, you're giving me a powerful headache."

Beth looked up, a small smile crossing her face. The two of them burst into laughter like they used to when they were younger. Beth threw her arms around JoJo, holding on tight.

"Thank you for finally telling me. I don't know how I feel about this. About all of this. So much has happened that I'm overwhelmed. And now we're homeless." She frowned and dropped her head, her lips quivering.

"I know how much the house meant to you, Jo. I'm sorry."

"You know, the funny thing is I'm not sad it's gone. It was just a thing." She shrugged one shoulder. "It was a comfortable place to live, and I had some good memories there." Thinking, she plucked at the blanket.

"I ... I guess that I wanted what a home represents, but Mother could never—would never give us." She glanced at Beth, who nodded. "But I felt that with Jimmy, you know?"

"Yes. I saw it. I was jealous of that, too. Especially since I had had that with Matthew."

This time, Jo looked back down, nodding her head.

"Jo, we'll figure this out. This isn't over."

She looked back up and studied her sister a moment. "Beth … what made you change?" Jo tilted her head. "You became nicer a couple of weeks ago."

Beth flushed. "I hated that Frank was getting closer to marrying you off. You should be able to choose your husband, especially since he's no relation to us."

Jo quirked an eyebrow at her. "Well, he is, but he doesn't behave like one."

Beth imitated Frank's voice. "I'm the head of the family, now."

Her imitation made JoJo laugh, and she joined in. When their laughter settled down, Beth's face went serious.

"I need to apologize to Mrs. Clarksen too. I owe her an explanation. She asked why I changed all those years ago."

"She'll understand, Beth. Despite all her goodness, she didn't really like Mother. She tolerated her. Most people tolerated her." Jo smiled. "Don't worry."

CHAPTER 51

After breakfast, Josephine and Beth—and even Mrs. Clarksen—felt lighter than they had in years. Mrs. Clarksen understood and accepted Beth's explanations, despite the hurt she had caused. Mrs. Snyder had been abusive and hid the harsher reality of it well, and all three of these women had felt it in one form or another. JoJo had borne the brunt of it. No one had really known until now, and they were soon to understand the full extent of that woman's depravity.

A knock on the door interrupted their reconnection when Mrs. Clarksen went to answer it. Pulling it open, she was surprised by the wall of men standing there, hats in hands. Travis, Jimmy, Matthew, and Mr. Patterson, of all people, were waiting patiently.

"Morning, Mrs. Clarksen. May we have a moment of your time? The ladies as well?" Travis indicated Beth and JoJo, who had come up behind her.

So many men at her door flustered Mrs. Clarksen, especially seeing the "missing" Deputy Merritt. She stepped back and swept her arm toward the inside while holding the door open with the other for them to enter.

"Please, come in. Sit. Would you like some coffee?"

Mr. Patterson smiled. "No, Lettie, thank you. I have some important bank business to share with Josephine, and the men want to have a word with the ladies briefly before I do."

"Well—" She looked around, feeling the need to chaperone but not wanting to pry.

Josie resolved Mrs. Clarksen's dilemma. Laying a hand on her arm, she softly spoke. "Please stay with us. Anything they have to say, you are welcome to hear. After this morning, we're beyond regular social niceties. You're family."

Mrs. Clarksen returned Beth's and Josie's bright smiles with a weepy one of her own. She pulled a handkerchief from her sleeve to dab at her eyes, and nodded thankfully as she sat down.

Mr. Patterson made introductions. "Ladies, this is Travis Henderson. He's a good friend of your Jimmy."

Jimmy was the first one to speak. "Merritt and I have talked this over, and we both want you to know that no matter what you find out today, it doesn't change anything between us—me and you Josie, and Beth and Matthew. We love you, and whatever you decide, we'll stand by you."

There was a lot on the line, and Jimmy swallowed hard. He didn't think the women would change their minds, but Josie was coming into a lot of money, and he had none. He had nothing to offer her. His eyes darted to Beth and back to Josie before looking down at his lap. The sisters shot each other furrowed-brow looks before uncomfortably turning toward Mr. Patterson.

Mr. Patterson cleared his throat. This whole situation was too much for him. Mrs. Snyder had made a mess of these poor girls' lives. And now this news, coupled with Frank burning down their home … Well, it was a lot to take in. He looked between them before beginning.

"I'm sorry about your home, ladies."

They gave him tight smiles, and he cleared his throat again.

"I want to make sure that you're fine with me sharing the news I've brought." He paused. "It's of a delicate nature."

The sisters clutched each other's hand, nodding.

"Well, Mr. Neilson has left a tidy sum of money for Josephine, as did Lena Kraus, Mrs. Snyder's late sister." He swallowed as he gauged their expressions. They sat immobile and bewildered, staring blankly at him. They didn't ask any questions, so he continued.

"Uh, well … Mr. Neilson and Miss Kraus are, are …" He cleared his throat. "They are Josephine's natural parents. They wanted to provide for her in the event that something happened to them."

Josie darted a glance at Beth, and she nodded.

"What happened to my, my mother?"

"She died shortly after childbirth."

Josie nodded. "Is that why my mo—my aunt took me as her own? Was she embarrassed that I'm a, a—"

Mr. Patterson vigorously shook his head, interrupting her. "JoJo, no. I'm afraid to tell both you ladies that Mrs. Snyder had been angling for her sister's inheritance long before she knew Lena was in the family way. Doc can tell you more about what transpired. Your parents weren't necessarily in the wrong—"

He cleared his throat when Mrs. Clarksen shot him a look.

"They loved each other." Flustered, he fussed with his cuffs. "Uh, yes. Well, Doc was contracted to care for your mother."

"I'd like to know, thank you. We'll talk to him." Jo squeezed Beth's hand to ease any guilt she might be feeling.

"JoJo, this is a lot to take in—and on top of all the other events you've had to endure. We can talk more about this later, but I don't want you to worry about money. You have it, and now you know to keep it away from Mr. Odin's greedy hands."

Josie looked thoughtful for a moment. "Mr. Patterson? Why didn't you tell me earlier about the money?"

He shook his head. "I meant to, but there was hardly a time when Frank wasn't there asserting his family authority."

Everyone gave a wry smile at that. Travis and Mrs. Clarksen shook their heads. Frank certainly liked to throw his weight around.

"But if I had given you the money earlier, Frank would've found a way to pry it out of your hands. He probably would've convinced you to willingly part with at least some of it. I was trying to figure out the best way to share this information with you before you were married, and it was too late."

Josie looked at Jimmy, who was frowning and looking quite pale for a man who spent most of his time outdoors. She nodded at Mr. Patterson.

"I understand."

Travis waited out the silence before interjecting his opinion. "Josie, you are your own woman now, despite what Frank says. Most likely, Carter Bass will try to take Frank down with him when the circuit judge hears the complaint against them. Their actions caused your house to burn to the ground. We'll have to see if we can gather any evidence of them starting a house of," he cleared his throat, "any sort."

He glanced at Jimmy and back to her.

"You get to make your own decisions now, despite all the

restrictions a woman faces. What you do with the money and whom you marry are fully your choice." He canted his head toward Beth. "Unless you'd like some sisterly advice."

Travis gave her a reassuring smile. "You don't have to make any immediate decisions, either. Everyone here will keep you safe."

CHAPTER 52

"Well, if there aren't any more immediate questions, I'm going to head over to the bank. We can iron out all the details and get you access to your funds whenever you are ready, Josephine. I'd like to give you some space and privacy to think these things over as well as the course of action you'd like to take." Mr. Patterson rose, tugging on the bottom of his jacket.

Mrs. Clarksen jumped out of her chair like someone had lit her bottom on fire. "Oh, Arthur! I'll show you out."

She scurried toward the front door and delayed her return. Travis stood as well. He held out a hand for Josie and then Beth.

"I can help with any legal details if you like. I'm a federal marshal, but I have clerked with lawyers and am available in case it's needed. I'll be in touch to get more details about Mr. Odin's treatment of both of you. I've already taken testimony from Deputy Merritt. You've been through a lot. I'll let you have some time to yourself." He nodded. "Ladies."

Also nodding to Jimmy and Matthew, Travis passed Mrs. Clarksen and Mr. Patterson, who were still in polite conversation at the front door. He left behind an awkward silence. The two remaining couples were unsure how to proceed, and shifting glances passed between them, accompanied by the occasional gnawing on a lip or chewing the inside of a cheek.

Matthew finally put that to a halt. "There are some things Beth and I need to discuss. I think we should give you some privacy." He angled his head, indicating behind him. "We'll go to the dining room where we can see you but not hear, in case you need us."

Jimmy's lips were tight as he gave Matthew a curt nod. Of all the situations he'd had to face, this one seemed to be the worst by far. He had much more at stake this time. He couldn't go back to living the way that he had been, feeling dependent on everything and everyone. He grasped Josie's hands. As he held them with arms outstretched between the two of them, he rubbed the back of her hands with his thumbs in a slow, soothing motion.

Josie longingly looked down at their clasped hands, his giant pair gently intertwined with her smaller ones while Jimmy watched her with a desperation of his own. Despite the generous size difference, these pairs of hands were equal. Rough to the touch, they bore the badges of their grit and determination. They were a blend of gentle and strong, much like their owners.

Jimmy's eyes roamed over Josie's delicate features, committing them to memory. He drew in a lungful of air as if readying to dive into deep waters and released it with a stutter before quickly saying her name.

"Josie—"

"Jimmy—"

They spoke simultaneously.

Jimmy released one of her hands, placing his on the side of her head. She leaned into his hand and closed her eyes.

Her sigh was contented, like a kitten settling into a comfortable spot in the sun.

"Josie, I'd feel a whole lot better if I could go first, this time."

Opening her eyes, she nodded.

"I'm not sure what it was, but since that afternoon I saved you from Gus and his cronies, I've felt something that I really didn't understand. It wasn't until I realized Frank was serious about keeping us apart that I knew I loved you."

His Adam's apple bobbed as he swallowed. His throat felt tight and his mouth dry.

"I've always promised to protect you, and I mean that. I'll always protect you. The problem is … I—well, I have nothing to offer you. I can't provide for you, and I don't want to be relying on your generosity like the rest of your family has. I don't want you to come to feel one day that I'm some sort of burden too."

"Jimmy, you could never be a burden to me—"

"Hold on. I have to say my piece. I love you so much, and I'll do anything for you. Anything, that is, but bring you down. And I'd just be bringing you down." His brow furrowed. "I'll help you rebuild and whatnot—"

"Jimmy, stop right now."

Jimmy stiffened at her scolding tone and set face.

"Your friend, the marshal, and Mr. Patterson are under the belief that I no longer have to be beholden to what another man wants. I have no family to tell me what to do."

Jimmy looked perplexed. Despite wanting her, he didn't want to be another man who ruined her life. He was trying to do the right thing by her, and here she was, getting mad at him. He didn't understand.

"You've done nothing but good by me, Jimmy. Why would I want you to go? I was the saddest I've ever been—and I've had plenty of sad times—when you weren't there just being with me. You are more home to me than that stupid house ever was. I love you. Why would I ever want you to go?"

Jimmy hung his head and shook it as he spoke. "You've got money now, and I have nothing to offer you."

"Have you not listened to anything I've said? I'd be the saddest I've ever been if you leave me—money or not. After all that's happened, do you think I care about money alone? Look what being greedy did to Frank and Mr. Draper. I wanted money to survive, and now we have that. That money will build a new home or help us start the life we'd like, if—"

The two jumped when Mrs. Clarksen began shrieking from the porch. They could hear scuffling and Mr. Patterson consoling her and almost turned in time. Dusty bounded into the living room, knocking into Josie, licking her and nudging her with his giant head. Jimmy reached out a hand to steady her.

"Oh, Dusty! You sweet boy."

Josie patted and scratched the excitable hound while his body wagged and wiggled, bumping into her and the table.

"Easy, Dusty."

The dog threw Jimmy a "mind your own business" look before begging for more attention from Josie.

"Dusty." Jimmy drew out his name and gave him a stern look.

Dusty proceeded to ignore him while rubbing his head against the side of Josie's ribs. Jimmy could've sworn the darned dog rolled his eyes at him while doing it.

But watching the dog who had adopted him with the woman who had nestled herself in his heart transformed Jimmy's stern countenance to a hopeful look. The very one that gave him the boyish look that was irresistible to Josie. One of the many looks that made Josie's heart flutter. She was fortunate to catch it as she glanced at him.

"Well, I—"

Matthew and Beth had watched Dusty crash into the room and interrupt the awkward dance Jimmy and Josie were navigating as well as hearing the end of their conversation. They endured listening to the shyest people they knew trying to say that they wanted to spend their lives together. It was painful, and they needed to be put out of their misery.

Josie couldn't very well ask Jimmy, but Jimmy was clearly out of his element. From what Matthew had heard from the others, Jimmy had done nearly everything a good husband could do for his wife while still behaving appropriately. He decided the gentle giant needed a big shove.

"Just ask her to marry you."

"Oh!" Beth's hand flew to her mouth, hiding her mirth and surprise.

Jimmy's and Josie's heads snapped in Beth and Matthew's direction, then back toward each other. Jimmy tugged Josie closer to him to look down at her. Her face tilted up, and her eyes shone brightly. She was trying not to smile—and failing. Trying to hold back her eagerness and joy.

Wanting so badly to reach up and kiss him was at odds with wanting him to ask her to marry him. She wanted it to come from him. She wanted him to choose her. She desperately wanted him to ask. So desperately that her head nodded a couple of times in a go-on manner despite herself.

Jimmy's smile was like the sun, and he burst into laughter at Josie's eagerness. Here he was doubting himself when his meek forest fairy wanted him just as much as he wanted her.

"Josie, I didn't know or understand what love truly was until I met you. I saw my brother being in love, but witnessing it isn't the same as feeling it for yourself. You see me for who I am, and you make me feel like I've come home every time I'm with you or even think of you."

Josie started to sniffle. Jimmy rubbed her upper arms and kept talking.

"I didn't understand what was happening to me. You were happening to me. No matter what, I love you. I love you, Josie. Will you marry me?"

"Yes. Yes!"

Josie threw her arms around Jimmy's neck. He lifted her, spinning her around. Dusty ran around them jumping and barking as Matthew pulled Beth into his side to watch them. Mr. Patterson and Mrs. Clarksen had sneaked into the foyer and were observing from a distance as Mrs. Clarksen dabbed her eyes. Looking wistful, Mr. Patterson smiled and nodded before whispering to Mrs. Clarksen that he was finally going to go to the bank.

Thrilled to finally be part of something joyous, Mrs. Clarksen stepped into the room, clasping her hands in front of her ample bosom. She winked at Beth because she was sure Beth wasn't going to let Matthew get away this time. Not when it had nearly killed her the first time. "Ladies," Mrs. Clarksen announced with delight, "we have some weddings to plan."

errance Draper's funeral was held two days after the fire. The small, rushed affair was filled mostly with the curious rather than the mourning. Word of Draper's death spread like wildfire, bringing with it the self-important Reverend Clarksen. The member of his flock without a shepherd confined to his "deathbed" had finally "passed," releasing the good reverend from his vigil, and allowing him to return to Linden.

After the burial was finished and cleaned up, people had gathered around Beth, Matthew, Josie, and Jimmy to congratulate them on their impending marriages. A few were formal introductions, but most were hearty handshakes and tears of joy. While no one would admit, or even suggest, that Draper's death was a blessing, there was something lighter in the atmosphere since the events surrounding the fire.

The stragglers of Watkins's gang had long dispersed, especially since so much law had arrived. No one wanted to be rounded up on anything. Especially anything related to George Watkins or Terrance Draper.

Van Der Kamp attended Draper's funeral for reasons

relating to Mack Pennington, as did Sheriff O'Donnell and Travis Henderson. They needed their eyes on goings-on, so to speak. They stood a respectable distance from the happy couples but still within hearing. That's when Reverend Clarksen ambled their way, puffed up with pride.

"Well, well." He spread his hands wide in a welcoming gesture. Jimmy tensed at his approach, and he could feel Travis and Van Der Kamp chuckling at his back. The tips of his ears burned hot.

"It looks as if I'll be busy officiating some weddings in the upcoming days. What a blessing. I—"

The good reverend never got to finish his sentence. Mrs. Clarksen marched right up to him like a tsunami making landfall, her eyes swirling with fury. He glanced at her and opened his mouth to chastise her for her inappropriate behavior, but she beat him to the punch, forcing him to snap it shut.

"You will do no such thing."

Her voice cut through the surrounding conversations and children running around. Dusty took that opportunity to sidle next to Mrs. Clarksen while watching Mr. Clarksen.

"You have some nerve coming here to officiate the funeral of a man who was holding your secret against you for so long."

Mr. Clarksen's eyes bulged. Lettie shook her finger at him.

"I've put up with your lies for far too long. The pandering to other women and leaving me alone to do God's work. I had guessed at it, but I now have confirmation that you are indeed not a reverend."

By now, a crowd with a mix of horrified and smug faces had gathered around. Dusty growled low.

"Now, Lettie, you hush. You're just overwrought. I realize

I've been working a lot, especially over in Adamsville. Why, we all know that—"

"Yeah, the flock without a shepherd." Mr. Kitchner crossed his massive blacksmith arms across his chest, daring Mr. Clarksen to defy him. Again, Dusty growled in a show of support. Mr. Clarksen darted a nervous side-eye at the dog.

"Wh-why yes. They have need of me." He held up his hands in a placating gesture. "They have no one to lead them." His hand extended outward.

"They have no need for a false prophet, David. No need."

Mrs. Clarksen vigorously shook her head at him. Steam was coming from her ears. Her voice went up an octave, and her finger went higher in the air.

"Those who do have need of you are your other wife and young children, David."

A collective gasp released.

"Or should I call you Daniel?"

Clarksen went pale.

"Daniel Cooke?" She put her fisted hands on her hips. "Which is your real name, or are either of them real? Harumph. The only clever thing you did was to keep the initials and the 'profession' the same. Less confusion for you, I suppose."

"Lettie, you were always a self-righteous woman who thought you knew more about God than I did. I married you for the prestige your father brought. I—"

Lettie's slap was loud and hard, and it knocked Clarksen off balance. He stumbled backward, not knowing what hit him. A red handprint glowed on his cheek. Lettie's fury and flat hand were like a lightning strike. Even quicker was her departure. She collected Beth and Josie in the ensuing silence, giving Mr. Clarksen—or Mr. Cooke—her back.

"You come back here right now. You are my wife and are to obey."

His face was apoplectic, and his body was shaking with anger and embarrassment. He jabbed his finger toward the ground as if that would be threatening enough to turn her around even though she couldn't see him.

Lettie froze at his words and slowly turned around to face the man she had thought she was married to. Her posture went ramrod as she tilted her head slightly before her verbal strike.

"You, sir, are most certainly not my husband. My father may have married us in a church of God, but by God, I do not know who you are. You are many things to different people. That will not do. And if we are married, then you are a bigamist and a lawbreaker. I do not associate with either. If you know what's good for you, you will leave. Immediately." Her voice went chilly as she turned on her heel.

Beth and Josie each threaded their arms through hers, leading her away. Mrs. Clarksen looked the most dignified she ever had while marching away from a life she had been afraid to acknowledge wasn't what she had thought it to be— no matter how much she had willed it otherwise.

The remaining townspeople turned to glare at the man who had failed to do his duty by them many a time. The man Lettie Clarksen defended tooth and nail. The very man who publicly shamed her and refused to admit any wrongdoing.

Clarksen raised his hands in a placating manner. "This is just a misunderstanding. A rare marital quarrel."

Mr. Kitchner muscled his way toward Mr. Clarksen because Lettie was a good friend of his wife. "Doesn't seem like any marital quarrel I've seen, *Reverend*."

Travis and Jimmy grabbed Clarksen's arms from behind while the blacksmith blocked his forward egress.

"Unhand me! What are you doing?"

"We're going to have a little talk. That's all." Jimmy shook Clarksen's arm, indicating what sort of talk he'd like to have.

"By what authority? Where's Colter? Where is the sheriff?"

Matthew Merritt stepped in front of him, his hands on his belt, legs spread. "Right here."

"No. You were disgraced and run out of town. What are you doing here?"

"For starters, repairing the damage that was done to my reputation and getting some justice."

"I want the sheriff!" Clarksen bellowed.

Merritt tipped his hat back, crossing his arms and rocking back on his heels. "Thing is, that's me."

"Where's Colter?" Clarksen spoke in an odd cross between annoyed adult and petulant child.

"He took an early retirement. Put me in charge until the town voting can take place. Been a lot of suspicious activity going on that he didn't have a good handle on. I'm sure you're aware of all that."

"I—"

"Look. We can do this in front of the town, or we can go to the jail and have a little discussion. Man to man. Your choice."

Clarksen frowned but gave him a curt nod. Jimmy jerked Clarksen away from the crowd toward Merritt, who took Clarksen's arm. Travis moved to escort them. Merritt nodded to Van Der Kamp.

"You all go on home now." Sheriff Merritt called out.

The crowd milled around for a few moments longer, murmuring among themselves. Little clusters left with their heads close together gossiping at yet another wild turn of events.

When the area had finally cleared, Van Der Kamp walked up to Jimmy with Sheriff O'Donnell at his side. Josie had returned to Jimmy after she and Beth had taken Mrs. Clarksen home, and she caught the ending. Josie stroked his arm with a soothing rhythm. She knew how much the "reverend" bothered Jimmy. Now she knew part of the reason.

"Jimmy. Miss Josie." Van Der Kamp nodded to each of them. "This here's Sheriff O'Donnell from the sister town of Weaver."

Jimmy and the sheriff shook hands, and O'Donnell tipped his hat to Josie. Van Der Kamp pulled up the corner of his mouth in a harsh sniff.

"He's Charlie's father-in-law."

Jimmy's mouth popped open, and Josie's eyes widened. Jimmy didn't know if Charlie and Annabelle had married or not. They hadn't been apart for very long, but long enough for many things to change.

"It's nice to meet you formally," Sheriff O'Donnell said. "Both Charlie and Annabelle have talked a lot about you."

Jimmy squirmed at being talked about.

"You, Van Der Kamp here, and that character, Goat."

They all laughed at the thought of Goat, because he was a character. It also served to shake Jimmy out of his shock and discomfort. O'Donnell was calming that way.

"I realize this is a surprise, but I wanted to let you know they are married and doing well. They're on their honeymoon." He scratched his head, looking at Van Der Kamp for assistance. "They were sad you and Travis weren't there to share the day with them, just so you know."

"Travis and I spoke with O'Donnell earlier," Van Der Kamp chimed in.

"I realize you have things to settle here," O'Donnell said, "and that you and your bride have some talking to do before you make any decisions. But I was wondering if you'd thought about work at all."

Jimmy's lips pressed a seam. He gave a curt shake of his head. Josie laid her hand reassuringly on his arm.

"Well … I hope this isn't too forward, but I'm in need of a deputy. Travis highly recommends you."

Jimmy went pale, wondering how much the sheriff knew about their situation. O'Donnell didn't give Jimmy a chance to run away with his panic and self-doubt.

"And if you're half the man your brother is, you'll do just fine."

O'Donnell paused, allowing that to sink in. Van Der Kamp took that opportunity for a jab at Travis.

"He keeps telling both of us every chance he gets what a great lawman you'd make." He gave a quick sniff through his right nostril. "Travis aside, I agree."

Jimmy's glance darted between Van Der Kamp and O'Donnell. He was incredulous.

"But I've messed up on all the tasks I was assigned."

"Like what? Lying low? Pfft. That was for O'Donnell's sake, not mine."

The sheriff shot him a look, making Van Der Kamp chuckle. "Look—I stayed outta your hair, didn't I?"

O'Donnell gave him a wry look. "That's one way of putting it, I suppose. I had an entirely different understanding of your plans."

"Bet you did, but no one's ever fully aware of my plans. Everyone's usually somewhat wrong when they think they know things."

"Fine. I won't split hairs with you right now. We need to let these two get on with their day."

Turning back to Jimmy and Josie, he said, "Tell you what —how about when you're ready to get married, you let me know. I'll send our preacher over, and you can have a real wedding with a real preacher. You can do it here with your people."

Jimmy and Josie looked at him wide-eyed.

"I'll have a job waiting for you if you want it. If you make up your mind earlier, that's fine too. I'm going to head over to the jail and see if they need any help."

Touching his finger to the rim of his hat, Sheriff O'Donnell sauntered toward the jail, leaving the three of them standing in the quiet. Everyone had left, ready to go back to work and finish off the rest of their day. No potluck or mingling to celebrate Terrance Draper. He was a temporary stain on the town's history. In contrast, the day was bright and the sun warm, a beautiful fall day. The few clouds in the sky were wispy and delicate.

"The way I see it, Jimmy, you are the law. You're fair, even with those who may not deserve it. I realize you got choked up about all the injustice around here, and maybe occasionally used your fists to prove your point, but never for violence's sake. You go out of your way to help those in need —that's how you found your woman." Van Der Kamp winked at Josie.

"You taught lessons only when you had to." Van Der Kamp grinned. "You had some adjusting to do, especially since Charlie left, and you had all that anger you needed to let loose." His eyes held an odd wistfulness. "You've adjusted, and it's time for you to be with someone who's always trying to stay on the straight and narrow—and that'd either be Travis or O'Donnell."

Jimmy's eyes were glassy. Aside from Josie and Travis— and now, unexpectedly, Van Der Kamp—no one, not even his family, had really seen him for who he was. Charlie loved him, but he was too busy feeling guilty and trying to protect him to understand him. He didn't blame Charlie, because he also was a casualty of their father and Pennington.

"You've got Josie here to think about, so O'Donnell is your better bet. No more moving around. You know Charlie and Annabelle want you with them." Looking at Josie, Van

Der Kamp added, "And I'm guessing they'd love a new sister, too."

Josie blushed as Jimmy smiled and looked down at his forest fairy. He thought about how Josie would love Charlie and Annabelle. They'd be a nice contrast to Frank and Essie. She nodded, smiling back at him. Jimmy looked back at Van Der Kamp before grabbing him in a bear hug and slapping him on the back with a couple of heavy thuds. While tall, Van Der Kamp was slender and was nearly swallowed by Jimmy's broad frame.

"Easy, you're going to break this old man."

Van Der Kamp gave Jimmy a couple of pats on his back before they released each other. Despite the awkward hug, they both beamed with familial pleasure. Their relationship was unique. They knew they had something special—something beyond the respect they had for each other. They were a different kind of family.

"I don't want to have to remind you—last mission." Van Der Kamp shrugged his shoulders, scrunching up one side of his face, pulling in air harder with one nostril. "I don't want to find you out doing other jobs. That's never what this has been about."

Nodding and grunting were his response.

"There's a big delivery going back East. Hit it before they meet the rails. Quickly divvy it up and ride in varying directions—split up and be done with this. Retire quietly because none of this ever happened."

Van Der Kamp looked around at the faces he'd been with for years—many he had directly commanded in the army. They expressed varying emotions: serious, sad, excited, and even emotionless.

"If I'm forced to cross your path, you're going to be very sorry. Don't make that happen."

Some riders rode out as others mounted. All of them either nodded to Van Der Kamp or touched the brim of their hats. A couple saluted. The thundering of hooves and horses blowing faded after a few minutes. Van Der Kamp remained without moving as the dust settled. He watched them ride away until they were out of sight.

Jimmy and Josie stood at the edge of Old Man Johnson's property watching Van Der Kamp, giving him space with his melancholy. Jimmy knew he was slowly dismantling the gang, keeping only a core group for the final leg of his journey. Oddly enough, he'd kept Harry back, not giving him the choice he gave the others. Harry had gone back to the barn, put out that he wasn't allowed a "last ride." Josie watched him go.

"He seems kind of young."

"Mmhm. Scouts found him wandering on the road on their way to the territory." When Harry entered the barn, Jimmy tilted his head in Josie's direction. "He's always been a follower. That's why he was with Gus, Cy, and Ned. They needed a minion as well as someone to make fun of, but he's too smart for that."

Jimmy took her hand as they walked back to the main house.

"Hmm. I'd have to agree." Josie nodded. "As frightened as I was, I didn't think Harry wanted to do me any harm. He kept trying to discourage the others."

"Sounds about right. I think he's next on Van Der Kamp's list. He doesn't want him to commit any crimes. He'll probably figure a way to get him out of the gang."

"Like he did for you?"

Jimmy gave a rueful smile. "Yeah. Like me." Jimmy was lost in thought when Josie interrupted it.

"Doesn't seem like much of a gang if he's helping the boys the gang kidnapped, an orphan he's found, and setting his men up to retire."

Jimmy chuckled. "He's a little odd like that. He formed the gang to make statements against the government and to disrupt big, corrupt businesses. He's disgruntled about the war—all the damage it did and the problems it didn't solve."

Josie nodded. "Yes, it did a lot of damage here, too."

She sighed hard thinking about how damaged the Reinhardt family was by the war and the rumors about Frederick being a deserter. Those thoughts were dropped when they heard Goat on the porch talking to Jaems. They weren't paying attention because they were busy drinking whiskey and smoking.

That's when it struck her that the very idea of standing here with her husband in the middle of a gang's hideout would've been incomprehensible to the woman she had been several weeks ago. Being married had felt beyond her reach, not to mention associating with known criminals. That stopped her in her tracks and Jimmy along with her.

"I should've been completely terrified of you when you rode in and saved me. Your eyes were black with anger, and you're built like a giant warrior. Look at you—you're huge. You rode your menacing horse like you were riding into battle. But you were calm and reasonable, and somehow always in control—even amid violence."

Josie was looking at nothing, remembering that evening.

"I rode home with a complete stranger and was both frightened and intrigued by you." She tilted her head, her eyes refocusing. "Even then I knew you were gentle and wouldn't hurt me, despite your size and strength. In just those few moments, you showed me more care and concern than my family ever had."

Josie gave him a lopsided smile that Jimmy bent down and kissed away. She reached her arms around his neck, and he leaned forward to press her closer. He slanted his head to get a better angle on her lips, making her gasp. He groaned when she ran her hands through his hair, and their breathing became heavy. Jimmy was just about to pick her up when Goat's voice intruded into their haze.

"Now knock that off, you two!"

They broke apart, jumping away from each other, like two kids caught stealing from the cookie jar. Josie's face was flushed, and her lips swollen. Jimmy's breath was harsh, the tips of his ears tinged red. They didn't know how to respond, so they just stared. Jaems chuckled as Goat continued to tease the two innocents.

"Yer putting me off my whiskey. Git a room, will ya?"

"Goat—"

Jimmy looked fit to be tied, but Goat held up his hand to stop him. He paused, then he waved them on in jest.

Jimmy looked at Josie, who hadn't moved, before smirking at her. He bent his knees and scooped Josie into his arms, surprising a squeak out of her.

"Good idea—I think we will. Thanks, Goat." Jimmy took off toward the house with an embarrassed Josie in his arms. She tucked her head in Jimmy's chest as they moved past a chuckling Jaems and a cackling Goat.

Dusty trotted up to the porch after them and plopped himself at Goat's feet with a dejected huff. Goat reached down and scratched the dog's head after he looked up at Goat with moon eyes.

"You best git used to sharing, Dusty. That boy is smitten."

THANK YOU!

Thank you for taking the time to read *The Lawman*! I appreciate your support and would love to hear from you. Let's be social and stay connected:

Ride out to my website, amihickenking.com. Read some of my Curiosities (blog posts) and sign up for my newsletter, *The Friday Tomfoolery*.

Email me at: ami@amihickenking.com

Instagram: @amihickenking

Pinterest: @amihickenking

Facebook: Ami Hicken King, author.

One last thing—Please take a moment of your valuable time to review my book. It would mean the world to me! I appreciate you.

GRATITUDE

All writing, no matter how big or small, is a journey of Self. You don't have to be writing about yourself for that to be true. It just is. And the creative journey is a powerful process that no one can fully traverse without guides, helpers, and loved ones along the way—no matter how solitary the writing and creative processes are. We need our people, and I love and greatly value all of mine, including you, dear reader. Additionally, I feel fortunate to have had the following people supporting and cheering me on both personally and professionally, through good times and bad.

My newsletter subscribers, The Fabulous Friday Fools. You read and engage with *The Friday Tomfoolery*, allowing me to share, connect, and experiment with my more spontaneous and off-the-cuff writing. You keep returning and responding, and I can't thank you enough for that. Keep finding the funny, curious, and thought-provoking things in your life to brighten your days and those of others around you. Your readership means the world to me.

My author friends, including Joyce A. Miller, Caren

Gallimore, Nancy Houser-Blum, and the PT Accountability Group, to name just a few. You are always encouraging, supportive, and helpful. You've picked me up when I've felt down and have provided all manner of thoughtful reflections.

Laurie Schnebly. You are an insightful and supportive teacher. Your classes and feedback are always helpful, and I appreciate your enthusiasm for this series!

My coaches, guides, mentors, and helpers. You are among some of the most patient and understanding space holders, helping me see myself through a fresh lens as well as become a better version of myself. You are honest with me in ways that are pointed, kind, sometimes uncomfortable, and always necessary. You have magic, tools, and skills that I'm so grateful for and are people I truly enjoy. Randomized and incomplete are these heavy hitters: Holly Lasky, Karla Lloyd, Clarissa Castillo-Ramsey, Cecily Sailor, and Tandy Gutierrez.

Lisa Norman. You fall under your own special category as friend, many-hatted mentor, and colleague with your one-woman show and skills of a wizard or at least that of a cat herder. Your generosity and knowledge are supreme, as are your friendship and support.

My skillful editors, Terry Cummings and David Lombardino of DLA Editors & Proofers. Thank you for your fantastic work and guidance. You crossed my path in the nick of time, saving me with your patience and understanding.

Roland Dalquist, my fabulous illustrator. Your work is wonderful, and so is your friendship.

Finally, my wonderful and patient husband and two sons. You get the unfiltered version of me and love and support me, nonetheless. You are loving, kind, and too funny for your own good. You represent some of the best of me, and I couldn't have done this without your support. I love you and feel so lucky that you are my clan.

443

ABOUT THE AUTHOR

When Ami was little, she wanted Andy Rooney's job. He was a smart curmudgeon who was funny and got away with breaking social etiquette. The good little girl and rule follower was fascinated.

Asking questions? Questioning others? Humor? Curiosity? She was all in—her inner rebel felt seen.

While she's a curious mix of rebel and rule follower, her quirky and whimsical side manages to coexist with her more thoughtful and serious side. She's an avid question asker-answer seeker and has a strong streak of curiosity that has yet to do her in. She mysteriously finds rabbit holes, loves connections, and enjoys people with a sense of humor—oh, and pretty, shiny things. She really likes those as well as wax seal jewelry, fountain pens, washi tape, and notebooks.

If she had a confetti cannon or a glitter gun, she'd use them to spread joy. She also entertains herself making silly "movies" with her stop motion app and believes that soup is a magic food and elixir.

You can often catch her with a hot beverage in hand, talking to her dogs, or watching the birds in her yard and the clouds in the sky.

She loves connecting with people and hearing their stories.

Ami frequently stands on the precipice, watching and observing, but when she's in, she's all in. She's your ride-or-die girl, Thelma to your Louise (or Louie, whichever the case may be).

Coffee or tea? Yes, please.